GUNS WANTED

GUNS WANTED

by

J. K. STANFORD

With illustrations by
A. M. HUGHES

· THE ·
SPORTSMAN'S
PRESS
LONDON

First published in 1949

This edition published in 1987
by The Sportsman's Press

British Library Cataloguing in Publication Data

Stanford, J.K.
  Guns wanted.
  I. Title
  823'.912[F]   PR6037.T164

ISBN 0–948253–12–6

Printed in Great Britain by
Redwood Burn Limited, Trowbridge, Wiltshire

To
PENNY AND JAMES AND SUSAN
who may never know
these diversions

CONTENTS

BOOK ONE. LONDON ONLY

BOOK TWO. NORTHERN INTERLUDE

BOOK THREE. TO SHOOT WITH STRANGERS

CONTENTS

ACKNOWLEDGMENTS

All the non-canine characters in this book are entirely fictitious. My acknowledgments are due to Mrs. George Bambridge for permission to use the quotations from Kipling, and to Dr. John Masefield, O.M., and the Society of Authors from whom I have also quoted. I have also used short extracts from the following books and am indebted to their respective authors and publishers for permission to use them: *Ciano's Diary*, Ed. Malcolm Muggeridge, Messrs. William Heinemann; *Reginald* by 'Saki', Messrs. Methuen & Co.; *Private Angelo* by Eric Linklater, Messrs. Jonathan Cape, Ltd.; *Farewell Victoria* by T. H. White, Messrs. Wm. Collins, Ltd.

Kingsclere   J. K. S.
31st May 1948

I. THE INQUEST

All the world over, nursing their scars,
Sit the old fighting-men broke in the wars—
Sit the old fighting men, surly and grim
Mocking the lilt of the conquerors' hymn.

—RUDYARD KIPLING

§ I

Colonel Roger Gore-Ambulance, F.R.C.S., grandson of the original Mr. Ambulance who had constructed the first "moving hospital following armies", was feeling annoyed. A patient on whom he had successfully operated had "died on him" most high-handedly, when he should have been convalescing at some expense and rendering tribute to his skill. He had had words with his wife, Rosamund, on the subject of her household bills, and had pointed out to her that pre-luncheon cocktails, besides being ruinously expensive, did nobody good, and, in the case of women approaching middle life, positive harm. And to crown all, Sir Michael Moffett, with whom he shared a receptionist, had dashed off on some rumour of a blacknecked grebe nesting, and landed him with three extra patients.

"I'd be greatly obliged if you'd just see them for me, old chap," Sir Michael had said in his engaging brogue. "I can't put this blasted bird off as she's just on hatching, and once the chicks are out of the shell, they'll be into the reedbeds and we can whistle for a glimpse of them! You will? Bless your heart!

13

There's only two old bags of insides, and a war neurosis from 21 Army Group. . . . Only I'd rather you didn't amputate till I'm after getting back! They're hardly surgical cases at all."

Col. Gore-Ambulance had disliked the suggestion that any operation carried out by him was at all unnecessary. *His* operations, like the quality of mercy, blessed both parties. He had never forgiven an infantry colonel who, in his early days, had refused him facilities for 'exploration' in a *sepoy* recruit. "I won't have one of my men," he had said, "made the *corpus vile* for any medical degree in the world! I'd sooner discharge him as not likely to make an efficient recruit!" The words had rankled ever since, as the operation would have thrown a flood of light on the whole question of disturbance of the blood supply in stimulating under-development.

Now, he had interviewed the two old "bags of insides", both interminably garrulous, of whom, had they been his own patients, he would have made short work. He rang the bell. The neurotics would not take long. He disliked them.

§ 2

Meanwhile the "war neurosis from 21 Army Group", Gerald Warde, of the Roan Hussars, was waiting uneasily in another room. Someone in his regiment had summarized him as a "desperate chap, always at the sharp end of everything. Got three M.C.s and would ha' got a D.S.O. if he hadn't told his brigadier to go to Hell. Did it on the blower in clear and the whole brigade heard it!"

He did not look desperate now. He felt, and had felt for some years "more like a knacker than a vet", and now the war was over that feeling seemed permanent. He had had strict instructions to see Sir Michael Moffett, whom he remembered of old (at Meerut), before he had gone on in glory, but the beggar was away for the day, so he had better get it over. He felt cornered in this gloomy room, with an unknown pundit waiting for him next door. He looked almost pale beneath the

gradually deepening redness which started high up on his forehead and reached the maximum at his collar, bitten in by the
winds of much travelling.

For so many years he had travelled light, without furniture,
or what the police called a "fixed abode", without any expecta
tion of life beyond the next day, ready to pack up and move
hundreds of miles with all the improvidence of a migrating
bird. There had always been so many new things to see that he
had little time to think, and none at all in which to brood.

And now his possessions, like his memories, were scattered
over the world. Civilian clothes in the basement of the Equestrian Club, some saddlery and horse-gear here, a few books
there, a dozen silver-cups somewhere else, some gun-cases, two
tin trunks of uniform and oddments, where were they all? He
had three saddles, now he came to think of it, in Muttra, or was
it Meerut? A couple of ponies in Cairo which he hoped someone
else was riding if they had not been shot. A dog or two elsewhere
which had long forgottten him for another owner. Some camp-
kit in Kashmir and the rest God knew where. But he had always
kept clear of impediments. No relatives. Above all, no women
or at any rate none that had not forgotten him completely.

And now this wait was getting him down. In the regiment,
if one had anything wrong and was not brought in on a
stretcher with it, one had a drink quietly with Bill Simonds in a
corner of the mess. And Bill would swallow drink for drink
with you, and tell you not to be a fool or, occasionally, to come
round and see him in his room next day. Bill would gain the
confidence of a rhino before he gave you some dope or scrawled
a note on a drink-chit which he would stuff into his pocket.
Gerald had seen him once, after a late night in the Club, trying,
while he shaved, to sort out a pocketful of those crumpled chits
and his memory, and murmuring: "Now who the devil was
the woman last night who told me her little one had a worm?
Maudie Anderson? Or Mrs. Preston? No, *she* must have been
the colic. Hell!"

At any rate, thought Gerald Warde, post-war England would not be seeing him for long.

§ 3

Roger Gore-Ambulance rose from behind his table as his patient came in, and what in a normal man would have been a smile made a gleam on his ivory countenance, like dawnlight on a glacier. The firm aseptic hand he offered looked as if it had been already prepared for an operation. His cold eye ran over Gerald's weather-beaten face as if to say: "I know all about you! You may think you are a son of God and heir to eternal life, but to me you are only a trunk and a few limbs, all readily amputable, and a collection of viscera indubitably the worse for excess, which I shall have much pleasure in removing or decarbonizing for you at so many guineas."

Roger Gore-Ambulance was an exceptional surgeon. A great advocate of Cæsarean section (holding that in these matters Art had long outstripped Nature), he looked forward to a time when state insemination would replace the processes which for so long had left their random influence on the human race. One day generations of surgeons, yet unborn, might trace their pedigrees back in tail male to himself, as racehorses do to St. Simon.

Gerald sat down and the Colonel took out a blank card.

"Name?" He unscrewed a gold fountain-pen, the gift of a grateful Lord Mayor whose duodenum, now in a bottle, was in constant request for lecture purposes at St. Jerome's hospital.

"Gerald Warde."

"Rank?"

"Don't know. I'd been a major for three years when I last heard of it, but in this war one's always popping up and down, especially if you go sick."

"Age?"

"Rising thirty-four."

"Regular soldier?"

"Yes. Roans."

"Address?"

"Glyn Mills."

It sounded rural. "What county is that?"

"Why, dam' it, Middlesex, isn't it? I mean the bankers in Charing Cross."

Col. Gore-Ambulance, who had long ceased to deal with army bankers, did not like people who implied that any question of his was stupid, and even more the houseless type of soldier who had no anchorage but a bank or a club. But he said nothing. His time would come.

"Married?"

"No, thank the Lord."

Roger would have thanked the Lord also if he had been able to say "No" to that question. His eye rose for a second from his card to the weather-beaten red face beside the table, and fire blazed suddenly up within him. Good heavens! This could be none other than the young devil of a horse-soldier who had cut him out so badly at Naini Tal in 1934, with Mary Todhunter, just before he retired. *The* only time he had really been in love with a woman in his life. He had seemed that time so well away, and then a spate of leave, a covey of carefree subalterns, sun-burnt and hard as nails up from the Ganges *Kadir*, and his care-fully-pressed suit was in tatters! And *this* was the young devil over whose goings-on he had ground his teeth with jealousy all those moonlit nights of April! He heard again the sound of the band coming faintly from the distant club. He smelt the smell of the roses and the watered lawns outside the verandah. He heard the crickets churring remorselessly in the kitchen of the forlorn house behind him. Even his ascetic heart still felt the scar of that hot weather. And to this young man it had probably been an amour as fleeting as that of a cat on a roof. . . . Well, well, the whirligig of time!

With an effort he controlled himself, and tapped the card with his gold pen.

"Do you drink?"

"When I can."

"Smoke?"

"Yes, a good deal."

Roger Gore-Ambulance, who had done neither for twenty years, snorted. He had been wont to ask certain of his patients if they womanized. On this occasion he did not trouble to put the question but inserted a tick in the column "W".

"Any serious illnesses?"

"Malaria once or twice."

"Accidents or wounds?"

"A few. Got shot up in 1941."

"Well, describe your trouble as briefly as you can."

He listened impatiently to a brief recital which included "General bloody feeling. . . . Always stiff. . . . Fearfully slack and stale at times. M.O. insisted on my coming home when the Boche packed in."

"Will you please remove your clothes? I want to make an examination."

Stripped, Gerald Warde revealed a mass of cord-like muscles which belied his slender appearance and a sunburnt torso beneath which his loins showed startlingly white. There were scars all over him. Very slowly, stethoscope in his ears, Roger Gore-Ambulance went over the young rip who had cuckolded him, tapping him with those firm aseptic fingers. Yes, there seemed definitely something wrong with the reflexes, and as he listened to the heart he thought "ah! systolic", though he had abandoned general practice for years.

He pointed to a six-inch scar on the shin.

"That? Oh, boar near Muttra."

"And this one?" It was a long wound from the thigh to the lower ribs.

"My own fault, in the semi-final of the *Kadir*. Horse came it with me; I went to the end of the reins and got messed up with my spear."

18

"Oh, and these?"

"Boche plane *stukaed* me in '41. We were on fire and I couldn't get out of the rozzy Marmon-Harrington."

"And that one?"

"Fell down a *khud* out shooting in Chitral in '32."

"Have you ever fallen on your head?"

"Often. If a horse falls with you at sixteen annas, I suppose you *ought* to land on your shoulder, but *I* always hit the ground too soon."

Col. Gore-Ambulance, who did not ride horses, and regarded them as anachronisms and their riders as morons, grunted again.

"Have you ever been unconscious as a result of a fall?"

"Yes, twice, once at polo; two of us took a bit of a jerk when I was crossed. I didn't know much about it for three days."

"When was the last?" Was he never to come to the end of the violences this young ruffian had done so casually to himself?

"Flew over in 1939 to Brussels, to ride a horse for someone. At the fourth fence the rozzy thing never rose an inch, and all the Belgiques did was to take my boots off and pack me in the plane for home. I never really registered till I got to Croydon."

The Army all over: and he had probably been out on the tiles the same night!

"Have you ever been X-rayed, as a result of a fall?"

"Not that I know of."

The Army again! Roger's ire mounted slowly as he thought back on his career. The Army spent millions in wartime making sure of the troops' drinking water and clean clothes, but their officers could break themselves up in peacetime and no one cared. And it was to one of these casual rips that he, a most successful professional man, owed his . . . .

"I have heard quite enough. Major Warde, to refer to one of my earlier questions, do you realize that every time you smoke a cigarette you knock two minutes off your life, and every time you drink a glass of whisky you shorten it at least a day. . . .?"

He leaned forward. His eyes glowed with ascetic fire as he let himself go at last.

§4

Rosamund Gore-Ambulance, on her way to her hairdresser, had met in the hall a thin young man, with a cynical mouth and a skin obviously ruined by exposure. His dreamy gray eyes had rested on her face, decided that her ankles were more interesting, and clearly did not consider either worth a second glance.

Rosamund was not accustomed to this for she was in almost full plumage again. She had, of course, been in uniform during the war, in an organization "affiliated to the war-effort", but its members, who had designed their own attire, had demobilized themselves with uncanny speed, the instant that the course of events seemed to justify it.

As she walked down Wimpole Street, where so many of her acquaintances had, at her suggestion, surrendered their teeth, tonsils, duodena, sinuses and other defective working parts to the faculty, Rosamund could not refrain from thinking about that young man. She must ask Roger later on. He had looked scared. Loose living probably, and now his wild oats were coming home to roost! She had heard strange stories of G.H.Q. in Cairo and Rear Army Group in Brussels from Tom Glenagony. That young man had hardly thought her worth a glance. She hoped Roger would find something wrong with him, something really painful and expensive.

In her father's day, Rosamund had been the first to encourage the young lovelies of Mayfair to have their appendices out as a precaution, and to bring in a friend or two to share their room and the tedium of convalescence. "Oh, you *must*, Celia," they had learnt to carol, "it'll be *such* fun if we're done together." The practice had caught on and sometimes there were three lovelies being "decarbonized" at a time. But old "Dripping" Gore, then at the height of his powers, had never made any reduction on a quantity in his fees.

Rosamund had often found herself wishing that some great man would discover a new organ in the human frame, a ductless gland or something and preferably above the belt, which could safely be excised to relieve the strain of modern life. Withal, she had so far managed to retain herself as God made her, subject to the decrees of fashion.

Then she forgot Gerald altogether. After the hairdresser there was a blouse to try on, tea at his club with Tom Glenagony, (who had blossomed into red tabs most gratifyingly after VE day,) and then a supper party with Sir William Boulogne. It was nice to get back to pre-war routine again.

II. AFTER THE VERDICT

At the end of this living the new lives begin.
—JOHN MASEFIELD

Gerald Warde entered the Club. He had been walking aim-lessly round the park for two hours and felt he wanted a drink. Sentence of death, by gum! And every cigarette or drink shortening the count of days he had left, if that bone-white image of a vet was right. A year or less and then . . . blackout, washout, *kaput*! Perhaps that was more than he had been used to, in practice. Since 1939 he had rarely looked more than a week ahead. He had lived all those years like a robin, with cheerful hardi-hood from minute to minute, and very little had worried him.

His mind ran down the long line of his friends in and out of the regiment, a pleasantly casual crowd. Tiny, who had written himself off at polo in a slow chukker; old George, who had got enteric when after a bison; poor Robin, the best fellow that ever walked, who had got himself seconded to Burma and died, mysteriously, up the N'Mai; Jerry, crashed when going on leave; Tom and Dick and Harry *stukaed* in the desert; Tony shot up in Crete, and a score of others whose ends had been as sudden and as lonely, and mostly "out in front". How they would all grin to see him when he cast up, but what a God-awful end! In peace-time he had always hoped he might die out hunting, or at polo with the thunder of hooves in his ears. But now he had to sit down quietly and wait for it to come.

As he pressed a bell and sank down on a sofa, a huge form loomed suddenly over him.

"Hullo, Gerald, well met!"

"Hullo! By God, it's Angus!"

Angus Cameron Somborne, usually summarized by his friends as "Pretty-hard-case-old-Angus", had been a horse-gunner, though he rode over fifteen stone, had retired and surprisingly become a beat-constable in Carlisle, and still more surprisingly Chief Constable of a county where he seemed to spend much of his time fox-hunting. He had returned to the service as a provost-officer with one of the new divisions during the War. Gerald had met him in the desert advances, always a bit ahead of where he should have been, his enormous frame jutting out of a jeep full of route-signs, marking out the axis for his division to advance. He had an uncanny knack of turning up early in newly-captured towns and cornering the supplies of alcohol. Gerald had not seen him for nearly a year.

"Drink, Angus?"

"Thanks. I say, have I got anything to apologise to you for?" Angus's eyes seemed to smoulder. His hair and moustache bristled, with the massive black George Robey eyebrows between, as if great vitality was forcing them through his skin.

"Apologise? To me? Good God, no! What for?"

"Why, last night?"

"But I was in a transit camp in Dover and a dam' badly run one too."

"It wasn't you? Then whose party was I at? I know we ended up at the 'Box of Dates', with a pretty mixed bag."

"But why the apology?"

"I generally do that. I haven't a clue how I got home! Complete blackout till about 10.15 this morning."

"Well, you probably owe one to somebody, but it wasn't me. Here's luck!"

"Luck!"

23

Perplexity was the main expression on Angus's ruddy and freckled countenance. These recurrent post-mortems were a great trial to him. "I haven't a clue," he said again. "I know I dined at the 'Ecu', with old Gus and a couple of girls Gus brought, and I had a hell of an argument later on with you, or someone in your regiment, about that mare Taffy Wynn-Evans jumped at Olympia before the war, three weeks after she'd had a foal. I made sure it was you. And then we went on. . . . No, my mind's going. I shall have to see my psychiatrist!"

Angus Somborne's psychiatrist had been famous in the Eighth Army. An earnest young alienist, credulous to a fault and bursting to disprove that there was any such thing as shell-shock or "bomb-happiness", Angus had installed him as his father-confessor and had told him, in confidence, some very startling things.

"Lord help us," Angus had once admitted, "the things that chap's swallowed about me would make a *mahseer* give itself up. But he just licks his lips and comes up for more. I found he'd only dipped into Havelock-Ellis (he knows Freud of course by heart but all the rest of his reading was ultra-modern). So I told him *I* was the bloke who'd gone round the world sampling the women of forty-seven nations as an experiment. He took it all down, hook, line and sinker, and got fearfully excited. I forget what particular form of neurosis I was suffering from, but it was one of the cruder ones that only really blossoms in Broadmoor! Bless-his-little-complex!"

Still uncertain how he had reached port overnight but re-assured a little, Angus ordered another drink and questioned Gerald about the last year.

"Well," he concluded, when the slangy recital ended, "for a man who's just come home on long leave after six years of war you're very glum. Seen your leech yet?"

"Not the one I was told to. But I saw *a* leech today and he said I'd got less than a year to live, Angus."

"Good God! I say, I'm sorry to hear that, old boy. What the devil have you got?"

"I gather it's just a general break-up. He used a lot of long terms but he didn't commit himself. But he seemed uncommonly positive."

"As how?"

"Well, I'd got a typical soldier's heart from oversmoking, alcohol, and general wear-and-tear, and no insurance company would take me for a second."

"If you're a bad life," said Angus, emitting a cloud of smoke, "*I* must be verging on suicide. . . . But don't worry, Gerald. Any company would have been fools to take you in the last ten years. 'Remember how they used to demand a 20 per cent. premium for a polo-pony or a pigsticker?"

"Yes."

"Well, any company that knew the life you were leading wouldn't have had a moment's peace. Think of your life, hog-hunting, polo, steeplechasin', *shikar*, climbing, not to mention the War. You were a pretty bad risk at your fittest, much worse than these beggars who sit on chairs and eat their way steadily to the grave. . . ."

He waved his hand round the Club. An Equestrian who had lived for years mainly by suction, to keep his weight down, scowled darkly as he overheard.

"Well, Angus, that doesn't alter what old Ambulance said, that I'm a caster. One more year to live . . . Where do I go from here?"

Angus smoked for a few moments.

"You're one of these healthy-looking devils who like the open air. Now if I could spell, *I'd* write a book in my last year saying exactly what I knew about the Quitechley Hunt and the Q Staff in Forty Corps and the War-Box and certain sections of society, and publish it privately. 'Make a terrific sensation! I should then pass away while the libel actions were still pending, leaving my literary executor to pay my debts out of royalties!"

"I couldn't write a book to save my life. I started to write one once about that trip I did up near the Shaksgam, and at the end of four days I thought 'Who on earth will ever read this bilge?' and I gave it up."

"Pity," said Angus seriously. "You know, with your life you've much more to tell the world than a lot of birds who *can* write and have never seen anything worth writing about. Look at that chap Percy Lorrimer, who publishes five crime-novels a year! I don't suppose he's ever seen a man killed in his life and, if he did, he'd take to his bed for a week with jitters. I'll bet that chap has never been five yards from a dictaphone or a confidential typist, but he can go on churning out thrills and adventure till all's blue and he slaughters his characters by platoons. Now you . . ."

"No, I'm not Mr. Percy Lorrimer, thank the Lord. I know his stuff. I should like to meet that chap. All his heroes drink like fishes and sit about all day long with tankards of beer or double Martinis in front of them, while detecting, and usually a girl into the bargain. Yet they can move like cats, stay awake all night, deduce anything in a fraction of a second, and kill a man by firing through their trouser pockets. Could *you*, Angus, unless you went into training for about three months?"

"Of course not! But that stuff is lapped up by millions. You'd have thought there'd been enough slaughter recently to put people off violent deaths for the next half century. . . . But still, that doesn't help *your* future, Gerald old boy. If I were you now. . . ."

"Well, what would you do? Come on."

"If *I* were you," Angus went on, "I'd borrow every bean I could and blow the lot. I would. Reminds me of poor old Freddie Hoolock. . . ."

"Never knew him."

"He crashed over Arras in 1918 and came out with a gratuity of £400, but all joggled up internally. The doctors told him the same as you, year to live and all that."

"What did *he* do?"

"He chucked his job in Ceylon, borrowed £2000 off his father and £500 from his bank and said, 'Well, if I've only got a twelvemonth more, it's going to be a cracker!' He proceeded to hit London and Monte the most imperial clout, seeing life with what Kipling calls a capital Hell."

"Sorry, Angus, I could do it for a week but after that it would bore me to tears. Did it hasten his end?"

"My dear old boy, he hasn't ended yet! At the close of Freddie's historic life-cycle, which was an absolutely non-stop beat-up, he went, wan and shaking, to the doctor who said, Very sorry, he must have had an earwig in his stethoscope or something, and Freddie, though much reduced by dissipation, would with care last another thirty years."

"Go on, this is interesting."

"Poor Freddie had got very firmly engaged to two different girls, feeling certain he would never come under starter's orders. One tried to 'get him for breach', as my charwoman calls it, but the other married him and he's been in Colombo since, sweating blood, with her standing over him, to pay back the money he owed when they reprieved him!"

"That's not likely to happen to me. This beggar was very definite and talked about progressive cardiac something. . . . Didn't seem to like me, I thought, though he seemed an un-emotional type. Sort of idea I'd seen him before somewhere."

"What else did he say? Avoid all excitement, animal, sexual, or mineral? No alcohol and so on?"

"He told me every cigarette I smoked took a minute off my life and every drink took a day . . . and as for women, I've for-gotten how many days *they* lopped off. Ascetic sort of cove! Gloomy beggar, I thought him. Talked about nails in my coffin."

"He said *that*, did he?" said Angus. His hair and moustache bristled. "Well, let's shorten our lives at once by a couple of days or so!" He pressed a bell.

The silver-buttoned waiter came and smiled at Angus.

"James Cameron," said Angus, "my mother was also a Cameron, and this is a very gloomy moment. I want two fighting gins. And let your hand tremble, Cameron!"

"I'll dae ma best, sirr."

§ 2

"I should see a bit of country life, if I were you," said Angus confidentially twenty minutes later. "You haven't been home for years and you'll find this country's changed."

He leaned back. He had just shortened his life, according to Col. Ambulance's reckoning, by something over five days. "You don't play golf, I take it?"

"I hope someone will have me put down before I take to that."

"Same here. You shoot, don't you?"

"A good bit in Kashmir, India, Mespot, and Egypt, but very little in this country. The doctor said I wasn't to hunt."

"Well, it might be worth your trying to get a gun in a syndicate. Have you any rich friends in what's left of the squirarchy or your regiment, who'd ask you out without paying?"

Had he? Bill had broken his neck at Sollum, Jock had had to let his place near Salisbury, Ambrose had stopped a mortar-bomb somewhere and the place had gone to a cousin, and old George was broke and sold up.

"Only an uncle with a small place, about 900 acres, in Harkshire, but I don't know what it's like these days. Bit late for a syndicate, isn't it, with August coming on?"

"Oh no! You may not get into a good one and they're all devilish expensive with beaters at about twelve shillings a day, keepers at a fiver and no food to rear birds on, but it would be worth trying. And look, I've got a pal up near the Borders who runs a sort of country-house hotel, for the fishing mostly."

"I'm not a fisherman. Wish I was."

"Well, he's got two or three goodish moors on the Pennine,

and two excellent keepers, and will probably have some grouse if anyone has. Why not try and get a few days with him? It's grand country and I'd sooner shoot one grouse than six part-ridges."

Gerald looked suddenly eager.

"Will you lay that on for me, Angus? I never shot a grouse in my life except one out of season in Connemara when I was after snipe."

"I do like," said Angus, "a Sassenach who admits he's hardly ever shot a grouse. To hear them talk you'd think they spent their time being asked to shoot grouse all over the north from Gunnerside to Glamis. 'Go to as much sweat to get invited to someone's moor as they do to get into the Royal Enclosure. They're the only people who are glad that grouse have done so badly in the last few years."

"Why don't you come up with me?" asked Gerald.

"I can't. I'm in a spot of bother with a girl. I had a few moments of what my psychiatrist calls schizophrenia in the 'Moribund Aunt' the other night. Anyway I ceased for the nonce to be a confirmed bachelor. And when I woke up next day I was engaged! Can you beat it?"

"Couldn't you tell her you'd made a mistake?"

"I affected the blandest ignorance of the whole thing, and she said she'd never seen me so natural or so sweet since she'd known me and she'd never been surer of anything in her life!"

"I expect she thought you were more malleable in a state of coma. But what does A do?"

"A," said Angus, "is going down there this week-end, and hopes to show her people how really unsuitable he is as a son-in-law. The sire is a brigadier and the dam even more so, if you know what I mean. The marriage will NOT take place but there may be a bit of blood and toil before we all break it off happily."

"Well, surely you can break it off before the twelfth of August?"

"She's one of the sheet-anchor type of women. Anyhow, let's leave it open. . . . Meanwhile we'll go to my other club. It's socially worse than this but alcoholically far superior. You'll see the last *abdomina* in London! A fat man in this country almost gives one a shock nowadays. But in the Savernake we still keep a few, in prime condition, as plump as a young partridge!"

He spoke proudly, as men once spoke of their hams or their cellars or their beeves.

III. AT THE SAVERNAKE

The stream is shrunk, the pool is dry
And we be comrades, thou and I.

—RUDYARD KIPLNG

§ 1

The Long Bar at the Savernake Club in St. James's is not as long as some others in the Empire but from six in the evening it is almost as crowded. With the exception of the head-barman (who broke down at Shepheard's after twenty years of cocktail-shaking and has suffered from laminitis and acute tennis-elbow ever since), the waitresses are all Displaced Persons in white coats and chosen for their beauty. The rules of the Club prohibit song but the drinking members like to feel that wine and women are to some extent still within their grasp each evening. Angus and Gerald saw a thick line of fattish prosperous men

> *with fevered jowl and dusty flank*
> *each jostling each along the bank,*

who all seemed to be talking about racing and the future of Lord's.

"Catch a chair over there, Gerald," said Angus, "while I get a drink. This is a major operation, on certain nights."

Gerald retired to a leather arm-chair in a corner while Angus towered over the crowd, his arm outstretched and making play

31

with his great eyebrows. He returned in a few moments with two glasses.

"Poppy said she couldn't serve 'doubles', so I said it shocked me to see so many members of the Committee drinking what must from their colour be double gingerales. That shook her, and also got the Chairman of the House Committee, who was next me, between wind and water. I think her hand trembled a little. Here's luck!"

"Now look here, Angus, if we're going to make a night of it, we've got to start slowly. I want to take my mind off that blasted vet but not all at once."

Angus nodded. "Right ho, old son! I've about had my whack."

'Whatever made you come in here then?"

"I was hoping to see a chap who might put you on to some shooting. Wait a moment till I get the *Squire*! We'll see if there are any 'guns wanted' advertisements."

Gerald thought, "There's one thing about Angus, the infinite variety of his acquaintances. I believe if I wanted a shot of hashish or a ride in the National, Angus would know just the man to see me through."

Angus returned with the paper in his hand.

"There aren't many these days. No one can afford now to run a shoot for fun or to entertain house-parties. You only get asked to shoot if you can ask them back, and I don't blame them. The days of the semiprofessional supershot who went from house to house are dead. My father asked one of them to Holton once. He was very solemn, never smoked, and never touched a drop, except one weak whisky a night. Worked out all his 'forthcoming engagements' like a Derby favourite. Scared the footman to sobs. He found him on his back on the floor when he called him one morning, and thought he was dead. But he was only doing deep-breathing exercises to clear his eye! That chap had a loader, three guns, three thousand cartridges, and one set of specially-made flannel combinations, with pleats under the arms, in order not to cramp his swing. They had to be ironed and aired every single night while we were at dinner. You could have grown tomatoes on them by the end of the week and, believe me or not, he left eightpence in coppers on his dressing table for the housemaid when he left!"

He commenced to read, "*Guns? guns? guns?* No, these are all poor devils who are trying to sell theirs. Um. . . .

> '*A few paying guests taken in beautifully situated house, North Wales; large acreage good rough shooting. . . .*'

Rough's the word. Two thousand acres of oak forest as steep as a house and one cock pheasant in the middle of them. A guinea fine if you shoot a hen but rabbits galore. . . . Mm. . . .

> '*Careful gun wanted for desirable low ground shooting, East Fife. . . .*'

I know *that* place. He'll be full of care by the end of the season. Under water for about six months a year and too wet even for snipe. If the owner wants a gun, it's a duck-gun. . . .

> '*A few guests taken October to January, Sussex. Good shooting. Home produce, h. and c. . . .*'

That means the guests come and go and it never has a rest all the season and I expect the home produce is disguised as pheasant *en casserole.* . . .

"Christmas! '*Two guns required complete party for coming season, Norfolk. Skill with gun not so essential*' (my-darling-Mabel!) '*as mellow comradeship. Excellent food and cellar. Apply Box X* 101.' . . . That must be old Bongo Bellemy, in the Green Dragoons! I thought he was dead! Only chap I know with an Old Plutonian game-keeper, Jammy Falkenham! 'Has him in after dinner to play chess, and they get tight together and argue a cow's hindleg off. It wasn't a bad shoot once, but now Bongo pops his guns in March and bails them out in September. '*Skill with gun not so essential as mellow comradeship.*' The Lord preserve me from the unskilled gun after lunch with Bongo! I'd sooner be shot by an enemy than a mellow comrade any day. You might get some fun out of that party but Bongo's an ace poker-player and you won't get out of it under 300 quid. He and his keeper will see to *that*! . . .

"Now what's this? '*Major Aubrey Bruisyard-Smith, O.B.E. late Caledonian Horse, still has vacancy for good gun in first-class mixed shoot in Bampshire*' . . .

"Remember that bird in Northern Command two months before D-Day? *The* perfectly-modulated staff-officer, the my-dear-old-boy-I-couldn't-agree-with-you-more-but-of-course-I'm-not-really-in-the-picture-on-that-one, but you couldn't get a sausage out of him! '*Excellent prospects.*' I'll bet! Troops all over it all the war and Jimmy Gammon told me when he had those hounds he took the shooting to rear a few spare litters of cubs in. Aubrey Bruisyard-Smith can go and sabotage himself. . . .

"Hullo! This is more like it. '*Experienced gameshot required to complete syndicate near Furzechester. Apply Mannering, Stoke Loyalty* 290.' I know that chap very slightly. He's a very nice fellow who farms a lot of land and ran a first-class bundobust before the war. . . ."

§ 2

There was a stir in the crowd round the bar and a sudden silence fell. Through it to a stool in the innermost corner, as to a stall in the theatre, walked a very stout short man with black curls draped closely round his ears. In his left hand he held an immense cigar between two stiffly-projecting fingers. He walked very slowly, bending a little forward as if to register the attention of his audience. A crimson carnation in his lapel set off the gleaming collar and cuffs, the dark pinstriped suit with its tawny waistcoat, and the swarthy face above. So might Jove have looked if he had ever descended on a London club. The newcomer settled himself on his leather stool with the deliberation of a bull-bison, inserted in the folds of his face an eyeglass on a thick black cord, and surveyed the line of eager drinkers

with well-bred truculence, "busied in his majesty", seeing
nobody he did not wish to see.

Poppy forsook all and without waiting for an order hurried
to lay before the newcomer a tankard of "Pimms". Into it he
dipped his massive jowl with delicacy.

"Behold the Lord Lysimachus!" Angus said. His knowledge
of Shakespeare was confined to the Falstaffiad and the more
censorable portions of *Pericles Prince of Tyre*.

"Who's he?" murmured Gerald.

"That," said Angus, "is Sir William Boulogne, late Lateral
candidate for Central Harkshire."

"What the deuce is the Lateral party? Never heard of 'em."

"Well, they bend so far in both directions that they're almost
horizontal. If the Communists ever come into power, when the
roll is called up yonder, they'll be there. And if the pendulum
swings back, they'll be there too, wearing Old Plutonian ties,
and blackballing people of whom they 'aren't sure' socially.
And they've so far been everything else in turn, Fascist, Liberal,
Unionist, old Uncle Tom Cobley and all."

"I see."

"I'm glad you've seen our William. He lends us tone. We're all a bit shabby nowadays but not William. No club is really complete without him."

"Gentile?"

"Almost, but very rich. Armenian at a guess but almost in the passing-out stage. *We're* rather interested in him."

"Who's we?"

Angus closed one eye. "Sorry, old boy, talking shop out of turn. Do odd jobs for a pal of mine in the force ever since I ceased to be a peeler." He looked at the Jove-like form and went on, rumbling under his breath. "I've always wished I could write, not a *Who's Who* of my acquaintances, but a *Why's Why* or *How's How* to answer the questions the books never attempt. You know, where does his money come from? How did he ever come to meet that woman, let alone marry her? How can he afford a peerage, or a Rolls, why did he ever get made a member of the Sausage Club, and so on and so on? That chap would make a very good type to start with. I've seen him wearing an old Plutonian tie but *Who's Who* says he was educated 'privately', which means he was sacked or else at some school he won't let on about. I have an idea he's a bit bogus. We're the most leaky collection of individuals in Europe and since Hitler came into power we've let in all sorts of queer folk, displaced persons and so on, while we others were all too busy. Now they're knuckling in everywhere. They're very adaptable."

"Protective coloration, eh?"

"Exactly. I've no doubt Bill Boulogne is marvellously documented and you'd find his ancestor was the original Guillaume Boulogne who first went in a coracle and discovered Folkestone in the year One or something, but . . . Let's try for a drink at the bar" (a slight gap had occurred in the fervent ever-shifting line) "and just make polite small-talk and keep your ears open. You're a naturalist! Well, you've got a chance to study a rare bird in full breeding-plumage."

36

"What the devil do I talk about?"

"Sport," said Angus, "the kind that means sitting in the Members' Enclosure or the County Stand or a ringside seat, and watching someone else do something. *Not*, my lad, the cruder type you and I have been accustomed to."

§ 3

Half an hour later Angus and Gerald went out. Gerald suddenly realized that he had not thought about that death-sentence of his for nearly an hour.

"You were right," he said, "about that chap being bogus."

"Oh, you spotted it too? How?"

"Well, I led him on a bit while you were backchatting with that Poppy, or whatever her name is. . . ."

"Camouflage, pure and simple. I didn't want Bill Bolony to think I was taking an interest in him."

"Why?"

"He may know I've been a peeler in my day."

"I see. I told him I was on leave and hoping to get some hunting later on."

"Yes . . . ?"

"Well, it wasn't long before he told me about a hunt he'd had in 1940 with the Quitechley."

"Not with the *Quitechley*?"

"He did. Most circumstantial account, too."

"Well, shiver-my-vertebrae," said Angus, as he fumbled with his keys, "if that chap ever indulged in the chase in *that* country, he was pursuing an heiress round and round the car park after a hunt-ball!"

"Do you mean that?"

"I do. Wasn't I Chief Constable of the county once, before they threw me out? I'll swear he never rode to hounds there."

"It didn't sound right but it was slick enough."

They entered Angus's rooms and sat down in immense arm-chairs.

"I'll bet it was. I know Jack Osgerby, the Secretary of that hunt, very well, and he'll pin that one down. Go on, Gerald. I watched you doing very nicely with him. Get any more gup?"

"Well, we just touched on shooting and he trotted out a few odd references to Langholm and Six Mile Bottom and Wemmergill. . . ."

"Did he? Well, these birds normally give themselves away by opening a bit too high. Like the heroes with the dud cheques, who always put up the V.C. or the D.C.M. instead of something that doesn't attract attention."

"What was he knighted for?"

"Services to the war effort!"

"What services?"

"Patronage secretaries are sometimes very mum. At a guess he was Chairman of the company that made seventeen million pairs of those Army braces, the kind that have about as much give in them as funnel-stays. *You* know! used to whip every button off your battledress when you stooped down to lace your boots!"

"I remember, frightful things!"

"And then he probably started a subsidiary company to make a hundred million relief trouser buttons at twopence each. You remember those sharp tin things that were taught to bite the hand that did them? Now I *am* beginning to get a line on Bill Bolony. I've wanted to for months. He may be just an ordinary liar but I'm beginning to think there's more to him than that. . . . Only keep your mouth shut, Gerald, won't you?"

"Of course. It's probably part of his protective coloration. He's a self-made man who doesn't want to let you in on his secret recipe. Oh, by the way, I've just remembered something else: he's taken a place near where my uncle lives in Harkshire. Says he's got some excellent shooting."

"You must go down there," said Angus, "and ask me too. I tell you what! I'll shave my moustache and eyebrows and go as your ex-batman, with a broad Scots accent. I'm rather good at ironing trousers! Let's get cleaned up and dine at the Equestrian."

IV. THE ROOT OF ALL EVIL

I have come to know that money is largely a fiction.
—JOHN MASEFIELD

"Have you any money these days?" asked Angus. They were sitting in the smoking-room after dinner. The bill had included two glasses of rather ordinary port, at a price at which they could have purchased a vintage bottle ten years before.

"So so," said Gerald, "thanks to the war I'm fairly flush. My bank had quite a shock when they realized that I was going to them for some of my own, for once."

"There's no such thing," Angus said severely, "as being flush nowadays. You may *feel* flush but it's an illusion, like love. Supposin' you've got £30000 in the bank in gilt-edged and what-have-you. It's only bringing you in a nominal £900 and that means you'll see £450. *And,* my lad, some black-coated son of sin in Whitehall is already planning to swipe that off you by 1950!

"And if they don't do it directly, they just let the flood of paper overwhelm them and then Government has to put in three other sons of sin, with ancillary typists and messengers, to keep abreast of the work. And there's fifteen new servants of Government, whose meal-tickets, pensions and every sort of leave, from privilege to maternity, you and I will have to shoulder for the next fifty years!"

He drank an inch of brandy.

"I tell you it haunts me! All down the years, Gerald, is a vista of little pale-faced stinkers who were in the Upper Bench when I was bottom of the Army Class, waiting to put a pistol to my head and pick my pocket! And then they get a K.B.E. for doing so. . . .

"One had one's chance with the old highwayman—a horse-pistol and a good horse and you *might* never meet them at all. But *now* some rozzy Minister, with his cerebellum in the clouds and bogged down to his hocks in class-prejudice, is *the* absolutely certain highwayman you and I must encounter. He doesn't know within forty-five million what it'll cost but he's convinced 'the masses' will stand for it. Sheep! that's all we are nowadays!"

An Equestrian in a neighbouring chair, who had almost convinced himself he was a horse, blinked and looked askance at the slur cast on him by Angus.

"Never mind," he went on, "whenever I spend a fiver on riotous living, I always say 'There it goes, confound you, my Lords of the Treasury, you haven't got it anyway.' "

"They've probably swiped half of it in excise-duty first," said Gerald. "And what about your children?"

"O them!" said Angus easily. "If this goes on, there won't be much to *breed* for. Bomb-fodder they'll be, or just tax-fodder, poor lambs! Perhaps marriage will be compulsory soon like vaccination. Then I shall be like one of those parsons who has squads of kids because birth-control is immoral. I shall go down in a welter of fecundity and bring the State down with me. D'y'ever read the report of the Royal Commission on Birth-Control?"

"Good Lord, no! Why?"

Angus was always confounding others with his ethnological studies which ranged from marriage-customs in the Sudan to the orgies of Travancore fire-worshippers. He was embarrassingly ready to give chapter and verse at any moment.

"The Antis," Angus went on, "were all laid a dead stymie on

that party. Supposin', they were asked, a man on £2 a week could only afford one child and then only save a halfpenny a week, and, supposin' there was no legal birth-control, two normal people marryin' young could expect to have fifteen children? How could they support them, and was it right to have them?"

"Well, how did they glance that one off?"

"In different sonorous phrases, but it all really boiled down to 'the Lord will provide'."

"He'll have to," said Gerald. "Only rabbits can afford large families nowadays, and they expect a thumping death-rate. I've got a cousin who's a parson. I'm always expecting him to be cashiered, with assets two-and-tenpence and a couple of prams, and liabilities five daughters."

"Let's drop these forebodings," said Angus, "and go to a night club."

"I don't know any. You forget I've been abroad nine years."

"We'll go," said Angus, "to the 'Tape-Worm'. It's by the old Taper Club, which had candles on the tables so that they could blow them out when they were raided, out of the 'Early Worm' which caught the bird when Ma Lebanon went to clink. The 'Tape-Worm' is quite an apt name for it as it's full of worms (disguised as lounge-lizards), and the management is inhibited by more red tape than any club I know."

"How do you mean?"

"Well, you can't bring a girl there unless you're married to her (and then they'll probably want to see your lines) or have been introduced by the King's Proctor to a member of the Committee."

"It doesn't sound amusing."

"You ought to see it! You'll see all the smart birds who've kept out of the really sticky jobs in this war. You'll see the top-layer of the Imperial race, pregnant with victory! They've all made money in spite of E.P.T., and they've all kept in the swim, while blokes like you and the Premier were stupid enough to think that making war meant getting as near the enemy as possible. I tell you there was no job so unmilitary that we couldn't find someone in uniform to do it, from hotel-keeping *de luxe* to entertaining ENSA stars! And that while you real soldiers up at the sharp end weren't wearing any uniform at all, growing beards and long hair and blacking your faces and putting on every damned unsoldierly gadget, like fur-coats and fishermen's sweaters." Angus spoke with warmth for as a provost-officer he had had to enforce some standards of "turn-out".

"But what's that got to do with the Taper Club, Angus?"

"Just a historical aside! The Club itself had a dim beginning until they got the second vulgarest man in London to stand up in spotless evening dress, and sing, very audibly, what he would have been turned out of most private houses for suggesting. Now it's absurdly fashionable: confidential lights, imitation-oak beams, a floor you can't swing a cat on, and whisky at three-fifteen a bottle. But it's quite a good *kala jugga*."

"What's the use of a *kala jugga*, if we've got no one to jug with?"

"I'll bet I know someone there," said Angus. "The rest will follow. I must just cash a cheque first. Have you plenty of money on you?"

"How much shall I want?"

"It's a question of how much *they'll* want. I should say it'll be all you've got and then you can bail yourself out by cheque. Come on, and curse-the-Exchequer!"

As they made their way up Bond Street, Gerald remarked certain ladies who stood bending forward slightly at street-corners.

"Lost a cousin of mine here one night," said Angus casually. "Most tragic thing! Magnificent ornithologist, only came up to London once a year from Cornwall to the Union dinner to talk bird-shop."

"Well, what the deuce was he doing in Bond Street instead of in South Kensington?"

"I was coming to that. It seemed he palled up at dinner with a female ornithologist from Kent (excellent naturalist but no oil-painting, y'know) and offered to see her home to her aunt's in Bruton Street. They walked all the way back, deep in converse about the difference between the songs of *Hypolais* and *Acrocephalus*, as sober as judges. Parted at her door with a promise to meet in May to look for *Upupa epops* breeding in Thanet. All as innocent as Eden. . . . But wait! down here, my poor dear cousin, who was the soul of rural courtesy, stepped aside off the pavement, at that very corner, to make way for one of those girls who was sort of cooing at him y'know, and a taxi came swishing round the corner and killed him! Well, if you'll believe me, there were only two eye-witnesses at the inquest, the girl and the taxi-driver, and nothing would persuade his widow that he hadn't been out on the tiles that night, instead of at the B.O.U.! My poor young godson, his boy, was brought up like a novice in a monastery, to regard all women as a menace and was never allowed to speak to one."

Gerald grunted. "Silly idea! What happened to *him*?"

"He was mad on birds too. He eventually ran away and is now a ghillie on the far end of Corrour with 50000 acres of damn-all between him and a woman! If a hiker so much as shows a skirt within three miles of young John, he takes to the high tops like a ptarmigan. 'Hid in the sanctuary when the new tenant wanted him to take his wife out stalking. I shall get my psychiatrist on to him, one day, if I can lure him up to Invernessshire!"

V. AT THE TAPER CLUB

What wafts of steak and kidney pie!
What blasts of Bantu melody!
—With apologies to the (untraced) author.

The Taper Club had, with the advent of VE-Day, abandoned its war-time name, "The Tape-Worm", bestowed on it by its most thoughtless proprietor when it had amalgamated with the ill-fated "Early Worm". It was now the most exclusive of the smaller supper-clubs in the Metropolis. Gigoleo was in charge of the restaurant, there was a negro band, and as Angus had hinted, the vulgarest wit in London in charge of its entertainment. Its members were sure of discreet lighting effects, of a company rigidly select, of hearing the very latest sultry story and, above all, of a competent staff-photographer, none other than Cyril de Bourbon.

Cyril it was who ensured that, when their portraits, two by two at meat, appeared in the appropriate journals, not only would their names be correctly given but they would not be looking "too fearfully goofy".

Cyril de Bourbon had begun life as a bird-photographer but, after several seasons of rain, mud, cramp and mosquitoes, had realized there was more money and less agony in portraying the rare birds of Society in their feeding-haunts. But he had never forgotten the first lesson learnt in the field of bird-photography—correct identification. "A pectoral sandpiper must *hate*", he said, "to be misidentified as a little stint or a dusky redshank. These Society birds are every bit as touchy." He had never slipped up even when Captain "Bunny" Girdlestowe had signed in a very distant cousin as his wife. They had duly appeared in the *By-Prattler* as "Among others dining at the Taper Club were Capt. 'Bunny' Girdlestowe, who goes so well with the Fattistock, and a friend." What Mrs. Girdlestowe had said later about the friendship was not evidence, and the cousin had since decided that she herself would "go" much better with the P.W.H.

A solitary amber light announced "The Taper Club" over a solid oak-door.

"They change it to red when there's a raid on," said Angus, "but they have such terrific graft that the red light is rarely needed. The limousine outside the door is a decoy. Only the manager can afford a car like that. Come on, Gerald. Let joy be unconfined but always the gentleman! Forget that leech of yours! We're early. The expensive people aren't out of the theatres yet."

They pressed a bell.

"I believe," Angus went on, "they're installing a television set so that one can be given the once-over before they open. . . . Now remember, Gerald, you're my cousin and give your correct rank and regiment."

A pale young man in purple uniform, with marcelled hair and two rows of medal ribbons, opened the door.

"*Hullo*, Tompkins!" said Angus, shaking hands. "Where was it we last met, Havre, Cairo, Tripoli, Naples, Bayeux, Brussels or Bad Oeynhausen?" The porter beamed.

"Why, it's Major Somborne! I heard you was a member. I've only been back a week. Brussels, wasn't it, we last met, when I was on the Welfare?"

Pte. Tompkins had followed the British Army faithfully round the continent of Europe and the Middle East, "marching to the sound of the siphons", as Angus phrased it. He had helped

45

to organize the officers' restaurant in Le Havre. He had been a mess-waiter at Cairo in a Service club, then batman to a brigadier at Gezira, and barman when they opened the Mehari Hotel in Tripoli. He had graduated finally by way of Algiers, Naples, and St. Paul's School, to be floor-manager in the *Splendide* at Brussels when it had been set aside to make other ranks on leave realize that this war was not as other wars. Tompkins had almost as many medals as the first Duke of Wellington or Sir Sam Browne, but the only shot he had seen fired was when, at Gezira, he had attempted to clean a fellow-batman's rifle for him without realizing it was loaded. The incident had made a great impression on him and in that hour he had resolved, finally, to abandon the sword for the corkscrew.

"Wonderful chap, Tompkins!" said Angus, as Gerald shook hands. "Night-porter in the Blitz before the war. Kept a case of whisky under the lift seat for people like myself, who came in late. Tompkins, those were the days, weren't they? *Labuntur anni!*"

"Annie?" said Tompkins. "I don't know where Annie's gone now, sir. You mean the floor-waitress we called 'Show-me-home'? Some of our girls didn't know enough to keep themselves out of trouble. But we've two or three quite nice girls 'ere, 'ostesses. But I forgot you was a member. . . ."

"I am, Tompkins. Private citizen now! No lights out or early parades. And did *you*, as a soldier for six years on active service, ever go on parade?"

Tompkins scratched his curls. "I can't recall doing so, sir. Yes, I did once, in Tripoli! I remember because I couldn't find me boots. We never 'ad much occasion for them in my job and they 'urt me somethink cruel."

Gerald laughed. "What ceremony was that for, Tompkins? Monty or Mr. Churchill?"

"Neither," said Tompkins, with an injured look. "It was an identification parade. Some feller pinched a million cigarettes out of a Naffy store, but they never found 'oo it was."

"There you are, Gerald," beamed Angus. "Six years soldiering in the greatest war in history and only been on an identification parade! And how did you get demobilized so early, Tompkins?"

"Oh, they took a few of us who were in the essential trades, like, out with Group One, sir."

"Sorry, I forgot. Lead on, Tompkins, to the receipt of custom!"

Tompkins flung open a second door. In an oak-panelled reception office, under a neon light, stood a ravishing blonde in a black dress, with hair which Professor Ridgway would have classified as pale wistaria blue.

"My God!" said Gerald involuntarily.

"*Courage, mon cher,*" said Angus. "Good evening, Jacqueline! I'm clocking in again. My cousin, who is going to be the new Under-Secretary for Power and Gas! Major Gerald Warde, Miss Binks."

Gerald Warde's cavalry training had taught him never to display emotion whenever man or horse did anything unexpected, but he blinked at this introduction, as he shook hands. Jacqueline gave him a limp hand, studded with purple nails which seemed two inches long, and pushed forward the register for signature.

"What's the cap, Jacqueline, for a male guest?" asked Angus.

"Two guineas."

Gerald was duly "capped", and they were passed on. Gerald was aware of an inner office in which a dark man in evening dress was taking down a book off a shelf.

"Don't be a bloody fool, Angus!" he said when they were out of earshot. "They'll spot I'm not an M.P. at once."

"Don't worry, old boy! This Government's far too young for them to know who two dozen new Under-Secretaries are. We can always say the appointment was cancelled. That bird will find you in the Army List!"

"But supposing that girl starts blathering?"

47

"Not she! Jacqueline is so dumb I nearly talk on my fingers to her. She's the original pin-up girl of the Dumb Friends' League."

"She looks a bit wet," said Gerald, "behind the glamour."

"Wet enough to shoot snipe off. If you sat out with Jacqueline in a draught you'd die of exposure! She's there as a decoy, looking lovely under that lamp. Everyone thinks they must all look as marvellous as that, inside."

"But why on earth say I'm a Labour M.P.?"

"Oh, it may come in handy. Now let's sit here and do what the books call 'take stock of our surroundings'."

The Club was only half-full. On the dais, the negro band was whiffling mournfully down its instruments, their gleaming teeth and shirt fronts and their henna-ed curls making the only spot of colour at the end of the room. Their orgiastic blare and thump would rise to its full diapason in about an hour. An empty table with very special decorations occupied most of one side. At a remote table Cyril de Bourbon, pale and languid with a blue kerchief lolling out of his pocket, was supping while one of the hostesses smoked a cigarette opposite him. Here and there a couple sat in earnest converse in a dark corner. Gerald's eye roved round the room.

"My God! Angus," he exclaimed, "I thought you said this was an exclusive club. Look over there. If it isn't that Monty Bitterne!"

"Who's he?"

"Monty Bitterne? One of the few Indian Cavalry men I couldn't like. He was one of the horrors of polo at Meerut."

"Oh, *that* chap! Handicap of three goals and a way with women. . . ."

"Which he didn't regard as a handicap of any kind, blast him!"

"I remember now. He used to address a girl as if she was a golf ball on a tee."

"But I thought you said this was an exclusive club?"

"I didn't say who they excluded. With that hair, Haroun-al-

Raschid's own nose, and Monty's ancestry, one is safe in any night-club in the world from Baghdad to Battersea. He's probably on the staff here or half-brother of the head-waiter. Dam' pretty girl he's with."

Gerald looked. "Healthy one too. Now tell me, Angus, why do the most awful men seem to get hold of such attractive women? Don't the women *see* or do they go for something we can never spot?"

"I have a theory we're all naturally polygamous, like bison, and women know it. They go instinctively for the biggest bull in the herd."

"I must say I should have to feel pretty polygamous before I went for Monty Bitterne."

"But then I'm not a woman, thank God! Perhaps he just *shikarred* her, and she can't get away. We'll see what we can do, before the evening's out. Come on, forget your leech, forget the whisky which is £3 15s. a bottle, forget everything for the rest of the ruddy evening. I always do. And mind! I never remember anything I say after ten o'clock at night!"

Angus's eyes smouldered and his mane and moustache stood up simultaneously. But Gerald thought, "Here I am: one year to live, and all England to see after nine years and my last summer running out inexorably. And this cacophony of negroid sound, this fetid atmosphere of flowers and sweat, Turkish cigarettes and *houbigant*, all this expensive fog which they hang so cleverly round the idea of wanting to be with a woman." Not for him, not after tonight anyway! The girl with Monty Bitterne looked a real nice lass, too. Much too healthy to be in that club or his company. Probably hunted. That complexion never came out of a bottle. And among the pale ones and the swarthy ones in that place, his lean red cheeks glowed.

§ 2

Slowly the Club filled up, and as the parties settled down Cyril de Bourbon rose and put on his languid, winning smile to make his nightly round with his camera. Wherever Society flocked, he was to be found. They were just like birds. One photographed them feeding, or preening on some quiet beach in the sunshine, one snapped them, almost before they knew it, when it was obvious they were going to pair, and later on one took them at St. Margaret's in the fullest of full breeding-plumage. And then a year later one followed them down to the country and they posed for you, like a great crested grebe on

the nest, leaning against the Adam mantelpiece of "their attractive country-cottage", or amid cushions with a background of family paintings, or playing with little Jennifer, the fruit of their union, on their "old-world" lawn.

And he thought, Birds! He had had it as far as *aves* were concerned. They hated the camera, they had kept him waiting for hours in agony and deserted their precious eggs rather than sit to him. Real birds didn't seem to want to be immortalized but these society birds did. And he looked savagely at Mrs. Simon Popkiss, who went to unparalleled lengths to get her portrait into the *By-Prattler* at least once a fortnight. She hadn't been on a horse for fifteen years, but there she always was, "chatting with the Master" at a Quitechley meet, wearing something very *outré* at a hunter-trial or a blood-stock sale, dining here, "helping to organize" there, at this hunt-ball, at that charity hop, in the enclosure at Ascot, on the Squadron lawn. Mrs. Simon Popkiss would be found graven in red asterisks on his retina when he died. And he thought:

"You wait, Mrs. Simon Popkiss, till we meet one day at a Fatstock Show, or some Breed Society's exhibition, and start shoving your dainty nose in. You'll get yours then, even if I have to superimpose one negative on another!"

There was a stir at the door, and a party chattered its way to the reserved table near the dancing-floor, preceded by the head-waiter under Gigoleo's personal supervision. Monty Bitterne, who had been leaning back confidentially in his corner, sat up and Gerald saw him draw a pencil from his pocket and swallow a very brown glass of whisky.

Gerald watched the party settle down.

"Funny thing!" he said. "I hardly know a soul in London and I haven't been in England for nine years, but I believe I've met three of that crowd today, though I can't put a name to any of 'em."

"I can," said Angus, whose acquaintance was world-wide and peculiar. "You met Bill Bolony in the bar at the Savernake. That's why I came. Who else do you recognize?"

"The fattish woman with the pearls."

"Stately, it's called. That's Rosamund Gore-Ambulance, wife of the distinguished Wimpole. . . ."

"My leech's wife, is she? I remember her now. I saw her in the hall just before I went in to him. . . . Showed me the white of her eye rather. Kicker, I thought. . . ."

"You've said it. We once had an argument about a mutual friend, and I told her she was a gossiping bitch!"

"What happened then?"

"Speaking as a gunner, we each put down a heavy concentration of gas and smoke and then broke off the engagement. But I was told later that poor Rosamund had been mortally wounded, and that if there was one woman in London who really was popular with and loved by other women it was her. I was, in short, bidden to apologise."

"What did you do?"

"I fell back on the old court-martial answer: I never remembered anything I said after ten o'clock at night but whatever I *had* said, I could assure her I meant. The correspondence was then closed."

Angus drank some whisky and closed his eyes.

"Do you remember old James Bunbury in India, the one we always called Jimmy Bundobust?"

"A little chap, rather a fusser about detail?"

"That's him, always worked everything out to the last trouser button, enormously involved operation orders covering every possibility; there was so much bundobust that no one had any time to get on with the operation, sometimes."

"I remember. I saw him sitting on his balcony once at Meerut swinging a polo-stick. He did it for two hours a day for six weeks before a tournament to strengthen his wrist."

"That's the chap! I've seen him hog his moustache before a steeplechase to get down to the weight, and if he went shooting he'd lay all his stuff out beforehand and have a kit inspection five times over."

"Rum fellow, but desperately keen and rather a good sort."

"Well, *her* sister Angela," Angus jerked his head towards the big table, "married old Jimmy Bundobust just before he retired. *The* untidiest woman in Harkshire and no more sense of time than a herring. Spends four hours a day on the telephone, another three reading in her bath, and the house is covered with unpaid bills and clocks which don't go. But she's got Jimmy Bundobust like *that*" (Angus flattened a thumb like a banana on the table) "and he's *mali, syce* to her children, bearer, *chaprassi* and sweeper to the household. I called on him once just before the war and he was fearfully pleased to see me. Trotted out the drinks and wanted me to stop to lunch and so on. But then Angela came downstairs, having just completed a brisk fifty-minute run on the telephone, and she very soon saw me off. She's quite good-looking but I'd as soon be married to a good-looking puma."

"How the deuce did James Bunbury come to do that? Marriage must call for a bit of bundobust, if anything does."

"My lad," said Angus, "let that be a warning to you. Houses and women! People take both of 'em on, and never work the cost of either out. The odds against one finding the house one really wants vacant, at the moment you want it, are almost as great as finding the right girl vacant at the right moment. The ones I want to marry I always find are bespoke two deep. And then I do silly things like that brigadier's daughter you wot of. However let's forget her. Who else do you know in that party?"

"That full Colonel in uniform I saw in the Club today. Lord Someone. . . ."

"Tom Glenagony, the perfect young staff-officer. Never been out of England (note the Medals) and never slept off a spring-bed all the war. There were very few like him in this war but they get my goat every time."

"I expect he was unfit." Gerald, now condemned to death, was ready to see hidden illnesses in anyone.

"Rot, Gerald. Did *you* ever have a medical in this war? I never did until after I got hit in '44. When I came back in '39, after being out of the army six years, a civilian M.O. gave one look at my face and said, 'Well, there's not much wrong with you, is there?' and signed on the dotted line."

There was a crash which nearly drowned the band. Monty Bitterne, dancing with the girl in the white dress and endeavouring to make notes about the centre table, had slipped on the turn and was flat on his back.

"Sunk with all hands," said Angus, "poor girl!"

Gerald watched the girl, pink with anger, pull herself together, smile and help Monty to his feet. She led him out of the eddy of dancers and proceeded to dust him down.

Angus rose. "I can see Monty's canned. This is where we step in." He walked over to the couple and had a few words with the girl. Before Gerald quite knew what had happened, he was bringing the pair back to his table.

Gerald rose slowly. He found himself shaking hands with the girl who said "My name's Ann" . . . something he could not catch, and then with Monty Bitterne who began "My dear old boy . . . Risshulpaw, wasn't it? I remember you onsh crossing me. . . . '

"You shut up about crosses, Monty," said Angus warningly. "You ought to have had a goal given against you just now, for that last foul. Miss Heriot, you don't look as if you needed a preen, I promise you, but I'm sure you'd like one, after that chukker with Major Bitterne."

Miss Heriot buried herself in her bag and "preened" into a small mirror. Monty, who had swallowed a whisky in less time than it takes to write, rose unsteadily to his feet. "Shsorry," he said, "Jush go and telephone my paper. See you later, Ann o' girl. Gobbless!" He swayed away.

Gerald looked at Miss Heriot. She was still rather pinker than usual with annoyance but it suited her gray eyes. There was a twinkle in them. "Miss Heriot," he said, "what on earth does Monty Bitterne mean by his paper? Is he out of the Army now?"

"I think so!" said Ann Heriot. "Though I only met him yesterday. He does all the hunting gossip for the *By-Prattler*."

"Well, well," said Angus who had been engaged in mysterious transactions with a waiter about certain "non-quota" bottles which he had apparently stabled at the Club. "Monty a journalist! But he won't get much hunting gossip here, surely?"

"I rather gathered," Miss Heriot twinkled again, "that he's deputizing for their special lady correspondent, Geraldine, who has gone to Paris this week."

"Now-sink-me-the-ship-master-gunner!" said Angus, "not *the* Geraldine who writes *My Social Whirl*?"

"I believe so!"

Angus looked solemn. He shook his massive head from side

to side and his brown eyes smouldered. "I would rather write that letter once, Miss Heriot, than sack Quebec. And to think that the palm has fallen to Monty. . . ."

A waiter leant over Angus. "Sir William Boulogne's compliments, sir. He wondered if you would care to join his party at his table?"

"Red-sky-at-night, waiter, this is indeed a good omen. Pray give our compliments to Sir William and say we will be with him in a moment."

VI. LITERARY PROFITS

Sir William Boulogne was annoyed. It was bad enough having young Monty Bitterne crashing into a Club of which he was not a member and trying to get free drinks for himself and his guest by representing that he was "Press". Worse, when he had hoped for a pleasant supper *à deux* with Rosamund Gore-Ambulance, she had not only inveigled him into throwing a large party, but had disappeared in the middle of it into the manager's office to answer a telephone call from Harkshire. The call had lasted forty minutes, while she had left him to entertain the bobtail of her acquaintants.

"You won't mind, William," she said at length, "I promised Angela I'd ring her up and then I forgot, so when she rang me, I told them to reverse that call!"

"Eh, what?"

"Reverse it! You know, charge it up here. My poor sister is broke as usual, she and her husband!"

"Oh! I see." But Sir William, smiling his dark smile, didn't really see at all. People deserved to be broke if they hadn't more sense of time, which was money, than that, and put through trunk-calls in the middle of the night to a club and then went on and on, all about an aunt. There was no future in other people's aunts.

Rosamund saw Sir William was annoyed. She unleashed her own smile, a much more brilliant affair, put her neat head on one side to show the pale streak, which was so becoming, and

said "Come on, William, let's dance. I'm terribly worried."
She had always found it more convincing to go into a clinch
with a man than to argue at long range.

And Sir William, who hated dancing and liked sitting at a
table where he could show his button-hole, his cuff links, his
signet ring, his wristwatch and his beautifully-manicured fingers
to all who cared to observe, had had to take the floor, like Jove
in a thundercloud, and plough round with a woman who
definitely wasn't a flier, and made his arms ache abominably.
She had nestled up to him, which had meant his carrying her
weight even more, and embarked on an interminable story
about Angela, and her efforts at palming off an ailing aunt on
her.

"It's frightfully inconvenient," she had said, "but the old
dear's been bed-ridden now for weeks in Angela's house. Of
course I'm her favourite niece and I don't want to cross the old
body, she's absolutely rolling, and not a soul to leave it to
except a cats' home! I shall simply *have* to have her and she'll
jaw my head off and I *was* going to stop with Mrs. Ikey
Malcolmson at Bembridge . . . sorry, aren't some of these
people *impossibly* clumsy? I suppose blood *is* thicker than water
especially when the blood has all that amount of boodle behind
it?"

Sir William had been poor enough, in his time, to know
what it was to have no blood and no boodle behind him at all,
and had never had an aunt; but he would have nursed his fingers
to the bone for one if she had shown any signs of leaving him
money. He grunted non-committally. And just when he
realized that Rosamund was definitely not in her first youth,
that she was badly let down, and not a free mover, and just as
her weight was beginning to tell, they passed the post or rather
the band. He immediately made a secret signal with his little
finger to Al Consomme, the band-leader, whose teeth flashed
an acknowledgment, and the band stopped with a crash. Then
he was able to walk statelily back to his table where he drew out

his famous crimson silk handkerchief and dabbed his streaming brow and dipped his jowl into a drink.

Only Al Consomme, Luigi the headwaiter, and Gigoleo knew that Sir William was really the sole proprietor of the Taper Club. He had had a varied business career, as we shall see, but he knew no investment which had on the whole paid him such spectacular profits, if only you watched your step and kept the right side not of the law but the police. A friend had once said to him, "I've got one, just one, of the old original hundred-pound shares in the Puss-cat Club. Brings me in £120 a year and don't I wish I had a thousand?" And Sir William, then plain Mr. William Boulogne, had said "Really! how interesting" and had kept his own counsel as usual. But some far-back ancestor of his, who had probably arranged for Syrian girls to dance before Haroun-al-Raschid, had nudged him secretly once or twice and said "There's money in this, my boy!" So he had gone on, starting in a very quiet way and always with someone to hold the baby if things went wrong. And now he was sole proprietor of a Club of his own, though he liked to explain everything to acquaintances by saying that he was "on the committee. They made me go on, and one likes to see the thing properly done." He only wished he had realized twenty-five years before what money there was in whisky and a heated atmosphere and twenty square feet of polished floor and negro melody, the four most potent short-term intoxicants he knew.

§ 2

This is not the place for a full study of Sir William's career. Suffice it that, as a young man, he had pressed trousers and turned on hot baths and cleaned buttons and run errands in an establishment which existed to transform the haggard mud-stained officer, fresh from the Somme, into a spruce being with money in his pocket ready to enjoy ninety-six hours leave. It had been for the owner, Mr. Salmon, a wearing and rather risky profession which blossomed imperceptibly into banking.

(You cashed their cheques and telephoned for theatre-tickets and tables for supper, and sometimes for pretty ladies to share the supper, and you showed them the ropes of London generally.)

And next morning young William had always hurried down to Cox's five minutes before the doors opened with a sheaf of cheques, in order to beat any of the pretty ladies to it before they brought in *theirs*. And usually he had won. William had learnt a good many things in those two years, including how to look after clothes really well, and how to make the utmost of his "turn-out". And on the whole singularly few cheques had rebounded towards Mr. Salmon. Until one day, a middle-aged man with a most convincing red face, and a tawny moustache brushed up like the Kaiser, had called William into the bathroom and smiled at him through the steam, and said: "I say what's-your-name? You can sew, can't you, Bill? Well, laddie, when you've pressed that tunic, just put up an extra pip and an M.C., a Mons Star and a coupla woundstripes, see? I've got rather a special date with a bird, so look slippy!"

Young Bill had done so, working overtime in a blaze of hero worship, and the hero had departed, as a Captain smarter than paint, and had tipped Bill ten shillings instead of the florin he had expected. He had popped in for a bath twice a month after that, and in six months his tunic had looked lovely, with a crown on each shoulder, the D.S.O., the M.C., the Mons Star, the yellow and black medal of the German Southwest Africa campaign, and three wound stripes. What a fighter he must have been! Until, very suddenly, there was a paragraph in the Sunday papers and the hero had finally departed to Wormwood Scrubs leaving a fiery tail of cheques, like a comet, behind him.

But William had never forgotten what a difference these little extras, an inch of ribbon or of braid, a gold watch or a pearl pin, seemed to make in instilling confidence, especially with the ladies. He had made up his mind that, when he himself prospered, he too would command everyone's attention and have what he termed an impeccable turn-out and a "few really class goods in his shop-window". But having started at the bottom of the tree, Sir William now did not like anybody to think that he had ever been near it. Fools boasted how low they had begun and thought it gave them added prestige on the heights to which they had attained. But Sir William preferred people to think that he had sprung full-fledged, as it were, from the foam of London, like Aphrodite, with perfectly-creased trousers, an Old Plutonian tie, a carnation in his lapel, and a gold wrist-watch.

Nobody else knew that under the name of William Bullen and Company he, and a couple of knowledgeable friends, had since 1940 been manufacturing the millions of new school ties and striped shirts which would be needed by the forces on demobilization. (For they had realized that whatever went in must come out some time or other, whether we won or lost.) So much so that he had recently formed yet another firm, entitled B. William Son and Company, whose purpose was (by means of representatives standing on the pavement outside "demob." centres) to buy for cash the neat cartons of clothing issued to the returning troops; and, having purchased them, to dispose of them, profitably, to persons equally in need, who had not been clothed for years by His Majesty's Government. This company had only commenced operations in a small way as yet, but there were Lateral Members pleading on its behalf in the House the sacred cause of demobilization. And once the outflow quickened, nothing could stop the chairman of B. William Son and Company, Merchants, from getting back all that he had been robbed of since 1941 in E.P.T.

So Sir William had, on the whole, no abiding cause for dissatisfaction. He sat back now and sipped champagne and asked Rosamund confidentially what she thought of the three hostesses' frocks, to which he and Gigoleo had devoted much thought. And luckily Rosamund did not reveal *her* thoughts, which were that both they and the girls inside them looked "too terribly common". And the band thumped and blared, as Al Consomme really got into his stride, and the night grew hotter and hotter until suddenly Sir William thought, "Dashed pretty girl over there with those two chaps. By Jove! I believe one's the feller I was talking to in the Savernake. Waiter!" After that it was only a minute before Gerald and Angus and Ann Heriot were ensconced at his table, and Angus (all previous hatchets buried) was trundling Rosamund round the floor like a milk-can. But after all, as Sir William smiled to himself, Angus seemed well up to her weight.

§ 3

"Well, red-tabs-in-the-morning," said Angus resignedly, as he and Gerald sank down on a sofa in the half-empty supper room, "what a party! That Rosamund Gore-Whatnot. . . ."

"I didn't go much on her."

"No. I did my best, and was as smooth as the B.B.C. but she was gently patronising about everyone in the room until at last she glanced pityingly at *your* new girl-friend, Ann Heriot..."

"Oh, yes." Gerald was not rising.

"And said she seemed a nice little thing but it was a pity she didn't know how to put her clothes on."

"*Did* she?" Gerald was still not rising but his rather sulky mouth had set in a thin line which a few people had learnt was a danger-signal. "I wish she'd said it to me."

"Well, *I* told her that with a *very* few women it didn't matter whether they knew how to put their clothes on or not, as they'd got everything else that mattered; and it was a pity the rest needed such expensive camouflage."

"Thanks, Angus!" Gerald changed the subject. "And who was the very long-necked woman with her mane banged? Lola Somebody? Came from Chelsea or somewhere."

"Oh, Lola Goldman! Her husband's a Lateral M.P. and she's an artist—something very neo-psychiatric, the new intestinal school y'know. And they're running a Bill, she told me, for the Abolition of Bloodsports, Gerald. You'd better watch your step if you want any shooting this year."

"She just started on that with me," said Gerald. "I told her I'd been the quarry for six years of quite a lot of Boches and Itis who liked bloodsports; and I found I didn't bear them any malice! But what does a woman like that *know* about bloodsports to start with?"

"Absolutely blink, but that won't stop 'em. *I* told her in confidence, that in the Quitechley country now, in order to avoid cruelty, we only hunted the carted fox. . . ."

"You bloody fool, Angus!"

". . . And that we were thinking of having the whole country electrified on the lines of Harringay! She lapped it up and said it was a pity people were so reactionary elsewhere."

"Good for you!"

"She's a red-hot Marxist and full of envy, hatred, and malice for all her fellow non-intellectuals, but as for illtreating an animal, oh dear no! But she made a hearty meal of trout. . . ."

"Which I'll bet were swimming about in a tank in the kitchen two hours ago."

"And went off in a Daimler with about £2000 worth of sable fur round her turret, and *they* didn't die under chloroform either! . . . I'm thinking there's a lot in going so far Left, Gerald, that when you spend a mint of money you're saying 'Yah!' to the capitalist."

"Rum crowd. Don't get enough fresh air."

"I saw you *shikarring* that girl, Ann Heriot."

"I *wasn't*!" said Gerald with some warmth. "She's a good sort, that girl. Healthy too. Hunts in Harkshire but I gather it's a washout these days."

He relapsed into his usual silence. He suddenly realized that he had not made any attempt to *shikar* Miss Heriot, as he would have *shikarred* without hesitation any similarly attractive girl he had met in the war. When Monty Bitterne had retired hurt, he had danced with her twice, avoided several attempts by Mrs. Gore-Ambulance to get him again on the floor, and had then seen Ann Heriot home in a taxi to the flat where she was staying.

Gerald had found himself talking quite simply to her and admitting that he had been "told to take it easy" and was probably going down to live quietly in Harkshire in the autumn. He found himself suddenly not fretting and extraordinarily at peace. What had Masefield said about "how the blood can run because of beauty"? He had never wanted a wife, living the life he did. He had wanted (what was it the Greeks had?) a *hetaira* more than a wife, someone who was content to be with you for a time and then would forget you as speedily as you did them, when you had to go off on some new quest. Same with horses. You loved them, and cosseted them and spent weeks "bringing them on" but in a tournament, or after a pig, you had to "ride 'em like a bicycle", and if they broke down, well, you turned them out and forgot them.

Women! And was polo or steeplechasing just a disease like making love, a frightful splendid excitement whose details you barely remembered afterwards? You played in certain matches, and rode in certain runs, when you were going flat out and really well, and at the end you could only remember two or three silly things that had happened in an hour. Women! One forgot them so quickly but neither they nor horses forgot.

What was it that drove one to women? And yet the clarity and ease of mind one sometimes got after being with them! He remembered irrelevantly a girl he had taken home from a party, one night during the 1938 Inter-Regimental. He could not remember anything about her now, except that it was on leaving her flat the great idea had struck him. Why not play that old, slow, really handy pony in the first chukker in what was bound to be mud? The fast ponies had gone skating and slithering about on their hocks all over the place, and he had turned inside everyone of them and scored two goals as easy as croquet before the others settled down. Women! and they could give you an inspiration like that!

Gerald awoke from his musing to find Angus engaged in argument with Gigoleo himself.

"But I tell you I must have another bottle. It's only 1.15."

"Very sorry, sair! You hadda the bottle you arranged for."

"Well, you tell the Manager to come and see me."

"Very sorry, sair! I *am* the Manager!"

"Oh, are you? Well, this gentleman, let me tell you, is going to be the new Under-Secretary for Power and Gas! You wait till your next allocation of business petrol comes up for that Rolls of yours."

"I'll see what I can do, sair!"

"There!" said Angus, cheerfully, as Gigoleo hurried away. "I knew that Labour M.P. business would do the trick." Three minutes later, a waiter appeared with a bottle. Nothing was said about payment.

"Steady on, Angus," said Gerald. "Isn't that blackmail?"

"Of course it is. Blackmail, according to the Oxford dictionary," Angus affected to search his memory, "is the 'tribute exacted by freebooters for protection and immunity', and also 'payment exacted for not revealing discreditable secrets'. We are all criminals in these restricted days. I shall give Gigoleo full protection and immunity for supplying me with non-quota whisky in prohibited hours, and I shall make no enquiries about how it comes to be non-quota at all and what else is in it. I shall also undertake *not* to reveal the fact that Sir William Boulogne is really the manager of this joint, and that he wears at times a tie to which he is not entitled."

"Is he really the manager?"

"He is. I had to go to Somerset House to find that one out and he would never have got into the Savernake if they had known that 'Company director', on his application form, meant 'Night-club proprietor'."

"I see."

"I will also bet that, if you do join this syndicate of Mannering's you will find him a member of it. Some people are fearfully touchy about admitting they have paid for anything, even in these days. Like being seen out hunting on a hireling. They hate creating the impression that their blue blood and charm haven't got them everything *gratis*!"

§ 4

The tempo of the club was running down but Angus and Gerald sat on. Suddenly they found Cyril de Bourbon, with his languid smile, looming over them, with a large envelope in his hand.

"Sit down!" said Angus. "Drink?"

Cyril de Bourbon coiled down lithely beside them.

"No *thank* you! One finds whisky is so bad for one."

"One does," said Angus, "but one shouldn't let that worry one, should one?"

"The fact is," said Cyril mopping his broad pale brow, "I've been looking everywhere for Monty Bitterne. I saw him with you earlier in the evening. Do you know where he is?"

"Been gone two hours."

"Oh *dear* me, what *shall* I do? I was to hand over my shots to him and he was going to do the captions and rush them down afterwards. It's vital they should reach the machines tonight." Cyril mopped his brow again.

"But don't they have to be edited or something? Monty was hardly in first-class journalistic trim when he left us," said Gerald.

Cyril launched into a torrent of explanation. The sub-editor was ill, Mr. Somebody was on holiday, Geraldine had flown to Paris for the first post-war dress-show, Tony Holman simply had to be at Cowes, and Derek at a dance at Claridge's; Monty had *assured* him that he could easily polish off the one remaining "para" of Geraldine's *Social Whirl* and the captions to Cyril's

E   65

harvest of photographs. He ended, "What *am* I to do? I really ought to be in bed, I get such *frightful* hay fever at this time of year, and these late nights are simply *killing* me!"

Gerald glanced at Angus. He seemed half asleep but his moustache and hair and eyebrows were rising very slowly till they seemed to stand up all round him. One eye opened for a second, smouldered, and closed again. Then he said, "Never mind, de Bourbon, old boy! Monty was a little high when he left us but we know exactly where to find him and we'll sort the whole thing. I rather wanted to see him. Friend of mine in India. Who are the printers?"

"Oh, Monty knows! They're Moon and Company, Night and Day Printers, in Holditch Street. They *must* have them by 4.30 a.m."

"O.K., old chap!" Angus was very reassuring. "Now you pop off to your beddy-byes and have a good night's rest. They tell me Malted Milk will induce Sound Wholesome Sleep. But I've never tried it. And don't worry! Angus will sort it."

He spoke like a mother to a fractious child. Cyril exuded gratitude and slid away, leaving the envelope behind him.

Angus sat up. He was wide-awake now. "We will with your good leave, Master Warde, this night write such a page in London's social history as shall not soon be forgotten. My flat is indicated. Waiter, the reckoning!"

As they went out Gigoleo himself met them at the door. He looked truculent. "Did I understand, Major Somborne," he said, "that your guest was the new Under-Secretary for Power and Gas?"

"I said he was going to be."

"Well," said Gigoleo, and there was a nasty gleam in his eye, "the real one's over there, Mr. Heinkel!"

He pointed to where a rather fat, very bald young man, with a long nose, was eating with passionate absorption.

Angus did not turn a hair. "Ah!" he said, "poor Rupert Heinkel! I had to deal with him once at school for cutting all the vital trouser-buttons off his O.T.C. uniform to avoid going on parade. But judging by the way he eats he'll find his way into the Food Ministry very speedily. And then, my cousin Major Warde will doubtless take his place. You wait till the next by-election! *Buona notte*, Gigoleo!"

And Angus stalked into the night.

§ 5

It was ten minutes later. Angus had discarded his dinner-coat for a silk dressing-gown and was sitting at his writing table with a sheaf of Cyril de Bourbon's photographs in front of him. At intervals he burst into his favourite song:

> *Only a ro-ose I . . . bring you!*
> *Only a rose . . . fading away!*

"Now remember, Gerald, we've got to have something bright, snappy and *très snob*. Now, who the deuce are these two? Take dictation, Gerald! '*Among others dining at the Taper Club were the Hon. Marigold and the Honourable Buttercup Rembrandt*'."

"Are you sure her name's Buttercup?"

"By no means, but we'd better put it in inverted commas to show it's her pet name. I'm sure of old Marigold, anyway. '*The Hon. Marigold was in a purple and yellow-flowered chiffon which matched her complexion . . . and her new utility eyelashes*' . . . (If you get your hunting and racing correspondent to do Geraldine's stuff, while she's beating it up in Paris, you must expect a technical error now and again.) '*They were with Captain "Fruity" Ingersoll, very jaunty (no,) genial in his new dentures.*' Well, look at 'em! A caption is supposed to explain what's in the photo."

"O.K."

" '*We also saw Lady Ingrid Stampling who goes like a train in the Fernie country, in a fascinating beige snood.*' "

"Rot!" said Gerald, "I met that girl once before the war and she told me she'd never hunted in her life, and thought it was a lousy pastime."

"That wouldn't prevent her going pretty fast in parts of the Shires," said Angus darkly. "Now don't interrupt, Gerald! *'Mrs. Rosamund Gore-Ambulance whose husband is of course* (you always say 'of course' in this sort of stuff) *the well-known Harley Street',*"

"Wimpole Street."

" *'Harley Street* (sounds much classier) *surgeon comma was in a Victorian dress of cream silk gros grain which had been worn by her grandmother* (they always put that bit in at weddings and it's probably O.K. at night clubs) *semicolon she looked a bit short of a gallop but should be watched for Ascot full stop.'* "

"Ascot's over."

"Well, Aintree then. She's up to twelve seven though she seems to hang on the bit, rather." (Angus had not forgotten his dance.) "Who's this in a fur-stole? Ursula Popkiss again! That woman can't keep her dial out of the papers for a week. *'Mrs. Simon Popkiss as usual created a flutter of admiration in her new vixen-fur from the South Notts country full stop.'* (She's a great pal of the Master's.) *'When at the close of her racing and dancing career she retires to the stud, she should prove an outstanding matron. She went in to supper escorted by the Hon. "Bubbly" Rake semicolon his father, Lord Binge, the first Baron, though almost gaga nowadays of course comma was in the famous turf-accounting firm which rarely owed.'* "

"Am I to put that last bit in?"

Angus drank some beer. "May as well! *'Among others dining at the Taper Club comma was Major Sir Giles Wallaby who comma it will be recalled comma cut such an attractive voluntary in the Brigade Heavyweight Race at Hawthorn Hill just before the war'* (it's about the only dashing thing he ever did) *'semicolon and Lord Glenagony who put in some fastish work in London all the war.'* "

"Did he?"

"Never left it for a day. . . . Lived at the Dorchester *con amore.* *'God give us Bases to guard or beleaguer!'*" said Angus, bursting into song again.

" '*Mrs. Lola Goldman, wife of the little-known M.P. for East Chelsea, is an artist whose portraits have such an individual stamp about them that they attracted the amused attention of the Hanging Committee at the Summer Exhibition this year.*' (Well, they must have! They hung three of the rozzy things upside down without realizing it and old Lola was livid. Carry on, Gerald!) '*Mrs. Goldman's husband is we hear taking a great interest in a scheme for hunting the carted fox in Leicestershire full stop.*' (That'll give him useful publicity, won't it?)."

"O.K. I've got that."

" '*Among the diners were Major Tom Beckenham M.P. and his attractive wife, the Hon. Mrs. Beckenham. She has of course a great deal of money but not as much as when she first met Tom full stop.*' (I'll bet she hasn't!) '. . . *Major Beckenham has recently espoused the Labour Party "en deuxièmes noces", as he thinks there is more behind it in the long run.*' "

Angus rose at last. "I'll just type these and then away we go to Messrs. Moon and Company, Night and Day Printers."

§ 6

In Holditch Street, a foreman compositor said slowly to a mate: "Room stoof soom of this. I suppose it's oke, lad. I rang oop Mr. Watson but couldn't get owt. 'E'd gone 'ome with stooma-cake, chap said."

His mate had no love for any social whirl. "These Society blokes always write a lot of bull," he said. "There won't *be* any of 'em left in two years from now. I'd let it go. That big bloke what brought it was a peeler once."

"Serve Monty right," thought Gerald fiercely as he turned in. "Shouldn't have tried to *shikar* a girl like Ann. . . . Nice name, Ann. . . . Rum evening. Only 364 of 'em more, if that vet knows his stuff. Dam' sure anyway I couldn't spend the remainder of 'em in London, beating it up with Angus!" And his thoughts swirled lovingly to certain rain-battered mountains 7000 miles away where very few Englishmen had been, and where possibly a new bear or a new pheasant were waiting for someone to discover them on the high tops above the trees. Then the pheasant suddenly took on the face of Miss Ann Heriot, and it said, "Of course, hunting's rather a washout these days but one gets a kick out of it still. . . ." Gerald was fast asleep.

And somewhere behind Sloane Square Miss Ann Heriot woke and thought: "I hope he won't go and spend all his leave in night clubs. What a fool I was to go there with Monty Bitterne when I hardly knew him! And I suppose if Gerald hunts this season it'll only be on blood-horses in Leicestershire, not our kind. I'm glad I didn't tell him I'd whipped in to the Mid-Harkshire, even if that *did* mean skinning horses and cows when the kennelman was ill. Ugh! Rotten job!" Miss Heriot too was asleep once more.

Not far away in Swan Street, Chelsea, Cyril de Bourbon removed the lanoline from his slim white fingers, and sprawled on his pale blue Louis Seize bed. He thought, "Perhaps I ought *not* to have let those pulls of poor old Marigold Rembrandt and Clarrie Beckenham go out. They never could be called photogenic, and they look even more hideous than in the flesh. Shooting folly where it eats! And a cave man like Monty Bitterne turned on to London's lovelies! What can a poor artist do? Lovely colour that girl Ann had, but a high colour is so often fatal to expression. Probably a 'sportswoman'. If so, damn her pretty eyes!"

Cyril de Bourbon slept without remorse. He had "sports-women" on the brain. When he had forsaken bird-photo-graphy, he had "done" the tournaments in quest of lawn tennis stars, and had lost his battered heart to the very loveliest of them all, none other than Jean Garganey. A taut little wheat-coloured automaton, with limpid blue eyes and a temper of forty degrees over proof, she drank only water for her game's sake, she could go on hitting a ball back till Kingdom Come, and was always thinking whom she was "bound to meet" in the round after next.

Jean Garganey had spurned Cyril's suit, after playing one mixed single with him. Blind with jealousy, he had laid aside for ever his buckskin shoes, his lily-white integuments, and his leash of rackets, and devoted his time to collecting the photographs which had informed and inspired Jake Dubison's far-famed *Sweaty Women*. Cricket, hockey, lawn-tennis and otter-hunting had all yielded him trophies of that grim chase. The private edition at three guineas in buckram had been sold out in under a week.

VII. GERALD GETS A LETTER

Though much is taken, much abides.
—TENNYSON's *Ulysses*

Gerald, waking next morning after a dreamless night, suddenly realized what lay before him and wondered how many days his evening with Angus had knocked off his "allotted span". For so many years he had never looked beyond the next evening. He had been a fatalist, as shortsighted as a hedge-sparrow.

He picked up a letter which the old Club porter had given him overnight. "It's been here for months," he had said apologetically, "we didn't know your address." It was from his uncle, old John Warde in Harkshire, his only near relative. Bachelor, doctor, naturalist, sportsman, traveller, he had lived a queer gipsy life. Antarctic expeditions, researches into Transjordan mosquitoes, an enquiry into *beri-beri* in the Kabaw valley, wanderings after animals in the unkempt edge of Asia, had all claimed him at times, but for ten years he seemed to have been anchored at Oakington.

Gerald remembered him as a pink smiling white-haired being with wrinkled eyes and an ineradicable desire to find out things for himself, and never to trust the written word.

It was a long letter. Gerald's eyes skimmed the neat close-packed pages:

"If this does not reach you before May 31, I may have gone

abroad. My old urge to wander has come over me again, over-whelmingly. In 1935, I thought I had finished with the East. But Kipling knew what all of us have felt:

> *If a year of life be lent her, if her temple's shrine we enter*
> *The door is shut, we may not look behind.* . . .

"I hope you will come home and look after this place. . . . Landed estates and their mansions are things of the past. But you are the last of our family; I have no wish to leave it to the Government. It has, in its 900 acres, most of the things which I look for in a landed property, from deep woods to a running stream and even a piece of marshland, from downland to corn-land, and you will find that I have put back into its maintenance every penny that I have received from it, and a bit more besides. . . . Old Dick Seymour, my bailiff, knows it from end to end. Listen to him! He will be worth a lot to you if you do decide to live here. His branch of the Seymours settled here about 1580, and they were lords of the manor for 150 years until they fell on evil times. Dick himself began by scaring rooks at 5/- a week, but I have often wished I could dress him up and trim his whiskers and take him to my club in St. James's Street. If he kept his mouth shut he would look far more of a *sahib* than some of the present members, for that blood is very potent and their features survive. . . .

"I have heard of you from time to time, from a lot of queer people, scattered about the world, and I was very glad to see you were living up to the family tradition. Only about fifty per cent. of the males of our family die quietly in their beds and they have all found it impossible to 'stay put' in this country. . . .

"They left this place very largely to itself and the Seymours, while they did strange things about the world, but they always came back to it in the end and each generation did something to improve and beautify it. That accumulation of family effort is worth seeing. . . .

"In the war I heard a lot of your regiment. . . . Much has

been said of the 'cavalry follies' of the older wars, the *arme blanche*, the wooden-headed swagger, the concentration on polo at the expense of war-training, the charge, the futile yells, the horses hocked with spears or mown down by machine-guns. But I have watched with amusement how our pre-war horse-soldiers came to the front of things and stayed there, unquestioned, in this war. The P.M. is of course the supreme example. You would expect that from a subaltern who could help win an Inter-Regimental with his arm strapped to his side. . . . But there were many besides him, whom polo and hunting and steeplechasing had *not* unfitted for war, but improved for it. (The infantry soldiers rarely seemed happy with two open flanks and nothing behind them. . . .).

"I never knew the explanation: a taste for speed, a sense of the urgency of the moment, of seizing the fleeting chance, a feeling for being in the foreground, of only going that way once, of not caring greatly what the next half-hour might bring? They knew what to do if they found themselves unexpectedly in a strange country alone, or with a polo ball in front of them and a split second to do something in. . . .

"The horse-soldiers are normally quicker thinkers than the run of us. And they have to learn to wait and not lose keenness, through months of patient training which may end in a moment in ignominy. Ecstasy and glory one second, and shame and disaster the next, with the mud from the other horses slapping down on you, or your pony putting his foot on the ball in front of goal. And not to turn a hair when you are yoked to a muscular unbeliever with an almost feminine mind, is good training for anyone. . . .

"Frankly I can't see much future for you in this country for some years. Sport, the kind of sport which involves doing something *yourself*, seems doomed except for the rich man and the professional. If you go to a local show in England, you find the ring full of professionals, or hard-riding children, while their parents sit around and watch them. . . .

"Also, it will not be many years before we have thrown away India and Burma, and there is still so much to find out, and so few people who want to go out and find it. . . .

"England has got to be much worse before she is better. You and your friends have won the war and now the smooth and cunning man will step on the stage, the glib and sonorous individuals, the huge anonymous societies run by God-knows-whom, the black marketeers and the mean ones. And everyone else will be too tired to kick them off. I know what you fighting soldiers said about planning staffs. You wait till our new Planners start! There will be a lot of prefabricated thought, cheap and narrow and rather shiny. . . .

". . . . No place for people with as few roots as you or myself, who have that incessant urge of wanting forever to know what is behind the hill or round the corner. That bent of yours ought not to be wasted before it is too late. Some of our guesses may beat all the museum theories. . . .

"So I am off. An American friend has signed me on with a unit trying to find the planes which crashed north of latitude twenty-six and left no survivors. We shall do a lot of flying, but in between some pretty tough foot-slogging." ("Good for the old man," thought Gerald, "seventy if he's a minute and in some of the most God-awful country in the world.")

"I will give you one word of advice: *Never marry unless you are certain your wife won't anchor you!* Anybody can have children. But the number of those who want to travel and collect and discover what is 'lost behind the ranges', is strictly limited. You are of that number. It means locusts and wild honey most of the time but it will be worth it."

Gerald smiled. What a piece of advice to get the morning after he had been condemned to death and met Ann Heriot!

He had turned in overnight with a curious sense of peace. Two years before, when on leave, he would have been drawing the coverts of Cairo or Alexandria for some girl as restless and amoral as himself. Now . . . one year to live and an injunction

75

on no account to anchor himself. And there was his old Ulysses of an uncle setting off for those heart-breaking gradients which the papers so unknowing, called "The Hump".

And for the old man "that untravelled world" would go on gleaming till he died, or found himself on the Mekong if his luck held.

Gerald folded the letter. He would savour England first. The "work of noble note", in his case, could wait. He wanted to shoot a grouse and a driven partridge and see Ann Heriot in her own countryside. They were petty ambitions but the untravelled world no longer had priority. In the war he reckoned he had travelled some 170,000 miles, one way and another, and slept in 600 different places since it began. It was time to anchor, if only for a spell.

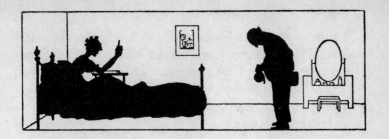

VIII. MISS GORE DISPOSES

"The young ravens cry for food. . . . ."
"And are fed. . . ."
"Which presupposes that something else is fed upon."
—*Reginald,* by SAKI

Miss Janet Gore's "man of business" came into the room with the air appropriate to an important client on her sick bed, shook hands tenderly, and hoped he saw her better.

"I am very ill," said Miss Gore, "and the events of the last few weeks have made me worse. I do not hope to survive the winter."

"My dear Miss Gore," said Mr. Catling, "you have, we all sincerely trust, many many years before you yet."

"Nonsense! Sit down. I wish to talk to you."

Both Miss Gore's bank manager and her solicitor had agreed, ten years before, that she was a "warm woman". Today by their estimate she was even warmer, though her nieces would have repudiated the adjective and she herself would have termed it indecent.

"To think," Miss Gore went on, "that I should have lived to see it. Poor dear Winnie!"

Mr. Catling was frequently slow in following his client's mental processes.

"You mean," he ventured, "your cousin, Winifred, the one who lives in Salop? I had not heard."

"I mean," retorted Miss Gore, "our lamented ex-Premier! The only Prime Minister for fifty years who knew a horse from a donkey-engine. How sharper than a ferret's tooth it must be to have a thankless nation! And to think that I danced with him once in India when he was a junior subaltern!"

"A good partner?" queried Mr. Catling, stalling somewhat.

"A fire-eater, a noble fire-eater! He could think of nothing but how to get away from his regiment to the Tirah, or the Sudan, or some such warlike place. Ah! what a man! Ichabod! or should I say Lucifer? I am altering my will."

Mr. Catling sighed. He had drawn Miss Gore a lovely will thirty years before, four folios without a single full stop until the end, and containing in its heart the clause: "*AND the capital* "*and income of such share or so much thereof as shall not have been* "*paid or applied under any trust or power affecting the same shall be* "*held In trust for all or any one or more exclusively of the others or* "*the other of the children of such niece at such time for the benefit of* "*such children or some or one of them as such niece shall whether* "*covert or sole by deed revocable or irrevocable or by Will or Codicil* "*appoint and in default. . . .*"

He liked to feel that he had, in his young partner's Army jargon, "buttoned everything up". Miss Gore had since added codicils at the rate of about one a quarter.

"The original will may stand, of course," said Miss Gore, "but there may be one or two more codicils for you to draw."

"I am sorry," said Mr. Catling. "To be frank, if the Court ever had to adjudicate in the matter of intention . . ."

"If the Court ever has to adjudicate," replied his client tartly, "it will be because *you* did not know your job! I have at all times made myself, I hope, crystal-clear."

"Too clear," sighed Mr. Catling, who disliked clarity on principle, "but at times, if you will allow me, a little conflicting or changeable."

"Perhaps," admitted Miss Gore, "but we live in a rapidly-changing world. Recall the clothes, for example, that your mother wore for croquet and those in which your daughters consider themselves attired for tennis."

Into Mr. Catling's mental eye swam a vision of himself, a spotty youth in a white collar and a Norfolk jacket, and of his mother, an almost circular woman in bombazine, driving his croquet ball relentlessly into the calceolarias. The companion vision of his daughters bent over a net with their lean hams clad in what they called divided skirts (in his opinion a Court would hold that they were wearing shorts), gave him little comfort.

"I agree," he said vaguely, "but what I meant was . . ."

"Never mind what you meant. I have, I think, left considerable bequests in my will to the Anti-Trapping League, the Dogs' Home at Battersea, the Council of Humanity to Animals, er, the two Royal Societies for Prevention, and . . ."

"Three, if not four, Asyla for Indigent Cats."

"Exactly, and the Horses' Home of Rest. Now I want to remember also another body, the Fieldsportsmen's Preservation League, or some similar name. They exist to preserve themselves against the future."

Mr. Catling, who was a Councillor of the Law Society, which existed for the preservation of solicitors, nodded.

"Well, I want them to have £1000 free of duty as well."

"Don't you think, my dear Miss Gore, that in the unlikely event of adjudication, the Court might consider some of your bequests mutually incompatible?"

"Why so?" said Miss Gore sharply.

"Well, so many of them are indubitably for the most excellent humanitarian objects, such as the prevention of cruelty to helpless things. But the Fieldsportsmen's Preservation League does not exist to preserve its members but to retain the right to take, kill or capture certain creatures such as foxes and birds by means of hunting. Your proposed bequest can hardly be called one with a humanitarian object."

"Mr. Catling, do you mind telling me what you had for luncheon yesterday?"

Mr. Catling started. "I had a lamb cutlet. A very small one."

"Even a very small lamb, Mr. Catling, must feel acute distress and pain when it is taken from its mother and is in the act of qualifying to be a cutlet. And have you ever been in an abattoir?"

"My *dear* Miss Gore!"

Mr. Catling was almost as shocked as when the elder Miss Makepeace had expressed a desire to bequeath £5000 for the endowment of a "model brothel" in Huddersfield under the impression that it was a form of soup-kitchen.

"Indeed," he went on, "I have not!"

"It is a pity. *I* have. No one should eat any food until they realize how it becomes food; particularly meat."

Mr. Catling had never visualized the genesis of caviare, or *pâté*, sausages or potted lobster. That he was forbidden to taste these delicacies until he had explored the method of their manufacture appalled him.

"But surely your argument would mean that no one should ever use coal who had not been down a coal-mine? That is, if it was carried to its logical conclusion . . ."

"It is a mistake," said Miss Gore blandly, "to carry almost any argument to its logical conclusion. (Even the Brains Trust never do. They say something irrelevant, or sweep on having a hearty laugh among themselves.) In the case of the meat-trade I am not sure what the answer is. To deprive this nation of meat, in these days of food ministries which exist to prevent us having food, might be too great a blow. In any case, vegetarianism is not the answer. . . ."

"How so?"

"Well, the vegetarian must cause a shocking amount of cruelty."

"Cruelty, Miss Gore?"

"Yes, to worms, slugs, snails and other humble creatures living out their blameless lives in rural surroundings."

"But surely they are very low forms of creation? and one must in reason draw the line somewhere!"

"But where? You know your Shelley?"

Shelley had never been Mr. Catling's Shelley.

"Not all of him," he said guardedly.

"Well, you remember the *Epipsychidion*?"

Mr. Catling was too old a solicitor to give himself away. As a matter of fact he had never got beyond the title of the poem and had wondered vaguely what it meant, ever since.

"Do you recall the lines which read:

> *the spirit of the worm beneath the sod,*
> *In love and worship, blends itself with God?*"

"Poetic licence," said Mr. Catling.

"Possibly. But in the after-life would you feel quite happy, vegetarian or no vegetarian, if you met a Godloving worm which you had riven asunder unwittingly with your spade, or thrown alive to the mercy of your hens?"

Mr. Catling jabbed back feebly. "I do not keep hens."

"No doubt, however, you are an ovivor, and you cannot shelter behind the cruelties of others. When Nebuchadnezzar took to eating grass, he must suddenly have realized what cruelty normal human food entails."

Mr. Catling was, in ring parlance, "out on his feet". A vision rose within him of himself in a collar and chain tied to a stake and browsing on the lawn.

"But let us be reasonable, Mr. Catling. Assuming that you have got to die and someone may benefit from your death, which end would you rather was yours? To be squashed under the boot of a vegetarian gardener? To race to and fro madly in your native element with a hook in your upper lip and to know that your last moments were going to be recounted in lyric prose by someone in an inn-parlour or a club for the next ten years? To have your neck wrung without warning when you woke up one morning? To have your throat cut in the sordid

surroundings of an abattoir? Or to be shot neatly in the face
as you swept over a fence, at the summit of your powers, with
the wind behind you?"

Mr. Catling shuddered. What frightful things these old ladies
did think up! On the only occasion when he had brought himself to visualize his own demise, he had hoped it would take
place in a darkened room full of spring flowers, with morphia

in the offing, his daughters in the background, and his partner waiting below with a copy of his own will (another lovely specimen) in his breast-pocket.

"I have not really considered," he began.

"Well, I have and unfortunately, as far as I am concerned, all these deaths are unlikely. But shooting is the least repulsive end. All things have to die some time and I would sooner take my chance of death by shooting if I was a bird than by disease or from a hawk, or from a fox when I was brooding on my eggs."

"But to make *sport* out of the death of an animal, to gloat brutally over the satisfaction of a blood lust! What was it Coleridge said?

Take not away the life you cannot give
For all things have an equal right to live."

"You had better repeat *that* quotation to the foxes and the carrion crows! All things *may have* an equal right to live but Nature does not recognize it. Our sweetest songbirds give beaks-full of living grubs to their young. . . . And have you ever thought of a garden with no thrushes because the cats had the upper hand?"

Holly Lodge, Mr. Catling's residence, had no thrushes, though it shared a blackbird on spring mornings with *The Laburnums*. But Mr. Catling was still undefeated.

"But surely, my dear lady, it is unethical to cause pain deliberately to any helpless creature?"

"Mr. Catling, the whole impact of civilization on nature is unethical. If you left things to nature, there would be chaos. To drink your daily milk, a calf is removed from its mother nowadays at birth, and if it is a bull-calf turned into veal at the tenderest age. To eat eggs, your hens are deprived for ever of male society, and bereaved daily of their precious offspring. The egg-trade, the milk-trade, the caviare-trade and the honey-trade all batten on the maternal instinct. How would you like to work hard and save all the summer, like a bee, and have your savings confiscated for someone else to enjoy? Do you keep cats?"

"One only."

"What gender? A male cat or a female cat?"

"Er, ours is neuter." Mr. Catling's wife had insisted on it.

"Is it humane, Mr. Catling, to neutralize a tomcat merely to prevent him disturbing your sleep with his love-affairs? Would you like any greater power to treat *you* in that way?"

Mr. Catling had had no love affairs since 1913. "I suppose not," he sighed, "but I cannot agree over field sports. To find pleasure in the death of a helpless animal . . ."

"By your own admission, Mr. Catling, you have often found pleasure *after* the death of a helpless animal. And not so very long after, either. . . . I refer to oysters. And when in your club some committee-member says 'We shall soon be having oysters back on the *menu*' and your eyes light up, are you not taking pleasure in anticipation of a helpless creature's death?"

"I suppose so. I had not thought of it that way."

Miss Gore went on. "If I were a bookmaker, I would give odds of nine to four on the fox with several hunts I know and I would sooner be hunted than trapped or poisoned any day. Also, let me remind you that the *raison d'être* of solicitors themselves, however blameless, is only because someone has died, or expects to die, or is in trouble in some way. You are the carrion-crows of Society though I hate to stress the fact! And I suppose you are happy in your work? I intend to leave my money so that this Government shall have as little as possible. You had better realize sufficient shares now to pay over my bequests to the Societies as direct donations. If this Government nationalizes charity, the supplies of it will be as difficult as you will doubtless find those of coal and food will be very shortly. I will sign the cheques."

"Do you mean that?"

"I do. I have a low opinion of my niece, Rosamund Gore-Ambulance."

"I am sorry," said Mr Catling who had been favoured in confidence with Mrs. Gore-Ambulance's opinion of her aunt, which was even lower.

"She and her sister, Angela Bunbury, fought like cats over my poor sister, Belinda, before she died. They courted her assiduously for what she was likely to leave them, and said their say about her behind her back. She was bandied from house to house by those two like an old, er, battlecock."

"Shuttledore, dear lady."

"Probably. And how that poor husband of Angela's, James Bunbury, has stuck to her all these years, I simply do not know. James is a tidy little man of great thoughtfulness. She is . . ."

"A woman of great determination."

"I call that a meiosis. *The* most unmethodical creature in Harkshire. He was a soldier with very high standards. He once showed me round his barrack-rooms when I was in India. A model. She must be *most* galling to live with. He is almost a menial in his own house. He scrubs, digs the garden, irons the clothes, cleans the boots, polishes and tidies up eternally after Angela. He is to have £2000 on my death *on the sole condition that he spends it on himself*. Please make that very clear. Also write to Mr. Robert Mannering, at Stoke Loyalty, near Furze-chester."

"One moment, Miss Gore, let me write this down!"

"Mr. Mannering is a nice man, who keeps a benefit society to provide shooting for indigent sportsmen with no land of their own."

"A syndicate, I think it is called."

"Never mind the name. The members or beneficiaries pay so much a year and they have parties so many times a season, and share the expenses and the game. I wish Colonel Bunbury and the dear vicar, Mr. Halliburton, to have two years' subscription to Mr. Mannering's club. I believe he has vacancies. Write to him and ask him to let you have a note of the cost which you will arrange to defray."

"But don't you think that Col. Gore-Bunbury may feel a little delicate about the matter, unless he knows where the money comes from?"

"He will feel positively uncomfortable. My niece will see to that! In fact if I sent him the money, Angela would make sure that it never reached its destination. You had better instruct Mr. Mannering to charge them a nominal fee, say £5 each, and explain to them that two other guns who have paid in advance, have failed him and so on."

"You go straight to the point, Miss Gore."

"I am amoral. The last two wars and the events of the last month have destroyed any sense of conduct I ever had. The vicar and James Bunbury shall enjoy themselves, once a fortnight, away from their homes while time remains."

"I see," said Mr. Catling who had had no such opportunity for thirty-seven years.

"The vicar is a widower but he is a keen bird-lover. A Saturday in the open will freshen up his sermons. And James Bunbury deserves a fortnightly break from that niece of mine! Do you understand?"

"I do," sighed Mr. Catling. "Your instructions will be implemented. *Au revoir!*"

Miss Gore leaned back on her pillows, but it seemed to Mr. Catling, as he tiptoed from the room that she only closed one eye. As he passed through the door, she called him back.

"Mr. Catling, I have forgotten one thing. I want £250 donated now to the Institute of the Horse. On one condition. That they arrange immediately for a course of lectures at all pony-clubs."

"Yes?" Mr. Catling was scribbling hard again.

"And that they get someone to write a book at once pointing out that not one girl or woman in a hundred can look well on a horse without a coat on. This new craze for jodhpurs and blouses or jerseys. Most unbecoming! Women have no sense of their own behinds. They should always wear riding-coats!"

Mr. Catling, whose gaze rarely wandered below a woman's throat, gulped.

"If the pony-clubs can drive that lesson home I shall have done something for my sex. Mencken tried in America, of course. You remember *In Defence of Women*?"

"Only very slightly, Miss Gore," said Mr. Catling hurriedly. Some of it had cut him to the quick, or what little quick had been left him by forty years of his profession. "I thought it almost, er, blasphemous."

"But *so* observant. '*The female body*,' he remarked, '*is very defective in form. It has harsh curves and clumsily distributed masses; compared to it the average milk jug, or even cuspidor, is a thing of intelligent and gratifying design.*' You should read it again."

Mr. Catling was accustomed with most of his clients to laying down the law suavely in their presence. To be involved in an argument with this elderly female philosopher among the by-ways of cruelty, vegetarianism, feminine contours and field-sports had shattered his acumen beyond repair.

"I fear, Miss Gore, I must away. I have another important appointment at 12.30."

"In your club luncheon-room, I expect! Don't forget what I told you about oysters and juvenile mutton! I once saw lobsters being brought, literally, to the boil in the kitchen of a French hotel. A quite human piece of brutality! I have never touched them since. Don't you appreciate now my reasoned adherence to shooting as the least objectionable means of obtaining one's viands?"

"I do, indeed! *Au revoir*, my dear Miss Gore."

Mr. Catling sped away though most of the Club's luncheon-menu seemed closed to him now. He wondered in what possible terms he could explain to the Institute of the Horse the condition that was precedent to Miss Gore's offer, and whether he could persuade the Club *chef* to short his lobsters before cooking them.

IX. MR. MANNERING LOOKS FORWARD

On a morning in August, 1945, Mr. Robert Mannering, J.P., farmer of Stoke Loyalty, went into his office with his letters. He sorted them quickly. For letters from His Majesty's Ministers and the Agricultural Committee he kept two trays, one labelled "Bilge" and the other "Business". The wads of useless stuff they sent out! Enough paper to paper a room on the subject of income tax for an old-age pensioner eking out his pension, who was not liable at all! But the permit for two tons of baling-wire, urgently needed, was still, apparently, in the womb of the "War Ag", and their gestation period was unpredictable.

He opened a letter in a notably eccentric scrawl.

Dear Mr. Mannering, it began,

> *My solicitor has under my instructions written to secure vacancies in your club for impoverished sportsmen on behalf of two of your neighbours who are friends of mine. Be sure and tell Colonel Bunbury to shoot his partridges in the head. Birds despatched in any other way must experience pain. He will shoot much better in the society of men, and his wife should be discouraged from attempting to accompany him. Like most farmers I doubt if you attend church, but when shooting with the vicar, impress on him that his flock appreciates a homely talk about the problems of village life (for example, how to keep hens and feed children without going to the black market) rather than about the spiritual approach to this or that.*

> *Yours very truly,*
>
> Janet Gore.

P.S. On my last visit to your village I observed that you kept sheep. I trust you do not lend yourself to the despicable practice of selling lambs at a tender age. I have little sympathy for mature sheep, which are old enough to choose for themselves. Nobody has ever distinguished clearly between the good shepherd, whose care for his lambs has excited the sentiment and admiration of artists and poets the world over, and the dealer in sheep for eating purposes, a distinction which I find myself appreciating in my old age.

Mr. Mannering mopped his brow as he threw the crabbed sheets into the tray marked "Miscellaneous". Who would run a syndicate? Club for impoverished sportsmen! And when it came to giving his guns advice on how to preach, and forbidding them to bring their wives out, and the lamb-sales! He hurriedly opened the second letter. The handwriting suggested that the writer had little use for a pen. It ran:

Equestrian Club

W.1

Ref. your advt for a gun in a Harkshire shoot in last week's "Squire" would you kindly send me particulars? Am home on leave and am supposed to be a safe shot. Please send to Dower House, Oakington, near Stoke Loyalty.

Yours ffly,

Gerald Warde.

Good Club, the Equestrian, thought Mr. Mannering, should be solvent; cavalry soldiers usually good sportsmen; thank Heaven for someone who realizes safety is a *sine qua non*! Must be some relation of the old Dr. Warde who had farmed there since 1934, and had left so suddenly for foreign parts, to the bewilderment of his bailiff.

He sat down and wrote:

I still have a vacancy for one gun in my shoot. I enclose particulars of bags, etc. for the last ten years. Our partridges hatched out well and we had a good stock in the spring but it is too early to say what we have at the moment until all the corn is cut. There seems to be a nice lot of wild pheasants as well. My terms are 75 guineas a gun, payable half now and half by Sept 27. I shall be pleased to have a walk round with you if you care to come over.

Better vet the chap! What a worrying gamble it was, this attempt to get the public to underwrite your game-risks. How many hopeful prospects had that seventy-five guineas winnowed away! He remembered the syndicate he had run in 1940, five desperately keen senior officers from the Command, who had begun by patronizing him collectively in his own house and ended by trying to beat him down ten guineas apiece on the price. They had paid up in the end after three or four surprise visits with fieldglasses, before the season opened, trying to discover how many birds there were. Luckily their first season had coincided with a bumper year and he had been able to shoot the place really hard without doing it any damage, though they had done their best to work in a couple of bye-days without payment at the end.

He had however wondered all the time why these gentry had taken the trouble to answer advertisements as, judging from their own talk at luncheon, they had spent each winter before the war going from country-house to country-house, and the summer in fishing for trout and advance invitations to shoot.

Mr. Mannering, who rarely went off his own farms, had had to listen, day after day, to such remarks as these, while they completely ignored his friendly attempts at conversation.

"Yes, it's a sweet little stand that. I fired seventy-nine cartridges last time I was there, but I shot like St. Dunstans."

"Hughie, the new Earl, is having all those tall trees down."

"He *can't* be, surely. It'll ruin the stand. What a *tragedy*!"

"It's hardly a two-gun day, of course, but they have one very intriguing little. . . . Almost a classic stand. . . ."

"I'm bound to be there next season and I'll tell him."

"Yes, he *does* show them prettily. I call him an artist. We had some screamers. . . ."

"A charming little 5000-brace moor, I hear."

"Poor Charlie! He lost most of his money y'know. No, I hardly ever see him now!" And so on.

They had expected all sorts of extras from Mr. Mannering, drinks, lifts, teas and accommodation for their noisy dogs, and he had even let them cut him dead in the County Club on a market day. But the cartridges had been the last straw. When cartridges had become scarce late in 1940 they had demanded that he should buy theirs in bulk and have enough ready for them each shooting day. Then the sapper colonel had fiercely disputed the price, which was exactly what the shop had charged him.

Mr. Mannering's blood boiled but he agreed quietly to take them back and get them something cheaper. That evening he went to the gunsmith in Furzechester.

"Sam," he said, "I want you to do a little job for me."

"In course I will and welcome."

"*And* keep your mouth shut! It's for a bet! I want 250 cartridges with No. 6 wads on them but no shot inside."

"In course, but whoi?"

"I'll tell you one day, Sam. You'll be amused."

Sam Hobson had been as good as his word. "There ain't a grain in any of 'em," he said, proudly, some days later, "but I've weighted 'em same as the tothers. I reckon they'll ha' to cut 'em open to tell."

Next week, the cartridge-bags of the five colonels were waiting for them. Seventy-five per cent. of the cartridges in each were blank.

His keeper, all unknowing, had protested before the start. "I ain't got enough bards left to go on hammering them any more. Can't we du a walk round the outsides and shute some hares?"

"Don't you worry, Beacon, we'll leave enough for stock."

The five Colonels had descended from their five Army cars, each with a companion who had come over to applaud and keep the score. It seemed that three of them being under orders for the Middle East, they had a bet on, which would shoot the most birds in the fewest cartridges.

Normally in early January, Tom Beacon could reckon on "losing" half his birds, back over the beaters or out at the flanks, without too much effort of his own. But that day it seemed to him, in spite of some very half-hearted flanking, as if the devil was in them all. With sick apprehension he watched pair after pair, covey after covey, of his precious stock birds rise and flow smoothly forward over the tall fence behind which the guns were waiting. Their cannonade hardly ceased for ten minutes. At the end of the drive Beacon strode dolefully through a gap in the fence. The five Colonels had six dead birds between them: two of them were disputing fiercely, with their satellites, who had accounted for the odd bird. Mr. Mannering had shot five brace. The rough meadow was strewn with cartridge-cases, but the young staff-officers had hardly been needed to keep tally.

The second drive had been very similar though a rising wind had begun to make every bird more difficult. The team would have begun to suspect something, had not Mr. Mannering himself been shooting with such obvious accuracy and assured them that his own cartridges were "out of exactly the same batch" from the gunmaker.

"It must have been the port," one of the young staff-officers confided to Mr. Mannering. "They scoffed nearly two bottles last night, making all those bets, and a round of brandies. I shall have to speak to the mess-sergeant! He must have been on the black market. I shall be for it with my old bird tonight."

"My partridges are rather special," said Mr. Mannering. He realized that the young major had never been shooting before. "They can change into top gear very quickly without one noticing it."

"Is that so? I must watch for that. I don't suppose *my* Colonel realizes it after last night!"

Mr. Mannering sincerely hoped this remark of his would not

be quoted. The CRA was a great technician who knew to a millionth of a foot-second the pace of shot, the varying speeds of gamebirds, and the whole gamut of forward allowances; he was a regular contributor to the *Squire* and the *Journal of Ballistic Co-Efficients*.

After the fourth drive, in which, as one Colonel put it, they had all shot "like the wrath of God", they stumped morosely into the granary for luncheon, and in awful silence the CRA sat down at the table. He took out a razor-sharp knife from his waistcoat pocket, and sliced an inch off a cartridge which he drew from his bag. But "by the blessing of divine Providence", as Mr. Mannering had confided to Sam Hobson, the cartridge he had tested was one of the undoctored rounds. Mr. Mannering almost sobbed with relief.

"Very unpredictable," said the CRA, "this wartime powder! Volatile, I should say. A few bad rounds here and there and all one's confidence goes!"

"*I* think," said the infantry Colonel, bluntly, "that it may have been the port last night."

The RAMC Colonel nodded. He had taken two aspirins the night before and had tested his own blood-pressure before shaving in the morning. The result had staggered him and he had been trying to compose a letter on the subject to the *B.M.J.*, without disclosing that the patient had been himself.

Mr. Mannering, with a beating heart, watched the heavy rain clouds burst suddenly over the tall beeches behind the granary. There was no more shooting, and the Colonels went home, having agreed among themselves that "all bets were off".

Mr. Mannering had hated that little bit of sharp practice. He liked to give his guests full value for their money, but that business of the cartridges had got him on the raw. How he wished he had a little more money and a great house to which he could invite his friends and only those he knew to be good shots, good sportsmen who knew what he and his keeper were attempting, and good friends!

He sighed, and went out farming. He had a very mixed bag of guns this year indeed, only one of whom, Major Ogle, had ever shot with him before. He looked forward to the season with apprehension, much more so than his partridges, dusting quietly along the firbelts of Stoke Loyalty, all unaware of the strangely assorted characters who were now interested in them.

X. JOURNEY NORTH

Gerald put his head out of the window and breathed thankfully a larger air, as the train swept through the early morning sunshine, between sheep-dotted fells slashed with stone walls running steeply uphill. This was more like it after the dim horror of London on a stuffy wet August evening! He wondered idly if the ghost of his grandfather was watching him. The old man had made as much fuss every year about his annual pilgrimage to the "moors", as any Mahomedan bound for Mecca. Every July he had read and re-read Stuart-Wortley's chapter in the *Fur & Feather* Series, beginning "*The lamps are being lit in Bloomsbury*" and then intoned reverently Patrick Chalmers' verses "*Mine eyes to the hills*". For the old man, like most of his comfortable kind, August had meant inevitably moors and deer-forests. Before the wars, the rich had made that pilgrimage after Ascot and Goodwood and Cowes as a matter of course, even as the bigger game of the forests flowed inevitably to their salt-licks in due season.

Gerald breakfasted in the Station Hotel at Carlisle, and found a message from Commander Teal awaiting him. Half an hour later, he came into the lounge to find a large square gloomy man with choleric eyes and a red beard awaiting him.

"R.N.A.S. for a fiver," thought Gerald. Aloud, he said, "Commander Teal? How do you do?"

"You're Warde, I take it. Thank God for something!"

"Why?"

"You'll know soon enough. You look at least as if you could walk up a hill. Got your traps?"

"They're all here."

"Good! Anything to pick up in Carlisle?"

"No, why?"

"You wouldn't believe," said the gloomy man, "what my guests can forget. If it isn't one thing, it's another. Dog-leads and dog-collars, reels and gaffs and flies, pull-throughs and cartridge-extractors, stockings and bootlaces and God-knows-what! Half of 'em expect me to make up their blasted kit deficiencies at Gallowgill. They don't realize we're nine miles from almost anywhere. And if I'm not dashed careful, they swipe half my own stuff when they go."

"Do they?"

"Why, I've known a chap come up by the night train all ready to shoot next morning with the stock of one of his guns and the barrels of the other. And one of our heroes left a new thirty-guinea denture on the rim of the top butt on Squarefell, and actually wanted me to send my keeper for it, in a howling gale after tea, as he couldn't possibly go in to dinner without it! My drying-room is full of odd socks and stockings and shoes and vests they've left behind, but one can't pop odd socks. I've known a feller write me five letters, before he came, about whether we had linen sheets and if his wife could get fresh fish for her Pekinese, and then forget to pack the fore-end of his gun! But you'll see it all soon."

"How long have you been on this job?" asked Gerald as the car started.

"You mean running a country-house as a fishing or shooting hotel? Nine years too long. My wife made me do it. We couldn't afford to keep the house up properly, and I had one goodish moor and an option on two more. Also Jean wanted a bridge-four occasionally and a bit of society in the wilderness. So I thought I'd had a brain wave—

G   97

make the public pay for one's fun and cut one's super-tax down a bit!"

"Very sound idea."

"Sound? My dear boy, it's murder! I've sunk thousands in the dam' place. I lie awake at night, dreaming of foxes and carrion-crows and stoats hard at work burgling my precious stock. When it's raining sleet or there's snow on the fells in May, I know my capital's depreciating, minute by minute, all through the night. How would *you* like to be a hen-grouse shivering on eggs in six inches of snow?"

"It must be good fun in a decent year," said Gerald. The gloomy man brightened very slightly. "It was," he said. "When we first started before the war, there was a nice stock of grouse here, and we had a bumper year in 1936. We killed 2500 brace that year and were shooting hard up to mid-October. I had the place full for weeks. The second year was nearly as good and the Lord sent me some very indifferent shots, just when I felt I had to go a bit *asti* with the stock. Also, I had a rattling good keeper who was a wizard at flanking birds out of a drive when we didn't want too many killed. The guns saw a hell of a lot and never guessed they were only intended to *see* 'em. And then the dam' place caught on! And ever since I've had every Tom Dick and Harry who hasn't ever shot a grouse, or is too unsafe to be anyone's guest, writing in to me. Grouse! grouse! grouse! I feel like that Irish family in Edith Somerville's book who gave up keeping a fish-shop because morning, noon and night people were bothering them for fish. I've had the Gaekwad of Swat and the Rajah of Rumbellypore, and the King of Canoodledum, and every chap with money to burn from Sam Cameron, the bookmaker who never pays twice, up to Mr. Sol Hammerfest of Milwaukee, all flocking up, with their under-and-over guns, and their Remington pump-guns, and one fellow brought a Paradox with lethal bullets in his waistcoat pocket, in case he saw a fox. And they want six days' fishing a week in the summer and four days shooting in the autumn and half of 'em have special attendants who need *halalled* veal, or kosher mutton, or parched gram and chillies and a mat to sleep on outside Master's bedroom door, or some b——y thing. Some of course are worth it. Old Canoodledum tipped all my staff in uncut diamonds, and when he shot a flanker he endowed his family for life. But I had one feller who got so fed up with a big trout which wouldn't take him for two days that he tried to shoot the poor fish with a twelve-bore!

"And to hear 'em talk! You'd think all the best moors had funiculars to take 'em up the hill. That's why I said 'Thank God!' when I saw you. You looked a fairly mobile type. What was your regiment?"

"Roan Hussars."

"Good God, can you walk?"

"I've done a good bit." Gerald smiled. "Even after mechanization, if your car brewed up in the desert, you might have to leg it for a hundred miles."

The gloomy man pondered. "Some of your chaps are very flat-footed, ain't they? My old uncle, the Admiral, ended up as a provincial Governor in Madras. He hated horses and believe me or not, the previous Governor left him two Indian Cavalry aides and a private secretary from your regiment!"

"That must have been Miles Entringham! When he wasn't looking lovely on a horse, he was looking lovely on a bar stool."

"Exactly! Well my uncle, after a lifetime prowling up and down a two-by-four bridge, was making up arrears of walking in his old age. He used to start out from G.H. after lunch and leg it across the paddyfields to the horizon, with two of his faithful staff in attendance. He broke the whole dam' lot down in two months, laminitis, sore shins, capped hocks, and whatnot. . . . But I'm glad you can walk. There's the Pennine!" He waved at a high grey-green wall far away, which seemed to carry the clouds along its dark crest.

"We're shooting the Slaughterhope side tomorrow and there's a pretty vertical mile and three quarters up to the first butts from where we leave the cars. That will weed out some of my guests! . . . But I mustn't talk shop. Have you anything to drink with you?"

"Yes," said Gerald. "About three parts of a bottle in my bag, but it's a bit early in the day, isn't it?"

"Oh, I didn't mean *that*. Jean—that's my wife—won't let anyone bring hooch into the house. She'll whistle that off you if you're not careful."

"Why, is your place T.T.?"

"Not quite. We run a club-bar for about two hours a night with limited supplies and you can always get beer at a meal. But Jean's mad about drink. She says people oughtn't to want it after a day in God's fresh air. Says it's bad for their eye and condition. She was Jean Garganey, y'know."

"Sorry! Never heard of her, I'm afraid." After years of exile, Gerald was always having to confess ignorance of those names which the Broadcasting Corporation thought it had made a household word.

"*The* Jean Garganey! Why, she had two match points against Alice Ivory on the Centre Court when she was only seventeen!"

"Oh of course, I've heard the name!"

"I sometimes wish I never had," said the red-bearded man gloomily. "There were so many silly jokes about the Teal and the Garganey mating when we were married. The sob-papers tell you a pretty wife is a good investment! My dear old boy, when I married her, I had to beat N.O.s off with a club. . . . And if she predeceases me, I shall put up a marble slab:

To Jean
for so many years wife of
Commander Andrew Teal R.N.A.S.

and underneath just four simple words, '*She gave him hell*'. Not but what she's a very good wife in some ways. Very easy on the eye, wonderful housekeeper, stands no nonsense with the maids, lives on milk and grapenuts. But all those years of sitting hard on her nerves and temper on the court, and being an automaton in the public eye, concentrating y'know, have been too much for her. Of course, she never plays tennis now. After her past, our local stuff would be a bit of an anticlimax. She breeds chocolate cavies."

"What the deuce are they?"

"Guinea pigs, y'know. About *the* most unathletic creature in the animal world. And her only game is bridge. It's the reaction. Do you play bridge?"

"No, I hardly know a spade from a club."

"You will," said the Commander. "Jean'll see to that! She insisted on my learning, when we took this place on; said we could make an extra 25 per cent. on our turnover without any extra income-tax, if we played a really sound game of bridge together as man and wife. Bought me Culbertson and so on. But I'm an ass with cards. I did my damndest but the first night we took any of our guests on, I revoked twice, without even knowing I'd done it! Now I'm not allowed near the table, thank God. It gives me time to carry on my own hobby of training gundogs. There's money in *that* nowadays. I'll sell you a fizzer if you can afford it."

They drove on in silence. They roared over a river hemmed beneath a stone-walled humped bridge, through a townlet of bare granite walls and slate roofs, and then the car began to climb.

"Four miles more," said Commander Teal. "But I forgot. We'd better do something about that whisky of yours."

He felt in his pocket. "I always carry a few labels, and a bottle in the boot. Which would you rather be, Gun-Oil or Hair-Tonic? Perhaps it'd better be Hair-Tonic. She may start sniffing if she finds Gun-Oil in your bedder instead of in the gun-room."

They spent five minutes transferring Gerald's whisky to a large square-cut glass bottle labelled:

GUNS WANTED

"Silly, all this subterfuge about alk nowadays," said the Commander. "Put that in your cartridge-bag till you know your bedroom geography and so on. The Americans had Prohibition once, and now they've cornered all the Scotch whisky in the world and are the only nation bar the French who can get decently tight. We aren't a free people any longer. We've got creeping paralysis of the national limbs and don't know it. If we grew twenty million tons more barley a year, some stinker in Whitehall would say we hadn't got enough except for export. I wish I was back at sea. Fifteen years ago, on the Malta station, I used to have twelve pink gins before lunch for a penny apiece and twelve before dinner. . . . *Sic transit gloria!*"

"I suppose," said Gerald, "one really would shoot better without it. Your wife's probably right."

"Don't you believe it! When I was a boy, I never smoked and never drank. I was as fit as blazes and could I hit a bird? About one in every ten. My gun used to come up in a flash and I wouldn't be surprised if I didn't miss some of those birds in front, the one thing the pundits say you can't do. My other old uncle down in Harkshire is one of the prettiest shots in the south of England. He's seventy-three and has done himself dam' well all his life. There's no pink of condition about him, I promise you! With the ordinary driven partridge, old Uncle Charlie barely bothers to get off his shooting-stick. It's just 'pat pat' and down they come as simple as kiss-my-hand. But you try it! Condition, my foot!"

The car turned a corner and Gerald saw a massive red stone building backing on the road ahead, with a great arched entrance.

"Here we are," said the gloomy man, " *'Childe Rolande to the dark tower came'*. Only—if you *are* a hunting-man, don't try any Childe Rolande stuff with your little slug-horn here."

"I haven't got one. Why?"

"It was in 1939," said the Commander, sadly, "we had a young Master of Beagles up here. He'd just taken 'em on and he couldn't blow a horn for sour apples. He came up here mainly to practise it before he started cubbing, or whatever you do to hares. He used to wander out in the middle of Gallowgill moor, and blow his little cheeks inside out, and make no impression on the b——y horn at all. Just a few mewing squeaks, like a bull-buffalo. (Ain't that queer, a great beast like that, with so little power of expression?)

"But one night, somebody slipped a bottle of rum in past Jean and we made an evening of it in the gunroom after most people had gone to bed. This young chap got a bit lit up. All of a sudden, I give you my word, the power came upon him. Sort of divine afflatus, y'know! Anyway he pulled out his horn from his pocket and without a second's hesitation he blew a 'gone-away' you could have heard in Carlisle. Talk of the trumpets round Jericho! Why, I tell you, we had Prince Boria (was it?) in the room above, and old Sir George Honeydew next door to him, and they manned ship to repel boarders like a blooming wasps'-nest. Old Boria fired a couple of shots with a twelve-bore out of the window before anyone could stop him, and then crept under his bed."

He paused and a melancholy smile lit up his pale countenance.

"My Jean's a tiger! I tell you, that young Master of Beagles heard what was likely to be useful to him in the after-years, and I got mine too. That's why she's so popsy about drink-imports now. Come on in and make your number with her!"

XI. HAPPY AND GLORIOUS

Gerald spent the rest of that day at Gallowgill Hall meeting
Commander Teal's other guests and doing what he called a
"recce" of his surroundings. Behind the tall severe prison-
aspect which the house presented to the road, he found comfortable rooms looking south over a far sweep of hilly arable
and woodland, and a park falling steeply to a trout-stream
below. He liked the quiet of the place with the call of a curlew
coming from beyond the apple-trees, and across the road
rough grass and heather running up illimitably to a ridge three
miles away.

He met the former Jean Garganey, very pretty, extremely
soignée, and perhaps not quite as lissom as she had been in those
summers, ten years ago, when every newspaper in England
had called her simply "Jean". He met also Mr. Ainstable, a
charming old gentleman with a white moustache, a life-long
member of "Lloyd's", who for years had rented moors of his
own in Scotland. In the old days there had always been grouse,
and once one put one's money down, there was sport to be had.
Now he was not so sure, but after forty seasons it was impossible
for him to forego the chance of shooting at least one grouse a
year, though he felt like a racehorse ending its days in a four-
wheeler. Yet he made no complaint and his eagerness for the
morrow was that of a boy. For him "the festival of Saint
Grouse" was holy, a day of renewal and rebirth.

Gerald also met the other guns, a farmer from Norfolk, who had made a fortune out of sugarbeet and had never seen a grouse, Mr. Pumphrey of Leeds and his brother-in-law, Mr. Harbottle, a silent pair with wives who knitted ceaselessly and discussed inexhaustibly the marital careers of their schoolmates of long ago. Mr. Pumphrey and Mr. Harbottle had made what they called "a bit o' brass" in the war and were spending it before the Government devised some new method of extracting it from them.

The last guest Gerald was genuinely surprised to meet and that was Sir William Boulogne. He had been relieved when Sir William had bowed statelily on their introduction, and had failed to recognize him as the young officer in the Savernake Club with whom he had talked of Langholm and Six Mile Bottom and Wemmergill. Gerald, sitting in a corner deep in a book, had been later amused to hear Sir William explaining to Mrs. Teal that he did not often come to hotels for his shooting, but that it "fitted in" conveniently before a round of visits, further north, on more impressive moors. There was rather more than a suggestion that everyone from the Macintyre to "the Duke" had been competing for Sir William's prowess.

Inevitably Sir William, being what he was, and Jean Teal, who in her heyday had "done" all the tournaments on the Riviera, drifted into what Gerald summarized as "snob-stuff". Of this and Paris Sir William displayed an uncanny knowledge, and brought out name after name of well-known people who, before the war, had divided their time between London and the South of France, all of whom he seemed to know. "Of course," Sir William would say, "poor Lord Charlie was very broke down there. I was able to be of a leetle assistance to him." or "Dear Clarice Gormathwaite, she's at Mentone now, without one penny piece to rub against another, now her son has come into the title. I hope to be shooting with him next month, it's a nice little moor."

Thus did Sir William's muse run on, his cigar in full fragrance, his cuffs and monocle gleaming. And Jean Teal, in the flush of reminiscence about the great days done, sparkled and grew prettier and pinker, so that Sir William found himself shelving his life-long ambition to be seduced by a really *svelte* brunette of unimpeachable origin, preferably in Claridge's. In that pursuit he had spent quite a lot of time since his business had prospered, lounging immaculately in the more expensive foyers and looking, as he felt, beautiful and lonely. But so far no brunette of the right type had swum into his ken. The nearest he had been to it was a most unsatisfactory encounter with a heavy-weight "At" in Shepheard's, when he had flown to Cairo to discuss with the Planning Staff the clothing required by the Middle East Forces on demobilization. She had giggled and kept on calling him "Billie-boy", and khaki drill most definitely did not suit her figure. Luckily for him, Rommel had reached the Qattara Depression, and the Planning Staff at G.H.Q., deciding reluctantly that even advance demobilization schemes must be shelved, had turned their starry long-sighted eyes elsewhere.

"Cartridges?" said Commander Teal, in reply to a question from Gerald late that night in the deserted gun-room. "I should take seventy and offer up a wee prayer. I know we've got a few grouse, but, though I haven't let on to the rest of 'em, I haven't a clue how the stock we left has done. That's the worst of a show like this! In good seasons you're tempted to go on and blue your capital and in bad seasons you live on overdrafts. We shall know more by four o'clock tomorrow and still more in a fortnight's time. My old keeper, Lumby, is very gloomy. Says half his sitting birds 'went out in fox-droppings'. This war has given all the vermin in the country, human and animal, their chance. Are you a hunting-man by the way?"

"I hunted a lot when I was a subaltern."

"Well, if you see a fox on Slaughterhope tomorrow, for the love of Mike forget the old hunt-button or tie, or whatever it is, and *shoot* the rozzy thing!"

"I certainly will."

"You wouldn't believe the sort of fellers we get up here," went on the Commander. "In 1939 I had a young Master of Hounds up here (the horn-blowing beggar I told you about) and he solemnly stood to attention and took off his little hat to three foxes—one after the other—which passed within ten yards of his butt in Wanfell Hags. He called shooting a fox (up here, too, where the nearest foxhounds are forty miles away!) 'worse than murder'. What I called *him*, I believe he reported to the Master of Hounds Association. Luckily our shepherds have some brain...." He broke off. "But I'll lend you a real good dog tomorrow. She'll find all you shoot and she's too old to spoil."

Gerald smiled. "I'll try not to spoil her."

"You wouldn't believe," said Commander Teal gloomily, "how quickly it can be done. I can make a dashed good puppy in six months, but it doesn't take six minutes for some other fool to ruin him in a day's shooting. This bitch has a few bad habits (to a dog they're like smoking and drinking) but she won't let you down." He yawned. "Tea 0700 hours tomorrow, breakfast 0745, start 0830. We've got an eight-mile run and then a climb. I had a party with old Sir William when he was told that part of the programme! I gather that to him and his chauffeur any hour of waking prior to 9.30 a.m. is nearly the middle of the night. Nocturnal sort of bird, what?"

Gerald closed one eye.

"Well, anyway, he's bucked Jean up no end. Says she'll have no difficulty in getting as much money as she wants in the South of France this winter. Why not come up here then? We'll relax the Prohibition Laws a trifle and get some fun with pigeons and rabbits and my flight-pond." The gloom on his bearded face lightened like a cloud passing away from the sun.

§ 2

Gerald stopped and with some difficulty turned the car at an iron sheep-gate set in a high stone wall. Behind him the round green hill which the road had skirted soared upwards for a thousand feet, dotted on the lower slopes with white dots which were sheep, and above, tiny black dots, too high and too far to see their colour, which were other sheep. Beyond the gate the stony track ran upwards between rushy pastures before it dipped into a stream. Beyond it a waste of grass and heather rose and rose nearly fifteen hundred feet to a great ridge whose crest and bony shoulders were smothered in cloud. There was no sound at all in the sunlight except the faraway crying of sheep. Cloud shadows patched the fellside lower down and there was a hint of rain in the west.

"Top of the world, it always seems like," Mr. Pumphrey had said to Gerald overnight. "You'll feel a different being there."

Gerald drew a deep breath and turned to look down the winding track for the other cars.

A minute later Commander Teal's shooting brake roared up to the gate and disgorged Mr. Pumphrey, Mr. Harbottle, Mr. Ainstable and the Norfolk farmer, wedged tightly in among a litter of gun-cases and three young Labradors. Far down the road Gerald could see Sir William's Rolls, driven by Private Tompkins (the veteran of Le Havre, Gezira, Tripoli, Brussels and the Taper Club), picking its way delicately up the stony track, like a duchess in a slum.

"He won't turn that 'bus here," said Commander Teal smiling. Out on the moor his gloom had changed to a cheerful cynicism, "unless he backs her down about a mile. But don't let's meet troubles halfway. We'll draw for places so that we can get going as soon as he comes alongside."

A minute later the Rolls arrived and Sir William descended with great deliberation. The seven-inch checks of his new Harris tweed coat and breeches made him look even wider than he was long. His high white spats and curled Homburg were modelled on a Royal photograph of the early nineteen hundreds. To conceive him crouching in a peat-hag was unthinkable.

"Sorry, Sir William," said Commander Teal, "you've drawn Number One. It's the top butt of the lot." He pointed to a faint dot on the skyline just below the cloud-curtain. "That's Number Eight this end but we shan't be filling that one, as there are only seven of us."

"But where," said Sir William severely, "are the ponies?"

"I've only one out, old Bill Garrowby's pony, and he's flanking in on the far side."

"Oh really! Then we *walk* there?"

"We do. I always feel it limbers the frame and improves the eye. Makes one ready to take on the birds on level terms. Don't you agree?"

"I do not," said Sir William firmly. "On all the best moors gentlemen are accustomed to riding to their places."

He spoke with indignation for in the Lateral Party Shadow Cabinet he was the Minister designate for Rationalization and Rural Uplift, when the party came into power as it was bound to do in the next five years. Then Sir William intended to build himself a stately pleasure-dome in Scotland, on the lines of Karinhalle, but on a good flat moor, such as was depicted yearly in the *By-Prattler* in photographs showing happy parties "on their way to the butts", riding well-groomed ponies. Nothing he had read had prepared him for this preposterous mountainside.

"Come on!" said Commander Teal cheerfully to his flock. "It's only just over a mile and a half and we've forty minutes before our only other grouse-bird is scheduled to arrive. Dinah! Heel-damn-you-Destiny! Here we are at 9.15 a.m. on the twelfth of August, 1945, the bloated plutocracy, gathering up our implements of slaughter and hurrying to God's gray and purple spaces all regardless of beauty, to pay homage to fashion and taste the vile joys of massacre!"

Sir William started and looked very severely at Commander Teal. This sounded oddly like Lola Goldman, who had made the suppression of bloodsports a potent theme in her husband's election addresses. Was he having his leg pulled, or was this a comrade all unknown?

"And there they lie before us," chanted the Commander, striding up the narrow track, "6000 acres of unprotected damn-all, all mine, and tenanted by 6 grouse, 5000 sheep, 17 foxes (or else my keeper's a liar) and 30000 hikers in due season."

"Six grouse?" said Mr. Ainstable. "I hope, Commander, there are more than that?"

The Commander looked gloomy again. "I always feel like that, Sir, at the start of the season. It's like looking at one's pass-book still in the envelope and not daring to open it, y'know, because one doesn't know if one's £500 overdrawn or six-and-elevenpence up. In my dreams that ridge is tenanted only by ravens and a few old bachelor grouse jeering at me from a peat-hag."

"It's magnificent scenery," said Mr. Ainstable, "this beats a lot of Scotland."

"Yes, but one can't shoot scenery."

"You're too despondent," said Mr. Ainstable. "After 1918 the grouse-stocks were right down but they recovered. Leave it to Nature and things will adjust themselves."

"Nature!" Commander Teal grinned explosively. "Every-one always says that! Nature's the one thing absolutely certain to muck 'em up. If I'd left my wife's complexion to Nature all the summer when she was playing tennis, what the devil would she look like at the end of it? See that drain?" He pointed beside the track. "That's been left to Nature for five years and see how it's clogged and over-grown, holding up water everywhere and a death-trap for any young grouse. Look at all that bracken! That's Nature, that is, and she hasn't taught sheep to eat it yet! These moors were left to Nature most of the war and what was the result? I shot over 100 pairs of carrions on the Gallowgill side this year and as for foxes..."

The silent farmer, Mr. Lee, put in:

"You've hit it, Sir! I left a brood mare to Nature this summer surrounded by about five acres of spring-grass, and she got so hog-fat she very near died of laminitis two days before the foal was due. I had to drag her into a yard and starve her!"

"Nature!" said the Commander again. "She always makes a bog of it. Give me Art every time."

Poor Mr. Ainstable, who had left things to Nature and his keeper for years, and could never understand why barn-owls and kestrels were so scarce locally, as they were really beneficent creatures, gave up the unequal contest.

"Hullo!" said Mr. Pumphrey, ten minutes later, "where's Sir William? He looks a bit lost. You'll never get yon lad into top butt on time, Commander."

Everybody stopped and Gerald, who rarely went out without fieldglasses, raised the pair he carried slung under his arm. Three hundred yards downhill, where the stony road petered out in the track they were on, Sir William was sitting panting, while above him Private Tompkins, a cloud of steam rising from him, rested on his arms reversed, as if at a funeral, the barrels well down in the mud of the road.

"On fire and sinking," said Commander-Teal, taking in the situation at a glance. "Who's Number Two? You, Warde? You take the top butt and if the old blighter does struggle into port, I'll say we're numbering from this end. But I'm blowed if I'll lend him Bill Garrowby's pony. I've only got panniers on it, not a *howdah*!"

Sir William was at that moment feeling that the only blood he wanted to shed was that of Lola Goldman. According to her, shooting was a devilish amusement, a form of torture inflicted by pampered modern savages, full of blood lust, on inoffensive and defenceless creatures, which had no chance of escape. But Sir William, with the sweat running down from his eyeglass to his flannel cuffs, and his pet corn on fire within his new shooting boots, felt that these Pennine grouse had chosen a pretty impregnable position, and that the agony was not by any means one-sided. When he did become the Minister of Rural Uplift, by God! he would choose a nice flat moor. And the moment he got back to the Taper Club, if any fool dared to order roast grouse for supper, he would, he swore, put the price up to 35/- a portion.

Private Tompkins, trailing desperately along behind him with Sir William's gun, 150 cartridges, the "unexpired portion" which Sir William had refused to merge in with the Commander's luncheon-basket, and two macintoshes weighing him down, was also seeing a new light, a red one. If this was sport, the favourite pastime of the idle rich, kings and princes and over-fed plutocrats, sating their lust for blood in a cowardly fashion, give him Harringay! Tompkins had won the war several months before, as his medal-ribbons showed, and had not signed on for any flaming route-marches in peace time. The tracts Sir William had lent him had assured him that the shedding of blood was a necessary "ingredient of pleasure" when on the moors. The only blood Tompkins felt he wanted to shed was that of his employer. Shooting cruel? He should just about think it was! Once the champion crooner of the Batmen's Club at Gezira, Tompkins found himself moaning deliriously beneath his breath:

> *Does the road wind uphill all the way?*
> *Yes, to the very end.*

No one, he discovered, had ever said a truer word.

§ 3

The path became a series of trampled clods leading through wet bog-grass almost straight up the hill. Mist billowed and swept about them and dissolved only to settle down deeper still.

"Blast!" said Commander Teal. "It's often like this on the top: you never know, even when it's clear down below! I've got ten small boys among the beaters and they'll probably lose themselves in this."

"Is it a long drive?" asked Mr. Ainstable.

"About two and a quarter miles. They bring the ridge parallel to this round in a half circle back to here."

Near the bottom butt, which Gerald noticed was still far from the top of the ridge, two figures were awaiting them. The keeper was an immensely tall bony man, leaning on a pole. His rain-washed red face and startlingly clear eyes were set off by a great beak of a nose. The child who stood beside him might have been nine years old. She wore a souwester, a dark-blue macintosh, and gum-boots, and came nearly up to the keeper's hip.

" 'Morning, Lumby! Hullo, Sally!" said the Commander. The tall man, who had been fumbling in his coat-tail, drew out a medium-sized alarm clock and held it in his huge fist.

"Yo're late," he said severely. "The lads'll be started this fower minutes. Yo'll need to hurry oop."

"Sorry, Lumby. I lost part of my convoy." Commander Teal looked back down the hill. The steep slope below hid Sir William and his attendant in their agony.

"Which of ye's One?" said the long man.

"Major Warde, here."

"Well, I want the wee lass dropped in Slaughterhope bottom. Hurry oop now!" He slid the alarm clock back into his pocket and strode off along the hillside.

"Will Sally be able to manage all right alone?" Commander Teal called after him.

"Aye. She'll twig owt, if there is owt." The tall man was gone.

"How old are you now, Sally?" said Commander Teal. "I always forget."

"Eight and a haaf."

"Good for you. You know where your father wants you to go?"

"Aye."

She smiled and her blue eyes sparkled in scarlet cheeks.

"I wouldn't care to flank on my own in this mist," said Commander Teal. "This ridge is all a mass of peat-hags and very boggy. A lot of people have been lost trying to cross it in winter. That's what *those* are for." He pointed to a line of poles, stretching away diagonally across the hags. "Well, here's Number Seven. We'll leave that for Sir William if he ever gets here. You'd better gallop on, Warde. Sally'll take you. And don't forget about foxes!"

Sally on her sturdy fat legs was well ahead of them all, with a home-made flag almost as big as herself on a pole. She was wet through from the knees to the waist but sublimely happy.

Gerald panted up to the top butt at last, and found that the ridge fell steeply away just beyond it. Sally gave him another beaming smile, said "Yon's you", and dropped over the crest into the mist like a mountain goat.

Gerald loaded his gun, placed his open cartridge bag at his feet and leaned over the edge of the butt. Somehow, even after that exhausting climb, he felt better here than he had done for some time. That "general bloody" feeling which had haunted him so long had departed a little. Here was a new land without end, which he had never seen or guessed at, though his view of it at the moment was limited to about five yards in any direction. Here were new people, a rain-swept bony race, who looked and walked and talked differently from any he had met in the over-populated south. And somewhere out in the mist was a new quarry, with which he had never tried conclusions before.

The mist swam and billowed and wet drops hung on every

grass-stem on the sods which composed the butt. But there was a rosy glint behind it as if it might be lifting soon. On his left was a blank wall of cloud; on his right he could not see the next butt but could just discern a post ten yards away, which warned him of its direction. A few yards in front the heather and rush grass sank away into mist again.

Gerald waited, wondering. Nothing he had read of grouse-shooting had prepared him for this. Dare he fire to his left front with Sally somewhere there, though he felt pretty sure she was a long way down the hillside? Would he ever be able to see a bird at all? He found himself recalling something Mr. Ainstable had said overnight, "The mistake beginners make with grouse is letting their birds get too near. You can start shooting when they're sixty yards out. They'll fly into it."

The wind blew keenly off the edge of the fell, and the mist eddied and dissolved and reformed in front of Gerald's eyes. Everything seemed out of focus. Fog dew gathered on his eyelids, and clogged his senses and his ears. Time passed and Gerald glanced at his watch. He had been there twenty minutes. He shifted his position and leaned against the left-hand edge of the butt and, as he did so, a black form, looking in the dimness almost as big as a turkey, swept over the butt within three feet of his face. Gerald had time to see a red rim above a bright brown eye, and every feather on the bird's immaculate frame. Before he could move, the old cock had vanished with a whirr behind him.

"That's that!" thought Gerald. "If they all come like that, I've had it!" Now fully alert, he leaned forward on the rim of the butt, his gun held ready, his wrists pricked by cut heather-stems. There was a faint radiance in the mist and gradually he could see the ground twenty yards out. The Commander's bitch, after attempting to scratch a dry place behind him, had curled up on the edge of a puddle and gone to sleep. This was pretty dull. Gerald wondered how many men scattered all over the world were envying him at that moment. How often in far places had he yearned, on that very day, to be doing what he was doing now!

He heard a faint wailing far down the hill on his left. Had Sally fallen into a bog? Was she dying in Slaughterhope bottom, or wherever she had "dropped" to? Slaughterhope! What a name! Perhaps someone had lost his all here, years before, with mining or sheep or something. Slaughterhope, Killhope, Bleakhope, Wanfell, Unthank, Flinty Fell, Duffergill, Hell's Hill, Bleaklaws, all those names, which Gerald had seen on the map overnight, suggested that someone had lost heart in places like this in the rain and the mist and the loneliness. Should he plunge down and rescue Sally? . . . The mist lessened for a minute, as if a curtain had gone up behind it, and suddenly on the edge of the hill in front were black forms that swept and veered across him thirty yards out, the flash of a wing like a pratincole, and then a huddle of grouse gliding down over his neighbour's butt and gone ere Gerald realized he had missed his own chance at them for ever. He heard two shots below him, glanced that way, and then as the mists cleared rosily, he saw a black dot lift and sink a hundred and fifty yards away. He blinked: was it a midge or only the fog dew on his eyebrows? Next second there it was again sixty yards from him, an old grouse growing and growing as it raced at the butt, a black bird which forged its way at him with a trudgeon-stroke of tilted wings. He put up his gun and pulled and missed it by feet. It whirred ten yards past the butt to his left and became a brown form *ventre à terre* disappearing among the hags. He fired again but it was gone. Only a feather or two hung in the air.

"Damn!" thought Gerald. "Old Ainstable was right. But what a mover!" More shots sounded muffled down the hill. He saw Commander Teal in the next butt shoot twice and something black and white crumpled at ground level in front of him. Again came the wail below but Gerald could see nothing. He heard shots again to his right and his eyes roved half-unconsciously down the slope among the hags. Then suddenly he was conscious of a score of dark forms which seemed to hang motionless in space above him on his left. It was too easy. They looked like a flock of rooks. He fired and fired again. Before he knew that he had missed them clean, they were gone over his head and down the slope behind the next butt. He saw Commander Teal turn and a grouse crumpled and fell out of the covey a hundred yards down hill.

"Damnation!" said Gerald savagely. He had missed duck like that at flight when they seemed to hang on the turn.

A minute or two later Gerald could see two of the drivers, splashing through the hags in front of him. He waited and, as they came in, unloaded. Suddenly, he was aware of Sally, scarlet and panting, standing behind the butt. "Nowt?" said Sally, cheerfully.

"Nowt, Sally! I missed 'em clean. There must have been twenty birds in that last lot."

"Twenty-seven. Ah counted 'em." Sally produced her wet red hand from behind her macintosh. There was a grouse in it.

"Where the deuce . . .?" began Gerald.

"Yon owd cock. Ah seen 'im fall. Yo' nearly missed 'im."

§ 4

"Might have been a fair drive if we'd ever been able to see 'em," said Commander Teal. "I shot like a fool and should have had three brace. Lumby says several lots have gone right, which he never had a chance to flank in, and some of the drivers got a bit lost at the far end and let some birds out as well. Hullo, Sir William, you got here all right, then? How did you get on?"

"A very badly-drained butt indeed," said Sir William severely. "You ought to speak to your keeper. My feet are wet through, and so are my man's."

The tall keeper spoke behind them. "There's half an 'oor from now. Now ye'll not sit blethering too long. Come on, lads. You too, Sally!" He was gone again.

"Lumby doesn't give a damn for anyone," explained Commander Teal, looking at the drivers trailing away. "He was head man to the old Lord Muggleswick for years, a very truculent old beggar. Lumby sacked himself at the end. The old chap was a bit eccentric, until Lumby told him in front of his guests, when he wanted to try some dam' silly drive, 'Ah'm none following bloody fool! Ah've been with gentry all my life but Ah've only just learnt there's two soorts.' He's only afraid of answering one soul back in this world and that's his wife. . . .

"Come on, now, gentlemen, we line those butts down there while they get round and bring in all that flat. We'll have time to sit down and have a smoke."

§ 5

"Well," said Commander Teal five hours later, leaning against a high stone wall beside Gerald. "It's been patchy so far but we ought to see a good few birds this drive. We've been shifting 'em over this way all day and this is the best heather I've got on the moor. What do you think of it?"

"Grand," said Gerald, "but absolutely different from what I imagined. I've hardly had a shooting-school shot all day, bar two, and those I missed. The way a lot will creep at you out of dead ground, for example. And then you see an old cock steaming along towards you two hundred yards out and he seems to go to ground and disappear. Then he pops up, faster than ever, out of a hollow just where you don't expect him! And they're all on a slant or sidling up or down hill with the wind. The one drive today where you could see a mile out in front of you, I was driven nearly mad by midges on the edge of the butt, and could hardly keep still."

"So was I," said Andrew Teal. "Your friend, Bill Bolony, had a bit to say about that drive! Thought we ought to have the butts treated with insecticide. He and Tompkins set *their* butt on fire before they'd finished, putting up a smoke screen, and I had a job to put it out. That peat will burn for days. And, of course, not a bird came near 'em! But you'll get some shoot-ing-school shots before the week's out. I've one grand drive on Crosshope, where we bring 'em both ways across a deep gully, and another on Hollidale where they put about 500 acres of enclosures over a belt of larch-trees. They'll be up in the air there, I promise you, always supposing I've got any birds."

He looked more serious. "That's what's worrying me! We haven't seen enough birds today. I shall have one more day on here in a fortnight's time, and we may see more birds than today—birds that don't get up on the first day's driving—but here I am with a list of people wanting to shoot with me for the next six weeks and I shall just have to glance off the lot! . . .

"I told you yesterday it was hell, this racket. This autumn I shall be what theatres call turning money away. Fishing's different. No one can tell what's in the blessed stream till we get submarine television, and many chaps don't mind whether they catch anything or not . . . perfectly happy casting for salmon and not rising a fish all day. But shooting's different! There are electric eels aren't there and electric hares? I wish to God someone would invent an electric grouse, for *hoteliers* like me in a bad year!"

There was a sudden whirr over the wall six feet from them and Gerald saw three grouse disappearing over the heather.

"Talk of the devil," said Commander Teal cheerfully. "Coffee-housing again! I'll bet old Lumby saw that and will tell me off about it later."

He snatched up his gun and ran on down the wall to his place.

§ 6

Gerald closed his gun, rested the tip of it against the wall-top and peered over. In front of him was a hundred-acre enclosure of heather and grass, surrounded on all sides by walls. Seventy yards out the ground sank out of sight and there was dead ground also to his left. Beyond the far wall the heather rose steadily and a mile away Gerald could see a wide semi-circle of purple hill framed in sunny haze. On its crest were four tiny figures, evenly spaced, which slowly dwindled towards him into the hill. All between was dimness, gray and purple, green and brown.

Five minutes passed. He heard a whistle from his right. Andrew Teal was crouching under the wall, only his cap-peak showing, and making little upward pointing movements with his left hand. Gerald saw far away to his left front two black dots high in air. Crows? Ravens? Then suddenly they were grouse, sweeping towards him statelily and very high.

Motionless, Gerald waited for what seemed minutes as they planed down at him. Dashed high, he thought at last, but just in shot. What had someone said to him once? "Up in the air they're never as high as they look." He swung at the leading bird when they were nearly overhead and saw the one behind it come crashing down to bounce sixty yards behind him in the heather of the pasture.

Better not say too much about that one, thought Gerald, as the Commander shouted "Well done, the Army!" Gerald re-loaded hurriedly.

Then he saw far away just inside the enclosure wall, a row of tiny black dots near the ground which seemed to stop and fling up and disappear, then more and more. That must be a big lot pitching in. He saw a flag waving on the hill, then a score of black dots against the sun-dazzle in front. He half-closed his eyes to see better and was aware of a covey, close-packed, sweeping towards the wall about two hundred yards out. As they came he could see birds rising out of the heather beneath them, till it was a phalanx of dark shapes creeping at him at terrifying speed. He put up his gun, saw it blot out the leading bird as he pulled, knew rather than saw that it was falling, and had just time to snap the last bird as they swerved across the line along and over the wall.

For Gerald, the next ten minutes was like some hunts he had ridden, or the finish of a fast game of polo. You were doing something with desperate speed and the keenest concentration, but time and all detail was a blur. The dead ground on his left and in front seemed for a few minutes to pour grouse at him at all angles, each lot a little faster and more on a curve. It was as though, while he crouched behind the wall, someone far away was catapulting great black objects at him, objects which skimmed and rose in a wave at the wall, whirred above him or sheered away sideways and were gone. He could hear the other guns shooting, and occasionally see far down on his right a string of black dots sweeping majestically on set wings for the horizon.

"I haven't a clue how many I've got down," he muttered at the end. "I know there were eight in front and four behind." . . . He counted his cartridge cases. Twenty-three, and he could remember four misses, all at slow hanging birds which seemed too easy. Luckily the bitch that was too old to spoil had collected two runners in that flurry without waiting for orders.

He hoisted her over the wall and called two of the drivers to him.

§ 7

"Well done!" said the Commander beaming, five minutes later. "That high one of yours was a fizzer. Was it the one you aimed at by the way? . . .

"I've picked seven brace and a half and three of those birds are probably yours. . . . A lot of birds went over the two guns at the far end but I heard very little shooting. Come on down and see what's happened. Luckily the heather's short here and it's the last drive. Noble," this to the under-keeper, "take these dogs of mine and hunt both sides of the wall carefully all along!"

Mr. Ainstable was in a state of beatitude. He said he hadn't had a drive like that since 1938 but they were getting too good for him in his old age.

"Ah shot," said Mr. Harbottle slowly, "three braace and a

half but God knows how many Ah shot at. There's still one to pick!"

"Well, blow-my-life," said Mr. Herbert Lee, climbing over the wall with two fistfuls of grouse, "they came at me like starlings. If that ain't a masterpiece! In Norfolk if we drives 150 acres in one drive we reckon that's a lot, but here you must ha' druv very near a thousand."

At the end of the enclosure, where a cross-wall divided it from the next, Mr. Pumphrey, holding a single grouse, was white and shaking.

"Commander!" he said, tensely, "right at the start I swung rather too near the line at this bird and ... and ..." he faltered, "I haven't heard a shot from Sir William once. Can I have killed him?"

Gerald and Andrew Teal hurried along and looked over the cross-wall at Number Seven stand. On the lee side, each on his macintosh, their backs against the wall over which so many grouse had come, reclined Sir William Boulogne and ex-Private Tompkins side by side. They were fast asleep. Sir William's gun rested against the wall, beside Tompkins' right boot, which he had removed to still the torment of his feet. Between them was a long-snouted green bottle which had once held Benedictine. Both were snoring.

After all, this was the first stand they had had all day which was out of the wind, properly dry, and on level ground. Through Sir William's dreams, the band of the Taper Club was thrumming on divinely-muted strings, while Al Consomme crooned into the microphone:

> *Home is the sailor, home from the sea*
> *And the hunter home from the hill.*

Tompkins, with his mouth open, was dreaming that he had just discovered Groppi's in Cairo, after that nightmare voyage he had made to the rescue of the forces in the Middle East. . . .

A tear of relief trickled down Mr. Pumphrey's cheek. He turned away to hide it. Andrew Teal took off his cap. "What do we do?" he whispered reverently, "hoist the Blue Peter and erect a cairn of stones over them where they fell? I always wondered what he kept in the boot of that Rolls."

Gerald was suddenly aware of a long scarlet face and neck, coming like a giraffe over the wall above where Sir William lay. With his beaky nose and clean-shaven cheeks, Mr. Lumby looked oddly episcopal as he gazed down from his great height at the slumbering pair.

"Mon and boy," he said solemnly. "Ah've served with gentry all ma life but Ah've never seen the likes of yon. Loup up, Sally lass, and tak' a peep! But," the episcopal look gave way to a ribald smile, "yon gowks are the stoof ye want, Commander, to ask oop here in a dom' bad season."

§ 8

"Forty-three and a half brace and three snipe," said Commander Teal to Gerald in the smoking-room, "and to think that the year before the war we killed over a hundred brace the fourth time over! But I don't think two of our guns today hit much."

"Well, that's that," said Commander Teal, an hour or so later, as the Rolls crackled majestically out of the archway into the night. "I must say I should like to know what 'other moors' he is shortly gracing with his presence. Said we didn't 'integrate' things in the way to which he was accustomed and wanted me to 'sublet' his gun for the rest of the week. Jean dealt with that one, I'm glad to say."

"Rum chap!" said Gerald.

"I couldn't agree with you more. He told me there seemed to be far too many 'wild sheep' on my moors and if I cared to dispose of any, he thought he could find a private buyer to take three a week! No black market, just a little 'gentleman's agreement' which would benefit all parties."

"I gathered it was nearly five days since the creature Tompkins had had his hair 'set'," said Gerald. "He must have thought he's strayed into the Long Range Desert Group here, by mistake!"

§ 9

"Good Heavens, Luigi," said Sir Giles Wallaby in the Taper Club, as he let his monocle fall out on the bill. "We seem to have been going it tonight. What the deuce . . .?"

"Very sorry, sair. You hadda de grouse. Very rare, very costly, very harda da get."

"But thirty-five bob, man! . . ."

"Not ordinar' grouse, sair. Very special. Mountain grouse."

"Not ptarmigan, eh?"

"I'll aska da Manager."

"Lousy things grouse, Giles," said Lady Ingrid Stampling, "the only time I was ever on a moor I remember being nearly eaten alive."

"Hullo, Sir William, back again?" said a desiccated man in the Savernake bar. "Been on a little holiday?"

"No, I've been up North, grouse-driving."

"Lucky man! I haven't shot a grouse since '35."

"Well, I have a few kind friends still, I'm glad to say."

"And how have they done this year?"

"Not at all well in most places. We had quite a pretty little day on the 12th."

"*Did* you? And what sort of a bag did you get?"

"Under a hundred brace but I forgot to ask the head-keeper the exact figure after the pick-up. The Duke . . ."

"You were up *there*, were you? How interesting! You must be an exceptional shot. I remember once seeing the old . . ."

Sir William drew out his other watch, a noble thing engraved with the new Boulogne arms, furnished by the College of Heralds (a packet-boat rampant on a sea proper. Crest, three dames passants, verts.). He shut it impressively.

"I must be going," he said. "I'm late for a tiresome Committee at my other Club! Good-night!"

"William," said Lola Goldman severely, half an hour afterwards, "what's this I hear about your grouse-shooting? I thought we'd agreed to *abolish* it?"

Sir William for a week had forgotten about the Lateral Party's programme.

"My dear Lola, one must be rational. There are certain sports, the virile ones, in which all the odds are on the side of the quarry, er, which no he-man with red blood in his veins, y'know, can readily forego." He drank a glass of Burgundy. "I think we must aim at rationalizing the game laws, when we get into power. There'll be plenty of control, I promise you! But the danger, the thrill, the huge open spaces, the hardship of pursuit, it's a pity to lose all those! I assure you, Lola, there was

I the other day alone in the mist, with a precipice on one side and an impassable quagmire on the other, and not a soul in sight! Grouse whizzing by all round me!"

"And did you shoot well?"

Sir William refilled his glass. "As you know I dislike boasting, Lola, but the old keeper did say (grand old chap, he used to be Lord Mugglewick's head man), he said to me after one drive, "I've been on a moor for fifty years, Sir," he said, "and I've never in all those years seen a gentleman who could equal you!"

"Good old William," gurgled Lola, nestling up to him admiringly. "Do you think Gigoleo could let me have just a bit more of that breast of grouse? If one *is* proposing to abolish blood-sports, one may as well in the meantime . . ."

"Luigi," said Sir William five minutes later, "tell Al Consomme to stop that frightful thing he's playing and put on that old song about the 'bony purrple heather'. I tell you, Lola, it gives you a wonderful feeling, all those moors. Limitless! My mother was a Mackintosh. It's in the blood."

"I think," said Lola, as the waiter hurried towards her with a fresh relay of grouse, "you'd look really sweet in a kilt, William. Pity she was a Mackintosh. Stuart is so much more becoming."

"Ration-al-iz-ashun," said Sir William an hour later. "Thash real way, Lola old girl, to deal with game queshtion. Integrate things! Uncoödinatedr brutes, groush. Ask George Kolynos get the Party office on to it! We must get groush down to the lower levels, less risk, less frost, less everything. Get I.C.I. on to formula for a good heather shubstitoot. Only matter planning. Shame with all game. If you caponized pheasantsh they'd be much better table birds, wouldn't they? It stands to reashun."

"And the keeper shed," said Sir William at midnight. " 'Sir William,' he shed. . . ."

"William," said Lola, adjusting her mink cape and powdering her nose, "if you drink any more vodka on top of port, I shan't let you see me home."

XII. SOUTH AGAIN

"What pleasure lives in height?" *the shepherd sang*
                                        —TENNYSON. *The Princess*

"Come again!" said Commander Teal, a week later, to Gerald. They had dined together in Carlisle before the departure of the night train. "I've given you one fair day, one patchy day and one dam' bad day (with rain curtailing play at luncheon, as the newspapers say) but you've seen nearly all the grouse we've got on 20,000 acres and that's more than my later guests will! Ain't it awful to advertise for 'guns wanted' and then not be in a position to *want* the blooming guns? . . .

"But come up later and we'll do a *chasse* of some sort while Jean's in Monte. We're still a free country but the Lord knows if we will be in a year's time."

"I'd love to come," said Gerald sincerely. He had taken a liking to this far-flung land of great winds and fells and silences, and the blunt long-striding men that lived in it. They seemed less cramped and worried and frustrated than in the south, and the shadow of the bureaucrat had not yet fallen so heavily upon them.

"That's a bet, then," said Commander Teal. "We'll have a crack at some of the barren old cocks (real old clubmen they are) at the very far end of Squarefell, where we've never been since 1939; and we'll try for a goose on the Solway too, and shoot some 'cock and rabbits and pigeons. My few pheasants this year have had to be 'retired to the stud'. Only don't come in the second half of October because the Ranee of Hunza (or is it Swat?) and my sister-in-law, Lulu Garganey, are converging on me then, armed to the teeth with the latest weapons."

"Dangerous, are they?" said Gerald.

"My dear old boy, if I knew for certain I would close the hotel or do something. It's the suspense which is getting me down. I doubt if either has ever shot before. The only way to bring home to them that they've fired a dangerous shot . . ."

"Is to shoot them back?" said Gerald.

"Yes, but one can't kill the goose that lays the golden eggs in my job without waiting for the goose to kill some other goose first. It's Hell! Why, when old Boria was here, he got so excited after his first day's shooting he wanted me to drive him round Langwith town at midnight and shoot all the street-lamps out with a high velocity rifle. . . . Said he did it every Saturday night in Rumbellypore and the State Engineer had to replace 'em all first thing on Sunday morning. . . ."

But here the train moved out, leaving Commander Teal to his destiny.

XIII. HARKSHIRE COMPANY

Softer than sleep, all things in order stored
A haunt of ancient Peace.

—TENNYSON

Gerald went down to Harkshire, anxious to see, after many years, the family home in which his relations had found it so hard to "stay put". His uncle had called the place "an accumulation of family effort which was worth seeing". Gerald had only stayed there once since his boyhood and he came to it with new eyes. He found a low-built white dower-house in a corner of the park, looking southwards over a river valley, with a garden sheltered by immemorial hedges of clipped yew. Six generations of dowagers had quietly beautified that house and garden through the years. Not far away was a great square of empty stables with living rooms above them, and further up the hill, an empty grey-stone mansion which still bore the traces of five years of soldiery, flanked by a great walled garden, where couchgrass and nettles grew everywhere about neglected trees. Below the manor was a lake surrounded with rhododendrons, and behind it the park rose steeply to the crest of the downs.

After five years of life in bivouacs and trucks, armoured cars and ruined houses, Gerald hardly knew what to do with himself in the neat dower-house where his uncle had roosted, rather than lived, for the last ten years. He was looked after by a silent couple, who lived over the stables. Mrs. Wiggins cooked for him and Albert Wiggins, who had been stable-boy to Gerald's grandfather, found time to clean meticulously Gerald's battered kit, to put a bloom on the young horse—a real 'chasing type, as Gerald observed—which old Doctor Warde had bred and ridden, and to tend a small garden.

Gerald spent a month exploring on horse and on foot his silent kingdom, the hamlet of Little Oakington nearly two miles away from Stoke Loyalty. He found farms, which for all the upheaval of the wars, had the same tenants, and many of the same labourers, as they had had in his boyhood. Gerald's father (in the few years he had owned the place before a Mahsud on the frontier had killed him), and later old Doctor Warde had put all the revenue from the estate back into improving the farms, as far as a steadily diminishing income would let them. It was as if they had seen the war coming, and the greater struggle of survival after peace, and prepared, as the old barons had done, to victual and fortify their private keeps against all comers.

Gerald heard that story bit by bit from Dick Seymour, a huge old man with almost classical features, who had begun life scaring rooks on a farm and now at sixty-seven was the estate bailiff. He could barely read or write but his daughter managed the estate office and accounts.

"Your pore uncle," said Dick Seymour, "a nice old gentleman he was, but that sudden! Went off last June at two days' notice and left us all in a muddle, like. I don't reckon we'll see him agen, pore feller. But your grandfather was the same and your father too. Couldn't rest nohow! And then back they'd come from furrin parts, having lived rough all them years, like foxes, and first thing they'd say was 'How much money is there in the bank?' and they'd lay out this and build that and plant the tother, and then off agen. I wouldn't ha' been their wimmenfolk for a thousand pounds—rare nice ladies they was, but as bad gipsies as ever your dad was. No rest at all."

"Well," said Gerald, remembering suddenly what Col. Gore-

Ambulance had told him, "unless the Army wants me back, I reckon I shall stay put for a year at least."

"And about time too. This here place want a lot doing to it."

"Things aren't in as bad order as I expected," said Gerald. "Even the big house."

"Ah! there was Army generals here nearly all the time and they kep' it tidy like. You ought to see some of the big places round here, niggers in and Yankees and Scotchmen and all. Why, them Scotchmen in 1940, they burnt the staircases in Fewdown House for firewood! No, we been lucky but we're right short of cottages. There's men on these farms what live three miles from their work, and there's one or two cottages what ought to be pulled down."

"Come on!" said Gerald. "Tell me what you think wants doing."

"I know what we wants but that's agin the rules nowadays. These here Councils and Ministries, there's no sense to 'em. They won't let you get on. You've been abroad too long, Master Gerald!"

"Come on!" said Gerald. "I'm not here for long and after six years of war I've got no conscience. A few regulations won't worry me. I'll risk it!"

Dick Seymour "came on".

"And you mean to say," said Gerald incredulously at the end, "that they'll give me a licence to put the big house straight and yet won't let me build cottages for farm-workers? They're daft!"

"In course! I never met a Gove'ment that wasn't daft yet, but this here one'll beat the lot before two years is out, you see if it don't. They're townsmen, like: never heard of the country except on Saturdays. No sense to 'em at all. Laäbour." It was difficult to exceed the scorn in Dick Seymour's tone. "Now you listen to me!" Gerald listened.

"Sounds all right, Dick," he said at last, "but where's the wood and paint, and so on, coming from?"

Dick Seymour laughed scornfully. "That ain't much use afarmen' unless you look three years ahead. I seed this acomen'. That happened after the last war every bit the same. I bin puttin' some bits o' stuff by. You come and see." He led the wondering Gerald to the lofts of certain thatched barns and the stables and showed him the "bits o' stuff".

"My daughter," he remarked, "she rid to me once in a book about them old chaps in history what lived in them castles and towers and places. They hadn't no ministries in them days hum-buggin' 'em around and wasting all before them, trying to pinch what a man had."

"Carry on then, Dick," said Gerald, "and mind, if there *is* a row, my uncle and I will carry the can. But in the old days, if anyone started nosing in, the lord of the manor used to hang him from the battlements, and remember we can't do that now."

"No," said Dick Seymour, the blood of his ancestors hot within him, "but I'd like to, and no mistake, especially that War Ag!"

§ 2

So Gerald found time to explore still more the corner of England from which so many strange quests had lured his family. They had been for a century tireless in pursuit of something new, this rare bird, that little-known beast, a range of hills, some secret river beyond the Subansiri or the N'Mai, a climate which few had sampled, a jungle tribe, a little war here, a revolution there, or a lost city of the desert. Their insatiable lust for the remote corners of the earth, from the Andes to the Gobi, from Samarkand to Tenasserim, had taken them again and again from "the place" in sudden migrations, but they had come back, like swallows for a brief summer, to beautify it before flitting off again. The great house showed it, in a score of ways, and so did the corners of the estate. This thriving covert had been planted for the pheasants, that great lime avenue sheltered the cattle and attracted the bees, that belt or hedge had been put there specially for partridge-driving. The hide on the little peninsula in the lake, with the swept path leading to it, had been made forty years ago to watch the nesting ducks and grebes, there was another opposite an otter-holt on the river bank, and yet a third, a glorious *machan* of a hide at tree-top level in the great oak wood, from which a Warde had once shot ninety-three pigeons on a windy January afternoon.

And as he walked or as he rode, Gerald realized again the truth of Commander Teal's assertion that Nature so often "makes a bog of things". The farms, from their thatched barns to their rickyards, were as tidy as they could be but old Dr. Warde's gamekeeper had died in the war and his place had not been filled. The unkempt woods, impassable with brambles and fallen trees, swarmed with jays and magpies, carrion-crows and gray squirrels, and Gerald wondered how much hidden slaughter, both of game and song-birds, went on in their silent depths. He had not met Mr. Catling, who was struggling hard to recast Miss Janet Gore's "testamentary dispositions", but if he had, Gerald would have joined issue with him on the subject of "all things having an equal right to live".

§ 3

One night Angus telephoned to him from London.

"How now," he said, "not dead yet?"

"No," Gerald replied, "and are you still engaged to that girl?"

"Disconnected, I think is the term! There were tripartite discussions on a high level and a unilateral declaration by the Brig. that I was no better than a false knave, and then what the totalitarians call 'a purge of reactionary elements'. I sank myself all right but, like Falstaff, 'I have a kind of alacrity in sinking', on these occasions. I'll tell you about it one day."

"Well, don't tie yourself up again in London."

"My dear old boy, I'm so scared of what I may say after ten o'clock at night, that I never go anywhere now without my married sister or my psychiatrist in attendance!"

"Must be fun for them."

"And if they leave me for a second, they put a notice on me: '*Blind. Do not interfere*.' I'm terrified. I haven't drunk a fighting gin for a month."

"How *is* your psychiatrist? The young one you had in Eighth Army?"

"Poor chap, he's suffering from acute anxiety neurosis himself. He's about due for treatment by one of his own kidney."

"Why?"

"Well, during the war there were always squads of chaps waiting to see him, to tell him all their Freudful obsessions in the hopes of not getting sent abroad or away from a base. He was worth a division or so to Hitler. And now the selfsame blokes are streaming at him to get passed A1 for demobilization. Like old Tompkins, whom you met in the Taper Club! And my leech sees his bread-and-butter going. Thinks he'll starve in peace-time for sheer lack of raw material. . . . I say, can I come down and stay with you?"

"Are you still a peeler, Angus? We're doing certain jobs here, that I don't want anyone to know about."

"Not dipsomania, is it?"

"Don't be silly! How can one get even reasonably tight in this country? Oh no, it's quite straightforward but slightly outside all these rotten rules."

"I", said Angus, "am not a peeler though I still take a keen interest in my fellow-men. In these days of controls, my dear Gerald, we are all petty thieves, petty grafters and petty lawbreakers, aren't we, even the police themselves? Otherwise how does a village constable keep hens, or a pig?"

"I suppose we are."

"Do you perchance need a keeper?"

"What sort of one?"

"Well, a male nurse and constant attendant?"

"Good Lord, no, why?"

"I met Rosamund Gore-Ambulance in the Taper Club one night. She carries very heavy armament, does Rosamund, considering her displacement. She asked me how you were and supposed you were drinking yourself to death in Harkshire."

"That woman ought to have a twitch put on her tongue. She must have been talking to her husband."

"Probably, but if Rosamund hadn't talked all her life, half London would still be in possession of its sinuses, tonsils, adenoids, appendices and what-not. I told her I was thinking of having myself operated on, to achieve non-belligerent status at parties, like one of those cats old ladies keep."

"Did she rise to that one?"

"She blushed slightly. She's frightened of me, ever since we wrote Geraldine's diary for her that night. They're all gunning for me in the Taper Club! Monty and Geraldine nearly got the sack, and poor Cyril de Bourbon was in tears for nearly a week. Anyway, Gerald, I want to come down to you for a bit."

"You can come down and kill some vermin for me," said Gerald. "We're lousy with jays and carrion crows."

"So's London, but there they're disguised as politicians, Lateral and otherwise. We are no longer an Imperial race. 'The sceptre has fallen from our nerveless fingers.' But gamekeepering would be quite my cup of tea. Good camouflage."

'You'd better go to Lichen Bross and see if they've got a keeper's suiting off the peg."

"I will," said Angus, "but," he added wistfully, "do your keepers wear livery, like they did in the old days? I mean, scarlet waistcoats, and bottle-green coats and buff billycock hats?"

"Good Lord, no!"

"Pity," said Angus, "I should have looked lovely dressed like that! Give me a chance to wear side whiskers down to my neck. That reminds me...."

"What?"

"You remember that chap, Bongo Bellemy, who advertised about the skill with gun not being so essential as mellow comradeship? I answered that advertisement and I've fixed up for us both to have a day with him in Norfolk in November, when he shoots his pheasants. It might be fun."

"O.K. but you stand my poker-losings!"

"I will. Has Sir William Boulogne asked you to shoot yet?"

"He hasn't got any shooting."

"What?"

"He's got about seventy acres of grassland round his house, very heavily overstocked by a small dairy farmer. If he gets a brace of partridges off it in the season, he'll be doing well."

"Have you seen the house?"

"I've passed it. It's a very modern country house with a chromium-plated cocktail bar and a swimming pool and that sort of thing. Big stables behind it, not used. All the shooting he's got is the syndicate we're both in."

"The old liar!" said Angus. "I say, can I buttle for you occasionally, when I come down?"

"It's not a usual combination, keeper-butler. And I haven't got any cellar worth speaking of for you to interfere with, I warn you!"

"Never mind," said Angus, "I won't let you down."

"You'll have to hog your moustache."

"I've hogged it. I feel dehorned, like a, like a . . ."

"Polled Angus?"

"Exactly."

"You'll have to bring your own black clothes."

"I will. I suppose in these days even a butler can smell faintly of mothballs? I must buy a dickey tomorrow. Cheerio, Gerald, I owe King George about seventeen bob for this call. When we go to Bongo Bellemy's, you'll see a genuine keeper-butler, not an amateur like me. So long!"

§ 4

Best treasure of all that Gerald found in that month was a smoking-room, ribbed with books to the ceiling, and holding a steel cupboard full of meticulously annotated manuscript. John Warde must have spent night after night for years compiling those notes. Here Gerald realized, tucked away in a corner of England, was knowledge irreplaceable and much of it entirely new. Gerald wondered in how many country homes, and in how many men's heads (the heads of the men of action and not the men of words), those priceless irrefutable facts were stored away.

He read John Warde's notes of his trips for forty years, and the correspondence those trips had begotten with learned men from Berlin to the Bahamas. Gerald, himself a naturalist as far as a young man's preoccupation with sport would allow him to be, read these avidly. 'Much have I seen and known', that might be the old man's motto, if he still survived; queer customs of trappers in the Chindwin, unknown routes here and there where no one else had been, notes on rare pittas in the Nepal *terai*, notes on scorpions and mosquitoes and takin, on flowers and the sandgrouse of the Karachi hinterland, notes on a dozen minor facets of history, and a file of notes on mysterious diseases from *beri-beri* to *kumri*, that would be priceless to any doctor or veterinary surgeon who chanced to read them. And always the old man had waited before publishing them because he was not sure. In some cases he had reached conclusions years before but had kept them, in the hopes that fresh evidence from some corner of the world might help to verify what he had determined.

Suddenly it came to Gerald that, if he had less than a year to live, he would edit those notes for publication and add a few of his own, and have them ready when he died. If we chucked away India, the chance might never come again. After those wandering amoral years, he would "settle down" for six months and see what he could do. The empty mansion up the hill, the silent pictures on the walls, all the unseen influences which hung about the house he lived in, seemed to urge him on. And night after night saw him in that library working till midnight.

§ 5

The neighbourhood displayed little interest in him. There had always been Wardes at Oakington, but usually they had been either just coming or just gone. He was lectured on the telephone by Lady Mary Wenhaston of Stoke Loyalty House, a vague elderly widow in whose mind so many trains of thought kept colliding that she rarely finished a sentence. Lady Mary suffered from hay fever and usually went to bed from May to early August, during which time all her Committees, from the Mothers' Union to the Village Club, ceased to function with incalculable results. There was also Bill Dimbleby, ex-Lancer and Secretary of the local Hunt, who had worn spurs all through the Kaiser's war in the War Office, and on the outbreak of Hitler's war had pressed very hard, in the *Times*, that mechanized cavalry should continue to wear these indispensable adjuncts to *morale* in order to distinguish *pukka* cavalry from the plebeian elements of the old Tank Corps. And there were a score of retired officers and civil servants, living on fixed incomes in small houses round the villages, grimly drawing in their horns like snails and preparing for the worst. Gerald thought wryly of Angus's phrase about "the Imperial race, pregnant with victory". They were not very noticeably pregnant.

Thrice he saw Ann Heriot, once jumping an old mare very competently at a local hunter-show, once very neat and busy, cantering round a wood to a holloa near Oakington with two bewildered hound-puppies at her side, and once at a cocktail party defending herself from the attentions of Sir William Boulogne. She and Gerald smiled and exchanged a few words but did not get much farther. In Gerald's regiment, if any officer showed signs of "nesting" or going on the Staff, when they were stationed in Cairo and Alexandria, the rest of the Mess were apt to throw him and his bedding out of the window when they returned home in the small hours. The custom of those rigorous years survived. Gerald would see what "the vets" said at the end of his year. If a woman was interested in him meantime, she would presumably come and get him. Meantime, he would sample his "country contentments" and do a job of work.

XIV. MR. MANNERING LOOKS BACK

When he was a boy amusement had been personal, sport had been rational and private. Now he had listened to the reading of a back page from the "Evening News".
—T. H. WHITE *in Farewell Victoria*

Mr. Robert Mannering sat on his grey cob on the edge of Farthing Hill and looked down over a field of barley sodden with dew. Eight a.m. and it should be fit to cut by noon. The combine would knock that down by six o'clock, easily. He thought of his boyhood forty-five years ago, when there would have been fourteen men mowing that barley from six o'clock onwards with scythes. Ah! those scythes, the sound of their whetting, the unhurried sweep as the mowers went on, echeloned each a little from his neighbour, the smell of cut corn and cut weeds and summer morning! And himself, a small eager boy with a large stick, waiting with soaking feet and hunger gnawing at him, for the first stir of a rabbit against the clean edge of the barley! The yellowed Panama hats the reapers wore, the sun on their brown and wrinkled necks, and the shoulders bowed by years of hoeing and ploughing and hedging! Eight pounds a man they got for a harvest then and now it was £4 a week all the year round, winter and summer, and only three horses on the 1700 acres where in those years he would have kept fifteen teams.

MR. MANNERING LOOKS BACK

If there had been a county *Who's Who* of Harkshire, Mr. Mannering would have called himself simply a farmer. His mother-in-law, whom he privately considered an imperial snob, would have inevitably prefixed the word "gentleman". To her, bred almost in the Close at Furzechester, a farmer was still definitely not "county", and only on the verge of Furzechester society, whatever he was or did.

Mr. Mannering (Bob Mannering to his friends) was no snob. His grandfather had been a working farmer in Suffolk, farming 500 acres of heavy land. ("I never want no rain except on Christmas Day: where you stamp arter rain here, that'll hang for a twelve-month.") He worked with his men and talked very much like them. He left his son, Charles, £25000, a farm on which no Government official had set foot, and the parting words, prophetic even in the early 1900's: "I doon't know what we're a-comen to, Charlie buoy. This here bleedin' Government, that's agooen to ruen us!"

Charles Mannering, the father, who had been to the grammar school at Mundingham, still kept up the heavy-land farm, but had been taken on as agent by the newly-made Lord Westleton, who was just beginning to discover that while his light land might still keep a stock of partridges, it was fast becoming a liability. The "old Lord" had turned his estate into a limited company years before most large landowners had done so. Charles Mannering had also sent his son to Sherborough, very quietly. Robert had grown up in the middle of a great game-estate, on which commons were heavily enclosed, and pheasants swarmed on the heaths, in the alder carrs on the marshland, and in the great woods beyond the marshes.

Lord Westleton had become extremely autocratic in his later years, as landowners could still afford to be, and Bob Mannering had seen what his father had endured. When both had died within a year of each other, Bob Mannering had taken his mother and some £30000 to Harkshire. It was not such a cold air in winter, nor so sleepy in summer as East Anglia, and a school friend, in the Indian Army, had been glad to find a long-term tenant to take over his land.

Bob Mannering had grown to love the warmth, the chalk, and the beech clumps scattered over the high and spacious land, and the farming-cycle which still revolved round the breeding-flock. He had an absentee landlord who treated him generously in the matter of repairs and he had got hold of the shooting at about half its market-value, on the one condition that his landlord shot with him whenever he was at home.

With Lord Westleton the tenant-farmers had had one regular day, usually in January when the birds had been severely thinned, and were very wild. On that annual festival there had been a good deal of forced *bonhomie*, a lot of beer drunk at luncheon, and some jocular apprehension expressed by the sons of the house at the prospect of being shot by a tenant. Those had been the days when farmers had worn bowler-hats and white collars on such occasions in the shooting field.

Alone of the tenantry Mr. Charles Mannering had shot five or six days a year with his landlord. Given, as of course, an outside place all day, he had "kept the bag up", the more favoured stands being occupied by peers of the realm, a baronet or two, and any mere knights or gentlemen who had been lucky enough to be asked. Robert had always felt he had done well in cutting loose from that environment.

He had lived since to see the wheel turn full circle. The small "rough shoots" of three or four hundred acres had faded out, for no one could afford to pay a keeper £4 10s. a week nowadays except on a place which was big enough to make it worth while. He himself could now afford to be a snob over shooting if he had wanted to be. He could keep a horse to ride and it got two feeds of corn a day and a grooming as well, when all most other people could do was to keep a child's pony at grass throughout the year. Old labourers pottered around the garden and kept it as neat as a pin with that peculiar tidiness so typical of the old school. His lawn was mown with petrol while the retired General in the house up the road was giving himself heart disease attempting to push a mower. There was new paint on the doors in the yard and on the pipes, and the whole place was what they called in Harkshire "up together".

But his neighbours, the ex-soldiers and the old Admiral, and the quondam civil servants, were either frankly living on capital, or had "drawn in their horns" so far that they were like snails with no visible activities at all, except a game of bridge. They did not ride, they could not afford to shoot or fish, and it was pathetic to have them asking him for a ton of hay for their children's pony or corn for their hens, and being polite to him when they met, in case he was "short of a gun" on shooting days.

Mr. Mannering himself, a county councillor and a justice of the peace, was the only member of that village community who was certain that he would get as much shooting as he could find time for, once the season opened.

He suddenly realized that it was nearly 8.15 by B.B.C. time on September 1st 1945. The First! What elixir of boyhood had once been distilled into those two magic words! And his mind flashed back over the years to a vision of his father and the three tried friends who had shot with him year by year on The First for twenty-five years: their guns, their clothes with great roomy pockets inside the skirt and a belt, their old fashioned slip-leads and wooden game-sticks for the birds, their heavy boots and gaiters (none of your new-fangled brogues and stockings in which you did not walk at all).

He thought of the slow line wheeling through field after field all the burning day, round acres of beet and mangolds and turnips, the slow crackling advance through maize higher than a man's head, the dew on the swedes and the coveys bursting with a clatter from the seed clover or standing barley to set a boy's heart thumping wildly. He could remember the old yardman in a smock and a yellowed Panama, who carried a cask of apple-wine on his back to quench your thirst at noon.

And his father in a high square gray hat, almost a compromise between a bowler and a top hat, leaning over a gate for the chance of a driven bird.

The magic of those days when a boy with a stick between the "guns" had time to "nobble" a rabbit crouching in the stubble, and see the blackbirds and the whitethroats slipping out of the potatoes, the landrail in the seed-clover, the turtle-doves coming to the stooked wheat, the whole rich picture of autumn serenely unfolded!

Then back they would tramp in the mellow afternoon to a dish of tea in the dark oak-panelled dining room, where there was always a bottle of "French cream" to lace the cream already in the tea! And outside behind the farm the scattered coveys calling their members together one by one!

Eight-fifteen on September the First! Old Peter Hawker at Longparish a hundred years ago would have had twenty brace by now, with his queer ragged bobtail of followers giving their "butcher's halloo" of three cheers, to deride the rival parties on the same ground. Marvellous sportsmen though, "quacking themselves up with *sal volatile*" and walking miles for a bird. There must have been then about one-fifth of the game there was even now. A pheasant near Longparish was obviously as rare as a fox : you chased him about "with cavalry and infantry" and "blew him down" at sixty yards range with black powder and then came home "very satisfied" and ate him.

And now! . . . there were almost too many wild pheasants on his main partridge-beat, though there were practically no coverts of any size to hold them. Tom Beacon disliked them: "Yew let them pheasants get up, sir," he would say, "and yeour puttridges'll goo down." At Littlebourne close by, where they once shot 300 partridges and thirty pheasants in early October, they would probably now get forty brace driving and 100 pheasants. Change! sweeping on inexorably and yet he had men here now who had worked on the farm as boys and their fathers before them! And the only signs of a six-year war on the farm were a few pillboxes half buried in nettles at certain corners and concrete emplacements where the anti-aircraft guns had been. The countryside swallowed a war as imperceptibly as it had swallowed a hundred years of peace. The weeds were at work to cover what was left.

Yet the wheel had come full circle. The county magnates had lost half their land and lived in precarious dignity in what was left of their own parks, in houses much too big, three-quarters of them shut up after the troops had done their worst in the war. And the local lordlings were the "War Ag.", as it was called, with their girl clerks and subordinates, with whom Mr. Mannering chaffered interminably for permits for this and permits for that till he was half demented. Luckily, they had one real farmer, a close friend of Mr. Mannering, on the Committee, and Mr. Mannering had managed, by devious methods of intrigue, to get what he wanted for his farm. Farming was a queer show now, with its spate of farmer-novelists all contradicting each other about what to do with "the good earth".

In the old days, farmers had groused at the weather because they were afraid of their landlords and "never knew what the beggars'll du next", like his grandfather. Now there wasn't a farmer in the neighbourhood who didn't show a loss on his income-tax returns, but they had a new enemy, far more dangerous and less predictable, the State, suspicious of their accounts, suspicious of concealed profits, but only on the fringe of poking its expensive nose in.

Rum show! thought Mr. Mannering. He did not like syndicates of strangers but for the last twelve years he had run one, to pay for the rising cost of keepering and beaters. Two keepers now on the 1800 acres, one at £5 and the other at £4 10/-, with cartridges at 32/6 a hundred where in his youth he had paid 5/6 for "Bonax", and as for beaters . . . !

He sighed. The old days when you could get the tagrag of village unemployment at half a crown a day, stiffened with a few horsemen, the thatcher, the under-shepherd, the groom and so on, had gone. And apart from being cheap they *had* known the job. They could walk, they knew the land, and if the keeper addressed them pithily in good Harkshire they knew what he meant. They could keep a line without being told, they did not talk or shout unnecessarily. They had a sort of natural instinct for the places where a covey or a cock-pheasant would lie.

But now! since 1939 Mr. Mannering had made use of soldier or sailor beaters from nearby units or the naval aerodrome. And what beaters! Long-haired, urban types, incessantly smoking cigarettes, drifting in talkative groups across a field, never knowing when to flag birds and half the time not seeing them, not knowing a rabbit from a hare, and wanting all that money and a bottle of beer at lunch. They had nearly broken his headkeeper's heart and reduced him to a state of blasphemy.

Mr. Mannering looked at his watch: 8.20 a.m. and time for breakfast. He could still afford to keep a cook but he could not afford to keep her waiting! There would, he hoped, be a kipper and some bacon of his own curing with a fried egg, and the nation grudged you those last two at whose existence they only guessed. And now he shot with strangers as paying guests to keep his expenses down and the Lord knew what would happen before the season ended.

But perhaps he fulfilled a need even now with his syndicate in our queer complex civilization, where so many people seemed to be trying to eat their cake and have it. Only eight days shooting a year. Perhaps one of those would be so wet that it would be impossible to shoot! Nearly four weeks more, anyway, before his first day.

XV. LIFE-CYCLE OF A
COLONEL

*"I do not deny that turkeys and geese, especially in winter,
lead a very dull and disagreeable and apprehensive life. So
do many human beings however. . . ."*
—Private Angelo by ERIC LINKLATER

*Me that'ave been where I've been—
Me that'ave gone where I've gone—
Me that'ave seen what I've seen,
  'Ow can I ever take on
With awful old England again?*
—Chant Pagan by RUDYARD KIPLING

The first member of the syndicate to be about on 27th September was Col. James Gore-Bunbury, D.S.O., widely known in India as "Jimmy Bundobust", who left his back-door at 6.45 a.m. with his retriever walking behind him. He held a steaming saucepan and a spud. He disbelieved in fowls, but now their feeding was his first early morning duty, which had superseded the cold baths of his youth and the physical exercises of his middle years, practices which, he found, merely promoted an appetite unsuited to post-war rations.

"Hens?" he would say to the vicar. "I dislike hens! But I suppose they do lay me an egg or two, and at least they get rid of my swill."

"My swill" had been a problem to Col. Bunbury for many years. Now his hens consumed the scraps of bread and fat, the horrid aftermath of porridge or stew, the fish-skins and the potato peelings which throughout his service had had to be got rid of somehow, lest they offended the eye or the nose of inspecting Generals.

"Swill!" he thought with a shudder! Extraordinary birds, hens, carrion-feeders in Burma and you got dysentery at once if you tried to eat the village-chicken. And yet you always ate their eggs whatever they themselves were fed on. His mind roved back to the old days with the odorous donkey carts crowding round the cookhouse door and the overflowing tubs after each "rationed" meal. A "rationed" army but how wasteful! If this Government thought they could cut down waste of bread by rationing, they would soon learn and want another 50000 civil servants to administer it. It was the first turn of the screw, though, as in Russia. And he thought of that frightful moment, when "Pop-eye" Pickering, who had been his brigadier in 1914 and had a nose like a setter, had winded all the swill-tubs which his serjeant-major had so cunningly concealed behind a hedge. And that still more awful time when he had served under "Gunfire" Samson, with hives of bees in his bonnet, who said that in a properly-run unit there was no such thing as swill!

Swill! There was precious little swill in a gentleman's household nowadays. As he added balancer meal and red pepper to the mess and stirred it, he could see a herring bone, and tea-leaves, and, God bless him, even a chicken-bone with gristle attached. That would be Doris, the pullet who had graced his wife's luncheon-party on Wednesday. Would the hens, those cannibals in spite of themselves, say "Alas! poor Doris!" as they pecked at her femur?

But Colonel Bunbury never felt any affection for hens, the Norman curve of their beaks, the enquiring eyes which rested on you sideways without enthusiasm, their toneless unmusical gurglings. There was nothing human about hens, as there was about horses or dogs, except when you saw them streaming down the orchard to their meal like women in plus-fours towards a 'bus-stop.

Angela, his wife, who talked of "her" hens, though she washed her pretty hands of detail, always considered it a waste of good food to introduce a cockerel among her pullets. The Bunbury hens were all, in fact, virgins, but despite that each brought forth about three and a half eggs a week, not one of which had the remotest chance of fulfilling its life-cycle.

"Angela's right, y'know," the Colonel had said once to the vicar, "it sounds unnatural, like putting them into a sort of compulsory convent, but when we had a cock in the run, he always came down off his perch in the morning much too full of himself. Chased 'em about, you know, dominant male and all that. Took the hens' minds off their work. They don't lay any the worse now, without one."

"Ah!" said the vicar, "I'm glad to hear that. They lay all right without pairing? My dear wife kept them in squadrons, you know, very new-fangled. I always thought it a bit cruel."

"Squadrons?" said the Colonel, "don't you mean batteries?" He was a stickler for technical terms.

"Batteries it must be!" said the vicar. "I knew it was some military formation. Each bird had an open-work cage with a wire floor where it stood all day and they lit it up at night. Nothing whatever to do but lay! Some of them, she told me, averaged two eggs a day. I suppose it was a tremendous effort at survival, like trees flowering two or three times a year. There's no doubt *homo sapiens* does think up some very ingenious devilries."

"*My* hens are very happy," said James Bunbury. "They're as free as air, and spend their day as they like, no fatigues, dusting themselves and pecking about. Unnatural creatures, though; I give them six nesting-boxes, but they only lay in two and queue up for those. But then they are absurd creatures—and this is an unnatural age."

"Yes," said the vicar. "Like some of my parishioners. I have one hen who always gets into my garden at the most awkward time of year, whatever my man Sam does to prevent her, but *can* she find the way back? Never! She goes into hysterics when he feeds the others on the right side of the wire but she never discovers the way back. Like one or two of my flock, who have fallen by the wayside. . . ."

"And when you come to think of it," said the Colonel, "the only creatures except man and the monkeys whose males are in rut all the year."

The vicar nodded. He was a naturalist and never minded other people making vulgar remarks in his presence, if they were the fruit of observation.

§ 2

The Colonel wiped the poker and put it carefully away above the cornbin. It was part of a set of fire irons, bequeathed to his wife by her Aunt Belinda two years before, along with some china, a Benares bowl, a pearl necklace and £500.

Angela and he had fought nearly to the death with her sister, Rosamund Gore-Ambulance, as a result. For years the two families had tossed their Aunts Belinda and Janet neatly backwards and forwards during the migration season from June to September, when it was warm enough for them to leave their houses. When Aunt Belinda had got really old and feeble and was unmistakably breaking up, each had felt that the other wanted "watching with the old lady", though each felt too that her illnesses were not really *her* concern.

But there had been no *rapprochement* except a momentary one in Brookwood cemetery when Rosamund, who had contrived to get a pre-view of the will, had offered to swap her newly-won Chippendale sideboard for the pearl necklace and, as an afterthought, the Benares bowl which was "just what she wanted for her hall".

The resultant contest in three rounds, one verbal and two epistolary, had been epic, and the Colonel, as referee, had suffered most of all. With some vague feeling of getting his own back, after that long martyrdom, he had dedicated Aunt Belinda's poker and shovel to the swill-bucket. The bowl had long lost its golden tints and sheen and now lay half-buried in the orchard, full of dirty water and little bits of grass, and that peculiar form of dandruff to which geese are prone. The thought that Rosamund had coveted it for visiting-cards in her hall gave him satisfaction whenever he rinsed it out. One day he would say to her: "I'm giving up geese. You can have that dam' bowl if you care to clean it, Rosamund!" She would have a job. Should he leave it to her in his will?

He stopped by the little gate into the orchard and looked at the dewdrops glistening on every bough. Then he opened the henhouse door and shouted, "Come and get it!" while he counted them carefully to see that they were "all on".

He was beginning to know them now. There was "Screwy", so called because she was so eccentric, a Buff Rock whose crimson comb and face showed her to be in the rudest health. "A very sound dependable hen: lays a beautiful egg," the Colonel would have said of her in a confidential report though she was the one marked individualist in his flock. She always tried to lay in the potting-shed, or the dog-kennel, in what the Army called "a disorderly manner". She would even arrive at the kitchen-door through the sacred garden to hasten her break-fast, though no one ever discovered how she got into the garden. But she laid 180 eggs, very large buff ones too, every year, and when she did sit (either on a china counterfeit or one of her own which, for the veterinary reasons I have hinted at above, had no earthly chance of hatching), she brooded in a defiant coma whose faithfulness appalled him, while nettles grew up all over her.

And there was Iris, a white creature, who laid about twenty-six eggs a year, but would adopt any other egg in the hen-house and peck him to the bone if he attempted to interfere with her; and Evelyn, a brown hen, always broody, who would lay eggs on her perch at night, regardless: a lazy hen who would have had a conduct-sheet as long as his arm if she had been under him of old!

"James!" Angela would say sternly at tea after her daily stroll up the garden. "That brown hen seems broody again."

Why was it, he wondered, that women, who, as Mencken had pointed out, had "no use for virginity *per se*", always disliked a dumb animal obeying the highest instincts of maternity? Just when they began to show devotion, or be in "an interesting condition", you whipped them off and put them in a coop or a saucepan.

Aloud he only said, "Sure she wasn't laying, m'dear?"

"Of course not. Deal with her! You know my method."

And next morning poor Evelyn would be incarcerated in a coop hung from a nail on a tree, which still had a label on it reading "BIBBY LINE, RANGOON. HOLD, NOT WANTED ON VOYAGE". This draughty cabin and short rations formed an effective deterrent to most broody hens. But not to Evelyn. She was at it again the moment his back was turned.

Women, thought Col. Bunbury, were far crueller and more ruthless than men, especially towards their own sex. They gave hens no credit or encouragement except as egg-machines.

The Colonel looked in the henhouse and recoiled at the atmosphere which met him. For twenty-five years of his life somebody would have been on the peg for that sort of thing! There would have been scrubbing and lime-washing and blow-lamps, and sweepers scurrying to and fro with dark threats of "*teen rupiya* fine". For the interior of the hen-house was not as hygienic as the Ministry of Agriculture's pamphlets advise. He had meant to do it last Saturday but what with pressing and ironing his Sunday trousers, exercising the old dog, digging potatoes, preparing his gun for the season, and doing the cross-word puzzle, the opportunity had come and gone. He knew now why his hens rushed out not to the swill-bucket but to drink deep draughts of water with their beaks raised heaven-wards. People in Belsen or Ausschwitz must have felt like that of a morning!

Then he suddenly remembered incongruously that it was a syndicate shoot today and the first day. What had Kipling said about "shooting with strangers being the same as war"? Marvel-lous old bird! Never shot a partridge in his life, but had hit the nail plumb-centre as he always did. He must take a field-dress-ing and some iodine, just in case.

§ 3

A muffled honking proclaimed that his early morning chores were unfinished. The geese! If the Colonel hated hens he loathed geese. They were like some smart batmen he had known in the Army, the dirtiest soldiers underneath. They left feathers everywhere, they fouled every place they frequented, they produced their own weight in guano in a week.

They were faithful parents but set all their efforts at nought by allowing their goslings to drown, by parading them in-cessantly to and fro from birth, by blowing them over back-wards in the slip-stream when they flapped their great wings, and by squashing them under their enormous leathery feet. Dam' bad parents, there was no other word, and unnatural, like most things if left to themselves!

Good mothers, but laying eggs so massive that the goslings exhausted themselves in their efforts to emerge, clumsy fathers, putting all their devotion at nought by gross carelessness, making great protestations of bravery but running away at a wave of the hand, bolt upright and looking over their shoulders.

He opened the door and let them out. Ben emerged and Eleanor and the one he called Lucy after his stupidest cousin. And as they came, the thought pierced his mind, "Oh God! I shall never, never, shoot a goose again!" Those old days in Connemara, as the stray gaggle came down to his setter, those misty mornings on the Chindwin with a skein in full cry above the fog, those evenings in Mesopotamia and at Cley when he had crouched shivering, and all life hung on their clanging as it came nearer. Shivering in ecstasy like the dog beside him, soaked and muddy and utterly content! He thought, "Great days, but I'm done for now. Two wars and almost no money of my own and these three filthy domestic brutes to dance attendance on!" Goose-girls indeed! A goose-colonel, that was all he was!

§ 4

The Colonel came back to the kitchen for breakfast. There were no pigs to feed at present. A succession of them, Debenham and Freebody, Marks and Spencer, and his latest pair, Fortnum and Mason, had passed to their reward and portions of what had once been Fortnum still hung, sewn up in one of Aunt Belinda's old lace antimacassars, in his larder.

Colonel Bunbury liked pigs in themselves and the way in which they helped out what he called "the commissariat", though for years their food supply had passed almost imperceptibly from the open to the black market, and he could never look them in the face for the last five weeks of their sojourn in his sty. He was, as he realised, much too soft-hearted to be a farmer. Most of his neighbours never lost an ounce of sleep from the fact that so many trusting creatures were awaiting death all round them. They fed them and tended them and often, in bad weather, slaved for them, and then one morning, without a qualm, the final act of treachery occurred, and nobody thought anything about it. You took on their successors, as calmly as new boys at a preparatory school, and hoped they would do the school credit by "going just under twelve score" at death. And yet farmers seemed to be the only people nowadays who could keep the income-tax bloodhounds at bay.

What a thing it was, this money-question, so that at sixty-two one was a slave to one's house, and doing menial jobs all day. He had tried everything he knew to enhance his pension of £800 and the £250 a year or so that his wife and he had between them, cutting thumbsticks, growing mushrooms, and even writing a book on his service in India.

He had also been to considerable expense just before the war to patent "The Country Gentleman's Dog-Chute", a simple form of padded slide, which could be lowered from a bedroom window by turning a handle, and by which incontinent pets could be put out on to the lawn without the trouble of going down and unlocking doors. Col. Bunbury had reckoned one freezing night that there must be, at least, 15000 gentlemen of England now abed who would pay three guineas each for this device. Fired by the prospect of wealth, he had suborned a friend to write a small brochure for him. He had received an expensively tasteful pamphlet which began

WONDERFULLY SIMPLE AND EFFECTIVE!

SOUND REST AT LAST!

SAVES TEMPERS! SAVES SLEEP! SAVES CARPETS!

YOUR PETS WILL APPRECIATE IT!

ONE TURN OF THE HANDLE AND THEY'RE IN THE GARDEN!

SHOULD BE IN EVERY COUNTRY HOUSE OR MANSION.

AN INDISPENSABLE ASSET.

Most useful in emergencies as a fire-escape or for
children's parties. . . . Nothing can go wrong.

(PAT. APPLIED FOR)

and underneath a picture of an Aberdeen terrier sliding happily down under a harvest moon into the outer world.

But alas! the first samples had not exactly swept the country and the Colonel had never gone into full production on a commercial basis. His only letter from a grateful customer (no less than the first Lord Aldeburgh) could hardly be used as a testimonial.

It ran:

Dear Sir,

It may interest you to know that I used your patent chute on my wife's Pekinese one night during the recent frosts, after years of sleepless annoyance. The little swine fell off halfway down and broke his blasted neck. I have had some shocking moments with my wife since but it was worth it every time. Supposing the dog survives the descent, how do you get him back in the house again? I enclose a stamped envelope as my wife is contemplating another pet.

Yours very truly,

Aldeburgh

With school-bills to pay and everything rising he was getting poorer and poorer with terrifying speed. He had no financial future of any kind until his wife's aunt died and nobody knew how she would leave her money. He decided not to stop for the post on his way down to the Valley Farm where the guns would meet. There never seemed to be any letters nowadays which did not contain bills, or demands for rates or tithe or income-tax. He was better without them. He remembered how dreadfully he had shot in 1939 at Preston Endever (an invitation day at which he had been most anxious to excel) on the morning after he had opened an income-tax demand for £67 15s.

The kitchen into which Col. Gore-Bunbury now went was almost as speckless as the potting-shed he had just left and a visitor would have understood why he had earned his name of "Jimmy Bundobust". In the potting-shed hung every variety of gleaming tool, burnished as in an armoury, and earth-oiled or painted every year. The old tin-lined saddle boxes, in which once his polo and hunting-saddlery had gone half over the world, still had

"Lt.-Col. J. W. A. Gore-Bunbury, D.S.O., I.A."

white-lettered across their lids, but they now held pig-food and balancer-meal and those blends of cayenne and curry powder which kept the hens' efforts at egg-laying from decline.

157

There were notices everywhere, one for use on the manure-heap at certain seasons, "DO NOT USE THIS END", another which forbade smoking in the old thatched barn, one for the carrier to call, and indoors there were neat typed announcements to his guests to prevent customs he disliked. There were two combs, for example, in the cloakroom, both neatly labelled, one for persons who used hair-grease and one for normal beings.

This week, with Angela away relentlessly nursing her last and most refractory aunt, Miss Gore (lest Rosamund Gore-Ambulance, her sister, should cut her out in the matter of yet another will), the Colonel was alone. For two years now he had been in sole charge of the garden, and there was only "a daily woman" who did not mind "obliging" in the house for two hours on Saturdays.

There had been a time in 1943 when he had "run to a land-girl" in the garden, a feckless blonde creature who was not considered strong enough for farming locally. Alas, his wife had regarded her entirely as someone who was likely to get him into trouble or the other way round. She had frequently upset their cook (now only a blessed memory) by coming into the scullery every hour to safeguard her cuticle and complexion. And every type of loafer, from American negro-soldiers with cigars and gold wristwatches, to hard-working farm-lads and married lorry-drivers who ought to have known better, had surged round his garden like storm-driven birds to a lighthouse. He had breathed a sigh of relief when she had gone, without scandal, to a market-gardener near Anderham.

Rapidly Col. Bunbury eyed the serried equipment on the table, the breakfast-things, the sandwich-things, his thermos, beer-opener, beer, apple and so on. He had plenty of time, for the meet was at 9.30 and he had risen at 5 a.m. But he thought wistfully of his subaltern's days, when he had been shaved in bed before daylight by his bearer, and of later spacious days with a Frontier Force unit in Burma. Then he had had eleven men-servants or orderlies about the place, he had changed his spotless clothes five times a day as a matter of course, and never worn the same shirt twice. It had been normal then to be helped into and out of everything from his polo-boots to his dress-ties. Great days, with two perfectly-groomed ponies waiting outside the house at the first glimmer of dawn, and battalion *shikaris* scouring the country for miles around to find him sport, once his short day's work was done.

And now it was his

> *To come in and 'ands up and be still*
> *And honestly work for my bread.*
> *My livin' in that state of life*
> *To which it shall please God to call*
>
> > *Me!*

And what that state of life would be in a few years time he could not bear to think. Marvellous luck, broke as he was, getting that vacant "gun" for a fiver, though Angela had been shockingly inquisitive!

He realized with a leap of the heart that in two and a half hours' time he should be waiting for a driven partridge. His mind veered suddenly to the coveys at Stoke Loyalty feeding in the dew-drenched stubble, not knowing it was a shooting day, their day of doom. Well, at any rate, they were dumb creatures without prescience.

Prescience? But could one say that dumb animals lacked prescience, when for the last hour a black shadow had dogged him never more than a yard away from his left knee, old Daniel, who had known ever since yesterday what was on? Though the Colonel still wore "fatigue dress", the corduroy trousers and the windproof smock in which he gardened and fed the hens, though he had not touched his gun for two days since its last loving overhaul, Daniel knew. He had shadowed his master since he rose, and even now those sad brown eyes, to whom the Colonel had been God for eleven years, were fixed on him unwaveringly, fearful that at the last moment he might be left behind. And they talked of animals lacking prescience!

One day early in the war, when he had been specially asked by his host not to bring a dog, the Colonel had tried to sneak out in his town overcoat with his gun in a paper parcel to deceive Daniel. But there had been no deceiving a dog who knew when the Colonel was going to church, whatever clothes he wore, and never attempted to come; who queued up an hour earlier than usual for his Sunday dinner because it was the best one of the week. Prescience!

He patted the domed black head to reassure those anxious brown eyes. "We're going, Daniel! but no hares, mind!" For even when half-crippled with rheumatism, hares went to Daniel's brain like champagne to a man's. Daniel had never got over the idea that, some day somewhere, a hare would slow down suddenly and, in racing parlance, "come back to him". No admonition, no black looks, not even a beating would ever drive the lesson home to him. The moment a hare got up or came through the fence, Daniel would say, silently and unmistakably, "Talli-o, Master! I know all about *them*! You just leave that one to *me*." And off he would go like an arrow. Only last season a cheap war-time belt round the Colonel's waist had snapped like packthread at the passing of a hare. In Daniel desire always outran performance, but he had never yet outlived desire.

The Colonel lit his pipe after breakfast and rose. Washing-up! Sandwiches! Thermos flask! Potatoes! Sprouts for Sunday! Two days' coal! Wood! Then get dressed and on parade. Thank goodness, Angela was away. He could smoke in the scullery and get away in good time without any last-minute "fatigues". He wondered who else, besides the vicar, was a member of the syndicate. Not, he hoped, a "flash" crowd, who might be supercilious towards him in his old clothes.

XVI. DAWN AT THE VICARAGE

And the poor beetle that we tread upon
In corporal sufferance finds a pang as great
As when a giant dies. . . .
           —SHAKESPEARE : *Measure for Measure*

The other local recipient of Miss Janet Gore's bounty, the Reverend James Halliburton, was asleep, with only his cherubic head showing, when his sexton-valet thumped at his door. In one huge hand Sam Westrup held two tin mugs, a red one and a blue, and in the other a pair of ankle-boots. He set down the blue mug on the bedside table beside *Studies in Bird Behaviour*, placed the red mug on the wash-stand, and roared: "Mornin', Vicar!"

There was no answer though Sam had been a longshore fisherman before his translation to the Church, accustomed to shout through gales with a voice suited to his calling.

Sam took from the dressing-table an instrument like a powder horn, screwed it firmly into one of the Reverend James's large pink ears, and roared again:

"Mornin', Vicar! Time you was up!"

This shot went home. The vicar blinked.

"Good morning, Sam! A fair day, I trust?"

"That that is. That's ablauen good tidily from the norard but that 'ont rain. The wind's agooen to back afore arternoon, but we'll hev a fine day."

"Excellent, Sam!" said the vicar, though his heart said *Alleluia!* He knew any weather-forecast by Sam was worth twenty by the Air Ministry.

"And, Vicar!"

"Yes?"

"Du yu put on them long woollen pants what I've put out. I've a put mine on, tu. That'll be perishing cold up on them gallops!"

"Sam!"

"Ah..."

"I deprecate the use of the word 'perishing'. It is used by Kipling in his coarser moments as a substitute for the unprintable."

"Ah! but you ain't got no substitute for them pants. Du you'll be wholly nigh frorn. Now I got to feed my pigs. . . ." He stumped towards the door.

"Sam!"

"Ah!"

"Will you be good enough to put me out a lay collar?" The vicar had always deprecated the fact that the clergy were so constantly in uniform on social occasions. It sometimes embarrassed and inhibited the company.

"I hev. They 'on't know yu from the tothers. Now don't you forget them pants. . . ."

"Sam?"

"Ah!"

"Was there any other detail of which you had to remind me?"

"Ah. Them chrysantums in the chancel Lady Mary is aduen'. I seen her chap last night. They aren't up to a sight but they'll du. Old Mrs. Crole's good tidily now, so they said in the *Falcon*. The doctor ain't acomen' today, so you needn't nowther. And doon't you bother about your sarmon till this evening! All our folks want is a good plain sarvice and cut out all the polyphanalia." By "polyphanalia" Sam meant some of the ritual which went on in neighbouring villages, of which he deeply disapproved. It kept back the village dinners on the most vital day of the week and when the sermon was unduly long, his hens always got into the garden.

"Very good, Sam!"

"We ain't aburyin' Tom Drury afore Tuesday, 'cos his son can't fare to git down from Lincolnsheer, so I needn't start adiggen today. Now don't you git them mugs mixed up. . . ."

Sam clattered downstairs. His last remark needs explanation. The vicar liked to drink tea while shaving and he liked his tea to keep hot, so favoured a tin mug in autumn and winter. But there had been many a day on which he had been surprised by his henchman lathering himself with a mixture of soap and tea, and contentedly drinking the shaving-water, while watching some bird in the lilacs on the lawn.

"Poor owd gentleman, he du get things whooly mixed up," as Mrs. Westrup, his cook, often remarked.

This morning all was well. The vicar had for years been cultivating his right eye as his "master eye" for shooting. His left, as his gunmaker had found years ago, was the stronger of the two but he abominated the use of a "cross-eyed stock". And Sir Ralph Payne-Gallwey had insisted that the master eye was simply a matter of practice, for when you threw a stone or pointed a finger at anything you did not shut one eye to do so. The vicar practised incessantly, and had nearly had a scene in Jermyn Street in June for winking at a pretty lady. (Her escort, who came from North Norfolk, had been quite unjustifiably abusive of the cloth.) But the Reverend James had explained the facts so earnestly, and with such a boyish blush, that he had been allowed to take refuge in his gunmaker's without a scandal. He was still uncertain which eye was master eye. But as he was equally uncertain what he did in those ecstatic seconds when he put his gun up to his shoulder and fired, it did not greatly matter.

Now, as he shaved and winked at himself in the glass to strengthen his right eye, he ruminated. A glorious morning, and he hoped to observe some migration during the day, rooks or lapwings or finches, and to bring back a brace of birds and a hare at the end of it.

§ 2

There was, he reflected, a busy week before him. Three services on Sunday and on Monday the Committee-meeting of the Helpers of the Church. His flock, particularly the "good churchwomen", adored committees and savoured every moment of them. They could talk for hours a month about a fund which had never exceeded £15 a year, collected in shillings and half-crowns. And Heaven alone knew what prolonged irrelevancies would crop up under what the secretary called "Mattahs arising".

Why, wondered the Reverend James, shaving his thin weather-beaten pink cheeks, did a Christian community squabble and argue so interminably over the little things when the big ones seemed to be ignored? Those dusky babies, for instance, with curly hair in the local perambulators. . . . Their colour was never attributed to the labour unit from Kentucky which had been stationed so long in the Manor House, but to some defect in war-time rations. And there were the war-time unfaithfulnesses which could no longer be concealed, the tendency for the young to abstain altogether from early services, and to regard marriage as an after-thought, the fact that no farmer ever came to Church even at the harvest thanksgiving.

And yet . . . in a time of real crisis, such as June 1940, no community could have risen more abundantly to the occasion! How could he now, at the war's end, tell them what he thought of them, and still "live in love and charity with his neighbours"? He was too sensitive to keep popping in and out of their houses, which seemed to him such an intolerable invasion of privacy, with all that bother of installing communications through his ear-trumpet. And nowadays they all seemed so busy, so harassed, and so short of food.

Well, he had done the parish some good in twenty years. Their hearts were all right, though their bodies ran away with them frequently. He had fought hard for them, in the matter of roofs and coppers and sanitation. He had stopped some gossip firmly, he had stopped the propagation of committees, he had taught five generations of school-children to respect young birds and helpless things, he had preached honesty and kindness and straight dealing, he had christened and married and buried them and, above all, there was no active cruelty to child or beast.

Cruelty? Only a lot of thoughtlessness, as in all rustic communities. And suddenly he thought: "Am I a hypocrite to be shooting partridges today, for the first time in six years?" Was it un-Christian to shoot? It was certainly not un-Biblical to take life. He shuddered at what a religious ceremony must have been once, in Sinai or Greece or Rome! Those hecatombs of slaughtered animals for "peace-offerings", the stoning of oxen, the mass captures of tired migrating quail? . . . "*At even ye shall eat flesh . . . and ye shall know that I am the Lord your God*". . . .

Queer that religion and slaughter went together all over the world! Those Kachin *manaos*, whose details of butchery had so horrified his son, the Mussulman *Id*, the Gurkha rejoicings at *Dasehra*, the mass-immolation of turkeys and animals which inevitably preceded Christmas, all ceremonies based on blood. Ghastly thought if the Buddhists were nearer the light than the Christians! And what a horde of slain creatures had bolstered up the law of Moses: "*Two lambs of the first year without spot day by day for a continual burnt-offering . . . and one goat for a sin-offering . . .*" down to the "*seats of them that sold doves*" in the Temple at Jerusalem. Blood, rivers of blood!

At least a driven partridge did have only a minute or so of acute fear or pain unless it was most unlucky; and they could have no remembrance of those moments, or they would not allow themselves to be driven every year over the self-same fences.

Those fences! The vicar's mind flitted to those he hoped to be behind today—the hedge which screened the gallops, the long belt, the railway cutting where on his walk he had seen Tom Beacon erecting hurdles, and the hawthorns in the farm-lane. He *hoped* he would be on the left by the tall beeches in that drive. He had watched a drive there once in the war. So many birds had tried to break out curling high and back over the farm-buildings. One bird shot like that would remain in one's memory, high in the blue air, for months and one did not have to bother about one's neighbours.

One's neighbours! He was paid to bother about them and Heaven knew they wasted little enough thought on him or the Church he represented. . . .

§ 3

Sam Westrup thumped at the door. The vicar, absorbed in his musings, raised his trumpet expectantly.

"Yar breakfast's riddy, Vicar," Sam bellowed, "and you ain't forgot them long pants what I said?"

He thrust his crimson face round the door. The vicar started and paused in the winding of his second puttee. The other puttee was on.

"No, Sam," he said, after some reflection, "I feel sure I put them on. Ah, yes! I did."

"Well, love my duzzy heart alive, Vicar, when I said to put them pants on, I didn't mean you not to wear no breeches! Now you'll ha' to taake them boots off agin, and start adressin'. If you ain't a masterpiece!"

"Dear me! Sam, I knew I'd forgotten something. Too many mundane details, I fear. I must have been thinking."

"Thinking? There's some as wouldn't call it that! Now, come you on, Vicar, du I 'ont get things tidied up afore we goo." Sam clattered downstairs.

"The owd masterpiece," he said to Mrs. Westrup, scratching his head in the kitchen. "Put them long pants on, I ses, du yu'll be wholly nigh frorn, and blast me if he don't go and forget his knickerbockers and starts to put his puttees on and all! And there's some as'd call him a duzzy fule!"

"Poor owd gentleman, he du fare to be half in the tother world, I reckon," said Mrs. Westrup.

She had an infinite compassion for the vicar ever since he had lured Sam from his fishing-nets and the East Coast to a part of Harkshire where there was no more sea. Since then she had done her utmost to entice Sam into family prayers which the vicar liked to hold every morning before breakfast. But Sam had resisted firmly. "My pigs . . . my hens . . . that duzzy heifer. . . ." Something on the vicar's little glebe always required Sam's immediate attention at the hour of morning prayer, and if he did come in he exhaled rich odours of the cow-house and the pig-pail. So now on most mornings she and the vicar formed a quorum and knelt stern to stern, like a covey jugging, she facing the window and the vicar towards the wall. He did this both as a penance and a precaution, for facing the other way his eye was too prone to stray towards the avian traffic at the drinking-pan on the lawn.

But the Rev. James looked very smart when he finally re-dressed and came down in his old suit of Harris tweed, and the "lay" collar for which he had hoped, with the silvery curls clustering round his large ears. He put his nose out of the garden-door to listen for the note of any stray migrant in the chestnut-trees. Nothing but the song of a robin, that vintage-song of the closing year. Something he had forgotten? Not his book on the Harkshire birds, now nearing completion! Ah! For once he remembered what it was. He had, he recalled, promised a friend some criticisms on his paper, *The Influence of Alcoholism on Empire-Building with special reference to the Eighteenth Century*. Clumsy title, queer subject, especially for an ex-bishop of Assam! But he had done scant justice to William Hickey. And it was absorbed in William Hickey's diaries that Mrs. Westrup found him, oblivious of family prayers, of his breakfast, and of the fact that he was going shooting, pursuing down some queer alleyway of history the promptings of his well-stored mind.

But that mind was still running on mundane matters when he knelt at last in the dining room. Throughout his clerical life the Rev. James had confided very frankly in the Almighty about his perplexities and had said almost anything that occurred to him when doing so. And now Mrs. Westrup, kneeling over her leather chair, heard him conclude a prayer: "*Eager to be happy if happiness be our portion and if the day be marked for sorrow* . . . and that reminds me, O Lord, if it be Thy will that I am near the beeches in the Valley Farm drive, may I please hold straight? And of Thy mercy grant that I do not fire a dangerous shot today . . . or cross the path of one, either. Amen."

XVII. OPENING MEET

GENTLEMAN—*Educated Eton and Cambridge, first-class all round shot, is prepared to consider* INVITATIONS *to shoot. Highest references and terms moderate.*

—*From* an Advertisement

Mr. Mannering stopped his car by the horse-shed at the Valley Farm and stood waiting for his "guns" to arrive. This was always the delicate moment in a syndicate shoot, when he had to introduce the members on the first day, and watch them sniffing rigidly around each other, like strange dogs and school-boys. Up to the war it had not been so bad, for he had had almost the same guns for several years, but this year few of his guns seemed to be acquainted.

At any rate they had all paid up before the season opened! He remembered what he had undergone with old Lord Drambuie, who had had two good days off him in October without paying a bean; and later had insisted the partridges had not done as well as he had been led to expect! And there was always one gun who felt that, having paid his money, he could be rude for the whole season about the management of the day's sport.

The first day was always a trial, finding out all about the guns, far worse than the vagaries of the game. One was always late, either constitutionally or because he could not read a map or start a car. He would arrive hot and bothered "marching to the sound of the guns", and disarrange all the numbering. The coveys in that drive always seemed to flow over the empty place where he should have been.

One gun, too, always hated shooting hares, which swarmed on the great open chalk-fields round Stoke Loyalty, however many were killed each year. Another abhorred wet roots and walking, and when the wind was wrong or a mass of head-strong birds insisted on breaking out, a gun with the drivers was essential. Another shot well in the morning but was un-predictable after lunch: like that frightful bookmaker who had graced the syndicate in 1944, and insisted on everyone having a "snifter" from his flask before they commenced. It had put everyone's eye out and old Mr. Aspirin, in a haze of un-accustomed alcohol, had shot a beater. Poor Charles Allingham in 1936 could sometimes shoot like a dream if he killed the very first bird of the day, but if not, he missed steadily all day long and rent his neighbours with melancholy post-mortems.

And there had been Mr. Challaby, who could not bear dogs out shooting, as they ran in and purloined for others the birds that he alone had brought down. He had, unhappily, come to the syndicate with Major Ogle, but he had not lasted so long. To the Major a day's sport without his faithful "canine com-panion", as he called a dog, was a day without any savour at all. He openly preferred a "quiet potter" with an odd bird to pick up here and there, to any of your "set" days when your barrels got too hot to hold. He always had two dogs out, one a young one "just coming on", to whose 'prentice foibles he would ex-tend an infinite compassion. (This was apt, in the case of a strong runner, to disarrange the time-programme terribly.) The other had been definitely "going off" for the last three seasons, a dog with bloodshot eyes, a mouth like an otter-trap and noticeable halitosis. Both the Ogle dogs had got very badly on Mr. Chal-laby's nerves all that season.

Mr. Mannering realized, suddenly, that the ideal syndicate would be composed of himself, five safe fellows who could not shoot at all, without any dogs, and one good shot with a competent dog, whose manners were not too offensive. This would, at any rate, ensure that five-sevenths of his partridges lived to fly another day. Tom Beacon had often pointed out to him that eight days' shooting in an average season was too much for the place to stand.

"I aren't got the birds," he would say, "that ain't a mite of use hammering them no more. Do we get a bad February, we're bound to lose some more and then where's my stock?" And he would employ all sorts of devices to ensure that they went back or out at the flanks.

§ 2

Tom and Fred Crane, the second keeper, had departed an hour before to "ketch up" the two big barley stubbles on the far side of the Stoke road and to bring their ninety acres in towards the railway cutting. It was a long drive but it saved his guns a walk and the beaters always halted on the road until they were in position.

For Tom Beacon, as for Mr. Mannering, there had been acute apprehension lest the main body of his beaters should not turn up. The farm could nowadays only supply six, three of them ancients who pottered about as flankers. Mr. Mannering had relied all the war on soldiers or sailors from nearby camps, and yearly it had proved impossible, even by giving the adjutants the most exact map-references, to get their men to the right place in time. They were quite likely to turn up, however well "briefed", not at the Valley Farm but at the Valley Farm at Little Welshney, miles away. Today Mr. Mannering, warned by tribulation, had sent Fred Crane to sit firmly at the camp-gates, like a deserted wife, from dawn onwards to waylay the beaters' lorry when it emerged.

Mr. Mannering sighed. Who would run a shoot and entertain strangers who regarded the country solely as a place to shoot in? Wearing and dangerous and after the season you never got a thank-you.

Ah! the guns at last! Two cars came jolting down the lane and from the first emerged backwards Brigadier Bowman, sandy and lean and with his tawny Guards moustache in full bloom. From the other came Major Ogle, in a deerstalker and a very old tweed suit with capacious pockets, followed by a cascade of black Labradors, inextricably confused with their leads, each other and Major Ogle's legs. Major Ogle was a pillar of the shooting world. He had invested several thousands in various journals devoted to the sport, so that he could read about shooting all the year round. Though only a third-class shot, he was a God-send to Mr. Mannering as, however loudly the horn blew, he never had a clue whether or not birds were coming, so that except at the start of the season, they were usually over him before he knew it. By the time he had risen from his shooting-seat, admonished his dogs to sit still, put up his safety catch and turned round to fire, they were normally out of shot.

Heavens! he had brought three dogs out, the old one "going off", the young one "coming on" and a third, a bitch which had been coming on last year and which he would try to sell as "finished" during the season. More complications, for Mr. Mannering would be appealed to daily as referee with "Remember-Mannering-that-time-she-had-a-running-cock-pheasant-of-yours-in-the-sewage-farm-last-year . . .? Wonderful find!"

But Major Ogle got much satisfaction out of his day's sport, beamed friendlily at all and sundry, and the same birds would last him all the season. This, as everyone who has run a syndicate knows, is desirable in an average year, and worth much fine gold in a bad one.

§ 3

Brigadier Bowman had recently settled in the neighbourhood and was not sure whether he could afford to "take a gun" in a shoot or not, but had decided to afford it for one season, hoping he would meet enough people to invite him out *gratis* for the following one. He had been careful not to bring out *his* dog, for a dog's gaucherie could ruin his master's prospects in such society as quickly as a lunatic sister at a cocktail party. He was also an exceedingly careful shot, as became a former instructor of the School of Musketry, and remained unloaded till the latest possible moment. In a partridge-drive run on proper Army lines, he felt there would have been a system of flags and field-telephones to insure that no one fired a hurried or a dangerous shot. In consequence, he shot little and rarely took a bird in front of him for fear of swinging too near the line.

Giles Bowman, despite his moustache, had been a Major in 1939 in a line regiment. In the swiftly-blossoming armies after Dunkirk, he had achieved by 1941, without effort, an independent brigade, charged with the defence of the Isle of Wight from invasion. From his stronghold in a small country-mansion Giles Bowman had based his brigade training on the twin pillars of "turn-out" and mobility. He had ensured the first by the simple method of accumulating five suits of battledress per man. As for the second, he had harried his brigade round the island month by month, attaining such speed on these exercises that, at times, owing to the island's geographical conformation, the leading wave of his attack had found itself involved with the rear of his "admin area" which had not yet moved. Unfortunately his units, by far the fastest and best turned-out in England, had been swallowed up as reinforcements for D-Day, and he had been faced with the dilemma of a Sub-Area or a bowler-hat.

"Red-tabs-in-the-morning!" said Angus Somborne, as the Bentley bumped round the corner a moment later, "if it isn't my very own Brigadier, the one I'm trying so hard not to be a son-in-law to! Now mind! Gerald old boy, remember the Badminton Library: 'kind and generous to servants but never familiar', and for the love of Mike don't call me Angus! If my name crops up at lunch, you got me through an advertisement and I'm supposed to drink!"

Angus had taken his position as keeper-valet very seriously. He wore a ready-made broad-cloth suit as stiff as a suit of armour and much too small for him, like his four-and-sixpenny tweed cap. He had shaved his moustache and begun to grow small side-whiskers. Failing to get a celluloid collar, as they were no longer made, he had had to compromise on a white "barmaid". He touched his cap to the party with a salute which was a reminiscent blend of the Royal Navy, the Polish Army and the Corps of Electrical Engineers.

The little drama of Gerald's arrival was spoilt by the arrival of Col. Bunbury and the vicar, both on old bicycles, which they bestowed in the cart-shed, the Colonel locking his hind wheel carefully with a chain. He had let Daniel run behind him for two miles, hoping this preliminary canter would "take the edge off him" and make him realize his limitations if they met a hare. Punctual to a fault, he had suffered agonies at the vicarage, first while the vicar hunted for his gun and cartridge-bag (both safely in the custody of Sam Westrup who had walked on by the fieldpath), and then because the vicar, stone-deaf to all human utterance, had detected from a tree in his garden a note which he felt sure must be that of *Phylloscopus inornatus*. By the time he had made certain it was not, they had had to pedal hurriedly to the meeting-place.

Gerald shook hands all round, while Angus put his gun together and addressed his Springer bitch in a Kirkcudbrightshire accent, and very seriously, like a headmistress beginning a new term. The eye of the Brigadier, from behind his monocle, kept sliding round towards Angus, as if unable to believe its evidence.

Ah! Mr. Lorrimer at last! Thank goodness! Mr. Mannering drew a leather case from his pocket from which peeped numbered ivory discs which he presented to each gun in turn. "We number from the left," he said, "and move up two after each drive. We shall be one gun short in the morning. Sir William Boulogne is arriving later."

As the other guns drew their discs and murmured their numbers one to the other, a shining Rolls-Royce purred down the muddy lane into their midst.

"How now?" whispered Angus, squinting down Gerald's gun-barrels. "Who have we here? Our Labour Member? The Lord Lieutenant?"

The Brigadier, glowering, looked at his watch. He always imagined that the first drive, when managed by civilians, would start before the guns were in position. Col. Bunbury drew himself erect as if for a salute. Even the vicar, his eye on a kestrel hovering beyond the lane, looked interested.

The Rolls-Royce stopped and from it a uniformed chauffeur descended, and stepped delicately round a puddle to the door. There emerged none other than Mr. Percy Lorrimer, the famous writer of detective-stories. He was a plump man of about forty-five, wearing an almost black and white check coat and a pair of gray flannel trousers. A pioneer in many things, he carried a very new golfing-bag from the top of which peeped the muzzle of an under-and-over gun. The chauffeur bent to the car's boot and removed from it a green canvas cartridge-bag and a small folding-stool, for Mr. Lorrimer had found, on his only other day's shooting, that the comfort afforded by a shooting-stick was contemptible for a man of his build. The short hairs rose on the Brigadier's neck and his moustache raised its wings in unison, so that he seemed a little out of drawing, though he said no word.

Mr. Lorrimer shook hands in the manner of those whose reputation has preceded them, saying "J'doo? J'doo?" as he did so. He wore no hat, and from his broad brow, the blonde hair swept back from its parting and lay in swathes over his ears. It looked as if it had never been cut but regularly rolled. His teeth gleamed in his olive cheeks: he exuded a faint but unmistakable fragrance of *eau-de-cologne*. A gold wrist-watch glittered on one wrist and on the other a gold identity-disc, a relic of wartime.

Mr. Lorrimer had served for several months in the Home
Guard until the fatal night when a new commanding officer
had, after one glance, said brutally, "Fall out, you! *You* can go
straight home and get your bloody hair cut before you come on
parade again."

Most of Mr. Lorrimer's heroes slew three cads a week in the
ordinary way of business, and were wont to witness or to evade
violent and almost inexplicable deaths a dozen times a month.
But on this occasion Mr. Lorrimer's eye, "the king of lethal
weapons", so often described in his books, had unaccountably
misfired. It had failed even to raise a mark on the Home Guard
Colonel, one of the crude kind whose spiritual home was clearly
in a Gurkha regiment or Waziristan. Mr. Lorrimer had fallen
out and left the Home Guard for ever, to command his own
battery of dictaphones and their ancillary troops, his three
adoring secretaries. He had returned thankfully to his profitable
world of murder and international intrigue, in which anyone
who was offensive to Mr. Lorrimer or his heroes was found
dead a week later with a bullet-hole behind the ear. He had
dealt faithfully with that Home Guard Colonel in his most
recent novel, to the delight of millions.

Led by Mr. Mannering and the chauffeur carrying the golf-ing-bag and the campstool, the party moved off towards the railway line. Mr. Mannering reflected that, though five minutes late in starting, this was good for the first morning. Tom Beacon would stop his beaters on the road till the guns were in their places, and the walk would loosen some of the party up.

The vicar, eyeing Mr. Lorrimer's startling checks, murmured to the colonel, "Not very *sub fusc*, is he? A good thing Mannering's fences are thick." The Brigadier's hackles were still visible, and he was being short with Major Ogle who, having failed entirely to catch his name or rank, had begun badly by addressing him as "Mr. . . . er . . ."

A walk of fifteen minutes over the flat down and across a stubble brought them to the first stand, a line of hurdles stud-ding the wire fence of a chalk railway-cutting.

There were the usual moments of indecision, while someone whispered, "Let me see, now, what number was I?" and the others asked again anxiously whether they counted from the right or the left. Then Mr. Mannering fired a shot in the air. The drive had technically begun.

XVIII. TWILIGHT OF A GENERAL

*"But all hath suffered change
For surely now our household hearths are cold."*

—TENNYSON

General Sir Bonamy Pickering, K.C.B., K.C.I.E., C.V.O., D.S.O. (*alias* among his contemporaries "Popeye" Pickering), stood alongside a gate in a fence leaning on a long stick. It is improbable that any of the thousands of officers and men who had, in their time, wilted or trembled or stood woodenly at attention beneath Sir Bonamy's gaze, would have recognized him. He wore a very old hat, some might have called it a shocking hat, which its eminent maker would have disowned at sight. Its stained brim hung limp, and what was left of its nap was speckled with the ragged marks left by the trout-flies of long ago. He wore an old muffler, and a still older black coat, almost green with age, in which he had once followed the Staff College drag. Its hunt-buttons had been removed, and its roomy skirts converted to hold "poachers' pockets", and below it were shapeless trousers of corduroy and navvy boots. Only in the waistcoat lurked still the General's gold watch, which had belonged to his grandfather, on a leather guard.

Sir Bonamy Pickering was without his eyeglass, his signet ring or his upper teeth, which now reposed in a leather purse in his pocket. (He could not afford repairs to a denture nowadays.) His moustache was carefully brushed down instead of out-

wards and upwards. In a word, he was pretty well unrecognizable as an officer or a gentleman, but he was content.

Years before, a mine in Tenasserim had swallowed up Sir Bonamy's private means as completely as if he had dropped them down its shaft. He would not have minded so much for, at that moment, the flood-tide of his career had seemed to be making steadily, and he seemed very sure of a Governorship in the fullness of time. But then, a year later, things had begun to happen. There had been simultaneously a Frontier row and a new Secretary in the Political department who did not know a Wazir from a wombat, and would have been shocked at finding himself close to either. Letters had arrived on which Sir Bonamy had said his say in no uncertain terms. He had told his frothing brigadiers not to worry and had taken things up, first with the provincial government and then, when the chance rose, with the Viceroy himself, for he had been taught that "to run a frontier show you have got to have your resignation in your pocket".

All would have been well, for these things blow over, had he not stayed a month later at Simla with the C.-in-C. and been asked to go down one morning to the Secretariat to "button up one or two things with F. & P.".

He had sent his card in by the *chaprassi* to the new Secretary, and the dashed heaven-born son of sin had actually had the nerve to keep him waiting in the corridor while he finished one of his classically-phrased minutes.

Perhaps the curry at breakfast may have had something to do with it, but Sir Bonamy objected strongly to standing about for God knew how long with a lot of Beluch *chaprassis* playing knucklebones all round him; with no *punkah* and only a confounded wooden seat used by the *chaprassis*, and nothing in the world to read except a board stating the whereabouts of "*Mr. L. M. G. Smith, O.B.E., M.A., I.C.S.*" behind a closed door.

Sir Bonamy had waited those ten minutes, while all the soldier's unexpressed scorn and hatred of the civilian had gradually mounted till he felt like an Esse cooker with all the heat hidden in its bosom. And the perspiration came through his silk shirt into his tussore waistcoat and coat, and the *chaprassis* went on playing knucklebones, until suddenly they found a rather sweaty General hunkering down beside them and asking in ungrammatical Pushtu if he could take a hand. Being frontiersmen and ex-soldiers they had good manners, and had not turned a hair, while they explained to him their rather involved rules.

So when at last the Secretary's bell had rung to announce that he was ready, "*Sabr*," said Sir Bonamy, who was getting quite keen on knucklebones, in other words, "let him wait". Five minutes later the bell rang again. Sir Bonamy told the *chaprassis* friendlily "not to bother", and they went on telling him with animation about their villages, one of which Sir Bonamy had recently threatened to bomb as a reprisal; though of course he did not mention this.

Three times the bell rang unanswered, till at last Mr. L. M. G. Smith, O.B.E., emerged angrily into the corridor and found his distinguished visitor squatting on the floor jabbering with three *chaprassis* in what Mr. Smith called "the vernacular".

That little scene had flushed Mr. Smith's heavenborn pallor to his spectacles while he began: "My *dear* Sir Bonamy! I *am* so sorry," though he *had* meant to keep the old boy waiting. Then Sir Bonamy had slowly unbent his ageing joints and said, with a gleam in his monocle: "Not at all, Mr. . . . er . . . Smith! Awful good chaps these! We were having a chat about their homes. Delightful fellers and such charming manners!"

Well, that remark hadn't gone down too well, and later some young fool of an A.D.C. had got hold of the yarn and spread it around the Club, so that Mr. Smith had even had his leg genially tweaked at Viceregal Lodge and had not kept anyone waiting for nearly a year.

But next time Sir Bonamy "went off the deep end", the Secretariat were almost waiting for him.

"Bit too eccentric altogether! After all, there's prestige to be considered and he's the last man to bother about that! About time, I suggest, we . . .?"

Then Sir Bonamy had found his next resignation accepted with regret, and was now in the limbo which awaits all public servants of India, however distinguished, between their official cradle and their grave. He had only his pension now and two unmarried daughters to support on it. So he had sold his guns, his rifles, his car, his saddlery, his horses, and his rods, and a few of his father's precious pictures and pieces of furniture. Then he had gone to a small white house in Stoke Loyalty surrounded by a high brick wall. One daughter had pledged herself to cookery on his behalf and the other to good works in the village; and the General himself was now settled in a monastic peace, devoting the evening of his days to gardening, and literary effort.

§ 2

His first book, *Soldiering or Smartness?* had been finished in 1939, but had had to be completely revised on account of the Long Range Desert Group's aversion to baths, hair-cuts and turn-out, and certain aspects of later Commando training. The General had wound up with a triumphant chapter on the "Chindit syndrome", to emphasize his life-long contention that "soldiering and smartness were not synonymous".

Well, dash it, were they? As a company officer in South Africa, "Popeye" had protested against the folly of condemning men clad in shorts to lie on the veldt in broiling sun with the skin peeling off the backs of their knees, so that after a couple of days they could hardly walk. As a Brigadier on the Aisne he had blackened his buttons and transformed the shapely contours of his hat into the original "Gor-blimey", to the horror of his brigade-major. As a senior Commander his training for jungle warfare had been revolutionary. "Damned nonsense!" he would rumble. "Who would survive in this stuff, the

Grenadiers or the Gurkhas? Smartness my foot!" And as a private in the Home Guard he had hastened his superannuation by sticking ears of corn and rushes in his steel-helmet to hide its outlines.

His son, a true Pickering, had similarly shattered the monotony of uniform in "Desforce" by going into action in battle-dress trousers, a yellow check hunting waistcoat under a leather jerkin, a blue spotted stock and a cherry-coloured side-cap. The revolt had spread by way of corduroys, fishermen's jerseys and furlined leather coats, to all the commissioned ranks from the Army Commander downwards. One illustration in *Soldiering or Smartness?* depicted a Divisional General of the Fourteenth Army in camp, whose only integument above the waist was an identity disc and some daringly erotic tattoo-marks on his torso.

General Pickering's second book, *Blunders of this War*, was still only in his mental womb, though he had amassed a body of notes for what would be a minor classic some day. He had caused a sensation by circularizing in 1941 every senior Commander, past or present, by means of a demi-official letter and a questionnaire which began:

"1. *What in your opinion were the two stupidest things (a) you (b) your* $\begin{Bmatrix} Italian \\ German \end{Bmatrix}$ *opposite number did during your campaign?"*

It had won him some rather peevish replies. There seemed to be an astonishing number of senior officers whose genius had "prematured" in various theatres of war, with unhappy effects on their headgear.

§ 3

But literary effort was not all the General's life. For four days a week, from September onwards to January, he now obtained employment as a beater on certain of the great shoots near Furzechester, since able-bodied farm labourers could no longer be spared from farming. For Sir Bonamy it meant a day's exercise, an income of twelve-and-sixpence a day *plus* beer on which no tax was payable under any schedule, and a chance to keep in touch with the sport he loved. Once a month he had a drink at the County Club, where he astounded his cronies with his inside knowledge of what went on at certain of the more famous places in the neighbourhood.

"Oh, he's a wretched shot! I've watched him," he would say, or "Yes, they got 102 brace the first day and about $5\frac{1}{2}$ in the pick up. Blew a gale the second day, and we knocked off early. . . . Very nice lot of birds! But their new keeper's a poor fish!" and, now and again, "Most dangerous fellow! Nearly bagged a beater last week. Inexcusable shot!"

Sir Bonamy had come to this side-line quite by accident. There had been a chance meeting in 1940, one evening, with a huge figure he recognized as Tom Beacon, one of the several hundred regimental serjeant-majors with whom he had had dealings in the course of his service. Tom had been overjoyed by the encounter, which they had celebrated in the *George and Horn*, while they discussed with rapidly-mellowing freedom a number of officers now dead, retired or in high command.

"Serjeant-Major," said the General, when they had finished the beer and were out in the lane once more, "I can't afford to shoot now but let me come out and beat for you next time you drive partridges. I'd be worth three of your boys!"

"Love my heart, General, I'd be right glad to have you. I don't hardly know where to turn for beaters. I can't get nobody, only Scatty Marsh, and that one we call 'Diddle-o' Dodman, (he properly craäze me, he's that slow) and three or four damn buoys and poor old George Savage, what can't hardly walk with the Arthur-itis. We can get all the army we want, but that's a rum army and no mistake. If you was to put 'em all out in a line here at twenty paces interval, by the time they'd git to the fudder fence, they'd be in column of lumps with their hands in their pockets. And they don't know a pheasant from a crow. *And* talk! I don't know what they teach 'em nowadays!"

"Very well, Beacon, I'll come out whenever you want me.

And you can pass the word to other headkeepers round here if they're short of men. Only remember! to you I'm plain Fred Smith. I don't want Mr. Mannering to know. And I don't want Scatty Marsh and Dodman and Co. objecting to me as non-union labour."

"Very good, General, I didn't serve four years as an RSM without larning to keep me mouth shut."

Tom Beacon had been very proud of having a real live Loo-tenant-General, as he said, under his command and on his pay-roll. But he had kept his secret, and sometimes taken the General's advice, when he murmured:

"Tom, you lost a hundred birds then by not doing it across the wind," or "Tom, why not run that covert out into the mangolds and bring 'em back with the guns placed there . . .?" and so on.

Once Sir Bonamy had come down to breakfast on Saturdays with an A.D.C., two *chaprassis* and a butler, all standing ready to obey his whims, and a carnation buttonhole waiting on a plate alongside a list of his engagements for the day and a chart of his dinner-party that evening. Now he sneaked out in his scarecrow clothes by the garden-gate, and down the path through the woods to a tryst miles away, and no one guessed who he was or whither he was bound.

And now that late September morning he had breakfasted and tramped three miles, thinking out the chapter on "Mistakes in the Desert". He was leaning on his stick on the flank of the first drive, ready to flag in any birds that tried to break out along the line of the cutting. He watched two big lots skim forward off the barley-stubble into the kale and thought how sick with excitement he would have been in the old days to see them from the "receiving end"! Crouching behind his hurdle with his finger sliding the safety-catch up and down, and continually opening and closing the gun to make sure he "was loaded"! And he thought, incongruously, of old days when he had stayed with Lord Westleton, and as they munched their way solemnly through their porridge and kippers and kidneys and bacon and coffee, there were forty beaters out bringing in a mile of stubbles beyond the park, and all they had had to do after breakfast was to walk out and sit on a shooting-stick and blaze away till all was blue!

And now his feet were wet and his gouty corn was hurting him. He had no chiropodist now: too expensive! But if a small boy got a corn nowadays they called it a *verruca* and his mother swept him off to have deep X-ray. Damned nonsense!

Incredible set-up a modern army too, with its T-forces and its Special Service Troops, its partisans, its "public relations", and its vast unwieldy tail, with no job so unmilitary that you couldn't find a soldier to do it, and your fighting troops wearing almost anything but uniform in action! And the "Prime" himself, the staunch old war-horse in his siren suit, heading the hunt over the Rhine into Germany! And to think he and the "Prime" had bumped each other as subalterns *con amore* on the polo-ground!

Poor old chap, though, to do a job like that for the nation, and then be thrown out on his ear! Ingratitude, by gum! and he must know it! Well, if things had gone differently in 1940 they would both have been in a concentration camp by now, or hanged. And perhaps some of his pals would find themselves in a de-Torification camp soon, having their outlook on Socialism purged! But not himself, not in that old hat and those scarecrow clothes! They couldn't teach *him* much about camouflage.

Ah! here they came skimming towards him, seven, eight, nine partridges and behind them a cock pheasant forging up to overtake them. That kale was too wet, they wouldn't have it! He raised his flag, watched them swerve towards the cutting, make as if to settle, then suddenly rise a little, put on speed and string out over the railway line. And as the first shots rang out a little tremor shook him.

XIX. THE DRIVE

"For to shoot with strangers I count the same as war."
—RUDYARD KIPLING

From Number Four hurdle facing into the wind, Gerald could see very little except a fringe of kale sloping away out of sight beyond the wire fence on the opposite side of the deep railway cutting below him. Angus was kneeling behind him, still practising his Kirkcudbrightshire dialect on the Springer bitch who, brought up in Harkshire, was quivering and looking at him with earnest suspicion. A thorn bush ten yards to Gerald's left, on his own side of the cutting, hid the view away to his left front and he realized that from this angle low birds could easily take him unawares. He glanced behind him, over Angus's loud tweed-cap, at the meadow running down to the larches behind them and the sweep of rising stubble and clover beyond the trees. Angus glanced too.

"Now why the deuce," said Angus in his natural voice, "don't they put us fifty yards back down this slope? We'd get some proper screamers over the valley that way."

"I expect," said Gerald, "Mannering knows what he's doing. He's had this place for years. Perhaps he wants to break it to us gently on the first day. A really fast high bird at the start would defeat *me*!"

"Don't you believe it!" said Angus, "it'd be up in the air: you can see it and swing without bothering about your neighbours.

187

You'll get some funny low ones here, I'm thinking. *Sit*, lassie, and dinna mak' eyes at me."

Gerald glanced along the line. On his left Major Ogle had pegged his dogs out in a row behind him and was giving them a lecture on behaviour in the shooting field, his hand up as if

pronouncing a blessing. He always appealed to a dog's better nature and never used a whip to enforce his commands, but the pegs helped. The vicar, his gun leaning against the hurdle, was wiping his fieldglasses and looking across the field behind him. Beyond the vicar, Mr. Lorrimer sat on his campstool, sheltered from the wind by the hurdle, puffing a cigar. Behind him, bolt upright, was the chauffeur examining with great interest Mr. Lorrimer's new gun, its muzzles pointing firmly towards Mr. Lorrimer's broad back.

On Gerald's right, the Brigadier and Mr. Mannering were in earnest converse, walking three yards up and three yards down, as if on sentry-go. The Brigadier's gun was propped on his cartridge-bag, open and carefully facing towards what he called "the target". Then came an empty hurdle, which should have hidden Sir William Boulogne.

Col. Gore-Bunbury, on the right, was alone preserving the traditions of the Badminton Library, "one of the right sort, ever on the watch for the stir of but a rabbit". His left hand on the fore-end, his right on the trigger-guard, his gun was "ready for instant use". His eyes roved incessantly in a half-circle from the thorn-bush twenty-five yards to his left to the alders in the dip thirty yards to his right. Within those limits any bird that crossed the wire on the far side would be his. Whatever others did, *he* was not going to be caught napping by any stray Frenchman running somewhere three hundred yards ahead of the drive, which would be over him before horn or whistle could proclaim its coming. At intervals he cast a sidelong glance of exasperation towards the Brigadier and Mr. Mannering, as if to say "Come on, the drive's started. On parade!"

Calm though he looked, Col. Bunbury was a quivering mass of apprehension. With a blank butt on his left, he feared that Sir William Boulogne would arrive in the middle of the drive, and upset him with belated preparations, or that its empty space would lure every covey to stream over it just out of shot of himself. He could not understand anyone paying good money for a "gun" and not being there on time. He hated crossing birds behind him which were just in shot but just far enough out to make them seem slow. Also he guessed there was a flanker somewhere out to his right, whom he could not see. If any birds did not face the cutting and skimmed sideways to the corner, one could not swing freely and that was fatal. You could blind a man at 150 yards, or so the *Fur and Feather Series* had said long ago.

A muffled coo behind him and a swallowing sound made him glance quickly down. It was Daniel. If he did drop one behind him, could he trust the old dog not to run in? He had been a paragon so far, his nose glued to the Colonel's stockings, but with dogs and women you never knew! Things went to their heads with such ghastly results, though in between no one could want greater affection or loyalty.

But . . . his mind flashed to the day when Daniel's teeth had met with a rending crunch on a bird under Lord Drambuie's nose (when he had been most anxious to comport himself well); the day that idiotic hare had come through the fence and dared him; that day when he had loosed Daniel at the drive's end, and he had shot off like an arrow from a bow, to gather a pheasant from behind the next gun but two. Dogs! And yet, like women, could one do without them?

§ 2

Far away on his left, Gerald heard a whistle. He saw Major Ogle, who had heard nothing, pick up his gun slowly, then turn with his hand uplifted to pronounce a final blessing on his three recumbent dogs. Gerald waited but could see nothing. His eyes slid to the right. Brigadier Bowman was glancing down the muzzle of his gun, to make sure the barrels were clear. Mr. Mannering, free at last of his guest's questions, was hurrying to his place.

Then suddenly far down on the left there was a covey, with the leading bird rising and accelerating smoothly, as they streamed over the cutting at Mr. Lorrimer, and behind the covey a cock pheasant, skimming and rising ever faster as he realized what was in front of him. Mr. Lorrimer got up from his campstool, seized his cigar in his left hand and reached for his gun. There was an acute moment of adjustment before he swung round and saluted the pheasant, now thirty yards behind, with both barrels.

Angus smiled. "Not as quick on the draw as some of his heroes, is he?"

"No," said Gerald, "but I suppose we *do* observe close seasons even in 1945 in a syndicate shoot? One's not *supposed* to shoot pheasants in September, is one?"

"Not we," said Angus, "but I doubt if that beggar knows there are any technical distinctions of that nature. My father, who was the second worst shot in Norfolk, always killed a few in September, preferably on the First, but they weren't fully grown and he never meant to. They got up under his feet out of standing barley and he simply *mowed* them down! He could miss any partridge which flew but pheasants had a fatal attraction for him. Always went down as 'macaws' in his game-book. Hsst!"

There was a flutter, like a dog shaking its ears, and five partridges, all coming towards Gerald at slightly different angles and very slowly, were over the wire fence on the far side of the cutting. He put up his gun at the leading bird and as he did so it dipped sharply into the cutting and he shot a foot over it. The second bird rose and swung back to his right along the cutting and he dropped it on the far bank and saw it run into the bushes. The next moment the others were gone but he could hear Mr. Mannering shoot farther down at the first bird which seemed to have skimmed out of sight along the cutting.

"Damn!" said Gerald, "and that bird's a runner."

"They come all ways early in the season," said Angus, "no point to make for. Those birds would probably have pitched in the cutting. Bred on the bank there most likely."

A horn sounded far off again and suddenly the air to Gerald's right front was full of partridges making high and straight for the Brigadier and Mr. Mannering, and picking up other birds out of the kale as they flew. Gerald saw three birds drop, heard again the whirring flutter near him and was just in time to turn round at a French partridge that had come at him screened by the bush on his left. Again he shot over it as it skimmed down the slope behind him, and, as he turned with an open gun to reload, two more whirred a foot over his head from straight in front, making him duck involuntarily.

"That big lot's gone right," said Angus, turning round, "and two more over Jimmy Bundobust in the corner. Bide a wee, bitch! If ye run in the noo, aiblins that Lorrrimer will shoot ye for a harrre!"

The horn sounded again. There was shooting on Gerald's left where both the vicar and Major Ogle, who were barely tall enough to peer over their hurdles, were being caught by birds which skimmed low over the cutting and were on them before they could fire. Gerald killed a hare as it came down the steep bank and as he did so, saw a partridge above him in the sunlight coming apparently from behind. He flung up his gun without thinking and dropped it in the cutting somewhere in front of the Brigadier.

"Well done!" said Angus. "That was a bird which old Ogle shot at, which wouldn't face the valley and turned back. You'll always shoot better when you've got no time to think. Losh! bitch, look at oor Perrcy!"

Mr. Lorrimer had risen off his campstool, discarded his cigar and raised his gun. The tall chauffeur was pointing. For thirty seconds the novelist took aim at something on the edge of the cutting, then very deliberately followed it round to his left.

Behind Gerald, Angus, the gunner, was muttering: "At battery-fire sweep one five minutes all guns. It must be a tank. He's *done* it!"

There was a bang and from somewhere near the hedge corner across the cutting an angry shout. A hare emerged beyond Mr. Lorrimer and galloped across the field.

"You won't be next to him all day, Gerald," said Angus, "but *that* won't make any difference. Wonder if he shot the chap or just scared him. That's the end of that lot. Let me have a look for that first bird of yours. It's a runner."

Gerald sat rather moodily, smoking, on his shooting-stick while Angus climbed into the steep chalk cutting and up the other side. He had had five fair chances, and only killed one bird, a partridge which had taken him completely by surprise. The first bird he had shot had probably run back into the kale and was miles away by now.

Major Ogle unleashed the middle of his three "canine companions", blessed the other two and, with stiff sweeps of his arm and clucking noises, cast it down the hill. The other dogs leaped simultaneously to do his bidding but the pegs held their ground. The blessing was repronounced. Below in the dip, Mr. Lorrimer's chauffeur and an old man, in a shocking hat and a long-skirted black coat, were exchanging personalities across the cutting. In the kale, Tom Beacon was shouting: "Now come on, all yew brushers! This way! Fred, you take six of 'em round them mustard. I seen two big gangs and a six cross out there early." Gerald could see the Springer bitch giving little jumps out of the dripping kale and standing still to listen with her hindquarters wriggling ecstatically, while Angus encouraged her in Scots.

§ 3

Angus appeared at last carrying both partridges and the hare. "It hadn't run far," he said, "but there's been the devil of a row between Percy's chauffeur and an old flanker. I found him fairly muttering. Told me it's the last time he'd come out abeatin' with *that* bastard! Reminded me of the I.C.S. claiming compensation for 'loss of career'. Come on, Gerald! Mannering's beckoning!"

But late though they were, they had to wait while Major Ogle perfected his all-round-my-hat cast for a bird with all three dogs. He had not actually seen it fall but he felt it ought to have fallen, and therefore must have fallen. With his red handkerchief on the ground he cooed and waved and exhorted, and held up everything till Mr. Mannering shouted angrily to them all to hurry on.

Angus stumped up to Mr. Lorrimer and solemnly touched his cap.

"Did ye pick yon pheasant, sirr?" he asked.

"What, my man?" said Mr. Lorrimer.

"Yon cock pheasant what ye shot at. I'll tak' ma bitch and seek him."

Mr. Lorrimer suddenly realized something he had read about pheasant-shooting being premature in September. But, as a veteran writer, he had specialized in dialectical repartee.

"That?" he said scornfully. "That wasn't a pheasant, my good man! It was an old cock partridge bringing up the rear of the covey, as they always do!"

"Och aye, sirr!" Angus withdrew routed behind the tall chauffeur and Gerald saw him blush.

XX. LUNCH AND MR. LORRIMER

"Luncheon now, gentlemen!" said Mr. Mannering. "That is if none of you have anything more to pick up."

The fourth drive was over. The beaters were clumping down the lane between its two high hawthorn fences, over which so many birds had come swinging from a field of mangolds. Angus had departed with the Springer to look for a bird which had towered in the wheat-stubble beyond the farm buildings. Gerald was standing with three other guns in a rough meadow watching Major Ogle who, fifty yards away, had his red bandanna spread on a tussock. He looked as if he was conducting a canine orchestra in the rehearsal stages.

The young dog, the one "coming on", with its nose to the ground, was flashing wildly to and fro in response to sweeps of the Major's arm and a series of mystic clucks: "G' puppy! gur-buoy, yur-seekim, hi-lorst!"

With his other hand Major Ogle was restraining the older dogs from participating, and also Fred Crane who, carrying four or five partridges in each hand, was anxious to assist.

"Let the dog hunt! Let 'im hunt, please, Crane!" boomed Major Ogle, like a traffic policeman. "Gur-puppy then! Yur-try-seekim, don't-foil-the-ground-with-those-birds, Crane! Give the dog a chance. Gur-buoy! *Sit*-Dynamo-I-told-you! Hi-lorst, old man."

It was, as Gerald said later to Angus, extremely bad form of one of Mr. Mannering's rabbits to seize that moment to join in the day's sport. He had been lying out pleasantly enough in the September sunshine, until the guns invaded his meadow. Since then he had been crouching flat in his tussock, only a few yards from where Major Ogle had been standing, surrounded by his dogs. It was still more tactless of him, when his nerve broke at last, to run as he did, not into the fence twenty-five yards away but towards the kale far across the meadow. More tactlessly still, he was an old buck-rabbit, in hard condition.

Dredger passed from scent to view in a bound and with his hackles up coursed the rabbit towards the kale. Major Ogle gave an agonized roar, holding up one hand to halt the dog, fumbling for his whistle, and making peremptory gestures to Dynamo and Bingo. These had risen to their feet but remained, crouching tensely, eyes on the rabbit, like a picture of lions by Nettleship.

"We'd better walk on to luncheon," said Mr. Mannering tactfully. As a boy, his heart had always bled for mothers whose offspring could not refrain from being sick at a party. Now each season he hated watching the earnest dog-owners in his syndicates being undressed, as it were, in public. He turned to Gerald.

"I saw you getting some nice birds at that stand!"

"Well," admitted Gerald, "I can hit them when they come straight at you over a high fence. But I missed all the curly ones. And that big lot was asking for it when they turned up the line, though the first bird I shot at was bung in the sun and I got the one behind it!"

"Ah," said Mr. Mannering, "they won't turn like that later on unless we're driving across a really strong wind. They'll just accelerate and go straight on. What happened was I got the old bird which was leading them and that made the rest turn. Pity! we've lost that lot for the rest of the day. But there's a nice few birds gone on."

"Shan't see 'em after lunch, I'm afraid," said the Brigadier, who felt that any "ops" which he was not personally conducting, were being mismanaged. "You won't get them to stop in roots after one o'clock."

But Mr. Mannering was a diplomat and had done this drive many times before.

"It's not very wet: I don't think they'll move just yet," he said pleasantly. "And some of my beaters have had nothing to eat since six. And these soldier-beaters . . ."

"You're right, Mannering!" said Col. Gore-Bunbury. "They say an army marches on its stomach. But some of 'em never stop! I told my chaps in '41 this war wasn't going to be won on tea and buns. Never saw such chaps! Stop work every two hours for a snack!"

"The desert army was as bad," put in Gerald. "The armour used to stop and brew up about seven times a day. Thousands of gallons of petrol spent entirely on makin' tea. Monty got very restive about it near Tripoli. . . ."

"Ah, Monty!" said Col. Gore-Bunbury, wistfully. They had been subalterns together. "Did you meet him . . .?"

They strolled towards the farm, picking up the vicar. His ears glowed with pride. The luck of the draw had placed him where he wanted to be, at the lower end of the line. His morning prayer had been heard and granted. He had achieved one really glorious Frenchman curling back over the tall beeches, and Sam Westrup was hunting for another which had planed down hard-hit into the farmyard.

§ 2

The first luncheon of the syndicate's season was always an ordeal to Mr. Mannering. His guests dispersed to their vehicles and emerged with little baskets and sandwich-tins and satchels in their hands. He thought of that dreadful day when his sheepdog puppy had eaten its way all the morning through Lord Drambuie's luncheon-basket and two layers of grease-proof paper, before regurgitating the sandwiches on account, probably, of the pâté.

Mr. Mannering, like all farmers a little nostalgic, sighed for the days when one had given one's shooting guests luncheon as a matter of course. Ah, those luncheons at the Blackthorn Farm in his youth, in the mellow warmth of early September or on some sparkling wintry day! Rounds of cold beef and apple turn-overs for the beaters and generous wedges of cheese, and indoors in the farm-parlour, a spread for the Gods! Cold roast chicken and salad and roast potatoes, or a glorious hot-pot, with an apple-pie to follow in its rich yellow crust, and a carefully-doctored Stilton and celery to wind up, and perhaps a plate of nectarines with the port before anyone thought of smoking! Carefree meals, and if they went "a little feelin' like", for the next hour, no one in his memory had shot any the worse!

But now, perhaps, austerity was just as well. Some of his guns were very poor shots and he could not really see them doing much execution, after a meal like that, at all those scattered birds waiting in the kale. They were better without it from the point of view of the bag, if not the stock of birds.

First into the granary came Mr. Lorrimer's chauffeur, staggering under an enormous black case which contained, as the salesman had assured Mrs. Lorrimer, all equipment necessary for a cocktail party and picnic luncheon for eight people at a smart race-meeting. It glittered with chromium and stainless steel, and it and Mr. Lorrimer took up nearly a third of the table. Mr. Mannering himself opened a small tin box, and feeling guiltily conspicuous, began on a cold partridge which he had shot on a neighbour's farm a few days before. He could see the Brigadier eyeing him between bites of a sausage-roll, and obviously thinking that Mr. Mannering had started killing the Stoke Loyalty partridges before the syndicate's season had officially opened. Col. Bunbury was eating sardine-sandwiches and cake, while the vicar worried his way through three currant-buns liberally centred with honey. He was chattering happily to Gerald about the difference between *Alectoris rufa rufa* (*Linnaeus*), the "red-leg" of Harkshire, and the chukor of Baluchistan.

"I don't think we saw quite as many birds this morning as I expected," said Brigadier Bowman. There was no harm as a paying guest in being mildly critical, as it might lead up to a rebate later on.

"We saw quite a fair lot," said Mr. Mannering gently, "and we've got a nice show of birds on the other side where we shall be this afternoon."

"I agree," said Gerald. He had been brought up to the rule that "on the turf and under it all men are equal". "I fired at twenty-three birds this morning and only killed fourteen of them and I reckon I ought to have killed twenty if I'd held straight. If all of us had done that . . ."

Col. Gore-Bunbury, whose "average" occupied him many hours of calculation every season, discarded his sardine sandwich, and began to work out something, making little ticks on a piece of paper, and lifting his head at intervals with closed eyes like a hen drinking.

The door was flung open and Major Ogle arrived, his three dogs puffing hard around him.

"Did you get it?" said Mr. Mannering. He was alluding rather tactlessly to the rabbit, but Major Ogle had forgotten all about the rabbit, now safely in the kale and probably enjoying the joke. He did not guess that Fred Crane, anxious for his lunch, had seized the opportunity, during the rabbit episode, to drop one of the partridges he had been carrying into the grass near the handkerchief.

"We did, indeed," beamed Major Ogle. "The old dog found it! It was stone-dead, stone-dead, I say, within three feet of where I'd marked it. Didn't you, Bingo, gur-boy then? Wonderful nose the old fellow has still! Can't think how the other two missed it! They can't beat the old 'uns, can they, Bingo? But then, of course, there's not much scent."

Bingo, pressing close to Mr. Lorrimer with his head on his knee, was gulping slightly and endeavouring to hypnotize him with his bloodshot eyes into sharing some fragment from his princely basket.

"Do you mind, Ogle?" said Mr. Lorrimer, loudly, pushing Bingo away with a fat white hand and producing a handkerchief drenched in *eau-de-cologne*. "Scent or no scent, dogs at meal-times make me feel a little faint!"

There was silence while Bingo and Major Ogle, both looking irreparably wounded, withdrew to the outer world and the dogs were "dropped" behind the granary. Major Ogle returned and edged his way silently into a seat, squashing everybody opposite Mr. Lorrimer up against the wall. He took out another red handkerchief, and from it produced a clasp knife, a large hunch of bread-and-cheese, and a raw onion. He had read somewhere that the famous Coke, his idol in the shooting-world, always gave nothing else to his guests at Holkham in the old days; plain honest English fare and only sybarites wanted more. One came out to shoot, not to eat.

Everybody munched in silence while Mr. Mannering busied himself handing round bottles of beer.

"You write, don't you?" said the Brigadier suddenly to Mr. Lorrimer, turning his tawny moustache towards him. He said it in much the same tone as that in which his aunt had once remarked to him, "They tell me you drink, Giles." As a man of action, Brigadier Bowman had a decided contempt for writers. He imagined writing books must be rather a cad's trick, though he read a few every year. His own literary efforts were now confined to appeals to his bank-manager and the regional petroleum officer, or a scathing letter to some tradesman or the telephone authorities.

"I think I may say I do," replied Mr. Lorrimer, with what would have been a smirk if it had not been masked by a jam-puff. He had published fifty-two novels in thirteen years and had three at the moment "in preparation". Only that morning he had dictated 4000 words of *A Gat on Loan* while still in pyjamas, and his secretaries would be busy all day with the dictaphone cylinders anent *Death at the Flowershow* which he had completed, overnight, while lying in his bath.

It was then that Major Ogle, all unwittingly, got his own back. The ejection of Bingo had given him the opportunity to insert his teeth which had been in his waistcoat pocket throughout the morning's sport, and in the glow produced by the old dog's achievement and some sherry from his flask, he entered the lists. He also wrote on shooting, in the correspondence columns of his favourite journals (contributions for which no one had ever thought of paying yet), so that he had the same awed admiration for the professional writer which some young women show towards a successful courtesan.

"Really!" he said. "Then I take it you are *the* Mr. Lorrimer, the novelist?"

As well ask William Shakespeare if one might take it that he was the one who wrote *Hamlet*!

"I am," said Mr. Lorrimer rather haughtily.

"Ah," said Major Ogle, "I am honoured indeed to meet you! I always read your works from cover to cover."

"I'm glad to hear it." Mr. Lorrimer's reply was smothered by the rest of the jam-puff.

"Yes, from cover to cover. Really, I never guessed we'd got such a famous writer in our midst, Mannering! I always think the most delightful thing you ever wrote, Lorrimer, was that one er, what was it called now er, I've half forgotten the title," he scratched his head, "that one about the Murder at the Villa Rose."

"Oh indeed," said Mr. Lorrimer stiffly. "I presume you're referring to that fellow Mason."

Major Ogle, in his confusion, used his clasp-knife freely on the onion. Unexpectedly Giles Bowman came to his rescue.

"I hear you've just brought out another one," he said. "How does one get hold of it?"

But Mr. Lorrimer was a veteran novelist. He had heard that one before. If there was one person he really disliked it was he who thought that a Lorrimer thriller was like opium, or hashish, or a copy of *Ulysses*, only obtainable through some secret and illegitimate channel. He fumbled in his pocket and drew out a stiff document.

"My royalty statement," he explained, "arrived this morning. Of the 40000 copies of *Gunman's Glory* which go to make up the first impression, only 35200 have been sold this month. It should be still obtainable at any reputable bookseller's."

Giles Bowman glowered. To him a book was something you borrowed, or got your wife to put down on her library-list, or packed surreptitiously in your suitcase in people's spare bedrooms and always meant to return. Most country houses in the Isle of Wight had contributed in their time to his little library. His wary blue eyes roved round to Gerald's weather-beaten red face, on which was the faintest glimmer of a smile. He swivelled his tawny moustache through forty-five degrees and opened fire.

"You, I gather, Warde, were in the desert?"

"Yes, Brigadier."

"Long?" Most of Giles Bowman's friends had lasted in the desert an average of three months.

"From '40 until after Tunis."

"On the Staff?"

"No."

"Not a very good party, was it?"

"So-so." Gerald was not going to be drawn. "We had an interesting time and we all learnt a good bit."

"And let me tell you," said Giles Bowman viciously, quoting one of his contemporaries, who had in the Eighth Army jargon achieved "a record for the course" in the matter of bowler hats, "there's nothing but false lessons to be learnt from the desert war!"

"What *does* he matter?" thought Gerald. "I shall be out of it in a year." Aloud he said, "Possibly. And it's a pity so many bloody fools never managed to draw them, isn't it?"

There was a shocked pause, as Gerald resumed his sandwich. Mr. Mannering turned to Major Ogle and asked him if he had ever met a case of coccidiosis in hares. Col. Bunbury upset his thermos-flask. Aghast at an open clash between a young major and a senior staff-officer, he began, "Of course, the equipment shortage in the desert up to Alamein made a lot of . . ."

The vicar had been listening intently out of his ear-trumpet and crumbling cake between his long fingers. "Desert?" he said. "And did you run across either *Alaemon* or *Galerida*?"

Major Ogle also put in his oar. Since 1939 he had only served in the Observer Corps but he had read widely and kept in touch with military things. Coccidiosis in hares could wait.

"Galerida?" he said. "Surely he was the chap who commanded 'em afterwards in Sicily?"

The vicar explained that he had meant a form of crested lark. The conversation died again.

There was a thump on the door and the huge form of Tom Beacon darkened the entrance. He handed a folded paper to Mr. Mannering and said, "We'll be agettin' on now, sir. I'll just bring that clover layer in on the way round. You don't want to be more than another ten minutes."

He shut the door and stumped away. Mr. Mannering sighed and went through the ritual of a sweep on the pre-luncheon bag.

Five minutes later Mr. Mannering rose. "It's time we were getting to the next stand, gentlemen," he said. The next drive was, thank goodness, an easy one, a walk for the nearest gun of only three hundred yards to a belt of ten-year-old firs and larches which flanked a seventy-acre field of kale. Thank goodness too, they had all lunched together fairly amicably. And he thought of old Lord Drambuie, who used to shut himself up alone in his great car and drink half a bottle of port after lunch, and then needed a great deal of waking and re-equipment before entering the lists.

Outside the hut waited the three henchmen, Angus, Sam Westrup and Mr. Lorrimer's chauffeur. Angus was standing at attention with Gerald's gun at "the order" and his great fingers held stiffly down the seam of his knickerbockers. Sam Westrup,

in his fisherman's jersey, hailed the vicar with "That's wholly
ablauen! You want to shute right ahid of 'em this arternoon,
Vicar. Now warn't I right about them pants?"

Then as an afterthought and in a loud whisper:

"We picked yar bird in the stacky'd. That dawg of the
Scotchman's ain't a bad 'un. I ain't acomen along o' you. Tom
Beacon, he want me as they ain't got enough brushers for that
there kale."

At that moment, a second Rolls-Royce crept statelily
into the yard. It held in its glossy heart the missing gun, Sir
William Boulogne.

Mr. Mannering sighed. There was always one late every day.

XXI. POST-PRANDIAL

It was five minutes later. Sir William Boulogne, beautifully dressed in plum-coloured tweeds with a rose in his button-hole, high white spats, and what Guedalla would have termed an Old Strombolian tie, had announced rather frigidly that he had not yet had luncheon. He clearly expected the proceedings to wait.

But on this point Mr. Mannering was politely firm, even at the risk of offending his most important guest on the first day. The partridges which they had put into the young swedes and kale in the last drive would not wait much longer, and would begin to draw back on to the stubbles to feed. So he made his apologies, murmuring to Gerald, "I wonder, Major Warde, if your man, Cameron, could stay behind and show Sir William where to go? Sir William will be Number One at this end of that belt."

"Certainly," said Gerald. "Ang . . . Cameron, I mean! Just stay here, will you, till Sir William's finished lunch? I'll take the bitch with me."

Angus fell out readily and assisted the gorgeously-liveried Tompkins to carry in a luncheon-basket almost as impressive as Mr. Lorrimer's.

The rest of the party walked out across a meadow towards a thickly-planted belt of larch and spruce-trees dividing the huge sweep of the kale from a still larger wheat-stubble rising to a

fence half a mile away. Brigadier Bowman ranged up confidentially alongside Gerald and said, "Have you had that keeper
chap of yours long, Warde?"

"Not very," said Gerald, "I got him through an advertisement." He suddenly recalled what Angus had said that morning. "They *tell* me he drinks a bit."

"Drinks?" said the Brigadier. The hackles of his moustache
rose with the word. "I should just about say . . ."

He broke off. Suddenly he realized that he could not "just
about say" what he wished. It was not easy to admit how
Angus had stayed with him as a prospective son-in-law two
months before. The remembrance of that week-end still
rankled. His guest had demolished seven-eighths of the Brigadier's tiny stock of gin and sherry as well as a bottle of whisky
he had brought with him, in an endeavour to show how unsuitable he was for any matrimonial appointment. The last
straw had been Angus's request for a siphon in his bedroom on
the Sunday night, at a moment when any right-minded young
man would have been sitting out on the lawn gazing with starry
eyes at Agnes Bowman.

"Have you any idea . . .?" he began again, looking round to
see that no one heard. He was obviously about to cross-question
Gerald still more on Angus. Any regular officer who had been
in the war from the beginning without getting on the staff or
rising to a high administrative command must, the Brigadier
thought, be pure ivory. But a regular officer with a bogus
keeper hanging round him must be protected from himself. . . .

"You want to watch out with people who answer advertisements," he went on, but Gerald was saved by the Vicar who
pattered up on his right, glanced at Gerald's tie and said, or so
Gerald thought.

"Got a perambulator?"

Gerald turned scarlet. What the devil was the old parson
after now? Did he imagine Gerald was a young husband, and
was he trying to sell to him, in the shooting-field of all places, a

pram? If so, it must be a real vintage pram, which had probably been at the vicarage since the 'nineties.

"Perambulator?" he said, blankly.

"Yes," said the Vicar.

If he does sell me one, thought Gerald, I'll bloody well make Angus march it home for me, with a leash of partridges in it and a hare. Aloud he said, shouting into the Vicar's eardrum and turning a deeper and deeper red: "I don't *want* one, sir! I'm not married!"

He was conscious that the other guns in the party trailing along behind him had stopped talking, except Major Ogle, who was still discoursing happily to Colonel Bunbury about the effect of sheep-ticks on grouse in Banffshire.

"Eh?" said the Vicar. He reached for his ear-trumpet and screwed it home.

"Damn and blast!" thought Gerald. Then he spoke again, very clearly: "No thank you, Vicar! I haven't got a *wife*! I don't *need* a perambulator!"

Mr. Halliburton flushed to the tips of his large ears. "I asked you was that a Perambulator? I was alluding to your *tie*! One m'self in the old days! We got some excellent country-house cricket in the Long Vacation."

"No," said Gerald, much relieved, "it's an Old Rugbeian."

"Terrible," boomed the voice of Major Ogle from behind, "they get all round the chicks' eyes and blind them. He tells me he's picked 'em up unable to see at all, poor things. Old days . . . lairds saw to it only a few sheep on grouse-ground. Now these War Ags! Monstrous! Soon have no grouse at all! And what will the rating authorities do *then*?"

To Harkshire people the fact that the shooting-tenants paid a high proportion of the rates in the Highlands might not have seemed a matter of vast importance but Major Ogle knew better. Coal and housing and demobilization might be priorities in Parliament. But in Major Ogle's world the restoration of *Lagopus scoticus* to its place of honour in the sporting calendar was priority number one.

"And quite apart from over-sheeping," he began again.

"Now, gentlemen, please," said the soft voice of Mr. Mannering, "the less we talk the better. There are a lot of birds in this drive."

He opened the gate. Ahead of them for five hundred yards stretched the belt of conifers. Along it at intervals in the stubble was a line of hazel sticks, each holding a numbered card.

"We number from here, leaving Number One peg for Sir William when he comes. The pegs are very close in to the belt as the trees are not too high yet. I must ask you to stand by your pegs and not move back."

In the old days, he thought, with guns who knew what was what, there would have been no need of such a warning. People would have kept strictly in line, and no one would have thought of moving. But now, unless he insisted, some ass would be sure to go back fifteen yards from his peg to give himself more time to see birds coming and if he did, someone further up the line would fire a dangerous shot.

"Much too close," said the Brigadier, who disliked being told to do things. "Shan't get a chance at any bird in front." He went sullenly towards his stick.

Col. Bunbury, who had hardly uttered a word since he left the granary, replying almost in whispers to Major Ogle's prattle, nodded to Mr. Mannering and hurried away towards his place, followed by the Vicar and Mr. Lorrimer.

Mr. Lorrimer, puffing a fragrant cigar, was deep in thought. He had suddenly realized that the 5000 words he had dictated overnight for *Death at the Flowershow* would all have to be done again. He had left his hero, Ronald Treston, the private investigator, in the huge refrigeration-chamber at the Towers, inexorably freezing to death, with nothing to save him but the memory of the secret de-icing formula used by the R.A.F. Research Unit, of which, as the result of a savage blow on the head half an hour before, he had forgotten the key symbol. Ronald Treston's brain was working coolly, as might be expected, but with lightning speed, to extricate himself against time from certain death. But Mr. Lorrimer, aglow with luncheon, suddenly realized that this episode, one of the most exciting he had ever penned, belonged properly to *A Gat on Loan*, with Tony Dunsterborne of the Secret Service as the hero. He sometimes made these little mistakes, due to pressure of work and the public demand for "Lorrimers", as his books were called.

Tony Dunsterborne, special agent, tall, blue-eyed, casual, had not had a very easy passage so far towards the inevitably happy ending of the affair. Coshed three times, then gassed by the second villain disguised as a County Vermin Eradicator, then savaged in the trigger-finger by a man-eating ape while reconnoitring the Towers, he had just been missed with a humane-killer wielded by the villain's parlour-maid, when she brought his early morning tea. In addition he had had to drink thirty-four double whiskies in three chapters while explaining the clues to his stolid companion from the Yard. But, in spite of it all, Tony was just getting his second wind, was still in the pink of condition, and was beginning to put in some pretty fast work with the raven-haired heroine who had so deftly eradicated the Vermin Eradicator with her "hunting-crop". But hang it, thought Mr. Lorrimer, all the names in that chapter would now need changing and other details as well. He walked on slowly. His brain, like Ronald Treston's, was working at lightning speed.

§ 2

Gerald went to his stick and dropped the bitch beside his cartridge-bag. He had Major Ogle on his left and the Brigadier was out of sight on his right just beyond two wheat-ricks which stood near the belt. Gerald began to think it was about time his own shooting improved. He had fired at twenty-three partridges before lunch, and only about seven had been orthodox "shooting-school" shots. He had found himself picking the "silliest" bird in a covey and then, as he fired, glimpsing three or four birds at a much more reasonable angle. And they seemed at this time of year to come "just anyhow". They slowed up, they accelerated, they turned back, they crossed each other, and now and again a covey had come at him with every bird at a different angle and pace. He loaded his gun, saw that his cartridge-bag was open, and looked at the fringe of the trees against the blue sky fifteen yards in front of him. Have to be quick here, with the belt so close! He sat in the sun and dozed.

Far away beyond the belt a horn was sounding. Gerald stood up and slid forward the safety-catch and half-crouched tensely. The horn seemed so distant that, he thought, the oncoming birds must surely pitch in the kale before they reached the fence. He waited a minute, almost another minute. Then suddenly, just as he relaxed, the air on his right front was full of partridges, twenty or thirty birds, skimming very slowly over the tops of the trees. He heard a flurry of shots and next moment was aware of a partridge rising and crossing towards him coming from behind the ricks. It was very fast and flying straight into the sun. He flung up his gun as he turned and saw the bird dimly in a haze of sunlight. Next second it had bounced on the stubble behind him. Another followed it but, as it saw him, swerved and planed back straight at Major Ogle who shot it as it swung back over the belt. Another flutter and a Frenchman (Gerald could see the chestnut markings on his flanks) was high overhead crossing from his left. Again a hurried snap and the bird dropped out of sight behind the ricks.

Two in two shots, thought Gerald, and in neither case did I have the faintest chance to think about allowance or what I was doing. It was just a matter of chuck-up-the-gun-and-chance-it. Perhaps that was the real way to shoot.

The horn sounded again. There was a rattle of wings beyond the belt, a whistle from the Brigadier on his right and a brown dot enlarging suddenly in front of him over the larch-tops. He pulled at it, saw it crumple and even as he opened his gun,

with a hand in his right pocket and the bird falling a foot or so
from him, a great wave of partridges broke over the belt,
creaking, chattering, swerving at all angles above him and on
each side. Gerald snapped the gun to, without reloading, pulled
at a bird twenty yards behind him and as he did so, realized he
was on safe. He swung on to another, pushing up the safety
catch, but they were gone, skimming up the rising wheat
stubble behind him. Damn! Then much nearer he heard the
horn again and Tom Beacon's voice, "Flag up, flags *up*, ye
beggars, blast ye!" Gerald let his eye slide towards the left
where he could see Angus holding Sir William Boulogne's
second gun, and a covey of brown dots breaking out high towards the beech trees by the farm. Then suddenly, without
warning, there were three partridges, very high, coming at him
on a slant from left to right. Gerald heard Major Ogle fire,
fired at the first, saw it start to drop, and swung on to the third
bird almost overhead, bending himself back as far as he could
go at the last moment. Something seemed to snap, he felt a
tearing pain just below his nape, and for a moment all went
black. He turned and could see a few feathers floating high in
air behind him. The birds had disappeared.

"Pretty work, sir!" boomed Major Ogle, touching his deerstalker. Then Gerald heard two shots beyond the ricks, and a
partridge appeared flying slowly past him about ten yards
above the top of the trees. Gerald swung very deliberately at it.
It was the easiest shot he had had all day. Nothing whatever
happened as a result of either barrel and the bird skimmed on
curling back towards the beaters.

The drive ended with a flurry of shots at birds which had run
up to the end of the kale and now came screeching low over the
trees and swerved along the line rather than face the great rising
expanse of wheat stubble. Gerald got two easy birds behind
him, then glimpsed the beaters through the trees. He felt better.
That tearing pain in his back had passed and the moment of
blackness that succeeded it.

§ 3

Angus strode towards him as he unloaded and turned to pick up. "I'm seconded, old boy, as Bill Bolony's loader. He's got that doorkeeper, Tompkins, from the Club out with him. The only time in the war Tompkins ever had a loaded rifle in his hands, he nearly shot himself, so he was terrified even of putting a gun together."

"Why the hell," said Gerald, "does Bill use two guns when everyone else is using one?"

"My dear Gerald, he must do the thing in proper style! We Boulognes ... the best people and so on. .... See you later!"

"Did he shoot anything in that drive?"

"One of our birds," said Angus grinning, "is down with anxiety neurosis, and I've sworn, in broad Scots, that I'll 'garther' it. Let me have the bitch, will you? She'll add verisimilitude to a rather unconvincing search."

Gerald picked three birds and turned towards the ricks. He was aware of Major Ogle hurrying up behind him, like a shepherd with his flock of retrievers.

"Can-I-help-you-Warde?" he boomed. "A-very-pretty-little-right-and-left-that-high-one-the-second-a-beauty-I-ought-to-have-had-one-but-I-was-on-safe. The-old-Lord-Walsingham-always-liked-that-quick-second-barrel-behind-the-vertical-sit-Dynamo!"

Gerald interrupted the flow.

"Never saw what happened to the second of those high birds," he said. "Did I get him?"

"Most certainly. Stone dead. Lovely one! Just behind the rick. I marked the exact place. Now Bingo, my darling, yur-trai-seek-him!"

There was a slight altercation with Brigadier Bowman, who insisted that he had picked one bird just behind the rick but that it was "most definitely" his missing bird. All three dogs were pressed into the search. The puppy, flashing wildly over half an

acre of ground, speedily found a bird behind the Brigadier's
peg which he had overlooked, and Dynamo recovered another
of Gerald's in some loose straw. Bingo, snuffling at a foot's pace
between the ricks, found and brought in very slowly a most
aromatic rabbit which had died three weeks before, and which
he yearned to roll on, rather than retrieve.

"Yours, Brigadier, I think," said Gerald politely. "I definitely
am not missing that one."

Giles Bowman glared. Major Ogle dropped all three dogs,
while he remonstrated with Bingo and endeavoured to remove
the rabbit from his ancient trap-like jaws.

"Guns this way, please," shouted Mr. Mannering. He and
Col. Bunbury had seven brace of birds between them and had
recovered them all except one bird which had run up the
stubble. Old Daniel, head up, tail waving, was pottering inconsequently up a water-furrow while Col. Bunbury watched
him, his heart in his mouth, guessing that the stubble was full
of hares, and praying that Daniel's better nature would rise to
the surface when a hare did. He breathed a sigh of relief when
the partridge suddenly fluttered out of the stubble under
Daniel's nose leaving his reputation still unsullied. He preferred a
dog to work like a Hoover, with his nose methodically snuffing
the ground, but with Daniel's technique, it was impossible to
tell when he was hunting a line and when he was just reconnoitring for something to hunt.

XXII. THE LAST DRIVE

The wind was blowing strongly down the line as the guns took their places for the last drive in a newly-drilled field of winter beans. Gerald, on the extreme right, found himself standing thirty yards back from a high belt of larch-trees, edged with low thorn-bushes. He could glimpse through the trees, a blue-green slope of turnips stretching down to his right.

They should be well up here, he thought, as he shuffled his feet in the soft loam, and anything coming down the line will have some pace on. That rending moment of pain and black-ness had passed. He had found himself shooting accurately and swinging freely in two queer difficult drives in which covey after covey had come sweeping low off seed-clover forward to hurdles in a thorny bank.

Up the line Major Ogle leant on his shooting-seat, the butt of his gun resting lightly on his thigh, his left hand far out along the barrels, his dogs couchant around him. It reminded Gerald of Nelson on his column with the lions below. Further up, beyond the vicar, Sir William had turned his back on the belt, and was talking earnestly with his hands waving, to Angus, who stood bolt upright, a gun under each arm. The vicar had cut down the corpse of a little owl from Tom Beacon's "gal-lows" on the edge of the belt. His gun lay on his cartridge-bag beside him. With a penknife he was busily dissecting what was left of the owl to see if the theories about its insect-eating pro-pensity had any foundation. Tom Beacon always insisted that there warn't any wuss varmin about than them there little cat-owls, drat them and that Lord what brought 'em into Northamptonsheer. Leave 'em be for a season and they'd ruen the countryside. The Vicar, a true naturalist, was not so sure.

Gerald was doubtful from which direction the main part of the drive was coming. Some at least of the beaters were coming in from far down the slope on his right front. Suddenly there was a flurry of wings far out in the turnips as a great pack of partridges, which had skimmed up from the right, settled in front of him. Then, before he knew it, a swiftly-enlarging black object, also coming from his right, was rising diagonally at the belt. He fired hurriedly as the bird topped the trees and a Frenchman crumpled and bounced down on the field behind him. Then far away on his left he heard the horn. A minute later a big lot broke over the trees, scattering high above the topmost guns. Another and another followed and Gerald could see birds dropping out here and there. With one eye roving along the tree-fringe and the other half-turned up the line, he was aware of a commotion behind Major Ogle. The French-man he had shot, winged and possibly only stunned, had picked itself up and was legging it across the huge bare forty-acre field. The young dog had been lashed to Major Ogle's cart-ridge-bag which he, expecting a "heavy drive", had left open in case he wanted to replenish his pocket. For a minute, which seemed to Dredger hours, he watched the bird recede. (Major Ogle was busy watching the belt, his pipe clenched in his teeth, for he belonged to the golfing-school which held that a pipe induced concentration on the object.) Then nature triumphed over art. Dredger "leapt to arms, unbidden", and after him surged and jerked the cartridge-bag, sowing its contents freely over the loam. Major Ogle gave an agonized roar which Dredger took as a hunting-noise of general encouragement. He mended his pace, stopping at intervals to turn round and snap at whatever kept bumping into his hocks.

Far up the line, Daniel had been trembling quietly behind

Col. Bunbury and taking in the scene. But this was too much for him. He sprang like a rival fire-engine to his comrade's aid. He, too, had been lashed to a cartridge bag, for the Colonel distrusted pegs in that soft soil.

The dogs converged at racing speed, leaving a trail of cartridges behind them, and only slightly hampered by the half-empty bags. They ran into their quarry head on, in a cloud of feathers. Daniel, realizing that the puppy had the lion's share and that the partridge was in safe keeping, trotted back towing his bag to Colonel Bunbury, his stern waving propitiation, as if to say, "Sorry, old boy. I simply *had* to see a dog about a partridge."

Gerald, who had been laughing too much to pay attention, heard a hoarse chuckle above him and was in time to miss a brace of very fast Frenchmen who were over him at tree-top level before he saw them. He reloaded and swung up his gun at another dark object rising swiftly at the belt and realized just in time that it was a hen pheasant.

The horn sounded again. Another great pack broke over the up-wind guns, and as they topped the belt scattered in all directions. A speck, far off, seemed to detach itself from the pack over the head of Number Four gun, hung in the wind for a second, then grew and grew on Gerald's vision as the wind caught it. Had that bird but known, it was asking for more trouble than if it had gone straight on, for Mr. Lorrimer and Sir William were unloaded; but, flustered and wind-driven, it did not know. It seemed unbelievable to Gerald that that on-coming bird, getting higher and higher as it came, should not turn back towards the belt, or be dropped by the vicar and Major Ogle.

To the vicar peering up through his glasses, it was in the phrase of his father, a "real archangel". To Major Ogle, his scattered cartridges forgotten, his left arm straight out along the fore-end, his mind buzzing with all he had ever read on the subject of forward allowances, it was "an-absolute-snorternever - saw - such - a - bird - in - thirty - seasons - looked - like - a-sparrow-I-laid-on-the-length-of-a-church-in-front-of-him-and-even-that-wasn't-enough."

It was over Gerald. He flung up his gun, jerked it wildly and fired, and the bird went straight up in the air. He jerked the gun again and fired blindly and, o joy! it was twirling round and round high in air on set wings, to fall dead more than a hundred yards below him on the edge of the belt. "Well, damn me," muttered Gerald, "I hadn't a clue about that one, and whether I shot above it, or at it, or in front of it, I shall never know." But it was, he felt, one of the high moments of experience, like scoring a nearside goal at sixteen annas under your pony's neck. Somehow he wished that Ann Heriot could have seen him.

A shriek from far away interrupted him. Mr. Lorrimer's plump chauffeur, his hand clasped to his thigh, was out in the field running as hard as he could towards the protection of his master. The Brigadier thirty yards away was just lowering his gun. And beyond the belt he heard Tom Beacon's roar, "Now you brushers! spreed out, spreed out, damn ye!"

§ 2

"I'm brimming with questions," said Gerald to Angus as, their farewells accomplished, the car bumped up the stony lane. "What the deuce happened, Angus?"

True to the Roans' tradition he had said nothing at all during those excited minutes at the end of the last drive when everybody else had appeared to be saying too much, around the prostrate chauffeur.

Angus tore open his stiff white collar, rubbed the red mark on his neck, flung his four-and-sixpenny cap into the back of the car and lit a cigarette.

"What a day!" he said. "Sixty-four and a half brace, seventeen hares, two wood pigeons and one various, to wit Eustace."

"You mean Percy's henchman?"

"I do. And to think it was Giles Bowman, late Chief Instructor at Hythe, who bagged *him*, with his own little musket! Why, if Giles had his way, nobody would be allowed even to load, until the red flag had been hauled down and the butt-officer had reported all clear."

"He struck me as safe enough with a gun. It's his tongue I didn't go much on." Gerald had not forgotten that conversation at lunch.

"He's so safe he shoots very little. And the gem of it is he'd insured himself for £500 against third-party risks knowing he was shooting with strangers! Never guessed *he'd* be the fire-raiser."

"But how on earth . . .?"

"It was Percy's fault. He at last shot a partridge, or rather one must have dashed itself against the pattern. Anyhow, by accident or design, he laid it low and sent Eustace scudding off to offer him tangible proof of his skill. My poor old Brig. wasn't expecting anyone to be free-lancing about, thirty yards behind the line. He swung round to take a hare, and pooped Eustace hip and thigh, before he realized anyone was in the fairway!"

Gerald grunted. "Might have happened to anyone."

"Exactly. Eustace got what he deserved. Screamed like a pig and bled like one too. Serve him right! I gather that young man had a very cosy war, in a supply depôt near Staines, with so much welfare laid on that there was almost no supply. Games for the lads, concerts every night with specially-imported floozies, seven blankets a man, and the hot-water bottles that should have been in the base hospitals when it was cold! Bandsmens' beds painted blue to match their pyjamas. No parades, and psychiatrists instead of serjeant-majors. And if you wanted anything urgently at Lewes they sent it up to Kilmarnock!"

"That sort of show, was it?" Gerald grunted with all the desert soldier's antipathy towards the base. "Percy Lorrimer seemed rather green at the sight of blood."

"He was. For a chap who bumps off as many people as he does in print, year by year, he was absurdly sensitive. Nerves all to blazes. He'll probably pile the Rolls up on the way home, with Eustace sobbing in agony on his face in the back-seat."

"There was one beater in the crowd," reflected Gerald, "as pleased as Punch when Eustace bled. Tall old shaggy chap in a frightful hat and a black hunting-coat. Rather a fine face. Kept muttering, 'Serve him dam' well right! He had the nerve to tell me, when I was nearly shot in the first drive, that it was *my* fault for getting in the way.' "

Gerald drove on.

"If anybody had been going to fire a dangerous shot today, Angus, I should have backed Percy down to odds-on."

"So should I! He was swinging through the line more than once today. I think Mannering has his eye on him."

"I don't envy Mannering's job. He can't possibly vet all his guns before the season starts. A feller may be a model husband and all that, and a holy terror in the shooting field."

"I agree. He's got a nice lot of birds. Rum guns, though."

"Do you suppose Giles Bowman spotted you, Angus, in that natty gents' rig-out?"

"I'm sure of it. If my engagement isn't off by tonight, I'll eat my new cap. Blatant impostor trifling with daughter's affections! Obvious crook, masquerading as a keeper, with designs on *your* money now. He'll put the police on to me. You watch!" said Angus cheerfully.

"And how did you get on as loader to Bill Boulogne?"

"We're improving. We shall hit something some day. We got off three barrels at one covey, two at once and one by accident when changing guns!"

"Did you, b'god! Any casualties?"

"Oh no, I saw to that. You didn't see our rabbit, though, after lunch?"

"No!"

"Pity," said Angus proudly. "You ought to have witnessed

our rabbit. I found it sitting out in the stubble, with my little eye, as we were moving to our places. I warned Bill Bolony, handed him a gun, said 'Ready, steady . . .' to the rabbit to get its hocks well under it, and gave it a kick in the right direction."

"What happened?"

"Bill upped with his cannon and missed the rabbit fore and aft, bracketing. The rabbit returned safely to its base. The poor

old vicar, thirty yards away, nearly didn't. He put up his ear-trumpet, the dear old soul, and apologized for being in the line of fire."

"What did Bill do?"

"He never turned a hair. He made an imperial gesture to me for his second gun and said, 'What the devil were you doing, kicking it up? *I* always regard rabbits as vermin, same as pigeons. One *ought* to shoot them sitting!' "

Gerald spluttered. "And you, my man?"

"I missed my cue. I should have said like the Watch to Dogberry, 'How if a' will not stand?' I forgot it. All I said was, 'Ah, weel, Sir Wulliam, I'll juist tell yon meenister you were no aimin' at him.' "

"Was he trying to sell you something in the last drive, waving his hands and so on?"

"Sell, my dear old boy, he was buying!"

"Not that cap of yours, for God's sake?"

"Lord, no! Apparently he only came here because he answered the wrong advertisement. He was trying to buy some drink. We've known for a long time that there was a chap in this part of the world who smuggled liquor across by motor-launch from Le Havre. He used to advertise under a box number in the sporting papers offering '*Excellent prospects and good accommodation in small mixed shoot, pheasants, partridges, hares, rabbits. . . .*' Which meant champagne, whisky, port and brandy. Sometimes it was '*Salmon fishing, three keen rods wanted March, April*', or words to that effect. If a real shooting-man or fisher-man answered, he choked him off politely and said the vacancy was now filled. And only a few, all in the black market for hooch, knew the truth. They popped down ostensibly to shoot, in a big car, with guns and all, and if there were any enquiries, they were strangers from London in Mr. Holyoake's syndicate. Well, Bill, seeking new markets for the Taper Club, must have been put on to this advertisement and got the box number muddled up with Mannering's. Apparently he never came near the place until he got a card saying when the first day would be. This other chap always invites his buyers down, gives them a damned good lunch and they haggle genteelly about prices and quantities afterwards. Bill was a bit bored at finding no lunch laid on, and being expected to stand out in a gale and shoot at partridges which seemed to have taken evasive action. When Mannering tacked me on to his chariot wheels, Bill imagined I was the go-between. Kept hinting he could manage 'thirty-six partridges and forty-eight pheasants' at least. I said the phea-sants hadn't come in yet, and pretended to be ultra-dumb. It was as good as a play! He gave me a broad hint that he was a genuine buyer in a big way. Eventually he began to get quite bitten with shooting, though he thought all real shoots had a group photograph as a matter of course, all ready for the *By-Prattler*."

"He went to a fair bit of expensive camouflage, pair of guns and all that," said Gerald.

"Yes, two guns in a new case but one was very old and one fairly new and there was inches difference in the cast-off."

"He's pretty quick off the mark," said Gerald. "Mannering tried to get me to take his own place next Monday at a brother-farmer's shoot near Burnford. Old Bill butted in and invited himself in my place, blast him! As if he was paying me a compliment by taking it! Mannering was too polite and asked me if I minded!"

"He may get there," said Angus solemnly, "but he won't do much shooting. *I* overheard that conversation."

"What the deuce do you mean?"

Angus fumbled in his pockets. "When we finished up, he tipped me a bob with an air and said, 'Just clean those guns carefully, my man, and see the case is put back in my car. Carefully now, they're most expensive!' "

"And did you?"

"I did," said Angus. "He won't shoot much on Monday." He ceased fumbling and laid something on his knee. "Alas, my dear Gerald, I made a gross mistake. I've got both his fore-ends here. He'll never think of opening the case till he arrives at the other end on Monday. Unless someone lends him a gun on arrival, he's had it!"

§ 3

In his bath that evening Mr. Mannering hoped things had gone well. They seemed an unusually difficult lot of guns and there were seven more days to go. The vicar was composing a note headed "Coleoptera in the gizzard of *Athene noctua*". Col. Bunbury, also in his bath, with a damp pencil and a postcard, his eyes closed, his lips moving, was working out how many cartridges he had fired to how many "head". He had already cleaned his gun twice, and given Daniel an aspirin in his stew. It kept the old dog from twitching in his sleep. Mr. Lorrimer, after a hearty tea, was dictating rapidly to his bathroom dictaphone a scenario for a new novel in which the villain, armed with a Winchester disguised as a shot-gun, succeeds in "bumping off" his principal rivals on successive days' partridge-shooting without exciting any comment except in the mind of the sleuth-eyed heroine. The Brigadier, with a whisky at his elbow and murder in his heart, was communing with Agnes Bowman's mother. And on the floor of his lobby, Major Ogle, the veteran, was sitting beside a basin of hot water and giving his dogs a slipper-bath while he searched their pads for thorns.

Sir William, speeding to London, his cigar in full fragrance, was deep in thought. For him the glory of his new shooting-suit was marred by a sore shoulder and the knowledge that unless he took immediate action, the Taper Club would soon be dry unless he came to terms with the non-quota wholesalers. None of them gave a thought for Eustace, writhing on his face while an amused young house-surgeon stooped over him with a pair of forceps and a swab soaked in alcohol. Nor of the few pricked partridges, who couched with stiffening limbs in the wastes of stubble, listening to the "cheep-wheat" of coveys which they would never join again.

XXIII. HASTE FROM THE WEDDING

But for pleasure and profit together
Allow me the hunting of Man.

—RUDYARD KIPLING

§ 1

Colonel Gore-Bunbury was turning out his wardrobe. What he called "full breeding-plumage", which he had worn for weddings, funerals and the pre-war Empire Garden-party, was laid out on his bed. He was searching for some silk socks to wear at a wedding and try as he would he could only find one. Angela hated mending and when her "little woman" was preparing his daughter Nora's trousseau for school, or being what she called "bad again", the Colonel's integuments flitted into Angela's mending-basket but all too rarely found their way back to his wardrobe.

He had indeed the second finest collection of odd socks in Harkshire, the others being in Angela's basket *sine die*, only surpassed by a neighbour, whose left leg from the femur downwards had been some portion of a foreign field ever since Passchendaele.

And as he groped and swore and decided on dove-grey spats to hide the fact that he was wearing odd socks on a ceremonial parade, he thought, Why the devil do they want society weddings in the year of grace 1945, with all the marriageable people still in the Army or out of a job? All the old birds round having to doll themselves up for some young couple who wouldn't give a damn if they came in gardening-clothes. There was surely nothing so unnatural as man! Could he possibly wear that old silk hunting-hat with the great scratch across its front where he had taken on that comic place out of Church-anger in 1937? He and the Whip had had fifteen minutes of the best after it, with everyone else pounded, but no one else would appreciate that wound-stripe right across the hat's nap. He would *not* wear the grey one which Angela had once insisted on his buying. Everyone would think he was one of those actor-chaps or a company-promoter down from London. Nor a four-in-hand tie either! Too dressy altogether! It was honour-able to look shabby nowadays—showed one wasn't what they called a "spiv".

§ 2

They made the church very late in a car closed down like a hearse, despite the warm afternoon, lest any breath of Heaven should ruffle Angela's hat or hair or top-dressing. The Colonel was perspiring when he got out. Half the county there and the worm-eaten old pews full of more morning coats than he had seen in seven years! Of course Angela *would* be late: it was more conspicuous to be late!

A tight fit, the Colonel found his pew, and he dared not kneel down properly lest his brace-buttons went. He leaned forward instead in what he called the "having-a-shampoo" seat, and wondered rather incongruously, with closed eyes, whether it mattered giving the fatting cockerels a portion of the hens' egg-spice with which he always salted the poultry mash, and what Angela's Aunt Janet had meant by the cryptic remark in her letter thanking Angela for her present of partridges. "*I always think,*" Miss Gore had written, "*the plumage of the French bird is so far superior to that of his English relative.*" Just like Angela to palm off a brace of Frenchmen on the old lady and expect her not to know. There were no flies on Miss Gore!

Meanwhile Angela, looking her indisputable best, her face momentarily hidden by very smart gloves, was letting her eyes range expertly over the serried ranks in front. As a huntsman gallops alongside his tail hounds and knows which are carrying the line, which are mute, which of his pack are missing and which going short or skirting, so Angela, with a few practised glances, could record for all time not only who was in Church, but what every woman was wearing.

The organ began and the congregation slowly rose. As it did so, a small pale moth fluttered very visibly up the aisle, crossed once from end to end of the chancel and came back down the aisle again, looking in vain for the coat that it had momentarily forsaken. Again the Colonel thought: Breeding-plumage in 1945, what a farce!

§ 3

The door opened with a creak, there was an altercation with the ushers, and up the aisle, preceded by Gerald Warde, who looked rather sulky at being an usher, walked a very stout and beautifully-dressed shortish man, who seemed, as of right, to seek a seat in the stalls. He sported a large crimson button-hole, an Ascot tie and carried a gray top hat. In his glossy black and white, he reminded Col. Bunbury of a Friesian bull. The Colonel wondered who he was. Angela beside him was wondering audibly too.

"Who's that, James?"

"Don't know, m'dear. One of the Press lords? He must be some pretty big bug to have a car like that." He indicated a vast and glossy limousine lining up outside behind the bridegroom's car.

It was Gerald who had returned to the back pew behind, who overheard him. The Colonel half-turned with lifted eyebrows.

"Who *is* that?"

"That? Sir William Boulogne! You met him shooting last week."

"Oh, of course. Is he a relative or what?"

"Lord, no! but he's the most important man here, next to the bridegroom and the parson. Between ourselves, he's laid on the liquid catering afterwards! Now this country's under prohibition without knowing it, a bird like that can chuck his weight about and get a front seat!"

"Hssh!" Angela objected to others disseminating scandal in Church, especially when she could not hear properly.

§ 3

The long file of guests wound their way into the marquee to shake hands with the bride and bridegroom. Col. Bunbury found himself listening to snatches of high-pitched truncated conversation before him and behind.

"Extremely pretty, I thought, and the little pages . . ."

"Was that the Lord Lieutenant in a vast Rolls?"

"Oh Lord, no! he's much too broke!"

"A very nice little day," boomed Major Ogle. "We saw more birds . . ."

"No, I don't suppose I shall get any shooting at all this year, now that poor old Jerome has passed on. . . ."

"Mine suffers terribly with her feet, she says."

"Poor Hetty! Yes, dreadfully tired! She'll be glad when it's all over, my dear. That terracotta . . . not a happy choice."

"Cubbing? Only a brace so far," boomed Major Ogle, "and they dug both those. But then this young new Master, y'know . . ."

"This 'do' must be setting poor old Richard back a bit. 350 guests, they tell me, and . . ."

"I simply don't know how people get it! My man in town lets me have two bottles every other month and . . ."

"Is that really *the* Percy Lorrimer? And his wife? He's not a bit like his books."

"I always imagined him as a very hard slinky young man with a super-lovely in tow."

"Really, I don't know what we're coming to!"

§ 4

"Good God!" said a voice in the queue, the voice of a young officer in uniform. "Look behind the buffet, Mary, among the waiters. If it isn't old Angus Somborne! I last saw him when he was a DAPM in Forty Corps."

"It *can't* be Angus!"

"It is. He's hogged his moustache but I'm certain."

"Not Angus! He had *pots* of money."

Another girl's voice said, "I believe you're right, Freddie. I remember now I saw him in the Carlton in uniform the other day, after the investiture. I meant to tell you."

"Pardon me, madam." It was the voice of Brigadier Bowman, and every hackle on his head, neck and upper lip was erect; for he, too, had spotted Angus among the row of butlers whom the bride's parents had collected from the neighbourhood. "I couldn't help overhearing what you said. . . . Would you mind telling me . . .? I'm Brigadier Bowman and I have reason to believe . . .

"Leave it to me," said the Brigadier, impressively, five minutes later. This was an "op" and it needed a senior officer to conduct "ops" properly. "There's been a series of robberies round here in recent months, and I think we've found the man. I'll have a word myself with the Chief Constable and I suppose there's a detective in charge of the presents. Obvious impostor! Keeper last week, butler now! Six weeks ago. . . . And you saw him in a restaurant wearing two rows of ribbons?"

"Well, sir," said the young officer desperately. His chance remark in the queue seemed to have "started something" which he could not stop. "Even if he was I don't think that means much. Anybody in this war could get those and without seeing very much war either!"

228

He spoke bitterly, for he had been in the original "Desforce", and by the accident of a wound in 1941 had not qualified for a certain numeral on his Africa Star.

The Brigadier quelled him with a glance. "*I* am dealing with this, and I trust that neither you nor these ladies will utter a word. Secrecy is what we require."

Captain Trogon, the Chief Constable, knew all the right people, and had once been an Assistant Superintendent of Police in Akyab, as well as a lifelong student of detective fiction. He was popularly supposed not to be able to keep his mouth shut, but, as Angus had once remarked, that was obviously a matter of conformation. He frequently lamented that, after Akyab, with its sixty murders a year, work in Harkshire was dull, but his eyes dilated as the Brigadier unfolded his tale.

"One moment, Brigadier," he said. "I'll just rope in Sir William Boulogne. He's on the committee of the Club that undertook the catering, and he may know something about the waiters. Most of them are genuine butlers from round here."

Sir William, in the glory of his wedding garments and his red carnation, his dove-grey waistcoat and watch-chain without, and two glasses of champagne making him feel, like the king's daughter, "all glorious within", was only too ready. He felt he was rapidly getting in with the county.

"I don't know the waiters." he said. "The General borrowed all the butlers he could lay hands on, he told me; but if it's that Scotch lout of young Warde's who loaded for me last Saturday, he's a crook! He went off with the fore-ends of both my guns. Lost me an excellent day's shooting on the Monday!"

"Your fore-ends, Sir William?" said Captain Trogon incredulously, his mind racing over a score of theories.

"Yes. They were returned to me by registered post with a stamped receipt for one shilling, signed Angus Cameron."

None of Captain Trogon's detective novels had prepared him for this. "A receipt for a *shilling*?" he said slowly.

Sir William suddenly remembered his tip to Angus on the

Saturday. Luckily, Providence saved him any further explanation. "Will you excuse me a moment?" he said hurriedly, looking out of the window. "I've just seen . . ." He had just seen the "sweet little pages" chasing each other round the house armed with umbrellas, one of them wearing Sir William's superfine grey topper, well down over his ears.

"Anyway," said the Brigadier, "not long ago, that chap was calling himself Major Somborne in London. And I hear he was in uniform wearing two rows of ribbons in the Carlton the other day, including the M.C. . . ."

The eyes of the Chief Constable glowed. "Leave it to me, Brigadier," he muttered, "I'll set the wheels in motion at once."

§ 6

Mr. Oldham, the social reporter of the *Mid-Harkshire Sentinel*, had faithfully recorded the list of distinguished guests, and was now having a quiet chat with the detective in charge of the wedding-presents. Both men were lamenting that nowadays wedding-presents had deteriorated terribly. It was all pots and pans and baking-dishes now, a dull lot of stuff not worth guarding, and certainly most difficult to pinch. So when the Chief Constable beckoned imperially to Mr. Jones, Mr. Oldham pricked up his ears. A decade on the *Mid-Harkshire Sentinel* eternally reporting livestock prices, Oddfellows' reunions, whist-drives, and the sagas of the Women's Institute, had never shaken Mr. Oldham's belief that he would have made an outstanding crime-reporter in Fleet Street—one foot in "The Yard", and primed almost to bursting with the gruesome inside details. When an hour later the machine of the Harkshire Constabulary sprang into action, Mr. Oldham was at the head of the hunt.

"What alibi did the Chief say this bloke was adopting last week?" he asked Mr. Jones, as their car pursued the police to Oakington.

"Loader to Sir William Boulogne."

"What's that, exactly?"

Mr. Jones, also, had not met any loaders in London.

"Sort of assistant gunman. He 'elps 'im shoot in battews."

At last! Already Mr. Oldham saw the headlines burgeoning in every paper in the land:

SOCIETY WEDDING DRAMA IN ALSCLERE
GUNMAN-BUTLER UNMASKED

§ 7

Gerald had hurried home from the crowd in the wake of the bride and bridegroom, and discarded his wedding finery for a tweed suit and a soft collar. He had managed a few "useful moments" with Ann Heriot and the new M.F.H., and had begged them to come round for a drink at six o'clock. He tidied his littered smoking-room and put out the drinks. Suddenly Angus, a dishevelled figure in his butler's attire, came racing across the park, and leapt the sunk fence. He panted into the room, tore off his collar and tie, and plumped down on a sofa.

"Red-tabs-in-the-morning," he exclaimed. "Anyway, I've given 'em a run for their money. I feel like Charles Stuart."

"Who's chasing you?"

"That poop of a Chief Constable, Algie Trogon. He's been listening to some yarn at the wedding and put his peelers on to me. Old Richard Ainslie's butler tipped me the wink, so I popped off through the orchard and came straight over the downs. I suppose I'm suspected of designs on all those utility casseroles among the presents! Sank my only decent shoes in that filthy ride through Oakhanger! For God's sake, Gerald, give me a drink before I go and change, and remember you got me through an advertisement."

He tore off his muddy shoes and dipped his great face in a tankard of beer.

"I'll hop up and change in a minute. Never realized before

how they only built one's morning clothes for standing about in! You try and run in yours!"

There was a crackling of gravel outside the door as three cars whirled in at the gate. Gerald saw policemen rapidly surrounding the house and at the window appeared the face of Mr. Oldham, white with excitement, shouting "Here they are, Captain! We've got them both!"

§ 8

The Chief Constable made a personal search of Angus's bedroom while the serjeant examined Angus below. Angus's library, which ranged from Havelock Ellis to the *Hog-Hunters' Annual*, from *Septs of the Clan Cameron* to the *Racing Calendar*, and *The Young Butler's Vade-Mecum*, interested him less than some framed portraits of ladies on Angus's chest-of-drawers. One of these he carefully marked "Exhibit A", and a crumpled card from the Lord Chamberlain relating to a ceremony a week before, which he found in a drawer, was "Exhibit B". He was exasperated to find neither jewellery, fur-coats nor stolen miniatures in the room, and there was not so much as a jemmy or a skeleton key. He descended in twenty minutes to confer with his serjeant.

"I'm not so sure, sir, we oughtn't to make other enquiries first. We may have made a mistake. 'Is discharge-papers seem genuine. Major, 'e was, Royal Ertillery. Says he changed 'is name—took a *norm de plum* like, when he 'came down in the world'. Didn't want 'is friends to know."

"They'll know before *I've* done with him," said Captain Trogon viciously.

"Says Cameron was his mother's name."

"If we all took our mother's names whenever we felt like it, there would be chaos." The Chief Constable spoke with feeling because his mother had bee none of the Herefordshire Nincoms. He had mentioned this in an unguarded moment to a man who had immediately christened him "Poop". The name had stuck.

"Leave him to me, Serjeant," said Capt. Trogon. "I can get most things out of him, or know the reason why."

§9

. . . "Taken down in writing and may be used in evidence against you. . . . Do you understand?"

"Vara weel," said Angus, "I suppose some fools will never lairn. I wasna as bad masel' when I was in the Forrrce. A little did sink in, whiles."

"Insolence won't do you any good, my man."

"Aiblins ye havena found that folk who are impairvious to reason are whiles extra-orrdinarrily sensitive to insult?"

"Do I write that down, sir?" put in the serjeant looking up from his notebook.

The interrogation proceeded.

"And how do you come to have a portrait of Lady Narrow-smith in your bedroom? She's . . ." (the Chief Constable hesitated and snobbery triumphed) "she's a well-known member of Society and a connection of mine by marriage."

"Puir gairl! She married on a felly from a vara queer family." Then as an afterthought, "She's juist ma sister."

They ploughed on.

"I suppose you'll be telling me you want to see your solicitor before you make a statement?"

"Ah'd sooner have a wee drink."

Angus got bored at last. He dropped his Scots accent and looked the Chief Constable in the eye.

"Look here, Chief Constable, we can short-circuit all this hu-ha. Will you ring up a number in London I'll give you and ask them about me?"

"I see no reason to do that. *I* am conducting this investigation."

"If you don't," said Angus, "you'll be sorry. It's an extension on Whitehall 1212."

The serjeant looked imploringly at Capt. Trogon. Then he

said, "I think, sir, I'd better nip back to the station. We've got a clear line from there."

"Very well. Now, my man, answer my questions. . . . I put it to you that . . ."

Three miles away, Brigadier Bowman was saying to his wife. "I think I've put paid to *that* young ruffian at last. I'm so glad Agnes couldn't come to the wedding. It would have distressed her greatly."

A mile away, in a call-box, Mr. Oldham, perspiring heavily and very short of change, was trying to get through to the Crime Editor of the *Daily Blame*.

Poor Mrs. Wiggins, in her parlour over the stables, was saying, "To think of the *police* being here, Alfred! We haven't had them here since Master's Gerry's grandfather was killed out hunting."

And Sir William Boulogne, speeding back to London with the knowledge that the Taper Club had "made a packet" out of the reception, was smiling his dark smile, knowing that the rape of his fore-ends had been amply avenged.

§ 10

The serjeant returned in twenty minutes. Angus's 'confession', which the Chief Constable had failed to identify as straight out of Havelock Ellis, almost word for word, had so far only reached the end of one foolscap sheet. He called the Chief Constable aside, but Gerald was able to hear what he said.

"Get through?"

"Yes, sir."

"Who did you get?"

"Mr. Troup himself, sir. He seemed 'ighly amused. The words he used were: 'What? old Angus in the calaboose? Whatever for?' . . .

"I said we 'adn't got anything very definite but 'e'd been disguised as a butler, helping with the drinks at a wedding. Ryebald sort of a gentleman for an Assistant Commissioner, sir. All 'e said was 'Good old Angus! Trust him to be at the fountain-head if there's a drink going! Give him my love, serjeant, and ask him if he's seen his psychiatrist lately!' Those were his very words...."

It was, in fact, even for Mid-Harkshire, a really disappointing day. The Chief Constable, however, would have been interested had he seen, five minutes after his departure, Miss Ann Heriot, with one of the bridesmaids and the new Master of the Mid-Harkshire Hounds, being ushered into Gerald's presence by a mud-splashed butler without either collar or tie, whose shoes were still in the fender of the smoking-room.

He bowed stiffly and announced his visitors.

"Cameron," said Gerald, "you're improperly dressed again! And get those socks darned before you come on parade again."

Angus went out blushing. *The Young Butler's Vade-Mecum* had prepared him for these "inevitable asperities of employers".

"He's only a learner," Gerald explained to the Master, evading Ann Heriot's eye. "Keeper by day, butler by night. He's apt to forget which part he's dressed for."

XXIV. VICAR'S SOLILOQUY

While we of virtue boasting at home in comfort sit,
The heathen man is toasting his brother on a spit.

—ANCIENT HYMN

"Consistency, my dear Warde," said the Rev. James Halliburton, removing the stopper from the decanter, "was never a
diagnostic field-character of *homo sapiens* of any subspecies. A
little more port?"

Gerald and he were sitting at an exquisitely-polished oval
dinner table on which a lustre was shed by four candles in old-
fashioned silver candle-sticks. The light gleamed, too, on the
vicar's velvet smoking-jacket and snowy hair, and on a mass of
silver. Mrs. Westrup, whenever the vicar gave a party, let herself go in the matter of the table appointments.

"Thanks, Vicar," said Gerald. "But I should have thought
consistency was our national failing."

"Well, all progress is inconsistent. Our delightful road
bridges, on which so much care and art were lavished, are quite
unsuited to the ordinary traffic of today. Those thatched cottages
of yours at Little Oakington were probably the last word once
in beauty and comfort. No one guessed that *homo sapiens*
would ever insist on what Sam Westrup calls 'indoor san'. And
all this silver . . ." he waved his tanned fingers at the sideboard,
"our forebears collected it with such loving care—carvers and
tureens and knife-rests and menu-holders and decanter-labels

236

and petty containers and contrivances for this and that, without realizing that within a century there would be no one left to clean it. It would become as redundant as the, er, human appendix."

Gerald was bemused. The talk at dinner had ranged from the courtship ceremonial of the eared grebe to the chemical composition of Stilton cheese and salt-licks in Nepal, from the strategy of Roper Barrett in a double to Lord Lonsdale's methods of gundog training, from the diaries of Pepys to those of Peter Hawker. On each subject the Reverend James Halliburton had shown himself to be deeply-read and prepared to talk till all was blue. Gerald sipped his port and inserted a word occasionally.

"Take our village activities," went on the Reverend James. "Improbable as it may seem, virginity is no bar to membership of a Mother's Union."

"I should have thought it was an, er, insuperable one."

"Oh, dear no! Poor Janet Ditherdale, who has never had a chance to marry, is one of our keenest Mothers, while Emma Gadwall, who has had five children in wedlock and one outside it, besides divorcing two husbands, is ineligible, as are certain unmarried mothers who even more badly need our care."

"I should think," said Gerald smiling, "Mothers' Unions give you a sticky time, sir! I'd rather run a commando of Bengalis any day!"

"I am only there in an advisory capacity: I fill in conversational gaps; I hand round tea-cups, and so on. But union is, I must admit, at times a misnomer for our little coterie of mothers. Is it the same in India?" He put up his trumpet hopefully.

"I never came across any Mothers' Unions in India," said Gerald, clinging hard to the thread of the discourse. "Are there any?"

"No, but what I mean is, and it bears out what I was saying just now about consistency, there seems no prospect of any union in India. Too many warring castes. When they say, 'India for the Indians', my son tells me they mean 'India for the Musulman'."

"And devil take the Hindu and the Sikh. You've hit it, Vicar, exactly."

"Ah! that's interesting. My son, a district magistrate at a place called Pindi something, assures me there will be a blood bath presently!"

"I'll bet there will. And the 'Pagets M.P.' here, who will have turned on the tap, haven't a clue about India!"

"And talking of blood baths, we are notoriously inconsistent here. Christmas, a season of goodwill to all men, is a period of noticeable illwill to the brute creation. I feel a hypocrite when we sing in Church

All things bright and beautiful
All creatures great and small."

"I agree, Vicar. I hope in Heaven we shall meet some of our favourite horses and dogs. I always feel not only miserable but a treacherous cad when I put one down."

"So do I. I gave up hunting years ago after the death of a very favourite horse. So many of my animals have exhibited much more likeable characteristics than a number of my parishioners; fortitude, loyalty, affection and so on. And yet, if we are to meet the rest of the brute creation in the hereafter, it will be extraordinarily embarrassing! I have, to be frank, shirked the subject in my sermons."

"One isn't given much of a lead," began Gerald.

"In Holy Writ, you mean?" said the Vicar. "I wish one were. The parable of the good shepherd, for example, always glosses over the ultimate destiny of the sheep. To be consistent about causing pain to animals one should, I feel, be a vegetarian, but thank goodness I am not! If one were, where does one stop? The Gospels seems to sanctify the slaughter of fish on a large scale in the human interest and the Baptist must have caused much pain in a quiet way to locusts. And yet excessive kindness to animals can verge on extreme cruelty. . . ."

"I don't get that, Vicar."

"Have you ever been in a *pinjrapol*?"

"A *what*?" Would this old bird never come to an end of his abstruse references?

"A *pinjrapol*, a Hindu asylum in which old, diseased and injured cattle end their days. Their religion forbids Hindus to put an end to them and they linger on for years. My son tells me the sight affected him far worse than an abattoir. Katherine Mayo makes the same point."

"I can well believe it. I see it won't be long before they try to stop bloodsports in Parliament."

"So I believe. Inconsistency again! There is very little cruelty to foxes in our local hunts (it must, I feel, bring a pleasurable excitement into the fox's rather dull life), but there again I wish we were given a clearer lead on the ethics, especially of trapping and poison. They are far more ghastly alternatives." He shuddered. "The anti-bloodsports people always insist that we shooting men take a 'sadistic pleasure in inflicting pain'. Surely in that case a bird which flies away wounded, and is not picked up, should give the sportsman a much keener pleasure than a bird shot dead? But is that the case?"

"Of course not. A bird I tailor always worries me quite a lot."

"And me too. I suspect it is not so much a feeling for animals that moves the doctrinaires against us as intolerance. My vegetarian friends are often most aggressively jealous of their fellows. Do you remember when Oscar Wilde edited *The Woman's World*? In about 1887, I think?"

"Sorry, Vicar, I was only born in 1910."

"Really? Well, Wilde remarked on the connection between vegetarianism and 'socialism, atheism and even nihilism'. He said it was strange that the most violent republicans were vegetarians and made some Wildeish epigram about brusselssprouts making people bloodthirsty. A sheltered life begets strange excesses. My dear mother in 1917 was always more bloodthirsty about the hanging of the Kaiser than I was when I was serving in an infantry battalion. Had it occurred, she would have applied for a ticket in the front row. But *homo sapiens* is a mass of inconsistencies! To Sam Westrup Stilton cheese is as repulsive as a dog to a Mohammedan, but he adores tripe and black puddings." The Vicar shuddered again. "I remember how grieved I was as an undergraduate to see a lady devotee of the stage in the Alhambra lounge, one of those who find virtue so difficult, dilute a glass of very sound port with what she called 'lemon'. Have another glass, by the way?"

"No thank you, Vicar!" Gerald looked at his watch. "Talking of ladies, hadn't we better join them?"

"The ladies!" The Reverend James flushed to the tips of his ears and tucked his ear trumpet into his pocket. "I *knew* there was something I had forgotten! I hope Mrs. Westrup has given them coffee! But we've had a most interesting chat and later I'll show you the specimens of *Acrocephalus dumetorum* I shot in the bad old days on Blakeney. The ladies! How remiss of me!"

But when they reached the drawing-room they found Mrs. Heriot contentedly knitting a sock and toasting herself beside a large log fire, while Ann, slim in a black dress with a thin pearl necklace, had dipped into Markham's *Country Contentments* and the *Diary of a Country Parson* and was strumming at the vicar's old-fashioned piano. Both were delighted that, for once, having had an excellent meal, there were no domestic chores of washing-up to spoil its memory. Mrs. Heriot began cross-examining the Vicar on recent crises in the Women's Institute, while Ann and Gerald wandered round together, looking at the Vicar's pictures and fingering his books. To Gerald it was in retrospect "one of the better evenings" until Sam Westrup in his Sunday suit struck the door a resounding blow with his tray and said, "I've brought your grog, Vicar; thar's only been a titty mite o' rain. And I skinned that sparrowhawk but I couldn't make narthen of her sex. I left the body on your writing table for you to see." Then as an afterthought, "Old John Cannon is whooly bad again: I shall start adiggen to-morrow." Sam, in his long seafaring existence, had always said exactly what came into his head, usually in a most audible voice.

§ 2

Not far away Col. Bunbury put down his *Times* with a sigh. They were going to make the greatest mistake about India, though after years of promises we could hardly back out now. There would be slaughter, you could mark his words. Any poultry-keeper could have told these Whitehall experts what would happen, even if the Pathans did not intervene. Your old geese never got on with your young geese. Your old hens gave the pullets and ailing fowls hell if they tried for "equal rights" at the food bucket. Hunter-Bunter, his late heavy-weight cock, had brooked no interference with his own "ideological tenden-cies", even from his own wives, however anti-social they might seem. Just as well expect the magpie to nest with the nightingale! All these warring *jats* in the bird world would never live quietly together, and the same in India. But those Whitehall chaps, with their black coats and horn-rimmed mentalities, had never had a chance to keep even chickens, let alone the King's Peace between warring tribes. There would be much pious hope, some sonorous froglike phrases and guff about "generous accommodation for racial minorities", "the goal of self-deter-mination", "practical statesmanship" and "an outstanding con-tribution to the political settlement of South-east Asia". But the result would be administrative chaos, blood and woe, and broken promises to any poor devils of officials kicked out in the process.

If his pension went, what then? Could he get a job some-where as a gardener, or a loader-valet? *That* would be the job! See the world, live very comfortably and discover how some of these supershots really performed. And perhaps a quiet even-ing's fishing on some first-class water while his master was playing tennis or "poodlefaking". Angela, of course, would miss her bridge and her incessant "sets" and "waves"—those *ondulations* which were guaranteed to be so *indefrisables* and which began to look like nothing on earth on the fifth day. Could she live on her expectations from Miss Gore, and on their small joint private income in a "home for distressed gentle-women"? For the first time he visualized the possibility of having to abandon her, one day.

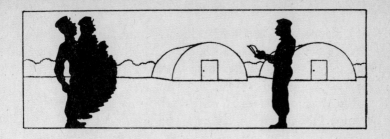

XXV. OPERATION PARTRIDGE

*"It was a splendid shoot. Everything was perfectly orga-
nized. The game was driven by four hundred soldiers commanded by their officers, and they all took their task seriously, as if it were a question of ejecting the Russians from
the forests of Wiesma or Briansck. If in Italy a Party
leader dared to use soldiers for a similar purpose, there
would be a tremendous scandal."*

—CIANO's *Diary for 25th Oct.* 1941

Alfred Budgett of the Royal Metallurgicals was in the Corporal's Mess one damp November morning reading the
pages of instructions which had reached him overnight from
the orderly room.

"Our something Adj.," he said to Corporal Jones, "ain't 'arf
a one for the written word."

"Ah!" Aneurin Jones looked up from the pages of the *Daily
Labourer.* "Thinks we want smartenin' up regimentally, does
'e? Teachin' us to get into bed by numbers soon!" He shook
back his flowing black locks. "Wot's it all about, Fred?"

"My something fatigue this morning. Parade 0800 hours.
Clean fatigue with gas-capes. Boots rubber knee. Civilian rep
to be at camp gates 0820. Sticks, flag to be drawn from
civilian sources. . . ."

"Ops, eh?"

"Ops. 'Operation Partridge.' Shootin' party, we are.
Ploughin' about in the something mud till dark."

"I was orderly corporal last night," mused Aneurin Jones. " 'Is table was littered with books, *Letters to Young Shooters, How to Drive Partridges, Rabbits for Pleasure and Profit,* and all that. He was getting ready to brief you, Fred, surely."

"*Brief* me? Brief my ruddy 'ead, Annie." Cpl. Budgett crumpled the closely typed sheets in his huge hand.

"And what will you be shooting with, Fred?" demanded another Corporal. "Two-twos?"

"Not something likely. *We* 'as to put the bastards up. 'Ence the boots, rubber, knee. Did it last year. Turnips up to me navel. *And* wet! Walked about fifteen something miles. Me feet came up in blisters white as lilies."

"Battew, eh?"

"Wot's that?"

"Battews, they call 'em. There won't be any more when *we* get going." Cpl. Jones waved the *Daily Labourer* menacingly. "They're the last stronghold of the bloated capitalist eera. They have them in flocks, not wild birds at all. They're preserved in coops and driven up to a hide-out. *And* slorter! They have seats to sit on, and two scatterguns, and valets to load for them, and ladies watching the poor creatures mown down. Don't you lend yourself to such practices, Freddie!"

Capt. Raymond Abersoch, the Adjutant, would have been shocked to the quick had he heard what Cpl. Budgett said of him when at last he left the Mess. An earnest young man, Capt. Abersoch had taken Mr. Mannering's request for twenty-five other ranks as beaters (on payment) very seriously indeed, had made a close study of the voluminous literature on shooting in the Harkshire County Club, and distilled their wisdom into two pages of typescript. Reluctantly he had cut out the sacred paragraphs with which all operation orders normally began, the ones about "infm" and the other about "enemy intentions".

But his beaters, he had felt, were going into action "beautifully in the picture".

§ 2

The detachment paraded at length twenty strong. Fred Budgett had nearly had enough of it by then. Three men, having heard what lay before them, had "gone sick" with verrucas, fallen arches or pyrexia of unknown origin. Craftsman Izzy Samuelson had claimed that on no account could he take part in any such ceremony on his Sabbath. Driver Conkinson revealed himself as a founder-member of the Anti-Bloodsports Union, and was dismissed from the parade on conscientious grounds. Storeman Botram, who had spent the war in a quietly clerical capacity in the Corsham Caves in charge of two million gas-masks, had developed an "anxiety neurosis" at the prospect of gunfire so close to him.

This is worse than a something Church parade! thought Cpl. Budgett. King's Regs did allow you to get 'em to the Church door and then let 'em fall out, but he couldn't leave his detachment littered about the something countryside today at 076352. He had wisely kept the haversack rations under his own hand, so once they were at the "conc" point they would probably stay put, at any rate till dinner-time.

He drew the "brief" from the thigh-pocket of his battledress, turned to the paragraph headed *The Drive*, and lifted up his voice.

"Properly at ease now. Squard, shun! Sta'at ease! Easy! Now pay attention. This what I 'ave 'ere is designed to put all ranks fully in the picture as to what is to 'appen. When we debus at the conc point, all ranks will be issued with a stick, flag, from civilian sources. . . . On the command 'Walk, march!' the drivers, that means you, will proceed in hextended order at twenty paces interval, with meself as the centre file and file of direction. There will be civilian reps on the flanks, acting as guides. We advance on an extended front, the five men on the left of the line, or the right according to the wind, keepin' twenty paces a'ead of the rest, sweepin' all before us. There will

245

be NO, repeat NO, unauthorized outcries which does 'arm by scarin' the game, quarry or what-'ave-you. Flags will be 'eld upright in one or both 'ands, and waved from right to left, or from left to right as requisight, in the event of game bein' observed. The purpose of the flag is to deter the game from approachin' the 'older of same. The cry 'Over'! is utilized to give warning of the approach of game to the sportsmen, who will be be'ind 'edges in hambush. In the event of an 'are or other animal turnin' back, it will NOT, repeat NOT, be persued. It is also forbidden to kill, maim or otherwise hinterfere with any rabbit, 'are or other species of game found *in sightu*, which means on its perch. In such event, the boot or flagstick may be employed to propel the quarry lightly, in the general direction of the advance, at the same time uttering the word 'Over'! in a smart and sportsmanlike tone. In some places," he perused the typewritten sheet, "a 'orn or whistle 'as proved hefficacious in announcing the approach of game. Well, we'll leave that bit out, 'cause I 'aven't got a bloody 'orn, and some bastard's pinched my whistle, so we will depend on the yuman voice. But remember no unauthorized outcries....! You there, in the front rank, stop scratching."

Craftsman Lancelot Carteret, an old Plutonian, who, since his call-up had insisted that the lumps he found on himself in the morning were not caused by mosquitoes, hurriedly ceased his researches and stood to attention. He was already known among his comrades as "Chatty" Carteret, as he could talk of nothing else.

Cpl. Budgett read on.

"On the conclusion of the movement, all drivers will 'alt, stand easy and await the order to close.... There will be NO, again repeat NO, attempts to fraternize with the shooters.... A serious view will likewise be taken of any driver bein' found in unauthorized possession of game.... Remember, too, success does not just 'appen, it is planned.... This *ain't a fatigue, it's a parade*...in a smart and soldierlike manner." He put the "brief" in his pocket at last. "Squard 'shun. Right 'tun! *Em*-buss! Now *asti* with that flipping tail-board!"

The detachment humorist, who wished most earnestly to be informed how one distinguished a rabbit from a hare, was told firmly to shut his something mouth. At the gate the lorry picked up the "civilian rep", Fred Crane, before proceeding to the "conc pt.".

XXVI. AFTERMATH OF A SPORTSMAN

"For to spy out the nakedness of the land ye are come."
—BOOK OF GENESIS

Major "Bongo" Bellemy, last of the Bellemies of Bottle-borough (so-called since he claimed to have been charged by an infuriated bongo), was going through his cellar on his return from Monte Carlo. It was a sad process and he felt like a dead Christian walking round the ruins of the Coliseum. Here blood had flowed so freely once but now there was no blood to flow. But he must do something about the empties. They covered the floor and had overflowed gradually all over the pantry. An independent brigade had even infiltrated to the scullery, with far-flung detachments elsewhere.

These gave housemaids and tradesmen quite a wrong impression. And sometimes when Jammy Falkenham, his keeper-butler, led his shooting guests through the back-premises to sell them a dog, (their best deals had been put through late at night for one couldn't expect to see a dog *worked* then), people fell crashingly over them.

Major Bellemy's pale blue, rather prominent, eyes watered slightly with melancholy in his plump face. His delicate nose, the gift of his lady mother, jutted out from it incongruously. He had clung to the adage that "a bottle a day keeps the doctor away", but now he was lucky if he got two a month. *Here was all the end of all that glory!* He had sunk in a night of yore what was now a month's super-luxury! To think that those platoons of noble shapes, gold seals and black labels and famous names and all, would fetch, empty, no more than a penny apiece.

What chances one had thrown away! Ten per cent. of those dam' bottles, bought by the dozen so lightly long ago, what would they not fetch now? Anglo-Eurasian Oils would have been chicken-food beside them.

"Bloody awful, ain't it?" he said to Jammy Falkenham, as he came into the cellar. "Makes you cry!"

Jammy Falkenham was wearing his keeper's boots and breeches under a pantry apron, and above was a striped waist-coat which had belonged to Major Bellemy's last footman. He fingered his school tie which he was allowed to wear on off-days when there were no guests in the house.

"Bottles, bottles, everywhere," said Jammy, "and not a drop to drink! And none till next Tuesday! I tried all over New-market *and* Bury. I even told Lady Dagenham's butler I'd swap our young bitch for a case of whisky!"

Bongo nodded. "*Did* you? Well, she's nearly as hard in the mouth, that bitch, as Milly Dagenham. Did he play?"

"Not he, the popsy old swine. Said in *their* house spirits were maintained for medicinal purposes only."

"Didn't you say I was an invalid, too?"

"You, Bongo?" Jammy Falkenham was allowed to call his master "Bongo" only in the cellar, and very late at night.

"Yes, I'm feeling hideous: something awfully wrong about that 'British port'. Last night I only had three glasses and, when I put it away in the sideboard, the dam' cork blew out and nearly shot me!"

"I noticed it smoked a bit when I uncorked it. It's hardly a vintage wine."

"I should just about say it wasn't. Couldn't we dacoit Milly

Dagenham? She'd probably think it was ordinary black market activity."

"She might, but it would lead to a lot of local comment. You'd have to hog your moustache, Bongo, even if you blacked your face."

Bongo's moustache had been a museum piece in his regiment. He jerked his upper lip to make sure of it and squinted down his porcelain nose.

"If this drought persists," he said, "I shall cease upon the midnight not without pain. Are you *sure* you did your best, Jammy?"

"I did. We never got farther than his rozzy still-room. I even gave him Cabinet Particulier for the November Handicap.   "

"I thought we'd been given that one in strict confidence. Didn't he rise?"

"Not a ripple. The old *soor* told me drink and betting were the curse of England. But then he went and backed the rozzy mare in spite of it!"

"How do you know?"

"You could have got fours about her yesterday. This morning I had hell on the blower with Bill Dale's office to get three to two. They said there'd been 'strong support' for her overnight. Lady D. must overpay her butler shockingly, sink him, to bring her down in the betting like that!"

"But, Jammy, what are we going to do about it this weekend. Two of our guns will be here tonight. Where is the 'mellow comradeship' coming from?"

"The *what*?"

"It was *your* advert. '*Skill with gun not so essential as mellow comradeship.*' "

"Beer, I suppose."

"You can't on beer. At least I can't."

"Farm labourers do, often."

"Hang it, Jammy, we want to send 'em out in a blaze of *bonhomie*, slapping each other on the back, and roaring with laughter when they miss a rabbit. I hope they aren't a lot of super-shots in hard training, who simply can't miss!"

Jammy Falkenham was holding a bottle up to the candle-light. His lean, dissipated-classic features, with the curls about his ears, looked almost angelic in the gloom.

"*Eureka!*" he said. "There's a quarter of a tot in this one! Let's get some glasses."

"Look here, Jammy," said Bongo menacingly, "this is *my* cellar. What about your traps?"

"I sprung the lot yesterday. You can't expect me to go gallop-ing round 3000 acres on a shooting morning before we start and its cruel to leave some poor stoat in them for twenty-four hours."

"Well, the number-cards and sticks for the stands, then? I don't want any nonsense about where the blinking guns stand tomorrow. Syndicates are bad enough but when they've never shot here before . . ."

"They're O.K. I did those yesterday."

"Well, buzz off, Jammy, there's a good chap, and tidy up the old racing-programmes on the library floor. It's inches deep in the dam' things and I want that girl to dust a bit before the party comes."

"It's done."

"What?" No one had dusted Bongo's sacred library to his knowledge since April.

"I heard her telling Mrs. Theberton she'd taken 759 matches, 137 cigarette ends, and twenty-five cigarette packets out of the Hoover and it wasn't able to cope with race-cards."

"Curse her cheek! I get through a lot of solid work on form there and I must have everything ready to my hand. . . . Refer-ences! I'll bet that girl has hidden my most important stuff."

"Your guests will prefer it." Jammy rose from his seat on a beer-crate. "Come on, let's milk the empties and get a drink."

"Look here, Jammy. It's time you did some keeperin'. What

251

about the 'excellent prospects' in our advertisement? Scout round the place and try to locate a bird or two."

"We've got plenty in the middle of the old battle-school area, but I can't put the beaters through that!"

"Why not?"

"It's stiff with mines, and those booby traps the Commandos left. If you drive that side you may get some birds but you'll lose a dozen beaters. You can get beaters for seven bob a leg on shooting days, but it'll cost you a dam' sight more if anyone hits a mine. I told you that last April!"

"I know I meant to write to the Command and get a UXB unit sent up here. Didn't I?"

"I'll lay you threes you never posted it."

Bongo Bellemy was getting frustrated and frustration with him meant anger.

"What about the other side, damn it, across the road?"

"It isn't lousy with birds. We shall have to work for 'em."

"But didn't our circular say we'd 'put down 200 hens and cocks'?"

"It didn't say what species. I put down the best part of 200 crows and jays, so it wasn't a lie. We didn't say we'd 'turned down' anything. One wants to be more careful over technical terms, Bongo!"

Major Bellemy flushed. "Rozzy fine shoot this and you're a hell of a keeper. If I beat where the birds are, I lose my beaters and if I go where they aren't, I'll lose my guns! What do we do?"

"Have a drink. You've got a gold mine lurking in these empties. I'll get some glasses."

"A glass," said Bongo firmly. "This is *my* cellar."

"Fair does, Bongo. You used to share my toast when you were my fag."

§ 2

The two spent an hour holding up bottles to the light of a candle and decanting the drops into wineglasses. By much concentration, Major Bellemy amassed two double whiskies, while Mr. Falkenham put together a glass full of gin, rum, sherry and port. It was not easy by candlelight but in 1940, Major Bellemy had fused the electric light for ever during an air-raid when he had found Jammy asleep in a deck chair beside the main bin, surrounded by *Race Form* 1939, the Wine and Food Society's journal, and two empty brandy bottles.

Refreshed, but still gloomy as to the future, they emerged at last into the hall.

"Cleaned my guns, Jammy?"

"I've cleaned it."

"What d'you mean, *it*?"

"I hocked your Number One gun in July; it's still with MacIsaac. But I've got the ticket."

"The deuce you have!" Bongo was really angry now.

"There were my wages and Mrs. Theberton's, and you still owed 'em for cartridges supplied in '39. We had to keep going somehow while you were beating it up in Monte."

"I was on special duty studying Welfare schemes for the post-war Home Guard. I told you that before."

"Anyway, you kept us very tight for money. How did the system pan out?"

"It didn't."

"But it's fool-proof, my dear old boy. We practised it for months, damn it, not only against the wheel but against the book. It never let us down once."

Jammy Falkenham waved towards the bound volumes at the back of the hall. Bound in blue cloth, with merely dates on their backs, they had been sometimes turned to eagerly by guests who thought they were the *Times Literary Supplement*, or the *Squire*. Actually they contained the recorded results of the roulette tables of Monte Carlo from 1871 to 1937.

"I played it three nights running and made my miserable 450 francs a night *à la Labouchère*."

"And then . . .?" Jammy smiled his ascetic smile.

"I met a girl in the bar on the fourth night, an absolute fizzer, with black hair and a red dress."

"Oh, yeah! French?"

"Very much so. And she told me she'd just made 47000 francs by her own system. She said yours was only fit for curates. She offered to teach me!"

"I'll bet she did. How much did *you* win?"

"We never got as far as that. Absolute Mata Hari! She swiped my capital."

"And how did you get home?"

"An awful nice barman cashed my cheques for me, through some merchant prince, Sir William Boulogne, going back to the Savoy."

"That still doesn't leave us with much hooch for tonight. Am I to do butler when they come?"

"Very much so. And you'll have to take off that tie and those gaiters."

"The apron hides them."

"You can't have a butler in gaiters, Jammy, except episcopal ones. Don't be obstinate!"

"Well, if I buttle, I'll ask them for their keys when I take the luggage. Some of 'em may have a bottle with them to drink in their bedrooms. I shall charge 'em corkage!"

"Corkage?"

Jammy Falkenham closed one wary eye. "You ought to turn this place into a club, Bongo. You'd get all the hooch you wanted then."

"Yes, with every blighter in the neighbourhood dropping in for a drink when he'd run out of it. No, thank you. I've forgotten who's coming?"

"Gerald Someone in the Roans and a gunner called Somborne. They're motoring."

"Not Angus Somborne who was in the Skewbald Troop? Fearfully hard case, even for them."

"May be."

"Rode seventeen stone and had a thirst like a fire-engine. If it's him we're doomed! But," Bongo brightened, "he's bound to have a drop of something with him."

"Leave it to me," said Jammy. "I'll get my little hazel-rod out and do a bit of divining when they arrive. If he's got any, he's had it, if you know what I mean."

"Do your best, Jammy, and take off that tie! We may be the strongest trades union in the world but butlers oughtn't to belong to a trades union."

They parted, Bongo to the library, Jammy to breathe on the silver tankards before polishing them with a gun-rag. The empties remained much as they had been before.

§ 3

To "Bongo", a shooting luncheon was a sacred thing. Breakfast he rarely ate; dinner had always been a form of blotting-paper after an evening at the Club or with some boon-companion. One ate it if one remembered it and one's cook had not fallen asleep at his post. But luncheon, as he often remarked, was "the" meal of the day and a shooting luncheon even more so. One had been out for hours in the cold air, and one came in to eat and drink heartily, to hear the latest story, or an inside tip, and to relax after the labours of the morning. To his ancestors the meal had similarly been a sacred rite, whether eaten in the Hall or served in some farm-parlour, or in a hut in the Great Wood.

They had suffered agonies on one of the larger estates near by, a shoot which still bore the impress of the famous "Coke". Here luncheon meant bread and cheese and beer standing up "with one's loins girded" in a ride, with cock pheasants swinging back over you during most of the meal. If one failed to deal with them properly one was not asked again.

Bongo had preserved the family tradition of doing his guests very well, though with rationing at least half the old-time glory of Mrs. Theberton's luncheons had departed. But one custom

255

had never lapsed, and that was the invitation, conveyed statelily by the butler to the headkeeper, to have a glass of wine with "the gentlemen" at the end. In the days of Bongo's father, the headkeeper had been an immense old man with side-whiskers and a glossy spade beard, resplendent in the scarlet waistcoat, the huge buff gaiters and the green velveteens of the Squires of Bottleborough. In he would stump, solemnly doffing his brown billycock with one hand and holding in the other the paper on which was written the pre-luncheon bag.

The pleasant ritual never varied. "Good afternoon, John, a glass of port?" the Squire would say, and John would tower over the seated guests and say, "Thank you kindly, Squire. Me humble duty to the gentlemen," holding the tiny glass in his huge fist; and the bag would be read out, and someone would produce a woodcock out of his game-pocket which he had pretended to forget, as a surprise, and while underlings were "bringing in" the next drive, a solemn discussion would take place between John and the Squire as to what it was best to do next. And then out they would all stump, and do the same drive in exactly the same way as it had been done for the last forty years.

Wartime had brought changes to Bottleborough, not least of which was the fact that Jammy Falkenham combined the dual role of headkeeper and butler. And among other changes had been a growing disinclination on the part of Bongo himself to go out after luncheon if the weather was inclement. At such times his compassion for the beaters' welfare verged on the excessive. To his father, beaters had been merely "bodies", who holloaed and "brushed" and stopped at 2/6d. a day, in smocks provided by the management. But Bongo imagined that if he felt pretty awful after lunch himself, it must be far worse for a beater, who had been wet through since dawn. It was kinder to sit over his port and perhaps a hand of cards, rather than face the weather.

On this occasion he had had quite enough of his guests by

luncheon. There were four, Major Ogle, an old friend of his father's, who had written him so many letters since 1939 that he had to ask him down sometime; Mr. Clewes, a retired Malay Civil Servant who had answered his advertisement; Gerald and Angus Somborne. They had listened throughout the meal to Major Ogle on the Political Situation, Major Ogle on Wet Food versus Dry for Young Pheasants, Major Ogle on Labour, Major Ogle on Gapes, Major Ogle on War-time Changes in the Shooting World, and Major Ogle on Tapeworms in a Golden Labrador.

"And I remember so well, Bertie," he was now booming, "how your dear father once shot nineteen cock pheasants at that very stand we did before luncheon in 1900, in twenty-two cartridges, dividing one bird with Lord Westleton. . . . And the old under-keeper, dear old Israel Cluckhorne, 'Squire,' he said, 'in all my born days,' he said . . ."

"FALL IN THE LOADERS!"

For a moment there was silence and everyone in the farm-parlour pricked their ears. Then through the wall came Jammy's voice again, full of martial fire. "Single rank! Smartly now! Put those second guns down! Properly at ease, the loaders! LOADERS, SHARN!"

"What *is* Falkenham doing out there?" said Bongo peevishly, taking the stopper out of the decanter again.

"Loaders, SHARN! As-you-were! Loaders, SHARN! For inspection . . . . PORT HIPE! Oh, my God! I said *Port*!"

"It's that or whisky," whispered Angus to Gerald. "I thought he looked a bit 'on' just now." He buried his face in his hands.

A year in the Brigade in youth had not altered Jammy's conviction that he was a fine officer *manqué*. He had discarded his apron and, resplendent in the livery of the keepers of Bottle-borough, was standing no nonsense from anyone.

"LOADERS, SHARN! Number Three! you're idling!"

"Hadn't we better be resuming, Bertie?" said Major Ogle hurriedly.

"I think," said Major Bellemy vaguely, "I'll just get Falkenham in and ask him about . . ." Anxious to put off the moment of resumption as long as possible, he opened the door a fraction and bleated "Falkenham!"

"Loaders, SHARN! GROUND HIPE. I said GROUND, that man! STA'AT AISE. EASY. MEN MAY SMOKE!"

Jammy put his hat under his arm, marched in, banged his heels together on arrival, saluted with a quiver of the right arm and said, "Loaders all ready to march off, sir!"

"Don't salute with your hat off, Falkenham," said Major Bellemy, old custom coming to his rescue. "A glass of port?"

As Angus afterwards remarked to Gerald, this was carrying coals to Newcastle with a vengeance. Jammy had, while waiting at luncheon, swallowed two whiskies, a quart of beer, and at least two glasses of "British" port. However he stifled a hiccup, said "Thank y' Squire, me duty, gentlemen", as was the tradition, and swallowed it. The effect was instantaneous, "like flooding a carburettor", as Angus remarked later. Jammy walked up to Major Ogle, placed a trembling hand on his shoulder and said:

"God-awful morning, wasn't it, Major?"

"Ah well," said the Major, flinching slightly, and glancing up, "we can't always have a good day, keeper. So often, y'know, luck, y'know, weather plays a great part in it."

Jammy Falkenham had reached the stage when he did not brook contradiction.

"I didn't mean weather," he said slowly. "Damn-all to shoot and a shocking lot of guns. We got these other three through an ad."

"Falkenham!" said Bongo sternly. He cast an imploring glance upwards but there was truculence in his keeper's eye.

"I tell you we did! Agony column of the *Shquire*! Saw replies myself." His eye wavered round the room. "My God, if it isn't old Angus Shomborne!"

At some period in their chequered school-careers both Angus and Jammy Falkenham had been nursed upon the self-same hill, and luncheon had given Jammy perception which had been denied him overnight. He rushed round the table, shook hands and plumped into a chair. Then he said audibly, "Tell Bongo to shove that decanter along." Bongo blinked and applied his delicate nose to his own glass of port. Everyone else pretended not to notice, while Major Ogle gave a spirited discourse on *Strongylosis* in Grouse with special reference to 1911.

§ 4

"Perhaps," remarked Bongo, fifteen minutes later, seeing that even Major Ogle's tide of reminiscence was beginning to ebb, "we'd better get going. . . . Unless," he added, "you fellers would care for a rubber? It's a rotten afternoon."

"My dear Bertie," put in Major Ogle, "plenty of time for that later. I suppose we do that charming little drive next, over the Squire's Belt on to the heath?"

"Er, yes," said Bongo. "The beaters have gone on. Falkenham!" He glanced down the table.

"He's asleep," whispered Angus. "The gentlemen" then left the room, leaving the headkeeper at the table alone in his glory.

They collected their loaders, who had without orders "taken up arms" from the mud in which Jammy had grounded them, and moved out through the farm towards a line of fir trees half a mile away. Bongo led the way up a footpath.

"My dear Bertie," said Major Ogle in surprise, "hadn't we better do as your dear father always did, and walk this heath in line up to the belt? There used to be a lot of birds on it and one put them into the drive."

Bongo knew there was something, but at that moment he could not remember precisely what it was. Deprived of his henchman he looked round and said irresolutely, "Perhaps we had."

"Good!" said Major Ogle, taking charge, "now-gentlemen-we–line-out-here-please-loaders-between-each-gun-and-keep-your-intervals-we-sweep-all-this-heather-in-up-to-the-belt. The-right-hand-gun-a-little-forward." Gerald and Angus, on the right, began moving along the edge of the heath, with Bongo following them.

Mr. Clewes was examining with interest a strand of barbed wire which ran along the heath ten yards from the path. On it at intervals hung small discs. "What are these little skull-and-cross-bone things?" he asked Major Ogle.

"17th Lancers, I suppose," said the Major. "Their regimental badge. They were stationed here during the war. Death-or-glory boys, y'know. Unit signs y'know. There's bound to be a lot of stuff in *this* drive."

It was Angus who saved the party from immolation. "I say, Bongo!" he roared in his great voice, "my loader says this is an uncleared minefield. Do we walk *through* the rozzy thing?"

"Oh my God," said Bongo despairingly, "I knew there was something!"

"Guns-this-way!" shouted Major Ogle.

§ 5

"Well," smiled Mr. Clewes to Gerald two hours later, "there's one good thing about today: one needn't worry how much to tip the keeper! I always hate that moment, don't you, when everyone gets together and whispers out of the side of his face to the next, 'How much ought we to . . .?' And nobody ever seems to know. . . ."

"Yes," said Gerald, "we are spared that moment this afternoon." Bongo was counting the bag among a group of beaters.

"Don't worry, old boy," said Angus suddenly. "You won't be spared it. Jammy is taking round the hat."

They looked round. Mr. Falkenham, rosy with healthful slumber, was standing just behind them, presenting his billy-cock like an offertory bag to Major Ogle and the bewildered loaders.

§ 6

"Poor Bongo!" said Angus later, as the car swept into New-market. "And to think that in 1930 he was one of the quickest things about a polo-ground you ever saw. Played Three for the Green Dragoons, and had a seven-goal handicap. Fine shot, too. Don't *you* go like that, Gerald my lad, if you're crossed in love!"

"Thanks," said Gerald, briefly, "but I don't think it's likely, even if the other solace was within my means. Whatever made you go there?"

"I couldn't resist answering that advertisement about the '*mellow comradeship*'! And that place was one of the classic estates twenty years ago. Only shot it twice a year—about a thousand head a day—and everything entirely subordinated to shooting. After dinner the butler used to read out the bag solemnly—together with each gun's individual bag. Tremend-ous function! Young men went into training for weeks when they were asked down there. Of course the Commandos

261

skinned it during the war. . . . And now old Bongo can't sack his keeper because he was his fag once and he'd blackmail him over pig-food or blackmarket whisky or something, if he did!" He smoked in silence as the car swept on.

"But I got a most useful line from him about our old friend, Bill Bolony. That man's everywhere! The universal Spiv! Sorry, mustn't talk shop!"

XXVII. DOMESTICS AND THE CHASE

Long ago, the Colonel's mother had promulgated the theory that all cooks, even in the best service, my dear, drank. It was a weakness peculiar to their calling. James Bunbury, then cramming for the Army at Wren's, had been awed to discover that, at Mrs. Bunbury's flat, the spirit-decanter was always carefully locked up to protect it not against himself and his boon companions, but from the onslaught of Mrs. Bunbury's cook, a pale good-looking girl whom James greatly admired.

Had it been, the Colonel wondered, simply thirst produced by the heat of the range? Was it, more likely, a longing for sustenance when her nature was revolted by the sight of the food she was preparing? Or was it some deep moral reaction against her calling which only alcohol could solace? He could not say but he had not forgotten.

When the domestic situation was very strained indeed, the Colonel would now bring out quietly what he called a "noggin", from his tiny store, to placate the wrath of the Goddess-Cook, as jungle men are wont to offer either *zu* or blood to the dark *nats* in whose control they feel they are.

"James! I want you!"

Even from the woodshed, where he was plucking a partridge, James Bunbury could hear that Angela was in one

263

of her moods. Ten years before, there would have been in the background, unseen but not unhearing, a dark being dressed in silk or spotless linen, moving on bare feet over polished floors, who would have answered such a call unfailingly.

"*Koi hai?*" she would have called and the unsleeping one would have hastened forward to minister to her whim. But now, James was the only *chaprassi* Angela could call on for ever more and she made the most of him. "James, must you always leave . . .?" or "James, what *have* you done with . . .?" or "James, I do wish you wouldn't . . ." with a second rhetorical question beginning "How *am* I . . .?" In Heaven, he felt, any ministering angel who wore the faintest sign of a *chapras* would have a very thin time of it from the moment of Angela's arrival.

As he went in, Colonel Bunbury realized that all over England that December morning there must be ex-colonels, and ex-generals for that matter, in the same boat. Gardeners unpaid, who "did" the boots, the coals and the washing-up, who fed the hens, cleaned the car and "mucked out" the pony's stable while their children went to parties; and who came in, as no paid gardener had to do, to get for ever the rough edge of the unpaid cook-general's tongue.

And what an edge it had nowadays! Frayed nerves and the feeling that their day was done, and that they would never more have the opportunity or the money to feel cool and poised and impeccably tidy again, it wore those fallen ladies down! All over England, he thought, battalions of unpaid cooks giving hell to their unpaid gardeners, and neither side able to "give a month" in retaliation.

But for once there was no "rocket", as the Army had it, for him to stop, even though he still wore his partridge-plucking apron.

"James, what's this about a lawn-meet at Stoke Loyalty House?"

"First I've heard of it, m'dear."

"Yes, on Wednesday! Lady Mary *might* have let me know."

"I expect," began the Colonel, but it was no use adding, "she didn't think it of great interest to people who don't hunt." Angela had never hunted but why rub that in? There would be a "smart" crowd and drinks and photography on the steps of the house and "*By-Prattler* stuff" with the Master, and Mrs. Simon Popkiss and Co. who had eyes like vultures for the social occasion. And the hounds would spend hours mucking about, there was no other word for it, in the wood behind the house, which was stiff with foxes, and the whole lot as straight as corkscrews. They might get a gallop of half a mile from Park Wood to Cockroaches, but not more. And if a fox was demented enough to go away towards the downs, he could almost see the phalanx of blathering mothers and motor cars along the Fewdown road. Normally, the local foxes knew what they were in for. No fox had been killed in Stoke Park Woods, except with a shot-gun, for years. They slipped from covert to covert and round and round, with a T.T. herd behind their armoury of wire on one side, and on the other eighty acres of dense firs, which held seven other foxes more wry-necked than the first!

And the Hunt would start digging about two o'clock, and give it up an hour later and go home, mired to their horses' browbands, and think they had been fox-hunting! But perhaps that young new Master didn't know what he was in for. . . .

Aloud he said, "Well, m'dear, suppose you go down to the Meet? I'll be quite happy with a sandwich that day."

"Perhaps I will, but I *do* think Lady Mary . . ."

§ 2

At about that hour the "young new Master", Captain Mike Pembury, was seated with Ann Heriot on Gerald's sofa lighting a pipe. He was a casual brown-faced creature, who had come out of a cavalry regiment with half one leg and a number of severe wounds which had not prevented him riding. With his arm in a sling and his face covered with plaster, he was blaspheming about a horse which had slipped up with him jumping on to a road.

"Clumsy swine lay on me, too," he explained. "Smashed this footling new shin of mine to atoms. Got to go before a Board for a new one next Wednesday. Gerald, you must help me out of a hole. Ann insists!"

Gerald was also filling a pipe. "What do you want?" he asked.

"Well, my kennel huntsman went into hospital with appendicitis yesterday and Ann here, who's whipping in, can't blow a horn and says she won't try and hunt hounds. She prefers to turn 'em. You've got to help me out on Wednesday. This seems the chance we've been praying for."

"What on earth?"

"Why, give 'em a drag! My committee are always grousing I'm not quick enough and I don't do this and that. Don't go well enough, they hint! I've had so much riot all the season I've *had* to go slow and get the rozzy hounds to use their noses. If they really went for a mile, not one of the blighters'd ever see 'em again. Isn't that so, Ann?"

"I believe," said Miss Heriot slowly, "some of the kids would see the end of it! They're as keen as mustard in my pony-club and dying for something to jump. One or two go very well. The rest think far more ..."

"Of their dam' pink coats and the social side. . . . Exactly ... They'll all be photographed on the steps and then be perfectly happy to footle around Stoke Park until teatime. Can't we manage a drag this time and take 'em straight up over the downs?"

"It's the best country we've got tho' there are practically no foxes in it," Ann put in.

"Won't they spot it?" said Gerald.

"I doubt it, if you're quick enough. I'll get Jimmy Welman to say he viewed him on top of the downs." Jimmy Welman was a young keeper who, in spite of his master, had endeavoured to keep a fox in that part of the country.

"It'll need some *bundobust*," said Gerald doubtfully. "Eh, Ann?"

"I believe we could," said Ann. "My brother will be down tonight and he was a good long-distance runner before the war. He'll keep his mouth shut. If he took the line Mike and I were thinking of, we'd get a gallop, and some quite reasonable places to jump. No one need know!"

"But what about the hounds? I've never hunted hounds since 1937 in India, and then I was a stopgap, and they were a pretty bobbery lot."

"Bobbery lot?" said the new Master. "You'll feel like comin' home again when you hunt mine! I've got a lot of sixth-season dogs with noses and no legs, and some second-season bitches with legs and no noses, and a few odds and sods which my committee think are the cat's whiskers because old Lord Purre more or less gave 'em away! They jaw at me about 'em for hours. My God! that *was* a draft . . .! that Verity, for instance! I never know what that bitch is running, a fox, a rabbit, a grey squirrel or a tractor which went past the place a week before. And Paragon! He ought to see our Paragon, oughtn't he, Ann?"

"By the Purre Paradox out of our Goneril," chanted Ann smiling, with her gray eyes on Gerald's ceiling.

"Goneril!" snorted the Master. "What a name for a hound! Where the devil do they get 'em from!"

Angus, who had appeared very silently during this outburst with a decanter of gin, bent with great solemnity over the Master.

"Gonerrril was a bitch in Shakespearre, sirr," he said. "By King Lear, if my memory sairves me, but I never knew the dam's name." He left the room, while Ann and Gerald and the Master got down to what they called a "bit of bundobust" in front of a large-scale map on the wall.

"Well, that's that!" said the Master at last. "Will you and

Ann come round and have a spot of food with me this evening and we'll button it up with Jimmy Welman?"

"Sorry," said Gerald. "If this wind keeps up," he glanced hopefully out of the window, "I'm doing a flight on Mannering's marshes, and God knows when I'll be back." He looked at Ann, hoping she would understand. No girl had ever, so far, come between him and a chance at a duck at flight.

XXVIII. THE PASSING OF A HERO

Ask me no more; thy fate and mine are sealed;
I strove against the stream and all in vain.
—TENNYSON: *The Princess*

A mile away from the main portion of Mr. Mannering's farm were some river-marshes which he used for summer grazing. In winter they were flooded, and near the river was an expanse of rushes and sedges and bog. Mr. Mannering had casually suggested at luncheon in November that if any member of the syndicate cared to "do a flight" for duck there at any time, they were welcome to go on them. Gerald's thanks had been swamped in the flood of wildfowling reminiscence loosed by Major Ogle about "the old days" at Keyhaven and Blakeney.

Of the members of the syndicate likely to be found there after eight o'clock on a stormy December night, Mr. Mannering would probably have put Sir William Boulogne last but one. But there he was indubitably, four days before Christmas, standing below the winding road, on a grassy marsh wall which fringed the drainage dykes running to the river. A nearly full moon was boring a pale yellow hole through dark and racing clouds, and at times seemed to race westwards with them.

Sir William wore his plum-coloured suit and the white spats which took his valet such a time to clean. But in deference to the weather, he had added a wadded leather flying-coat (the

269

gift of an airman who had slept the clock round in the Taper Club) and fur-lined gloves. His fingers could barely get inside the trigger-guard of his gun. He was stamping his feet, which felt bitterly cold in his nut-brown polished brogues. The dyke beneath him also shivered in the icy wind and there was a faint hiss of reeds from the edge of the water.

Never before, in his enterprising career, had Sir William yearned so deeply for a confidant as he did at that moment; although his latest venture had seemed quite straightforward, so far, beginning with the visit of the quartermaster-serjeant who had known Private Tompkins in Cairo, and ending with a dinner in Soho with old Ikey McLeod.

"Club nearly dry, d'yer say, Bill?" Mr. McLeod had muttered with a glance of his queer sidelong eyes. "Well, a few days now, and you won't know y'self, or Gigoleo either! Swimmin' in it you'll be, and good stuff too. Now remember! 'Ave your gun with you, and if anyone asks anything, you're shooting!"

"At night? What can you see to shoot at night?"

"Flighting, they calls it technically. It's ducks you're after: nocturnal bastards, sleep all the blessed day somewhere, only get up for supper. Wrap y'self up well! It'll be perishing cold. And the dough in pound notes! And look 'ere, just in case, mind yer, I'll throw in a bit o' camouflage, a real duck to 'ave with yer, a wild one. My dear boy, there can't *be* a hitch, and once inside your stables at Littlemersh . . ."

Ikey McLeod had kept his word. He had come back from Leadenhall next day and slipped into Sir William's car a large dark-brown duck, obviously not a farmyard bird. Sir William had carried it a few minutes before from his car, before sending Tompkins off to wait down the road. It felt limp and heavy, cold and thoroughly repulsive. But it lay at his feet, the indubitable proof of his marksmanship, the object for which one "flighted". It was, as always, the little details that counted in the picture.

Sir William looked at the racing moon, shivered again and

thought: Flighting! What a pastime! Only savages would come to this outlandish place at such an ungodly hour to shoot. What barbarians the English gentry still could be! And he thought with longing of Tompkins in the car, his feet on the electric warmer, Sir William's own rug round his knees, and the harsh world shut out by the genius of the Broadcasting Corporation.

§ 2

Never again, thought Sir William, next time Gigoleo can come. Only if anyone did happen along, he supposed Gigoleo on the edge of a marsh, attired for the chase, would give himself away at once if he did not die of exposure first. They needed someone like himself, a hard virile type, who would dress like a sportsman and look like one too.

Down near the pollards on the river bank, Sir William could discern the gleam of flood water under the moon. From it he saw suddenly two faint spurts of light and then the reports of a gun came to him on the wind.

Some other sportsman must actually be shooting down there, waist deep in water and slime! Sir William glanced down at his white spats and shuddered again. To him shooting was something you did on a sunny autumn day, or for a few hours round about noon in winter. You sat on a shooting-seat with ladies behind you, and were "snapped" for the *By-Prattler* "in action" against a parklike background, with a pheasant just falling to your unerring aim. That moment had been one of Cyril de Bourbon's favourite "shots", the dignified amusement of a gentleman.

But whoever had invented flighting must have a hideously distorted intellect. To Sir William wild duck had hitherto been things that dived for crumbs in St. James's Park, or something on a card—*canetons sauvages rotis aux petits pois*—and you cocked eighteenpence on the price on account of their being *sauvages*. But now, having seen how one had to come by them, he would make that surcharge two-and-ninepence the moment he got back to Maddox Street. It was like the "mountain grouse" about which Gigoleo and Sir Giles Wallaby Bart. had had a little dust-up in August, though nearly everyone had accepted the extra charge resignedly in a bad grouse-year, and Mr. Heinkel, the Under-Secretary for Power and Gas, ate grouse regularly at every meal, having considerably more money to spend than he had ever earned before.

But wild duck in future in the Taper Club would have to toe the line like grouse. When the Lateral Party came into power, they would "rationalize" the duck-question beginning with St. James's Park. Sir William liked to feel that one day he would stroll out of Downing Street followed by two loaders, and stand on a good asphalt path while all those useless park ornaments were put over his head. Then he would pull them down out of the skies, watched by adoring thousands. But for the moment . . . an icy gust swept across the marsh and he shuddered again and fumbled in his pocket for his flask.

It was a good flask, one of the silver-necked tapering kind affected by hunting people, and Sir William had sometimes recounted to urban admirers the terrific hunts he had had with the Quitechley when carrying it on his saddle. It was now full of cherry-brandy, almost the last bottle in the Club, and Sir William swigged it gratefully.

Ah! that was better! The loneliness, the night, the tearing wind and the racing moon swam once more into proper focus. This was adventure! For a man of spirit there were endless opportunities. The blood of those ancestors, who had run cargoes of Syrian lovelies from the Lebanon to Jerusalem, throbbed again in Sir William's veins. This was only a legitimate diversion of Army stores destined for the officers' messes of the transit camps at Le Havre or Calais. The Army always had far too much at absurdly cut prices. Besides . . . . there wouldn't *be* any officers' messes in ten years time, for the Lateral Party meant to abolish officers when they rationalized the forces, "in order not to exacerbate class-conscious-ness". And it was the greatest mistake to waste good alcohol on young officers on the eve of demobilization. Just when they ought to be entering, clear-eyed and earnest, on the austerity of their new lives, the Army sent them out with a hangover or in a state of muddled optimism. That was not the spirit at all, when peace was going to be far worse than war. Any diversion of alcohol from the forces' messes to the Taper Club clearly helped on the national effort at recovery. He took another swig.

As he replaced his flask, he felt the great bulge of notes in his inside pocket. For £1250 down he had been promised 1000 bottles and by George, thought Sir William, if that outlay didn't bring forth some fivefold, some fiftyfold, before the New Year, he didn't know London. What a power of good could be accomplished by a man of free enterprise, prepared to risk all for his vision! In an hour that cargo would be safely under lock and key in his stables at Littlemersh, ready to be sent up to London, batch by batch, in the great boot of the Rolls. And when it reached the Club, what a change would come o'er the spirit of so many people's dreams! With a fluid ounce of that in their bosoms, and Al Consomme's baritone trembling on their ears, men would love women, and women's eyes would glow divinely at men, there would be generous afterthoughts and noble resolutions and lucrative deals put through in a glow of mutual understanding. Minds would take fire, and wits would flash and sparkle, and poor Dryden Moggs (who had written his only masterpiece thirty years ago on black coffee and now could barely register except after a pint of kummel), might even give the world a worthy sequel to *Honey-moon Tremens*.

Once that cargo reached London, the shares of Man, Limited, warworn, depressed and under par, would go to a premium. It was not sleep but alcohol which was Nature's soft nurse. Sir William felt already like Jove motioning to Bacchus, pater-nally, to "carry on".

He took another sip and his thoughts raced up and onwards with the racing moon. What couldn't he accomplish in the next two years when he had done so much already! The new school-ties and shirts which his company had made before de-mobilization were flowing forth steadily into the quickening mainstream of ex-soldiers. He was almost ready to sell the fac-tory. His other clothing company, sub-piloted by Ikey McLeod, was doing very well, buying the clothes back for cash from the soldiery, as they whistled their way out of the de-mobilization centres. His visit to Gallowgill had enabled him to start a very prosperous little new company, Boleyn and William Limited, which delivered pork and mountain mutton and rabbits from the fells in plain vans to clubs with a busy luncheon-membership. And there was always the sunshine of the azure coast awaiting him, and a horde of people who wanted only 5000 francs to "square up" against cheques to be cashed in London.

> *And moving on from high to higher*
> *Becomes on Fortune's crowning slope*
> *The pillar of a people's hope,*
> *The centre of a world's desire.*

That would be his destiny yet, when the Lateral Party held the reins. He looked down at the savage marshland under the moon and thought, "Not much in the portfolio of Rural Up-lift! You couldn't do a lot with people who were so brutalized that they could find amusement in places like that!"

Again came the report of a gun from the flooded waste below, and then again. That madman still shooting away down there! Must be starving to keep on like that!

Come to think of it, thought Sir William, his real cup of tea would be the Ministry of Repopulation. That only needed integrating: control of the stage, the film and liquor industries, broadcasting, holiday camps, swing-music, cosmetics and women's dressmaking, all those facets of modern life which helped to keep the vital sex-urge of the nation at fever heat. He would put the birth-rate up or he wasn't William Boulogne! He saw himself resplendent in a superb lounge-suit going round the factories, giving pep talks on Repopulation, accompanied by Mona Joy, and other film-stars, revitalizing the nation. Yes, by gum, Repopulation was the portfolio for him!

§ 3

Someone in heavy boots was splashing towards him. Sir William posed himself alertly, as if waiting for birds to come, the stock resting lightly on his thigh, the dead duck at his feet. A dim figure with a gun on its shoulder edged its way across a narrow plank which spanned the dyke, and clumped up on to the marsh wall. Sir William saw in the moonlight a young man, dripping and muddy, who wore a cap-comforter over his ears, thigh boots, and a leather jerkin. In one hand dangled a sodden muddy bunch of birds.

"Hullo!" said the figure. "Any luck?" Then with a start, "It's Sir William Boulogne, isn't it? Good evening, sir!"

"Good evening! Who are you?"

"Gerald Warde. I never guessed anyone else was here. I stayed on long after flight-time—perishing cold, too—because they still kept coming in and the clouds were just right against the moon."

Most of this was Greek to Sir William. He said, "Indeed."

Gerald looked at Sir William's gleaming spats. "Did you get a shot *here* at all?"

"I shot one duck," said Sir William grandly, indicating the dark-brown form at his feet. "And you?"

"Eleven teal, four tufted and a mallard," said Gerald. "And I knocked down a shoveler but couldn't pick it."

Sir William had not realized how many technical terms of this nature there were in duck-shooting. He looked at the sodden row of birds which Gerald was turning over. They seemed very small compared with his own. "Young ones, I see," he said rather patronizingly.

275

"Young ones be damned." Gerald flashed his torch on the duck at Sir William's feet and said "Good Lord!"

"A very fine duck," said Sir William impressively.

"I agree, sir. I should think it must be a record."

The older man said "Really?" Over his mental retina passed a slide of a large brown duck in a glass case with an inscription beneath it, "Shot by Sir William Boulogne on 21 Dec. 45 on Loyalty Fen." He saw paragraphs in the *Squire*: "*A magnificent specimen of well-whatever-duck-it-was-technically was shot recently in a gale on Loyalty Fen, Harkshire, by Sir William Boulogne, the well-known sportsman. It weighed . . .*" He must get it weighed when he got home.

So he said, "Er, Major Warde, what did you say was the technical term for this duck?"

"Khaki Campbell," said Gerald. "I'm pretty sure it's the first time anyone's shot one at flight in *this* county. Good-night, Sir, *bonne chasse!*"

He slung his gun over his shoulder, picked up the little ducks, and thumped off in his thigh boots towards the road.

A Campbell was it? A Scotch duck! Good, his mother had been a Macintosh. He seemed to have heard of Scotch woodcock but did not know they also had their own ducks. Exclusive beggars, the Scotch. And once again, his mind roved to the question of what tartan he would wear in the fullness of time.

§ 4

Far away where the lonely road curved round the side of the wooded hill, following the indentations of the marsh, he saw at last a radiance in the sky and then the headlights of a vehicle coming slowly towards him. They vanished, then re-appeared a little nearer. Five minutes more and that precious cargo of inspiration would be his. He fingered the notes in his pocket and tilted the last of the cherry brandy into his mouth.

Then he climbed the stile and stepped on to the road. What

was the pass-word Ikey had taught him? Some Urdu word, *"Mila-gya"*, meaning "Got it?" The lorry rounded the corner. Sir William stepped out of the hedge-shadow, the duck in his hand, his gun under his arm. The lorry stopped as if expecting him. There were three men on the front seat.

"*Mila-gya?*" said Sir William.

"*Mila-gya!* Sir William Boulogne?"

"No, William Bullen."

"O.K. guv'nor. Hop up in the back, will yer. It's all on."

It was with difficulty that Sir William obeyed this injunction on account of his build, especially when that build was encased in a wadded flying-coat and cumbered with a gun and a dead duck. But willing hands hoisted him up into the lorry, and he found himself sitting on a wooden case with tiers of other wooden cases reaching to the roof above him. Good, four tons of it at least! There were men sitting squashed in the gap down the centre of the lorry between the tiers of cases. The lorry gathered speed.

"*Mila-gya?*" said Sir William again politely.

"*Mila, sab teek hai.*"

Sir William had not been in India but he knew that *sab teek* meant "O.K." or words to that effect. He looked at his wristwatch. Twenty minutes to get to Littlemersh, fifteen to unload, and five to settle up! The glow of the cherry brandy and the icy December wind warmed his cheeks.

Inside the lorry, out of the wind, all was warm and peaceful. Port after stormy seas! It was the last "flight" he ever intended to do except in St. James's Park, and that would be after the Lateral Party's accession to power. He thought of that wretched young Warde, trudging homewards in his great thigh boots, soaked and muddy and thinking that the puny ducklings he had shot were worth the agony of obtaining them. "Nocturnal bastards—only get up for supper," Ikey had said. Ikey knew. If a fly settled on Ikey, it scalded itself, he was so hot, someone had told him. But one thing Sir William also knew: those bottles surrounding him would be worth £5000 to him before he'd finished. They held the divine motive spirit without which London night life did not really move.

The lorry bumped on to the main road. Two miles along it and then the Littlemersh turning. Sir William's heart leaped up in the glow of the cherry brandy within him. Only about seven minutes more! He lit a cigarette, tapping it impressively on his great golden case. In the light of the match, he glanced at the man in front of him, squashed between the tiers of cases. Great hulking ruffian with ear-rings and a duffle coat and one of those peaked yachting caps such as seafaring men wore. Off the docks probably, for the lorry had been "diverted" on its way to a ship loading up for Le Havre. Handsome ruffian, too, with brown regular features which seemed somehow familiar. . . . The match went out. Suddenly he realized that they had passed the Littlemersh turning, and he said, "You've passed it!"

A quiet voice answered from the gloom: "That's all right, Sir, we know exactly where to go!"

They must be taking the Chawborne turning, a mile longer but a better road. Sir William relaxed. What restful stuff that cherry brandy was! After his icy vigil he felt sleepy.

Suddenly the lorry stopped. Sir William pulled the tilt aside and glanced out. Above him was a severe row of houses, on the end window of which gleamed in blue letters the words:

HARKSHIRE
POLICE
OFFICE

A heavy hand closed on his shoulder. "I wouldna flee, Sir Wulliam!" said the voice of Angus. Another quiet voice spoke in his ear.

"I am a police-officer, Sir. Would you be good enough to come in for a few minutes? We have reason to believe . . ."

§ 5

Hell must be like this, thought Sir William, with glaring lights and hard chairs and large, lounging unbelieving men, who looked at you like a butterfly on a pin, and on whom your finery made no impression at all; who gave warnings, and asked questions, and wrote down all the answers; who simply would not believe that you had just "thumbed a lift" home, after an exhausting night's wild-fowling.

The sweat trickled down into Sir William's astrakhan collar. Irrelevantly the Superintendent said: "What did you say you were doing down there?"

"Flighting for ducks." Sir William pointed to the brown corpse.

"You shot this?"

"Of course."

"On the wing?"

"Certainly."

The Superintendent picked up Sir William's gun and stared for twenty seconds up the barrels against the glaring lamp. Then he said, quietly, "Well, I suppose someone's seen a Khaki Campbell flying, and I suppose some people clean their guns the moment they finish shooting, but I never met either yet! Watson, get a newspaper and pluck that bird carefully on to it. I want to count the shotholes. Don't make a mess now!"

The little details! He had always been such a one for those. How much they counted! What a fool he had been, over an hour with nothing to do but fill the flaming duck up with shotholes!

He pulled himself together. "This is a monstrous mistake. I can explain everything at the proper time and place. I decline to make a statement until I have consulted my solicitor."

"O.K., but he won't love you much for this one. Can we have his address and we'll telephone him?"

Sir William had a vision of his Mr. Hyams, tucked up safely

in bed with two hot water-bottles and his massive spouse, oblivious of the throes in which his most spectacular client was writhing. It was followed by a vision of his first interview with Mr. Hyams, also writhing in a chair and moaning: "But my dear Sir William, surely you *didn't* . . .? and you *said* . . .? Oh dear! oh dear! oh dear!"

And then the clinging mist of the cherry brandy swept across the whirlpool of his brain. He was back in the Taper Club, with its soft lights, its discreet attendance, its confidence and warmth and harmony. Al Consomme was at the microphone, his white teeth gleaming in his great black face, the spot-light focussed on his hennaed curls, and a tear of genuine passion in his eye as he crooned the Club's theme-song which they had borrowed without acknowledgment:

So fold thou up, my dearest, thou and slip
Into my boo-som and be lo-o-ost in me-e!

If only he could! Another tear trickled down Sir William's wind-whipped swarthy cheeks. Somehow the Portfolio of Re-population seemed a little further away even than 1950. He wondered dizzily where Tompkins was.

Tompkins at that moment, his name and all particulars having been taken in another room, was speeding up the London Road without waiting for his employer, like a hunted fox, his mask set for the Taper Club. His face was white and every hair was quivering beneath the frozen waves which held them in their place. He had only been on parade once since 1939 and that was that identification parade in Tripoli in the matter of a million cigarettes. Just at the moment, it looked very much as if Tompkins had been "warned" for another parade.

§ 6

Gerald had been to sleep in his bath and now in a dressing-gown was reading by the smoking-room fire, his weather-beaten face redder even than usual. To him entered Angus, still wearing his duffle-coat and a peaked cap which was two sizes too small for him.

"Hullo, sailor!" said Gerald. "Back again! Would you like to be a butler for a few minutes and get us both a drink? There's beer and I believe there's still a little rum in the sideboard."

Angus came back with the drinks and sat down in a chair to light a pipe.

"Any luck?" said Gerald. To him it had been a "super" evening in a place where no one came, with Fate slinging swift black prizes at his head out of the wrack of clouds against the gleam of the moon, to be snatched before they vanished for ever. That was flighting, a hidden rapture which so few really knew!

"We bagged two birds," said Angus, "and the second I fear was an even finer one than the first, a member of your Syndicate."

"Tell me all about it," said Gerald.

Angus began. "I felt rather a cad," he concluded, "but I promised Reggie Troup last July I'd lend him a hand. Never guessed it would end up on a marsh within a few miles of here. Poor old Bill Bolony! Almost I find it in my heart to pity him; but when I think of you and me, Gerald, goin' round the desert in '42 with our tongues hanging out for one drink a week and ten cigarettes because NAAFI supplies were short, I'm not so sure!"

"How did you get on to him?"

"Oh, he's got irons in every fire and he's marvellously covered up, like all the Lateral Party. One day someone will rumble his pet racket of financing holiday-makers in Paris and Cannes with francs which I believe were pinched by the German Army in 1940. But that won't be yet! Queerly enough, what gave us a line on him was that remark he made to you at your first meeting with him about a hunt he'd had with the Quitechley."

"I remember. In the Savernake." It was that faraway evening after Gerald had been sentenced to death. He had been wet through tonight for three hours in an icy wind but somehow the thought of his impending doom had ceased to worry him.

"Well, I wrote to Jack Osgerby, their Secretary, and found out Bill Bolony had subscribed twenty quid one year during the war, though the only time he was ever out he was superbly mounted on a heavy-weight black limousine. But when the Hunt got into difficulties over catering for their wire-fund ball, Bill said he knew a 'little man' who might do it. So they got a licence and along came the little man with lashings of drink; and Bill turned up in a pink evening coat at the ball wearing some rather dim hunt-button which Jack Osgerby thought was the Lanphysiog or the Epping Forest Bloodhounds. And afterwards there was a hell of a row about certain NAAFI supplies disappearing from a divisional headquarters, but by that time so had the little man. And then everyone was too busy with the war to enquire."

"I shouldn't have thought that got you very far," said Gerald.

"No, but it gave me a line. And I had one already. Do you remember when I told Gigoleo in the Taper Club you were the new Under-Secretary for Power and Gas, and *ghabraoed* him into giving us another bottle?"

"Yes, you old blackmailer."

"Well, he popped off and sent us a good one out of store; most of their stuff is a bit adulterated by the time it reaches the client. Thought we should be useful later, I suppose. And they had barely time to change the original label and slapped on a wet one which came off in my hands. I'll bet you that cargo of his tonight would have increased mightily by the time it reached the Taper clubmen, except his own special pets." He yawned. "My job is over for the time being. I'll ask Mannering if I can take Bill's place next Saturday. Why not come up to town for a night and have a beat-up?"

"Sorry, Angus. I'm hunting hounds for Mike Pembury on

Wednesday, and I've got to spend tomorrow in the kennels with Ann Heriot and Mike, learning their blasted names! There's already been a row between Mike and his committee because two of them think they're Heaven-sent huntsmen and want a chance to show it. It won't look well if I haven't a clue which hound is which. And by-the-way, Lady Mary rang up tonight, to borrow my 'manservant' to help with the drinks at the meet. It's a lawn-meet with the County in full force, so I said you would. She said you *must* be properly dressed."

"I will," said Angus. "I will have my last fling as a butler and give them good measure."

"You'll have to take off those ear-rings," said Gerald. "And keep your collar and tie on this time."

XXIX. LAWN MEET AT LADY MARY'S

Went the day well? We died and never knew.
— From an Epitaph

An American, soldiering in England during the war and observing the tribal customs of his ancestors, had once attempted to join the Mid-Harkshire Hunt-Club, to the consternation of the Committee. He had described it later, in a University journal, as "a form of secret society, designed ostensibly for the destruction of foxes", though, he was careful to add, "its primary function seems in danger of falling into desuetude". In an appendix he had devoted much research to ascertaining the numbers of "foxes killed", "foxes missing, believed killed", and "foxes otherwise captured" in the last twelve seasons. But the social activities of the Hunt had survived immutably through two wars, and constant changes of Master, and as yet no farmer had been admitted to membership or the right to appear at the hunt-ball.

Fields in 1945 were small, and were composed mainly of the Committee, children home from school and farmers who made a living from show-jumping and horse-dealing, with occasional business-men from London who kept a horse at livery and hunted one day a week. Some of the elderly lawgivers on the Committee had not ridden a hunt for fifteen years.

A lawn-meet, however, at Stoke Loyalty House, by special invitation of Lady Mary Wenhaston, was one of those functions which everyone endeavoured to attend. Even old Mr. Francolin turned out, resplendent in the "full fig" of the nineties. He liked to say that he had hunted for fifty seasons, though it now needed four strong men to help him mount, three on the leg side and one on the off, lest Mr. Francolin should miss the horse altogether in the act. There was Major Ogle, the main repository of the hunt-traditions, a tribal vessel of Mid-Harkshire lore, and his brother-in-law, Captain Sparrow, late of the Yeomanry, who wrote accounts of the hunt's activities under the pen-name of "Spadger". Both had once forty years ago whipped in to the London University beagles and on the strength of it had been decidedly critical of all professional huntsmen ever since. The other members of the Committee had been more or less "grounded", like aircraft, on account of structural defects or obsolescence. John the runner was also there, an untidy old man now far gone in drink, who had once been huntsman and lorded it over his field, smart as paint, for years until the fatal day when, savage with toothache and the loss of a favourite hound, he had damned his Master's eyes for an "interfering fool". Since then poor John had gone steadily down the ladder, but he usually managed to be there or thereabouts with the hunt-terriers in winter, and in summer earned a precarious living by selling programmes at agricultural shows.

And among the crowd of adoring children who surrounded the hounds was Master James Bunbury, the Colonel's son, on a stout bay pony with a crest like a bull, which came in on hunting mornings for a feed of oats and was turned out after hunting to groom itself in the manner peculiar to grass-fed ponies.

Among the foot-people, Colonel Bunbury was there, in a neat tweed suit and fieldglasses, wistfully recalling the days when he had spent his leaves in Northamptonshire with three horses and no family to care for. Rosamund Gore-Ambulance was also there, for she and Roger had been invited down for the week-end by Sir William Boulogne. His arrest and the refusal of bail had greatly disorganized their plans. They were now roosting precariously in Angela's house and at any moment the argument about Miss Gore's money might, as the newspapers put it, "precipitate a crisis". Col. Gore-Ambulance, pale and ascetic in a blue overcoat, turned his cold eye on the chattering throng, as if he was quite prepared to operate on the lot of them without anaesthesia.

In spite of his dislike of "sportswomen", Cyril de Bourbon was there too, garnering copy for the *By-Prattler*. Most of the members of the Hunt needed no urging to pose for Cyril on the steps of Loyalty House, in attitudes of careless ease which contrasted strangely with some they displayed ten minutes later on a horse. And the inevitable Mrs. Simon Popkiss, who had swooped down specially with her adolescent daughter, saw to it that she and Lady Mary were in the group. After that Cyril, wavering round with his camera and notebook, was shocked to find that his suspicions at the Taper Club of Miss Ann Heriot had been correct. There she was, very neatly dressed in a dark blue coat and a velvet cap, among the very hounds! Cyril was so disgusted that he only took one snap of the pack. He was careful to include in the picture both the huntsman, Gerald, and his lady whipper-in, lest the hounds should eat him in the process. But he shut his eyes when focussing and hoped sincerely that Ann would not come out.

Angus was also there, very solemn in his black coat, and taking round trays of drinks. He managed to slip a double rum to old John the runner, another to Rosamund Gore-Ambulance disguised as a dry martini (which led to words between herself and her husband about "alcoholism" later), and a third to Gerald, whom he suspected of having cold feet. After the photographs, he found himself with his tray close to Mrs. Simon Popkiss and Angela Gore-Bunbury. Both ladies were talking loudly as if the silent villagers who surrounded them did not exist. Mrs. Simon Popkiss (still smarting under the recollection of that July paragraph in the *By-Prattler* about her vixen-fur from the South Notts country), was careful to appear this time, well in advance of local fashion, in a white duffle-coat attributable to the Royal Navy, and a pair of fur-lined flying boots. She had borrowed a pony for her own daughter from a small girl in the village who had broken her collarbone, and was now watching the daughter's ungainly efforts at mounting it.

"I can't think, my dear Angela," said Mrs. Popkiss loudly, oblivious of the fact that the small girl was standing only a yard away, "what possessed anyone to buy that child an old mare like that?"

The small girl blushed scarlet and turned aside to hide a tear of shame. Was her adored "Bumps" really as bad as that?

"Nor can I," said Angela with equal scorn. "She's frightfully badly let down. . . ."

"By her rider, ye mean, mem?" said Angus, in a still louder voice, appearing at her elbow with his tray. "Aye, but one day your wee gairl will lairn to ride, and then ye'll see what a grand awld jumper the mare can be!"

Angela and Mrs. Popkiss drew themselves up to their full heights and glared at Angus, like queen cobras at a cockatrice.

"That's cherra brandy, mem, in the wee glawsses," Angus went on imperturbably. "Ye'll hae a drap now? Forbye, in the cauld weather, it doesna gang to a body's nose." He ambled away amiably with his tray.

§ 2

Gerald, in a borrowed pink coat of Mike Pembury's, and surrounded by a ring of adoring children on every sort of pony, was conning over the hounds whose names he had learnt on the previous day, and fretting at the delay. He was feeling "unusually bloody" that morning, as he had done so often before a race or a polo-match or a battle, and the sight of Col. Gore-Ambulance's pale face at the meet had suddenly brought home

288

to him that he had "less than a year to go". Both he and Ann guessed there was a scent at the moment, but how long the drag would last and whether it would hold on the chalk at the top of the downs, they did not know. To him appeared Angus again with a tray of drinks.

"Buck up!" said Angus over his horse's wither. "The old Cock-Spadger was frightfully curious about you and wanted to know if you'd ever hunted hounds before, so I told him you'd hunted the Buccleuch in their record season in 1936. He's now in the library trying to verify that out of Bailey."

"Blast you, Angus," said Gerald. "I wish they'd let us get along."

There was a stir at last in the chattering throng by the House and the villagers surged over to witness the time-honoured ceremony of hoisting old Mr. Francolin on to his horse. Major Ogle trotted up to Gerald.

"I expect, Warde," he said importantly, "you'd like me to go to that little place I always watch in the first draw."

Gerald, mystified, glanced at Ann. Her left eye seemed to flicker for a second.

"Thanks," he said, "if you wouldn't mind."

"I'd better get ahead then," said Major Ogle and clattered off up the park to his outpost. (He had once viewed a fox there and had never forgotten it.)

"Where *has* he gone?" said Gerald out of the side of his mouth to Ann.

"He thinks we're going to draw Park Wood," said Ann. "It's usually the first draw."

As the hounds, preceded by Miss Heriot, jogged out of the park into the lane, Captain Sparrow reined up alongside Gerald.

"I expect you'd like me to act as Second Whip today, Warde?"

"No, thank you very much," said Gerald, forewarned by Mike Pembury. "I think we can manage." He turned to look at the cavalcade behind him. Squashed into the ditch among the leading horses, was a small pink boy, with very large red ears standing out almost at right angles beneath an old velvet cap. Ann Heriot had told Gerald about him overnight. "You're James Bunbury, aren't you?" said Gerald, beckoning. "I want you to help me in the wood, James my lad, when we draw."

Tears of adoration came into Master Bunbury's eyes, and he almost dropped his new whip. As the cavalcade trotted past the gate of Park Wood, Gerald could hear the murmurs break out behind him: "Where the deuce is he going to ...? We never... We always..." Capt. Sparrow tried again.

"Wherever are you going, Warde?" he shouted. "Park Wood's the first draw and then Cockroaches."

Again, as when a brigadier had crossed him at polo, Gerald took mental refuge in the saying, "On the turf and under it all men are equal."

"Well, we're not assing about there today," he said shortly. "We're drawing Morshanger."

Five minutes brought them to the edge of the steep down. Gerald turned again to Capt. Sparrow. "Keep the field, please, down this bottom side. Get on, Ann, to the end, will you!" They had agreed that she should keep round the lower edge of the hanger at first in order not to arouse suspicion.

Followed by James Bunbury, Gerald rode up the sloping path. Fearing what the Master had told him about riot, he planned to keep his hounds together until they got near the dense patch of thorns from which Ann's brother, Bill, had commenced to lay the drag. As he rode, Gerald's mind was a quivering mass of apprehension. Mike Pembury had assured him that some of the "bobbery lot" would run almost anything that moved or smelt. Supposing they wouldn't run a drag? Supposing his old hounds, the ones "with noses and no legs", wouldn't own it? Supposing there was a real fox there, or the place was lousy with rabbits? Random and Canopy had already slipped into the wood and he dared not delay things by rating them. Supposing the drag had failed while they were coffee-housing ...?

"Oh, hell," he said at last, his cavalry training coming to his rescue. "It's no ruddy good supposing. Let's get on ahead and see what it's like!"

Then as he cheered them into the bushes and heard the sudden tangled chimes break out above him, he knew that suppositions were, as usual, in vain. And less than a minute later from far up the hill came the voice of Ann (miraculous Ann, thought Gerald, to have got round there in the time) hollering "Gone away—away—awhaii!"

Blowing his horn furiously, Gerald cantered up the steep path watching the ever-widening gap between his horse's saddle and his mane. Behind him thundered James Bunbury, tears of rapture in his eyes, the bay pony pulling like a train, his saddle slipping back as far as it would go. And from the crest of the down came a full-throated roar from Jimmy Welman, the keeper who had been instructed, in strictest confidence, to "view him".

Two minutes later Gerald scrambled up to the crest and saw the hounds three hundred yards ahead running down the side of a great thorn-fence. Ann had waited. "So far, so good," said Gerald. "We've lost Random and that white-ticked bitch (Canopy, ain't it?) at the start but the rest are all on." He looked down and could see his field, some thundering up the path, a score at least of the knowing ones galloping eastwards along under the down.

"Come along, Ann! I'm afraid the pace'll bust 'em even if there was nothing to jump."

§ 3

"Well, that's that," said Miss Heriot, pulling her mare alongside Gerald's, as the pack threw up in a ride near the centre of Druid's Wood. "Don't you think I laid you out a very nice little jump-course?"

"You did," panted Gerald. "What happens next?"

"Bill's lifted it here for 300 yards. Let's keep 'em together or they'll be all over the place! Warrior, *Warrior*! I must say Mike and Will have got 'em much fitter than I thought they were, but I believe old Chancellor knows it's a drag. We turn left-handed here, and have about three miles more with a little lepping to the *Rose and Crown* at Winnington Scrubs, where our survivors will probably need a drink badly."

"But are there any survivors?" said Gerald, looking up towards the empty down.

"I'll back two of my Pony Club to get here," said Ann, "even if they've lost their ponies and have to walk." She counted the pack quickly. "I make it Random, Canopy and that bitch Verity short. Otherwise, much to my surprise, we seem to be all on! *Chancellor*! G'bike to 'im, Chancellor."

Old Chancellor, regardless of the rate, was moving up the slope into the trees, his stern lashing furiously. A moment later they heard him speak above them in some bushes.

"My God Almighty, I do believe it's a fox!" said Gerald, as the hounds rushed from him. "What the hell does A do now?"

"A," smiled Ann, catching her mare short by the head, "won't argue with the dispensations of divine Providence. Come on, Gerald, it *is* a fox!"

§ 4

Master James Bunbury, aged ten, sat on his steaming pony in his sister's cast-off "reach-me-downs", outside Druid's Wood, unseen by all except perhaps by the shade of his grandfather who, like the Colonel, had "gone really well" to hounds. James's velvet cap was covered with mud, and his face was freckled like a moorhen's egg with mud-splashes, but it and his full-sailed ears were brimming with health and achievement. No one (except perhaps his grandfather) had instructed James Bunbury where to go or what to do, when he had struggled up the last slope to Druid's Wood, but he had decided that someone ought to look out that side, and it was the down-wind side where he hoped to hear the horn or hounds if they did go out in any other direction. James had already taken two falls, once "complete with pony" and once slightly in advance of the pony, when it had jumped a post-and-rails which had effectually stopped most of the field. James reflected with satisfaction that he had only one more fall to make up the thirteen, without which, someone had assured him, no one could really claim to be a horseman.

All was silent in the wood, for the drag had been lifted and Gerald, Ann and the hounds were having their momentary breather below in the main ride. James did not know this but he sat still and listened with both his large ears. He heard a sound behind him and a white hound cast up, trailing along in the indeterminate way stray hounds so often affect, as if they knew exactly what was going on and where the rest were, but were in no hurry.

"Purity!" said James fiercely under his breath. He knew it was Purity or Verity but his promotion to Second Whip that morning had been rather sudden. He yearned to crack his new whip at her, but again the shade of his grandfather intervened. Purity (or Verity) sat down near him and had a good scratch, her head back with her hindleg to an ear—in an attitude which reminded James of his mother telephoning.

Suddenly, fifty yards away on the bank of the wood, a very slight movement caught James's eye, and he and the bay pony stiffened simultaneously. A fox was crouching there, a huge fox he seemed to James, his back to the pony, his head turned sideways to look back into the wood from which he had come. James held his breath, his heart dealing hammer-blows against his ribs. Then he saw the fox very deliberately pluck and eat some blades of grass from the bank, as a dog will do in a garden. Seconds passed and suddenly there was a single deep note and then a full-throated clamour down among the trees. With great deliberation the fox was sick, with a delicate neatness of his open jaws which reminded James of their cat at home. The clamour came nearer and the fox, lightened of his last meal, crept down off the bank into the field and turned towards James, sneaking along with a ripple of muscles.

It was then that Verity (or Purity) came into the picture from behind James's pony. She had in her time run many live things, fowls, smaller dogs, grey squirrels, hares, pheasants, a goat once, and many rabbits. Rabbits were fun. They lay about in brambles and if you lost one there was generally another. But so far she had never been on coursing terms with a fox. It was, however, moving and to an aromatist like Verity smelt delicious. Her hackles went up and she charged.

The fox, busy with his own thoughts and listening to the

noise behind, was suddenly aware of a white hound coming at him head on, and of James and the pony stock still a little further away. He jinked from Purity with that deliberate easy sidestep which looks at once so purposeful and so casual, as if he was thinking of something else, and turned away. He obviously intended to slip back into the wood but the clamour among the trees was approaching and he heard Gerald's cheer. He jinked again and went off down the slope, and generations of Purity's ancestors screamed with her after him in hot pursuit. The shade of James Bunbury's grandfather also unloosed itself in a shrill "Whai-i-i!" He forgot all the Pony Club had taught him about counting thirty before he halloaed. As he did so, the rest of the pack, headed by Chancellor, burst over the bank.

Gerald and Ann, bucketting up with their heads bent over their horses' withers through alder and thorn, found a small boy, white with excitement except for his scarlet ears, holding a ramping pony short by the head and trying to gather up his whip-thong.

"What was it?" roared Gerald, praying that it wasn't a hare.

"A fox! A most enormous fox! I saw him. He was sick!"

"Sick!" said Gerald. "What's wrong with him?"

"Sick like I was on my birthday," said Master James in a blaze of candour. "On the bank. And Purity nearly caught him!"

"Purity's not out, James," said Ann Heriot as Gerald raced on. "Must ha' been Verity. Good show your keeping quiet till he was away. Now off you go, while I put the tail hounds on."

She turned back towards the covert, but for the second time that day the Mid-Harkshire were "all on", except Random and Canopy who were still rabbiting in Morshanger. Her cries, however, brought two small girls on the scene.

"Are you all that's left of 'em?" said Ann.

"We haven't seen anyone else," was the reply. "They all went round at that post-and-rails, and Capt. Sparrow said he was bound to swing left-handed. I jumped it and Mary's pony crawled under it!"

At the foot of the slope, half a mile below Druid's Wood, a six-mile belt of larch and fir-trees runs north-east and south-west across the spacious downs. The Romans went that way of old, and when it became a grassy track running through a country of large down farms, two far-seeing squires planted the line of it with trees to break the great winds which swept across the downs. A later magnate had kept the belt for par-tridge-driving, and his keeper saw to it that foxes west of Druid's Wood did not easily survive.

The fox intended to reach the shelter of the trees where a farm road cut through them and then turn left-handed down the wind towards Winnington Scrubs. By chance he met at the bottom a farm mechanic, who had come up to retrieve a tractor spanner left behind. The man shouted at him and the fox turned right-handed instead, up the line of the belt. From there he was in cover for the next five miles with no other wood within a mile of him on either side.

"Hold hard, you children!" said Gerald twenty minutes later as they emerged from the belt and saw hounds feathering across the Rowborough road. "We're having a devil of a hunt. Don't spoil it." He rode on with Ann. "I believe this blooming fox is clean out of his country and has lost himself. He ran the belt because he didn't know where to go!"

"Never was over here in my life," said Ann. "It's all par-tridges here. I must say they've hunted extraordinarily well. This mare of mine has just about had enough of it."

"So's this horse," said Gerald, "but we're not far off our fox. Look at Chancellor! He says he's on. Let us pray!"

"Poor old Bill," said Ann, inconsequently. "Think of him waiting in the *Rose and Crown*. We're eight miles from him if we're a yard."

§ 5

What a ruddy muddle a fast hunt was, thought Gerald, no clarity about the thing and all the details a blur like a polo-final. He supposed professional huntsmen knew what they were doing and had it all mapped out clearly in their minds, but for him it was just snatching at something momentarily urgent which needed to be done, with irrecoverable loss if you made mistakes. You went on and on, without a clue where you were or how far you had come; you guessed and guessed wrong and the hounds or Ann guessed right, and you scrambled after them, managing somehow to be there, with your sweat-sodden reins slipping like soap, and whip or horn always in the way.

They were twisting now from hedge to copse, from copse to wooded ditch, down in a closely-fenced valley. Ann had viewed the fox twice and said he was very dirty and tired, but scent had miraculously survived, when it should have been failing. They were all at him now, clamouring round a dense wood of ash and hazel, but the hazel stems were too close for the fox to get his wind and he slipped out on to the down again. Gerald galloped up a muddy ride and above its end could see five couple of hounds racing along the steep field across his front. Even in that glimpse their shapes seemed altered, for all their hackles were up. And he found himself thinking, "Bobbery lot be damned! If only Mike could see 'em now!" Then he saw Ann gallop across the end of the ride. *She* looked different, too, for her cap was off and she was cheering. Gerald sat down and rode his tired horse at a solid mass of bushes which blocked the end of the ride to keep out sheep. Many a time he had driven a beaten horse into a jump, and in that moment when the fence seemed to disappear he had sat still and prayed. The bushes sank out of sight beneath him; then he was conscious of the twang of a hoof hitting a wire, and of turning very slowly over with his horse in the air. Pelvis or back, blast it, he thought, for a fiver! There was a rending pain behind his neck as he hit the ground, a whirl of stars slow-circling, and then oblivion, complete.

He came to to find Ann kneeling beside him, slashing at his stock with a most business-like jack-knife.

"Don't swear," said Ann. "I made certain you were dead. It

took me about two minutes to kick the horse off you. Mike always said he got too close under his fences, that horse. Are you O.K.?" Gerald's bay horse, black with sweat, was standing with his head down three yards away and his saddle almost upside down.

"I haven't a clue what went," said Gerald inconsequently while his head swam, "but something did and yet I can move my back and legs. Did they kill him by the way?"

"Very much so," said Ann. "Three minutes ago. They're eating him now. I heard that toss of yours and went back. Are you *sure* you're all right? You were completely out."

"No," said Gerald suddenly. Like James Bunbury, he had a sudden rush of truth to the mouth, "unless, Ann, you'll . . ." Then he thought, "Hell, what's the good of asking the girl if I'll be dead in six months?"

"Yes?" said Miss Heriot, looking away. She was pinker than usual.

There was a sound of galloping in the wood, a rending crackle of branches, and out of the tangle over which Gerald had fallen, appeared James Bunbury, flying through the air. Behind him through the bushes showed the outraged face of the bay pony. He was clearly wishing that Master Bunbury would learn what was and what was not a feasible jump for a grass-fed animal of 13.2.

"Does that count, sir?" asked James anxiously, attempting without success to tow the pony over by his teeth, his eyes on the worry at the edge of the wood. "Can I say I was in at the death?" Then with another shattering rush of truth to the mouth: "Anyway, that makes up my thirteen falls."

"It counts all right, James," said Ann. "If those hounds have left anything of him at all by this time you shall have it. Where are the two girls?"

"They've gone home. Major Ogle told Mary yesterday no horse ever ought to be out of his stable for more than four hours on a hunting day."

"Oh, blow old Ogle!" said Gerald. He got up and walked towards the worry, wriggling his shoulders. Somehow he felt looser, if not fitter, than he had done for some time. "I wonder if the old blighter is still watching that corner of his in Park Wood." He looked at his watch. "Only 1.50 by gum, it seemed like hours. And we must be fifteen miles from kennels!"

§ 6

"Goodnight, Ann! Goodnight, sir, and thank you."

"Goodnight, James. Now mind! take that pony home slowly and give him a good rub-down while he's eating."

"Dam' good kid that," said Gerald. "I don't suppose . . ."

"He'll ever have a run like that with these hounds?" laughed Ann. "No, not if he lives to be the oldest member. I *would* like to know what happened to the rest!"

Gerald laughed. " '*Saul he went to look for donkeys and by God he found a Kingdom.*' Yes, I wonder where the other poor donkeys are? By-the-way, who's was the beautiful lawn we galloped over near the end, and jumped a sunk fence with an old boy shouting at us. I've only just remembered it!"

"I haven't a clue!" laughed Ann.

"But as I was trying to say, Ann," went on Gerald, "just after I took that jerk, when that young devil James interrupted me, do you think you could possibly . . .?" The high colour, which Cyril de Bourbon considered so fatal to expression, got deeper.

"I might think about it," smiled Ann, "subject to warranty, as dealers say. Vet's certificate essential, my dear. The yarn going round when you first came here was that you were drinking yourself to death and Angus was your male nurse from the Home."

"Who the devil started that one?" said Gerald.

"I think," said Miss Heriot, "Angus himself did, but I got it through Angela Bunbury, who probably got it from her sister!"

299

"Bless 'em all," said Gerald largely, "and you too, Ann! I don't know what's happened to me, but I can move my blessed neck for the first time in about five years. I feel pounds lighter somehow in every way. I say, Ann . . ."

"It's time these hounds were back in kennel," said Ann severely, "and our boiler-room after hunting is no place for dalliance."

§ 7

Master James Bunbury, hacking away from the road, his soul swimming in glory, the bay pony's ears set for home, kept repeating to himself the words with which he would greet his father on his return: "We killed . . . we killed . . I tell you, we killed . . ! And I got the mask . . . A most enormous fox. . . . I viewed him . . . and the Huntsman said . . . And Ann said it was seventy-four minutes from Druid's Wood. We killed, I tell you . . . and no one had ever been there before!" James at that moment had abandoned any desire to be a bishop, or an admiral, or a tractor-driver. He was going to make a million pounds by winning the Grand National and then be Master of the Mid-Harkshire. He turned in the frosty sunset to look his last at the hounds jogging over the hill. Then he looked away again hurriedly for what he saw had shocked him to the core of his professional soul. The Huntsman and the First Whip were riding side by side and seemed to be holding hands.

None of them gave a thought to the young dog-fox who, after a hearty meal of rabbit overnight, had been more or less "bounced" by Verity, easily the biggest skirter in the pack.

§ 8

Much of interest had happened in those few hours at which we can only glance. Mr. Francolin, after hacking about for forty minutes with his groom, had sent his horses home and motored round to get a glimpse of hounds. He had cast up eventually at the *Rose and Crown* and actually had a drink with Bill Heriot without discovering what Bill's role had been. Major Ogle, after waiting in vain like Sister Anne at his "usual corner" for about an hour, had found his way to Morshanger by way of two mothers who were gossiping amicably in a car until their children's return. Finding all quiet, he had gone home in a huff. One of the farmers had jumped eight fences with his cunning old fleabitten grey and had then decided that if he took her home now, and put her in cotton wool, he had the Farmers' Race in his pocket in April. John the runner, pleasantly full of rum, had contacted Jimmy Welman and speedily divining that it was a drag, had put himself and the terriers to ground in the Wenhaston Arms where they spent the rest of the day carousing. And all over the neighbourhood Mother was ringing up Mother to say, "Has your Pamela come home yet? No more have mine. Where *have* those children got to? But don't you think Paul looked sweet in those new jodhpurs? What? Oh, the earth and eight coupons but what *can* one do?"

Most anxious of all that multitude was Capt. Sparrow. When hounds had first gone away he had made certain that "their quarry", as he always called it, would turn left for Squeers, and he had ridden accordingly. Finding this guess incorrect, he had hacked on to what was bound to be the afternoon draw, and finally home. From there he had rung up the kennels (twice), Lady Mary (once), and all the members of the Committee without obtaining any information. And it was, of all days, the day on which his weekly article had to be posted to go to press. Too maddening! He breathed heavily on his fountain-pen to warm it, and began:

Mid-Harkshire

These hounds had a disappointing day from their Thursday venue at Stoke Loyalty. There was a sizeable field to enjoy the usual lavish hospitality of Lady Mary Wenhaston, to whom all lovers of fox-hunting owe a debt of gratitude. With such a good-scenting day we had expected better sport. In the absence of the Master, Capt. "Mike"

*Pembury, and his kennel huntsman, Will Jelf, Major Warde was
hunting the mixed pack. He speedily found, as amateurs are apt to do,
that conditions in the south are by no means as easy as they are across
the Border. That good sportsman, the tenant of Morshanger, soon had
a stout fox afoot which took us straight over the hill towards Fewdown, where hounds were speedily brought to their noses. Running
on right-handed with a grand cry, the varmint . . ."*

But there he stopped. What could he say? He went to the
telephone. Not a whisper, and the hunting world waiting for
his report! Finally he could bear it no longer, with the post
going out at 5 p.m. With a map and his book of cuttings, Capt.
Sparrow decided to "gag". He had done so before. Slowly the
well-known phrases trickled from his pen:

*Finding again in . . . swung left-handed . . . skirting Laundry
Wood . . . across the Underton—Hollowshot lane . . . scent poor in
covert . . . nearly to Squeers . . . not accounted for. . . . An un-
enterprising fox . . . back to Squeers . . . sinking the wind . . . Pool
Wood obliged as usual . . . our pilot's point . . . hounds unable to
press . . . fresh foxes intervened . . . the closure was applied.*

As he returned from the post, his telephone rang. It was
Major Ogle brimming with news. "I've-just-been-through-to-
the-kennels-and-they're-not-back-yet-but-then-I-got-on-to-
Angela-Bunbury-and-would-you-believe-it-that-boy-James
-has-just-got-in-and-says-they-killed-at-Flux-Weston."

"Flux Weston?" said Capt. Sparrow. "The boy's daft!"

"Flux-Weston-he's-quite-sure-says-there-were-only-three-
up-and-it-was-a-great-big-old-dog-fox-and-they-had-seventy-
four-minutes-of-it-from-Druid's-Wood-can-you-beat-it?"

"I don't believe it," said Capt. Sparrow. "Angela Bunbury
told me herself that feller Warde, who was trying to hunt 'em,
is almost a dipsomaniac. He must have imagined it. Never on
your life! That yarn about the Buccleuch. . . . Can't find it in
Bailey at all. Anyway my report has gone in. It's too late to
alter it now. They know ME well enough on that paper."

"Never mind," said Gerald a few days later, when the indignant Ann showed him the journal in question. "Who said 'History is bunk'? Every show I've ever been in, polo and Alamein and so forth, some rozzy correspondent was simply bound to get hold of the wrong end. They haven't a clue!"

"I don't care," fumed Ann. "I'd like to shoot that dreadful Sparrow!"

"Try jumping on him next time out," suggested Gerald.

"He won't give me the chance. He's a chicken-hearted chap and if he saw me coming he'd shout 'Make way for the Whip', and expect me to give him a lead."

§ 9

"That young Warde looked fit enough when I saw him at the Meet today, Roger," said Rosamund the same evening. "I thought you told me in the summer he'd less than a year to live. . . ."

"Blood-pressure probably," said Roger Gore-Ambulance, "or may be alcoholism. That high colour is very deceptive. . . . And certain cardiac conditions. . . . But I trust you haven't mentioned that to a soul, Rosamund?"

"As if I should," said Rosamund. "Have I ever let you down yet?" She hurried off to tell Angela to keep *her* mouth shut.

Meanwhile Col. Bunbury, meticulously wisping the bay pony before he turned him out, was murmuring with passion, "And I not there! And I not there!" But poor little Jim could never afford to hunt when he did grow up, even if they hadn't abolished fox-hunting by the time he did, so he did not grudge the boy his ecstasy now.

XXX. THE FINAL DAY

Mr. Mannering was anxious to give his guests a good day just before Christmas. It was the last but one of the season, for he never shot after his partridges began to pair. Two days had been spoilt by heavy rain, and an afternoon gale which had put large numbers of birds off the ground. He still had a good stock of partridges, thanks to certain of his guns, and so far they had not accounted for the numerous pheasants which lurked in the huge fields of kale and swedes he kept for sheep-feed.

"We ain't seen half the birds in that drive," Tom Beacon would say. "I seen one gang of forty goo back at the onset, and a nine and a seven slipped out agin the rail-road and where that big lot was we saw last time I'm beggared if I know. And we've got a master lot of pheasants. Last Tuesday morning when I was up by them young beans, I seen forty-three. Yet time we druv it, we ain't put up more 'n six."

"It's the beaters," said Mr. Mannering.

"Ah! We used to teach sowljers to walk in line at so many paces interval. They don't fare able to du that now. Sowljers!"

Mr. Mannering throughout the season had used every device to show his guests sport. The first drive, for example, where birds so often skimmed up to the railway cutting and turned aside, he had tried in two different ways, without much success. On account of the boundary he could only drive them west or south, and on the only occasion when he had tried the last, he had lost a lot of birds off the corner. If he wanted to kill some of

304

his pheasants by walking a field of roots in line Major Ogle expressed objections to tailing birds—"much better birds the other way, my dear fellow"—and Mr. Lorrimer refused to walk through dripping kale in his trousers. If he wanted the outside guns to go with the beaters and deal with some head-strong coveys, which got up at three hundred yards range and came straight back over the line, it was usually Sir William or Mr. Lorrimer on whom the lot fell, and they never hit anything except rabbits. Also there had been murmurs about Mr. Lorrimer's "safety" and even the vicar, who seemed to move in a world of his own, had whispered something. Two beaters had on successive days complained of shots fired straight at them in a drive and Mr. Mannering had at last been compelled to speak.

"A dangerous shot?" said Mr. Lorrimer frigidly. In his world there was no such thing. You were dead with a bullet neatly behind your ear before you knew anyone had fired. "My dear Mannering, I am the best judge of that. Only I can see what my gun is aimed at. It must have been a ricochet from some other weapon."

"Nobody else was shooting at the moment, so Fred Crane said," answered Mr. Mannering desperately.

"These yokels are very stupid," said Mr. Lorrimer. "When I shoot someone it will be time to complain."

"It'll be too late," said Mr. Mannering miserably. It was harder to accuse a man of being a dangerous shot than of being a swindler. That sort of thing was like halitosis.

He prayed that this would be one of the days when birds "showed themselves" well. He knew that his guest, Sir Charles Teal, could be relied on to shoot more than his share all day. Col. Bunbury and Gerald Warde likewise did not care how difficult the birds were if they were up in the air. On the other hand Major Ogle, the expert, with all the theory of "forward allowances" at his finger tips, rarely hit them, as apart from supervising his dogs, he was so busy calculating whether the bird was thirty or forty yards up, and what the Shooter's Calen-

dar had told him about shot-charges, muzzle-velocity, and foot-
seconds at various ranges, that he was very apt to miss. Similarly
the Rev. James was usually occupied with small birds or cleaning his spectacles, and rarely took the fast high chance. Mr.
Percy Lorrimer would sit on his campstool and treat the tall
ones contemptuously as "outsiders", not worth having a bet
on, and Sir William Boulogne, before his disappearance, had
done little better. Brigadier Bowman was no longer in their
midst. Chagrined that Angus was still at large and finding
retirement expensive, he had left the syndicate, to explain
demi-officially "the English way of life" to the inhabitants of
Nicaragua. Mr. Mannering was now involved in an acrimoni-
ous correspondence with him concerning a refund of the money
the Brigadier had paid. In it, the "queer ingredients of the
syndicate" had been stressed—the word "bogus" even crop-
ping up once—and the number of cartridges the Brigadier had
expended during the season. Mr. Mannering stuck to it that he
had shown plenty of birds, and still had them to show, that no
syndicate could be run if the guns came and went as they chose,
and that the Brigadier was welcome to put somebody else in
his place. This would have involved him telling a third party
what he had paid for "his gun", a detail locked in the bosoms of
himself and his bankers.

§ 2

Major Ogle was much looking forward to the day. He hoped
to buy extra game from Mr. Mannering to make up his Christmas presents, and he was on the verge of selling to Col. Bunbury the puppy Dredger, who had been "coming on" by leaps
and bounds (metaphorically, of course, he was careful to explain). In transactions involving an animal, sentiment played a
considerable part in the Colonel's choice. Daniel was getting
very pottery (though he still imagined on shooting days that he
was a match for any hare in Harkshire), and the Colonel was
slowly awakening to the fact that sooner or later the sickening

moment would come when he would have to "put him down". The mere thought of it made the Colonel feel like a murderer as he looked into Daniel's eyes. He could never explain to himself why he could shoot partridges and pheasants without a qualm and yet feel caddish and hateful when killing any domestic animal or condemning it to death. The deciding factor in his mind had been the discovery that Dredger's mother had been a bitch who had been lent to him once for six months. Pedigree, performance, training, all sank into insignificance compared with the fact that Dredger was "out of Dinah"—a golden bitch with a nose like a foxhound and the sweetest manners in the world. The only things the Colonel was now worrying about were, first, how to pay Major Ogle's price—for haggling among gentlemen was not done—and how he could conceal from Angela what he had paid.

§ 3

Gerald and Angus arrived at the meeting-place in high spirits. Gerald was feeling stiff and sore about the neck after his fall, but "pounds lighter" as he expressed it. Something seemed to have got back into place, he could turn his head and move his shoulders, and the old *malaise* had gone. "I shall probably shoot like a bad dream today, I *feel* so well," he told Angus. "Was it Tilden who said that when you feel fit before a show you're usually stale and it's when you feel rotten beforehand that you play well?"

"When the cavalry start enlarging on how they feel," retorted Angus, "they're usually tight or in love! I thought they taught you chaps to suppress all emotion, except those of sympathy for your horse?"

"Blast you, Angus!" said Gerald. "I see for once everybody's here on time."

Mr. Mannering was all ready to move off and beside him on a shooting-seat was a pink plump old gentleman, in a neat brown suit, with a neat Labrador behind him. The butt-ends of the other "guns" were protruding from their cars as they extracted their belongings. Mr. Mannering had warned them overnight that he was "laying on lunch" at his own house. He introduced the neat old gentleman as "Sir Charles" . . . something Gerald could not catch.

Col. Gore-Bunbury was wiping the damp of the morning off his speckless barrels but he seemed in low spirits, for he was accompanied by his sister-in-law, Rosamund. Her husband was in Furzechester, dealing with somebody's recalcitrant duodenum. Col. Bunbury had been aghast when Rosamund had actually suggested ringing up for Sir William's gun and taking his place herself. "My dear Rosamund, you *can't*!" he wailed, remembering a dreadful day at Overshot years before, when somebody's wife had appeared "under arms" just as they were moving to the first stand and said, "What number's Derick? Six, is he? Well, I'll be Six A," an incident which had caused her host almost to swallow his monocle.

"What nonsense, James!" Rosamund had said in answer to his protest. "They'll be glad of an extra gun, now poor William is away." Only the discovery that both Sir William's guns had been temporarily retained by the police had rescued the Colonel from a prospect which appalled him. Women never knew when they were redundant nowadays! And he guessed that with wild partridges and wilder cock-pheasants, Rosamund's chatter would cut down his own chances considerably, quite apart from her criticisms of his shooting.

Cyril de Bourbon was also there, for Sir William had asked him, several days before his own arrest, to come down and photograph the shooting party. Cyril had been roosting in Furzechester since the lawn-meet, and had already photographed Rosamund in her new "saddle-stitched hand-tailored two-piece, unbelted, with the breathlessly attractive pleats and vanishing side-buttons, a classically-formed suit that could never date". Rosamund had seen it in a catalogue as worn by a very lissome lady perched on a shooting-stick, her knees together, the muzzle of her gun resting lightly on the ground between her feet, the butt supported against her classic thigh, while she lit a cigarette in a nine-inch holder and a covey of partridges whirred over her head.

"Too attractive, my dear," Cyril told Rosamund, peering up from his view-finder, "though of course I hate the very *idea* of sportswomen, except as onlookers."

The brief visit of Rosamund and Roger Gore-Ambulance had reduced the Colonel to a condition of quiet frenzy. It meant four times the washing-up, twice the coals, more than twice the vegetables and extra boots, apart from the cleaning which the ceremonial glass and china had to undergo. Only by getting up at 4.30 a.m. had he encompassed his chores that morning, and if one dug one's hens out of their houses before 9 a.m. you weren't going to get winter eggs! Luckily his small daughter was laid up, as on hunting mornings he had to do everything from feeding her pony at dawn to tying her stock, and putting the stable to rights after she had gone.

Mr. Lorrimer for once was punctual, driven by Eustace who, since the afternoon when he had fallen a prey to Brigadier Bowman's gun, had declined firmly to enter the shooting-field proper and remained, nursing his wounds, in the car. He had, however, with great self-sacrifice lent his only son, aged ten, to carry Mr. Lorrimer's golfing-bag and campstool, with orders not to move on any account from under Mr. Lorrimer's lee. Mr. Lorrimer gave everyone on arrival his rather lordly salute, for his mind was busily at work. He had completed his shooting novel and was now engaged on the scenario of one about hunting. In it the noble Master was scheduled to "bump off" three rival candidates for the Mastership with a loaded hunting-whip while drawing certain lonely covers. The bodies were to be picked up later by the kennel-van and disposed of to the hounds. The grim scene in the feeding-yard one Sunday afternoon (when the young new Secretary first detects a human tibia in the hounds' trough), had great possibilities. He must arrange for young Pembury to show him round the kennels after Christmas, to get his local colour right.

Last of all, pedalling down the lane with his gun across the handle-bars, came the vicar. He was glad to be there, for it was execution day for his young geese and the Christmas pig. The vicar could never get used to this rite to which Sam Westrup always looked forward keenly. He would even lean over the pig on Sundays and discuss amicably, in his presence, with friends, how many score he would "goo". The vicar again felt grave doubts whether we were, or were not, complete hypocrites at Christmas. Was he himself, while shooting, a sadist? He could not agree, search his conscience as he would. There were certain things you knew in your heart were wrong, lying, adultery, ill-treatment of children, neglect of an animal or "a robin redbreast in a cage". He could understand that, though the "friend of man" was the most pugnacious and totalitarian bird in any garden. Would Masefield have written *Reynard the Fox* if he had thought hunting was a cruel sport? And the poets were so often nearer the truth than the divines. The Rev. James Halliburton postponed this question, which had worried him, not so much because of what he himself felt, but because of what others had written. He could never get over that "great draught of fishes" gasping their lives out in the boat for the delectation of the multitude? Montague had spoken of those "disconcerting bombs" of the Christian teaching, which courageous divines kept rushing in to pick up and throw away. He was only a simple country parson. The dilemma must wait.

§ 4

Gerald sat on his shooting-seat and looking up the slope of the meadow. He could smell the invisible kale beyond the brow, where the wire fence of the railway cut across the grey sky. A train puffed out of sight through the cutting, only its wreathing white smoke clouds marking its passage.

Mr. Mannering had at last, as an experiment, put his guns far down the slope away from the cutting, with a dense hedge of thorn and larch-trees in the dip fifty yards behind them. Gerald, shuffling his feet to keep them warm, was thinking of what Ann had said in that boiler-room at the kennels which was "no place for dalliance". "I'm not going to think of it till you've seen a vet, Gerald, a decent vet. And I shall expect you to win the Heavy-weight Race now on that horse of your uncle's. You'd better start qualifying him at once. You'll have to put up a lot of lead, of course . . ."

A year ago any girl, who had dictated to Gerald like that, would have been told firmly "where she got off". Was he going soft, or was this just a sign of "nesting"?

A whistle far away interrupted his musings; then he heard a horn from the unseen line of beaters beyond the brow, then low down through the wire he saw eight, nine, ten partridges skimming across his front, to stop suddenly and disappear. That covey had done it twice before on other days. They wouldn't face it and would go back when the beaters came on.

The horn sounded again or was it the wind in his gun-barrels? Some verses Gerald had read overnight shaped themselves to new words in his mind:

Dim forms skimming and a horn half-heard
And somewhere in a nameless field a nameless heart has stirred.

Pity, he thought, that Chesterton and Kipling had never shot or hunted in their lives. They might have given one something as unforgettable as the *Maltese Cat*. What was happening? Was another lot creeping forward to pitch in the kale or about to burst over the brow?

He saw a smear of yellow-brown and white high in air which meant a covey breaking back. Then the horn sounded again. Away on the right of the line a cock pheasant appeared, Heavens high and still rising. He had made good use of his time from the moment he was flushed and now he was over Angus.

Gerald saw Angus stand up and shoot and shoot again. The

old cock commenced to plane down, unscathed, his tail at a
steep angle. Angus turned his leonine head to look after him. So
might a lion in the Coliseum have looked at a disappearing
form and said "Snorting good Christian, that one! I never saw
a better".

Fizzer, that, to start the day with, thought Gerald, and as he
did so a wave of partridges swept over the brow opposite himself, not chattering, not swerving in all directions as they did
early in the season, but flowing on smoothly as a breaker and
accelerating every second. Gerald snapped at one in front, saw it
start to drop and as he switched on to another above his head
he realized it was the last of the wave. Next second they were
gone, climbing the air over the larch-trees towards the rising
ploughland beyond it.

Another lot broke over the railway seventy yards to his left,
skimmed twenty yards down the slope and turned smoothly as
a destroyer in a curve towards him. He saw the pink old gentleman on his left half-rise off his stick, lean forward, and two
birds fell almost simultaneously far out up the hill. Even as
Gerald missed the nearest bird, conscious that it was on the turn
and rising, the whole lot were gone, streaming like grouse back
over the cutting.

Again the horn sounded and two small coveys broke over the
right, all swerving right-handed and swinging smoothly back
towards the cutting. Gerald, his eyes on Angus and Major Ogle,
heard a whistle from his left and was aware of a cock pheasant
skimming down the slope at him at the level of his waist. It
was past him before he could think. He swung round and snapped
at it as it rose steeply at the larch-trees. Miss, he realized, but
next second it had crumpled over the top of the trees fifty yards
behind him. Gerald turned towards Sir Charles on his left and
touched his hat. This must be one of the "professors" of whom
Andrew Teal had spoken, ancients who behind a quietly
untrained appearance hid surprising aptitudes.

At the end of the drive Gerald walked over to the old gentleman who was sitting placidly on his seat watching his dog which had never moved during the drive. He had fired six cartridges and the dog was just bringing in the last of his five birds, the cock pheasant from the larch-trees.

"I'm afraid I didn't catch your name, Sir," said Gerald.

"Teal, Charles Teal," said the old man, smiling.

Gerald recalled Andrew Teal's remark about there being "no pink of condition about his Uncle Charlie".

"I think," said Gerald, "I met your nephew this autumn up at Gallowgill."

"Ah! poor Andrew!" smiled the old gentleman. "Trying to make his living out of the unpredictable: all demand and no supply! Steadily diminishing assets, poor chap! He's a gloomy soul, and I should be, too, in his position. The last straw for him this season was when the Government sent up a minority delegation from the hinderparts of Empire, who had come to talk Dominion status. Whitehall was bored with them, so gave them a cocktail party, and sent them up to Andrew with instructions to show them the British way of life. Thing these Whitehall chaps *would* do! Andrew got them into their butts (in October, mark you) on a freezing day, and then the mist came down and the beaters lost themselves. One of the delegation thought it was all a Whitehall plot to abandon them, rather than give way to their demands, and shot himself in his butt out of sheer misery. Well, well, Mannering wants us to get on!"

§ 5

The next drive was a long field of kale lying on the brow of a hill. There was a wood half a mile away to the west and another almost as far to the north. The kale was full of pheasants, and Gerald, walking with the beaters, watched bird after bird rising into the wind, stand almost still for two seconds in the air and then give itself over on stiff wings to the gale at sixty miles an hour. Only Sir Charles Teal seemed happy. He barely rose off his shooting seat and took them a long way out in front with a quick deftness which left Gerald astounded. He made those curling birds look simple, even as a billiards professional never seems to be taking anything but easy shots, but Gerald could see that he was shooting far quicker than the other guns.

Major Ogle had much to say at the end of that drive.

"I don't think I was giving those birds quite enough allowance. Three-foot-six at least, the books say, but I reckon those pheasants were doing much more than forty-five feet per second, don't you, Sir Charles? Much nearer seventy feet and that means at thirty yards . . ."

"I wouldn't be knowing," said Sir Charles amiably. "I never know what I do when I'm shooting. 'Squirt at 'em,' my father used to teach me, 'and keep the gun moving.' After all, when you hit a tennis-ball, nobody knows how fast it's travelling or what your own muzzle-velocity is. It's a question of eye, not radar!"

"Of course," said Major Ogle. He was, as always, brimming with theory, "there's one school of thought which says you should point your body at the bird and fire as soon as the gun comes to the shoulder."

"God forbid!" smiled Sir Charles, looking down at his comfortable contours. "I'm the wrong shape to point at anything, aren't I?"

§ 6

Mr. Mannering listened to the babble of conversation down the table. He had given his guests sherry, followed by soup and roast pheasants, and things were going for once reasonably well.

"Oh yes, poor chap," said Col. Bunbury, in reply to Angus, "he *had* retired; resigned all his clubs in Bombay in 1938. And then his wife took up children as a form of war-work; she had four under five, including twins, and now the poor old chap's had to go back again and rejoin all his clubs and start saving once more."

"Let that be a lesson to you, Gerald my lad, if you're thinking of nesting," said Angus.

"Oh, too devastating," twittered Cyril de Bourbon to Rosamund. "I'd just got him beautifully in my view-finder with a Colourchrome film in, when the wretched horse lay down with him, my dear, on his poor leg. Apparently she'd done that before with her previous owner. It *ruined* poor David's lovely white breeches, and he's got such a *perfect* seat. I could have cried." Cyril drew out a large silk handkerchief and blew his nose as if about to do so.

"What? Brigadier Bowman spreading the English way of life?" said Angus, lifting his great face from his tankard. "That'll make Nicaragua think twice before joining the United Nations, won't it? He'll probably launch a series of hate-films, sort of Odium Circuit, y'know, not a kiss in the whole reel! Well, well."

"*Humus?*" said Col. Bunbury. "Don't you find, Mannering, that these farmer-writers contradict each other so often?"

"I don't read them," said Mr. Mannering. "Haven't time! I'm too busy farming."

"I should like to take some of them and show them what my garden can produce. If you dig it, it's all broken bottles, and bricks and stones and chalk, no *humus* at all, yet it can grow weeds three feet high. I found a linnet nesting in them when I got back from the war."

"Always-been-a-basic-principle-of-covert-shooting," boomed Major Ogle, "a-judicious-blend-of-deciduous-among -the-other-trees-but-then-no-one-ever-lays-out-coverts-properly-these-days. All commercial."

"Only 100,000 so far," said Mr. Lorrimer, who had been very busy eating, down the vicar's ear-trumpet. "But the film rights are not to be sneezed at."

"Jammy Falkenham?" said Angus to Major Ogle. "He's almost in quod at last, and not before he's deserved it. Some Old Plutonian met him in a pub. Hadn't seen him for years,

and invited him to shoot. Jammy took French leave from
Bongo, hired a gun from a gun-maker for a quid, sold it to
another gun during the week-end for 150 guineas, and then
pouched thirty-three per cent. commission!"

"Of course," said the Vicar to Gerald, "the white on the
inner secondaries of *Pyrrhoplectes* probably makes it look as if
they had a white rump, unless you see them flying."

"A nice bitch, yes," said Mr. Mannering to Gerald on the
other side, "she was one of Lord Warracombe's."

"She seems well-broken," said Gerald, "but has she any
nose?"

Mr. Mannering smiled at Gerald with new respect. "Good
for you! She's got no nose at all and she's terrified of going out
more than fifteen yards from her handler. Any bird outside
that magic circle is as good as lost."

"That's-what-I-always-say-about-field-trials," boomed
Major Ogle. "I-shot-at-one-last-year,-my-dear-old-friend-
Herbert-Umbrage's-in-Wiltshire,-and-with-four-of-these-
championship-dogs-all-round-me,-I-never-lost-so-many-birds
-on-any-day-in-my-life. Keeper's dog at home would ha' done
better. Over-broken, that's the trouble, and no brain! Quite
apart from nose."

"Of course," snorted Major Ogle again, "that feller's not
really Labour, he's a crypto-Lateral! When-he-stopped-at-
Chequers-he-shot-the-garden-cock-pheasant-out-of-the-bath-
room-window-while-it-was-strutting-about-on-the-terrace
-early-one-morning. Ghastly chap!"

"I saw your little girl-friend at the meet on Wednesday,"
said Rosamund compassionately down the table to Gerald. "I
thought she was riding in your pocket a bit."

Gerald's mouth set in its sulky thin line but his eyes smiled.
"Not a bit," he said, "I was riding in hers for the next two
hours. She goes dam' well, that girl."

"Rather pathetic, I thought, the whole show," went on
Rosamund sweetly. "Of course, after the Quoddon . . ."

Angus sailed in to Gerald's rescue, landing, as he expressed it later, well over both hocks.

"Looks all right, doesn't he?" he roared down the vicar's trumpet, his eyes on Gerald. "Brought off a deuce of a hunt on Wednesday. All these stiffs on the Committee left at the post! And only six months ago some BF in Wimpole Street told him he was cats' meat!"

"We'd better be getting on the move," said Mr. Mannering hastily. He did wish that when people were joined in a common pursuit of pleasure, they wouldn't always say something which led to a squabble.

The vicar, used to the rivalries of his Mothers' Union, was thinking the same, though he put it differently. "It's curious, isn't it, Warde," he said, as they walked out, "how closely-allied families like the laughing-thrushes, all living in similar terrain, evolve quite specific feeding-habits and plumages, as well as songs, and don't interbreed? Is it the food, do you suppose? If half my parishioners ate bread-and-jam and the other half bacon-and-eggs, would there be plumage and other specific differences? Is the public-house habit of *homo sapiens* cause or effect? There's good material for a monograph there."

In the cartshed, the older beaters, sitting on trusses of straw, had been talking also.

"And as for that fattest one," said the old horseman, wiping his mouth on the back of his hand, "he couldn't shute a wind-mill, not if it was ever so close. What sort of a job may his be now?"

"Books," said Sir Bonamy Pickering *alias* Fred Smith, with his mouth full of bread-and-cheese.

"Bookmaker, is he? They maäkes some money, blast 'em. Them bastards wouldn't give me no odds at all last June about that 'orse of the Agger Can. I only got threes to half-a-crown."

"A fairish lot, the tothers," said Fred Crane. "Of course, Sir Charles is a wunnerful pretty shot. The old Colonel, he's a nice shot too, and that young sowljer, Warde, is acomen on."

"Ah," said Tom Beacon, filling his pipe. "That's a rare good plaäce, Oakington. Dick Seymour was atelling me what that young chap is adoin' for his tenants. Gipsy like, though, he 'ont be here long."

"I didn't go a lot on the tother fat 'un what ain't here," said the horseman slowly. "Was he a bookmaker, like, as well? The one what's been pulled by the police?"

"Nar, London chap, treated us as no more 'n a lump o' dirt. Whisky, he was! Stole it off the Army and sowld it in them night-pubs, they calls 'em, what never cloose. You can get a drink all night long there down in London, only you has to put on your Sunday clothes. They pulled him, and no mistake!"

"Well, if that ain't a rum 'un. The gentry ain't what they used to be." Fred Crane put his jack-knife back in his pocket. "We'd better fall back round that barley-stubble and then ketch up them swedes into Dean's Wood, hadn't we, Mr. Beacon?"

"And all you chaps look out for yourselves good tidily this arternoon," said Tom Beacon, busy with a stump of pencil. "They've got a rare good dinner in their bellies, and them two fat 'uns ain't never been saäfe all the season. If they shutes some of my Army beaters, that wouldn't do them a mite o' harm, blast 'em, it's the only war they'll ever see—but I don't want you poor beggars off the strength."

XXXI. MR. LORRIMER TAKES OVER

*Masters, it is proved already that you are little better than
false knaves; and it will go near to be thought so shortly.*
　　　　　　　　　—*Much Ado about Nothing*

Fred Smith, *alias* General Sir Bonamy Pickering, K.C.B., etc.,
leant on his flag-wrapped stick near the rough thorn-fence
which fringed the gallops. The late afternoon was dark and
stormy with a strong wind and General Pickering, had it been
his own shoot, would have stopped proceedings half an hour
ago. But they had put a lot of birds into the drive and the wind
was right. Silly to disturb them just when they were on the feed
before a night of rain! Pearls before swine, too! he thought,
peering through wrinkled eyes under his shocking hat, as he
saw the dark racing forms rise and scatter over the high fence.
Only one gun in the team, except Mannering, could really deal
with fast December birds on the wind like that, and that was
Charlie Teal, who had been one of his old commanding officers
before he came into the baronetcy. Charlie Teal could shoot his
share in a gale and a bad light, but it was like asking the rest to
stand up to fast Test-match bowling when they were only up
to club standard. Another covey swept towards him, swerved
at his flag and hurtled rising over the fence. Bang! bang! bang!
Nothing down that time, but the end guns were Angus
Cameron, who hadn't had a chance to shoot all the season, and

that fat writer-chap, the unsafe one, with whose chauffeur he had had words on the first day, the one who couldn't "shute a windmill". They were standing a long way back from the fence but at that pace it was not too far. Another big lot poured high over the centre of the line and he could see two birds crumple and drop from where he stood. That must be Charlie Teal, taking 'em as early as that! Beautiful shot he was, broke to the wide but asked everywhere, and as safe as houses. A covey rose far out on the stubble, and skimmed low towards the fence, rising just enough to clear it and stringing along the fence in his direction. There was a fusillade of shots and one bird, hard hit, swerved back over the blackthorns, with a curious swaying action and dropped dead in the bushes on his side. He would pick that up after the drive. These syndicate chaps got bewildered in a heavy drive or else didn't care what they had down. It began to sleet heavily and he could see, through the fence on his right, a great tide of sheep stemmed by the shepherd, waiting to be driven up the gallops to their Sunday pasture.

The beaters closed in at last and hurried, crouching from the sleet, towards the straw ricks at the other end of the line. Sir Bonamy saw Tom Beacon and Fred Crane force their way through the blackthorns to help pick up. He himself stumped slowly, for his corn was hurting, towards where he had seen the wounded partridge fall. Ah, there it was, right in among the thorns, crouching in the tangle but stone-dead. He wormed his way under the bush towards it. With one hand outstretched he suddenly heard a shot and knew, as one knows without question, that it was fired in his direction. Something spattered a yard away from him in the undergrowth and he thought "Clumsy ass! Loosing off after a drive! Ought to be unloaded! Chap ought never to be asked again." Then there was a stunning blow on the side of his temple and this time the sound of the gun seemed to fill his head.

He did not see the chattering sportsmen get into Mr. Mannering's shooting-brake and go home to tea, nor the beaters wending their way with Tom Beacon to the Low Barn to be paid. Sir Bonamy lay under the thorns, his hand still grasping the bird, a trickle of blood running from the ribbonless and shocking hat and making a little pool among the dead leaves. The brain that had been feared and respected by Boers and Mahsuds, Chins and Wazirs, Prussians and Turks, Sikhs and Dogras, Secretariat officials and "Whitehall warriors", and the motley ingredients of His Majesty's line-regiments, had ceased to function. The rain beat down on him and formed a little pool in the pocket of his old hunt-coat. The hawk-eyes which had helped him to hit pheasants and polo-balls, snipe, bison and flighting duck, which had scared a thousand commanding officers and sent men scurrying about the Empire, were half-closed. *Blunders of this War*, now in its penultimate chapter, would never now be finished.

§ 2

"I don't think," said Angus to Gerald as they walked towards Mr. Mannering's shooting-brake, "that our friend Percy touched a feather all day. But he did bring off one most incredible shot at a rabbit which got up out of the grass just after the last drive. Missed it clean with the first barrel, and turned it over stone-dead with the second at about sixty yards just as it disappeared into the fence. Did *you* connect at all in that last drive?"

"Five," said Gerald. "Proper snorters, weren't they? I fired thirteen cartridges for those. And you?"

"I never got on to 'em properly, but I killed a brace in seven cartridges. Charles Teal and Mannering were pulling them down beautifully. Look, Gerald, I'm going down to the barn with Tom Beacon when he pays off the beaters. He's promised me a spot of strychnine for your magpies. It'll save me a lot of hu-ha signing the poison-book in some chemist's at Furzechester, and I know the chap at Stoke Loyalty hasn't got any. You carry on and I'll follow."

§ 3

Mr. Mannering always gave his guests tea after shooting once a year, usually at Christmas, when everyone wanted some extra game for the house or to give away. Tom Beacon would be busy for half an hour paying the beaters, counting the bag and tying up birds. Rosamund and Cyril had fled for home, overwhelmed by the elements, so Mr. Mannering was able to produce the whisky and say, "Now, gentlemen, a little of this won't go at all badly in our tea!" There was home-made jam and scones and butter "off the ration" and such milk as only farmers in those days ever saw. Everyone settled down to eat heartily, except the vicar who was whispering over to himself the opening phrases of his sermon, and Col. Bunbury who was wondering if Angela had fed the hens.

"Wonderful drive, that last one," said Major Ogle twenty minutes later. "Fine show of birds too. I-remember-in-1923-when-I-was-shooting-with-old-William-Titmouse,-married-Lady-Susan-y'know-first-rate-little-place-down-in . . ."

"Titmouse?" The vicar abandoned his sermon. "I saw both *ater* and *coeruleus* today in that drive out of Dean's Wood but the hard weather has hit the longtails very badly."

"Yes," said Mr. Mannering to Sir Charles, "the fox-hounds had a wonderful run from Morshanger last week. Killed at Flux Weston, about the first fox they've killed in the open this season."

"Extraordinary run," boomed Major Ogle who had now decided to "adopt" it. "Some of us were thrown out early on, wire y'know. . . ."

"Do you mind passing the jam?" interrupted Mr. Lorrimer, who was still eating steadily, "*and* the butter. I suppose, Mannering, you get all the butter you want? I wish *we* did."

"I wonder," said Gerald to Col. Bunbury, "where the deuce old Angus has got to?"

"Yes," boomed Major Ogle, "he's turned *his* place, too, into three syndicates, one for each beat, one all peers, one all stock-brokers, and the third half bookmakers and half jockeys from Newmarket. Gets three days a fortnight for nothing, about £150 a gun, and some wonderful tips. Needs tact, of course! Couldn't do it m'self."

There was a knock at the door and the huge form of Tom Beacon entered. His white forehead contrasted strangely with his weather-beaten, rain-washed face.

"Ah, Beacon," said Mr. Mannering, "brought the bag?"

"No, sir, I ain't had no chance. There's been a rare nasty accident, sir! General Pickering's been shot!"

"*Shot?*" said Mr. Mannering aghast, "but how?"

"Why, in that last drive right at the end."

"But where was he? I never saw him."

"He's been abrushin' for me these five seasons," said Tom, "the one we called Fred Smith."

"That was General *Pickering*?"

"Ah, he said I warn't to say narthen."

"And you say he was *shot*?"

"Right through the side of the head, hole size of a pea, like. I couldn't make out why he never come in with the tothers, so I went back. He was aly-en right in under them thorns. One hole in his head and the blood adrippen!"

"Dead?" said Mr. Mannering in a hushed voice. This would "put paid" to his syndicates of strangers.

"He looked as dead as a nit when we found him but he was just breathin'. Major Somborne was along o' me and we stopped a car on the road and sent him straight into hospital."

"But how?" "Why?" "What on earth . . .?" "Not poor old 'Popeye'?" There was a chorus of questions from the other guns. But a new voice chimed in majestically and silenced them all: Mr. Lorrimer had finished his tea.

"Murder, quite obviously," he said, wiping his mouth with a silk kerchief. There was calm self-possession in his voice. "One hole, you say, keeper?"

"Ah, as big as a pea."

"A .32 Colt automatic, I expect," said Mr. Lorrimer. "They make a very small hole." Mr. Lorrimer was rising to his full stature. This situation arose about twenty times a year in the course of his work. To him it was nothing new. Most of his characters were found like that, sooner or later.

"But who could have *murdered* him?" said Col. Bunbury. "Poor old Popeye!"

"We shall, of course, look for the motive," said Mr. Lorrimer. "*And* opportunity. Investigation will doubtless show who had both."

"My poor old friend," said the vicar. "I am deeply distressed. I must break it to Miss Pickering." He moved towards the door.

"You do not realize, Vicar," said Mr. Lorrimer frigidly, "that this is murder. I am afraid I must insist that none of you gentlemen leave the room."

"But ..." Col. Bunbury was thinking of his hens.

"There is no but," said Mr. Lorrimer. "You are all suspect, gentlemen, in some degree. Here we have a dastardly murder committed almost certainly by someone in this room, under circumstances which reveal careful planning." His cold eye swept round the assembly. "There seems to be one gun missing. Ah, Major Somborne!" There was deep significance in his voice. "Where is he, may I ask?"

"He went with Beacon after the last drive to borrow some strychnine," said Gerald.

"Strychnine! Indeed ..." said Mr. Lorrimer; his mind was seething. Here was an absolutely first-class murder mystery in real life and he, Mr. Lorrimer, was by the greatest good fortune on the spot to solve it. He had always wanted such a chance. The country-house party, with several suspects, who were all gradually "eliminated" or eliminated each other, was a favourite situation of his. But he must not betray excitement. He changed the subject.

"You did very wrong, keeper, to move the corpse at all."

"He warn't no corpse, though he may be now. Love-my-heart, we couldn't leave the poor old gentleman lying there in the rain now, could we?"

"It is the usual practice," said Mr. Lorrimer. "You have probably destroyed very vital clues, my good man. Are you sure he had nothing in his hand?"

"Narthen, only a partridge. He must ha' crawled in under them thorns to pick it up."

"A partridge?"

"Ah!"

"Put there doubtless by the murderer to disarm suspicion."

Col. Gore-Bunbury rose. "I really must go and shut up, Mannering," he said. "My hens, y'know. Foxes, y'know. And my wife wants the car for bridge."

"No one," Mr. Lorrimer gave a basilisk glare at the Colonel, "will leave this room till I have completed my investigation. You are all at present suspect, some perhaps more than others. I shall have to eliminate you from the enquiry, one by one."

"Well, why not yourself?" said Gerald. "You were there too, and you're the only soul I've seen fire a dangerous shot all this season."

"Me?" said Mr. Lorrimer, pursing his lips. He was all too familiar, in his world, with these attempts to avert suspicion. "*I*, Major Warde, am the best judge of that. In any case, I do *not* propose to leave the room. I am now going to ring up the Yard." He moved majestically to the telephone in the corner.

"Surely the local police?" said Mr. Mannering. "I'm a J.P. and they know me well."

"And I," said Sir Charles Teal, who had been filling a pipe, "am, now I come to think of it, a Deputy Lieutenant of sorts."

"The local police! Faugh!" said Mr. Lorrimer. In his experience the local police were imbeciles, responsible for at least three chapters of false clues, while the reader waited breathlessly and several more people were "bumped off" in the interval. "We can afford to disregard them in a case of *this* kind."

He took out a gold pencil-case and dialled with it impressively. His mind was still seething, like rich milk in a churn. He had always wanted a chance to get inside "the Yard" and this looked a heaven-sent one. He could already see the Murder-Squad fawning round him, showing him with child-like pride their impotent little gadgets and methods, and saying, "Well, I'll be damned! A very neat little solution, Mr. Lorrimer. Who'd ha' thought it? Of course, we've learnt a lot at times from reading you . . ."

"You will ring me. Good! And treat the call as a clear-the-line one. Lives are at stake. . . ."

There was silence, broken only by the scrape of matches, and Mr. Lorrimer lit a fat cigar. Suddenly the telephone rang.

"Yes, yes, is that Whitehall . . .? Yes. Can you please put me through to . . .? It's extremely urgent. There's been a murder down here. Yes . . . yes. Who? Ah, detective-serjeant, this is Mr. Percy Lorrimer speaking. I've just had a very neat little murder-case down here. 'Where?' Stoke Loyalty! By shooting but there's more than a suspicion of poison too. The victim is a disguised General. 'Who's speaking?' I told you! Mr. Percy Lorrimer, *the* Mr. Lorrimer, the criminologist. Good Heavens, L for Lovely O for Onions R for Rabbit R for Rabbit I for Idiot M for Mother . . . What? *The* Mr. Lorrimer! Never *heard* of me! Well, then, put me through at once to someone who has. . . ."

"The old story!" said Mr. Lorrimer to the room. "Police of the purest ivory." He bent again to the 'phone. "Ah, good evening, inspector! Mr. Lorrimer, the criminologist, speaking. There's been a murder down here. General Sir Bonamy Pickering shot through the head with what appears to be a .32 automatic. No question of suicide! There are eight suspects. I have them all here under my hand with one exception . . . yes,

yes . . . I expect in fact to have the whole riddle complete by the time you come down. The principal suspect is at the moment missing but I have often found that in these cases the principal suspect is not . . . Exactly! But he is in possession of deadly poison and will not hesitate to use it. A good many lives are at stake. He will certainly commit another murder within a measurable space of time. The local police? My dear sir, surely you, with your experience of rustic forces . . .! Exactly. You will, I presume, send down two of your best men at once. My number is Stoke Loyalty 290. At once, please!"

"And now, gentlemen," Mr. Lorrimer looked up with a pad of notepaper in his hand, "perhaps you will be good enough to answer my questions."

§ 4

The interrogation had already covered six sheets of note-paper. Suddenly there was the whine and scrunch of a car drawing up on the gravel outside the house. The dining-room door opened and a very large figure in a wet macintosh filled it. It was Angus. His cheerful brown face seemed more serious than usual. Behind him was a slightly smaller stout man who also nodded to Mr. Mannering.

Angus said, "Sorry I'm late, Mannering. I see the *post mortem's* begun. Any arrests yet?"

Face to face with Suspect No. 1, believed to be in possession of strychnine, Mr. Lorrimer gulped a little as he looked up from his notes. His eye, that "prince of deadly weapons", wavered, but he said calmly, "Sit down, Major Somborne, I shall have several questions to put to you in a moment."

The stout man behind Angus interrupted. "You are Mr. Lorrimer, sir, I take it? I'm Serjeant Williamson from the Furzechester police."

"Indeed," said Mr. Lorrimer with icy condescension, "well, you will be relieved to know that *I* have already been through to the Yard. They are sending their own men down."

327

"I heard about your call, sir. They were on the blower to me just now."

"Indeed! and what exactly did they say?"

The serjeant opened his notebook. "My operator logged it 'ere, sir. *'Find out 'oo the blighter is at Stoke Loyalty 290 wot was shooting his mouth about a murder AAA Instruct 'im where 'e gets off AAA Name o' Lovely Onions something message mutilated AAA Take suitable action message ends.' . . ."*

"As I expected," said Mr. Lorrimer, flushing with annoyance. "One learns never to rely on the police. However, my investigation is nearly complete and I can place my hand on the criminal."

The serjeant was holding a green cartridge-bag. He drew out of it a 12-bore cartridge, and held it up to Mr. Lorrimer.

"Excuse me, sir," he said, "but is this one of yours?"

"It is," said Mr. Lorrimer, looking at the bag. "I always use six shot."

"Number Six, sir?"

"You heard what I said. Six shot."

"But this is LG, sir!"

"My good serjeant, if you cut open one of those cartridges you will find there are precisely six pellets in it."

"But where did you get it from?" pursued the serjeant. "There's a broad arrow on the case."

"I retained some," and for the first time there was a faint shade of embarrassment on Mr. Lorrimer's brow, "when I severed my connection with the Home Guard."

"In that case, sir," the serjeant rose, "perhaps you wouldn't mind coming along with me to the station? We're making enquiries about 'oo shot General Pickering and you seem to be the only gentleman 'oo could have done it."

Mr. Lorrimer's face had flushed but it might have been the tea. He was still undefeated.

"Very well, serjeant, I would prefer to tell you what I know in privacy. But I warn you, if any more deaths occur, you are leaving behind a most dangerous impostor, who is in possession of deadly poison."

He strode majestically from the room. For the first time in his career as a criminologist he was, for better or for worse, "in" with the police.

§ 5

"He'll live, poor old chap," said Angus. "They're operating on him now. But LG.! can you beat it? No wonder Percy mowed down that rabbit at sixty yards."

"But what I don't follow," said Col. Bunbury, "is how Lorrimer was so glib about its being 'six shot'. I never counted the pellets in a cartridge in my life!"

"I can explain that," said Angus. "When I was at Larkhill in '44, a friend asked me out to shoot and I couldn't lay hands on any 12-bore cartridges for love or money. Eventually someone suggested my ringing up the local Ordnance depot and they told me they had thousands of 12-bore cartridges doing nothing and could let me have as many as I wanted. I asked what sizes and the chap said at once 'Six shot'. I rushed down, having promised the R.A. Mess I'd lay on a thousand for them, and found they were all buckshot, LG or SSG, called in for the Home Guard in 1940! Their idea of sizes was to count the pellets!"

"My dear Mannering," said Sir Charles, "please don't apologize! I haven't had a day like this for years. Some first-class birds and then to be suspected of murder. I'm always terrified that I'll fire a dangerous shot without knowing it. (Sort of halitosis complex, y'know.) I was fascinated! I used to read quite a lot of those 'who-dun-it' books, but this is the first time I've seen the culprit deliberately draw down on himself the attentions of the police. He won't shoot again with you, that's one good thing!"

"Poor Mr. Lorrimer," said Mr. Mannering, "he told me today he had always wanted to see the 'police-machine' at work from the inside. He will now."

"Most interesting," said the vicar. "I shall preach tomorrow on '*Judge not, that ye be not judged*'. I have never before been suspected in a case of murder. Arson, once, yes, when the Senior Proctor sent for me after certain bump-supper celebrations round the Martyr's Memorial. And poaching, of course, frequently, in my shore-shooting days. But murder, so far, no! *Homo sapiens*, like the larger primates, is prone to the strangest inconsistencies. . . ."

"LG. in a partridge-drive!" snorted Major Ogle, "dam' feller ought to be shot!"

"No good advertising for *Guns Wanted* in *that* firing-party," said Gerald. "There'd be too many applicants from this syndicate."

§ 6

The Colonel went home brimming with excitement but found Angela much annoyed.

"Really, James," she said, "you might think of me occasionally. You go out day after day and enjoy yourself and leave me to do everything. . . ."

"Sorry m'dear. Where's Rosamund?"

"Gone up to town. Apparently Aunt Janet is not expected to last the night and Rosamund wants to be . . ."

"In at the death. Well, *I've* just been cleared of a murder-charge this evening, which is why I'm late. . . ."

"If the old body does leave it all to Rosamund, I could kill her. She's done nothing but fawn on her for years."

"Do, m'dear! But why not lure her into Mr. Catling's office and shoot it out with her? I'll lend you a gun."

"James, have you been *drinking*?"

"Yes, m'dear, and what's more I'm going to have another one. It's not every day one's suspected of murder. Did you shut up the hens?"

XXXII. NEW HORIZON

I have seen flowers come in stony places,
And kind things done by men with ugly faces,
And the Gold Cup won by the worst horse at the races
So I trust, too.
—*The Meditation of Highworth Ridden* by JOHN MASEFIELD

It was Easter Monday, a clear sunny evening with thrushes singing and daffodils in the springing grass under the apple-trees.

Col. Bunbury, his colour heightened by the April wind, was walking round his meadow with old Daniel pottering at his heels, and the young dog flashing here and there, nose to the ground, as each successive scent went to his brain like wine. Dead spit of his mother except for his colour! What a lovely bitch she had been! But too much needle in his nose, definitely.

The Colonel had come back from the hunt Point-to-Point, to which he had walked across the down. His wife had lunched out but he had made an excuse about feeding the hens. He had met more people whom he knew than he had anticipated, he had enjoyed sunshine and the sight of galloping horses jumping out of their stride, and his only bet, on an old mare which he had chosen because she looked so ugly but was a real hunter-type, had paid seventeen shillings on the tote. It was a grand course, in a lovely sweep of country where you could see clear away to

Sarum and almost to the Island, and, there being no irony in the
Colonel's soul, he had not commented, even inwardly, on the
fact that they had selected for the course a part of the country
where no fox had been hunted or killed, with the exception of
the luckless creature in Druid's Wood, for fifteen years. But he
had rubbed shoulders with every facet of the county, from old
Lord Drambuie whom he had met, unexpectedly, in the
Farmers' car park, to Bill Nineteen (what a name!) with his
pale Jewish face and greasy curls in the ring, and the horseman
from the Valley Farm who had made a week's pay in half-
crown bets.

What a packet the Point-to-Point Committee must have
cleared, with subscribers' cars at £2 a car and £1 in the other
park! And where did all the money come from? The Colonel
disliked watching a point-to-point, for ten years ago he would
never have dreamed of any meeting being complete unless he
had been having a "bump round" himself on his own horse,
and "scrounging" one or two other rides as well.   It filled him
always, that well-known scene, with the acutest nostalgia. He
felt, as he put it to himself, like an elderly chorus-girl in the
stalls watching the ballet. And what a ballet! Hardly a hunting
man in any of the races and the only pink coat was worn by an
old soldier of fifty-eight. Only *quasi*-farmers could keep horses
nowadays, because no one else could get the fodder. A lot of
farmers' sons riding in jerseys and drab breeches, with vast horse-
boxes which seemed part of their farm equipment nowadays.
He had overheard one of them. "My Dad," he had said, "has
got fifteen under rugs at present." Fifteen! and a gentleman
could barely keep one! God knew how they accounted for the
oats that kept up a stable like that.

But it was a straightforward course. The Colonel had walked
it conscientiously, yard by yard, as he always had done, and
except for that gruelling piece of plough near the end, like soap,
uphill to the last two fences, he could have jumped it "on his
head".

§ 2

He dropped the dogs and went in to collect the eggs. Good girls they had been, eight and a bantam's, and there was old Screwy sneaking away from behind the roller. That would make ten, half-a-crown dividend on that small investment of his, and half-a-crown a day was £45 a year. What other industry paid that rate of interest on a beggarly £20? Not bad, and the young dog would earn his keep, too, next season. Was doing so, by Jove, already! Embarrassingly so.

Out on the down on the Sunday afternoon, we had better admit it, the young dog which he had bought from Major Ogle had suddenly put his head down and, ignoring the Colonel's whistle, had flashed at full gallop for two hundred yards along a bank covered with rough grass.

The Colonel's heart sank to his boots. A hare for a fiver or a fox! No discipline at all but what a nose, to take it straight down the wind at that pace! And then, oh horrors! a lightning turn into the wind and up got an old cock pheasant out of the grass to fly low over the down with the dog in full pursuit. In the next thirty seconds those months of patient training seemed to have sunk without a trace. Shame and anger tore the Colonel. But the dog had known better and the old cock too. He must have been a pricked bird, shot by someone months earlier, and after flying a hundred yards into the wind barely a foot from the ground, he had turned back for the fence and slumped into it again. Three racing turns in the grass, a dive round a bush, and the puppy was cantering proudly back to him with the bird in his mouth.

"Goo' boy, Dredger, bring it, old son! Ge-e-ently, my dear!"

Almost before the Colonel knew it, he had knocked the old cock on the head, and was crouching in the grasses of the bank to see if anyone had observed him. Those old boyhood tremors, when keepers were ogres and game was sacred, and he crept on sufferance round a land over which The County reigned, made his heart beat again. Not a soul for a mile, thank God, and that lambing-pen was just round the corner of the down, out of sight!

They had crouched there, Dredger wildly excited and licking his quarry, his gleaming yellow eyes recalling his mother, while the Colonel methodically buried the tail-feathers and bestowed the rest of the old cock in his mackintosh pocket.

Always before he had hated Easter and Whitsun, with the countryman's dislike of the towns, which spewed out their population to trample down corn, to loot the nesting birds, to ravish the daffodils and the flowering pussy-willow. But now, suddenly, the Colonel felt a vast and kindly fellow-feeling with them all, as if he and they had for once beaten the unseen book-makers who had inherited the earth. He would have been shocked if the vicar had told him that it was symptomatic of the general loosening of moral standards after the war. He a *poacher*! and on Easter Sunday of all days in the year!

> *Never, oh God, let the neighbours say*
> *I killed a cock pheasant on Easter Day!*

But he had, and he had sneaked across country home, glassing the fields spread maplike below from the crest of the great down, to avoid any keeper. Now the tailless old bird hung in the larder, waiting for a fit occasion.

Angela, of course, had had her grumble. "Whatever are you doing with that, James? Hh! I suppose it's a diseased bird. And I suppose *I've* got to pluck it!"

"Yes, m'dear, I hope you will. It will help out the meat ration," said the Colonel. But she would do it, sooner or later. Heart of gold, though her tongue ran away with her, poor girl, like that young dog's nose at times.

§ 3

Suddenly the telephone rang.

"Look, James, I went home with Lady Mary for a drink and

she wants me to stop and sup and play bridge. Do you mind?
Can you manage?"

"Of course I can, my darling. Did you have a good day?"

A good day at a Point-to-Point with Angela meant a winning bet, the realization that her hat, her coat, or her boots were
definitely in advance of local fashions, recognition by people
preferably above her station, and an opportunity to talk rather
loudly in a crowd.

"Oh, so-so! I made two pounds. That's all right, then?
You'll shut up?"

"Of course! Good-night, m'dear!" As if he didn't "shut up"
for 364 days a year, but Angela never got over the idea that the
establishment hinged on herself!

Good! There would be sardines on toast, a spot of cheese and
his own special coffee, and time to cast up his game-book, his
invariable custom at Easter-time in the old days, and a melancholy task in all conscience for the last few years.

And by George! there would be another bird to add to the
tally, another entry to make in the diary which he would read
in after years when the "young dog" was now the old dog and
grey under the muzzle, his faithful soul looking out of eyes no
longer masterful but mournful, as Daniel's did.

James Bunbury busied himself laying out methodically the
preparations for his meal. And suddenly the front-door bell
rang. His heart sank. The police, come to enquire about that old
cock pheasant? He shut the larder door. His cousin Eileen and
her barrister husband? Neither of them had hunted in their lives
but they never missed a point-to-point within thirty miles. He
always wore riding breeches at them and she went to incredible
lengths to insert their car into the subscribers' car-park, if possible at cut rates. They would sit there for ever, quizzing his
shabby little sitting-room, bringing their family memoirs up
to date, and drinking him out of house and home. Oh, Hell!

He went out, his vision of a peaceful evening torn to shreds.
But it was only Gerald Warde, in an old green hat and a tweed

coat above his bleached corduroy trousers, Gerald Warde whom he had seen in the last race coming in on a very tired young horse, about thirty lengths behind the fellow who had won.

"Good evening, Colonel! Can I come in?"

"Jimmy Bundobust" opened the door very wide and beamed. "My dear fellow, of course! Delighted! Come in and have a drink!"

He bustled about, drawing his ceremonial cigarettes from their lair, lighting the electric stove, and banishing old Daniel, whose smell was only noticeable when visitors were present, while his mind flashed, as it always did, to the problem of what he could offer Gerald to drink. The gin? finished by Angela on Saturday. The sherry? Gone long ago. The dregs of the whisky but Angela would have forgotten the siphon. The rum! that sacred bottle which he had hidden a year ago as a medicinal standby when brandy became impossible.

Some body in rum, and just the stuff for an evening like this. Thank God for a bit of bundobust!

He sat down at last, and looked at his guest stretching his long thin legs by the stove.

"Have a good ride?" he asked eagerly.

"Oh, so-so."

"That plough near the end looked a hideous thing to jump into after a mile uphill?"

"Yes. He's an honest horse, that, but he was stone cold long before then and I thought he was going to lie down on me anywhere in the last half-mile."

The Colonel grunted. His fieldglasses had not betrayed him. "He hit the last two fences a bit of a crack?" he ventured.

"You could have ridden a bicycle through the rozzy things by the time we'd finished with 'em! I can't really think how he stood up."

"Rotten job, isn't it, pushing a tired horse? I wonder you bothered with that chap so far in front?"

Gerald Warde smiled and the wrinkles showed redly on both sides of his eyes.

"Well, I shouldn't have done but for one thing. As you know, that chap and I were the only two left in. He and Mark Billingham had a bet on. They'd been riding pretty jealous all the way round and he slipped one on Mark at that very boggy place coming down by the old barn."

"I saw it," said "Jimmy Bundobust" quickly. "I walked the course, always do, and I thought to m'self, 'Someone will come it, there.'"

"Well, Mark Billingham jumped a bit early and wrote himself off and we went on alone from there."

This was what the Colonel wanted to hear: some inside "gup", however fragmentary and ungrammatical, about what had been going on by one who had been "in the forefront of the battle". Something that none of all that crowd had seen, except little coloured dots moving up the downland a mile away. The Colonel would rather have heard of any historical event from a yokel, one of those whom the Greek dramatists used so successfully, than from any professional announcer in the world, so polished, so omniscient and so null. All he said was: "Most interesting. Another noggin?"

"Thanks. Well, I went on lengths behind with the young horse blowing like a sealion and suddenly came to a fence where there was a weight-cloth lying on the near side. Couldn't believe my eyes! Thought it must have been dropped in a previous race! Why, that chap had about seven people fussing round him when he saddled up, from his head-groom to his girl-friend and his aunts, and I simply couldn't believe he hadn't got all that side of it taped. Apparently he'd forgotten his surcingle and his saddle had slipped. So I thought, 'Well, someone's goin' to get disqualified!' and I plodded on and when I got in, he was arguin' with the Stewards as to whether he could weigh in with the bridle. We were so far behind him, he'd have had time to get off and pick up his ruddy weight-cloth and *still* win."

The Colonel, having started homewards just as the last race came in, had not guessed at this story at all. He beamed and raised his glass.

"So you won, eh? Congratulations, my dear fellow. I'm delighted to hear it. Genuine hunting man. . . . Not many nowadays. We're all too poor, for our sins! Hope next year you'll show us all the way. . . ." The words bubbled from him.

Gerald Warde smiled and shook his head.

"I'm off, sir. This country's hardly my cup of tea at present. I was only staying at home because some ass of a doctor told me I'd got a year to live."

"Really!"

"Yes, I went to the wrong vet by mistake in Wimpole Street last summer who said I was just about ripe for the knacker! But old Mike Moffett was watching the races today. . . ."

"Mike Moffett! Not the Colonel Moffett (I believe he's got a K now) who was DDMS in Meerut?" The Colonel could never quite get over the modern cult of Christian names. They sounded too familiar, almost disrespectful.

"That's him. I had a date to see him last July, only he was out, and some other bloke" (he hesitated, suddenly realizing to whom he was talking) "saw me instead and put the wind up me properly. Wrote me off like that." He snapped his fingers with a sideways motion.

"Good Heavens! my dear fellow!"

"Well, today Mike Moffett came into the tent after my race and said, 'Why the devil didn't you write and tell me, young man, that I'd forgotten your appointment last year? I've just watched that finish of yours. If you can hold a beaten horse together like that, there can't be too much wrong with you. Let's have a look!' And he borrowed a stethoscope from the M.O. and laid me out on the table like that."

"I can see him doing it."

"Spent about ten minutes on me, with all the odds and sods looking on! Then he said, 'There's some bloody fools of gynaecologists I wouldn't trust to diagnose a broken ankle, but I'll stake *my* reputation there isn't much wrong with you! I think there's been what we may call an erratic diagnosis. A bone-setter on that neck of yours and a month's massage and you wouldn't call the King your uncle.' Then he went on rumbling. 'It's my belief about twenty-five per cent. of the women that come to us want their main girders straightened instead of some fool muckin' about with the plumbing!' "

"That's just like Moffett," said the Colonel, not realizing that Gerald had been talking of his own brother-in-law, "always said there was too much specialization, and the pundits would get themselves in an awful tangle if they had to do a G.P.'s work for a day."

§ 4

Gerald Warde looked into the fire and out at the sunlight on the new-mown grass. He seemed to have something which he hardly knew how to say. Then, very slowly, he began.

"Look here, Colonel, I'm off. I'm pretty sure I can get another year's leave and we shall be down to cadre strength very soon. I don't want to muck about with peace-time soldiering in Germany or Aldershot after the last five years."

The Colonel nodded. "Very wise, too. 'Gather ye rosebuds while ye may.' "

"As I see it, we're going to chuck India and Burma down the drain in a couple of years, and I want to look at a few odd corners of both before we do."

"Lucky devil," grunted Jimmy Bundobust. "I wish *I* could." He thought, "A hundred years work by generations of us thrown away for ever. That heritage of hill and woodland, river and plain which the Indian never wanted and which meant so much to us, the Kadir, the Manchar, the Himàl, the Terai, the N'Mai hills, sunlight and great spaces, freedom and a shirt-sleeves job to do." And into his mind came the words at whose meaning he had barely guessed:

Far to southwards they wheel and dance,
The million molten spears of morn—
The spears of our deliverance
Which shine on the house where we were born.

But all he said was, "Very wise you are. It'll be a scandal if they let it go."

"Now, sir, I want to do something about that empty house of mine, the Manor. I've got a friend coming into the dower-house, David Logan. He got *stukaed* in Libya and he's only got half a leg. He'll look after things for me and he's thinking of nesting."

"Nesting", indeed, and "*stukaed*"! What queer slang these young men did use!

"But the Manor's a bit on my mind. It's been empty for fifteen years, except for the troops in the war, and it's such a waste, especially as the War-Box have just done it up for me."

"The Government may lay hands on it for the Coal Board," said the Colonel. He was nervously making conversation.

"That's just the sort of silly-ass thing they *would* do," replied Gerald. "It's only about 200 miles from any coal. But I doubt it. Now I don't think the big house even in a small village should lie fallow like that. . . ."

The Colonel gasped. Whatever was coming now?

"Well . . . I've been looking round and several things are clear. The first is we won't get these farms right in under five years unless we make more cottages available. This rozzy Ministry seems determined to stop any landlord building or reconditioning cottages. So I'm going to fill the stable cottages and the north wing of the manor with seven or eight old couples who will turn out of their present houses to make room for younger men. I put it to them very frankly and, rather to my surprise, they agreed. They'll live rent-free and I've put a lot of work into that place since last August. They'll get electric light and much handier water and drainage than

340

they've got in the old cottages. Also a lot of them worked as housemaids and gardeners and stable-boys there in the old days and have a feeling for the place."

Still the Colonel could not see. Did Gerald Warde want him as manager of this queer feudal almshouse? But all he said was, "Sound idea. Some of those cottages, picturesque enough, but must be very out-of-date. Have another rum?"

One drink with him nowadays was an exception, and three sheer dissipation, but for once he decided to break his rule. The third rum did it.

"Well, Colonel," said Gerald slowly, his lean face redder than usual, "this is what you'll probably think the most God-awful impertinence, but looking at things here, it seems to me that what they used, in my father's day, to call 'the smaller gentry' have got to combine in self-defence. You've been worse hit th n anyone, and you're ground between the upper and the nether millstones with fixed incomes, and rising costs which, if things go on, are going to swamp you all one by one. You can't suddenly pack in and start poor, because you can't leave the neighbourhood. I can't help seeing it, being a bachelor still and likely to remain one."

So that nice girl, Ann Heriot, must have turned him down! Poor fellow!

"Well, this is where you'll probably kick me out! All your houses in Stoke Loyalty would let easily nowadays to Furze-chester lawyers and merchants and London chaps who week-end, and if five of the local families here moved into the Manor, you'd cut down your overheads a lot on a community basis."

At last light dawned on the Colonel. A chummery, b'God, a sort of married mess! But all he said was "Overheads? I don't quite follow you."

"Well. Five or six telephones, which each of you wants for about ten minutes or less a day. Six sets of repairs, insurances, rates, taxes, lighting bills, and every form of labour from daily helps to chimney sweeps, six motor cars where one would do, and all that howdy-de-do whenever one of you wants a four at bridge or to go away for half a day. If five or six of you, and your wives, combined to run a joint show, in a decently-built large house, I believe you'd get much more for your money than you do at present."

The Colonel saw his own case to the uttermost farthing. Hay for his ponies and a quiet park to canter round, without ever going on the road. Wood fuel to be cut and carted happily on autumn days, a view of the downs from a room which a great architect had designed, his own pet midget-tractor making short work of that great walled garden; somewhere to potter round with a gun and young James; forty good hens in the little paddock and some help about the house. If this new Government was determined to kill off the 'smaller gentry,' they might as well die comfortably in decent surroundings! Then all the objections rushed, crab-like, into his mind. Would Angela yield up her suzerainty, unquestioned all these years, over the telephone? Wouldn't she and Mrs. Heriot or Miss Pickering fight interminably over little things?

"It's a great idea," he said, "and I do appreciate your offer. But I doubt if, even on our combined incomes, we could afford the rent."

"Blast the rent!" said Gerald. "I want that house lived in. It seems such a waste. It's a marvellous site! Our ancestors *did* know where to build. And it's produced some pretty adequate types in its time, though I say it as shouldn't. That house gives you a good feel, y'know. . . ."

"Yes," said the Colonel, "but you're a venturesome young chap. You've come through this war but supposing anything happened to you? If we got shut of our little houses, we might be in Queer Street in three years time."

Gerald nodded. "I'm willing to let you occupy the Manor at a nominal rent and make the lease legally binding for, say, ten years, by which time this rozzy country may have settled down."

"It'll want consideration," said the Colonel. "Women don't

342

live too easily in communities. They've all had a wearing time in this war and the last few years have played havoc with their nerves and, er, they're apt to say things they don't mean. . . ."

Gerald smiled and the wrinkles showed all round his eyes.

"All right, Colonel, I understand! I had an old aunt m'self who nagged my head off years ago."

The Colonel blinked, as that shot went home. The word "nag" was one he was forbidden to mention. He had never looked it up in a dictionary but he liked to think that "nagging" was an equestrian term, for "keeping a young horse up to his work". Any further implications were barred.

"Do you really think it could be done?" he said eagerly.

"I do. I want to throw a party in a week's time and broach it to the five or six households I had in mind. You'll come, won't you, and Mrs. Bunbury?"

The Colonel was moved, but all he said was: "Of course. Delighted. Now one more stirrup-cup before you go? No? Well, you've opened up quite a new prospect for some of us! I hardly know how to . . ."

"O.K. Colonel, then don't! Thank *you* and good night!"

And as he closed the door and returned to the kitchen he thought, "Lucky young man, but how lonely! I wonder what he does for women?"

Then his mind roved back to the "bundobust" of his long evening: sardine-opener, cheese, margarine, coffee, shut up the fowls, a glance at the pony, the greenhouse, change the water for his gumboots at the side-door, hen-food in the oven, windows, lights, and the barn door. There was always something. And slowly he got down his cooking-apron from the scullery door. It would need a lot of bundobust and the Lord alone knew what Angela would say.

§ 5

On the crest of Farwarren in the dusk Gerald stopped the car gently and turned to Ann. "I always like this place," he said.

343

"You can see for miles here up and down. I want to talk to you."

"And so do I," said Ann. "For example, where did you get to after the Heavyweight Race? I couldn't find you anywhere."

"Sorry, Ann. I was getting that warranty you insisted on. First class vet, too. Galloped me for wind and everything!"

"Oh," said Ann, "and what did he say?"

"A lot of blemishes but not likely to affect my usefulness, that *sort* of certificate. From what I can make out, I've had more or less a broken neck, or a dislodged vertebra for years, and that jerk I took with Mike's horse that day at Flux Weston straightened it out for me. I've got to have an X-ray and probably a bone-setter on it. After that a mild blister and perhaps a year at grass."

"I see," smiled Ann, "blemished but sound and likely to make a good hunter. And what may you be asking for him?"

Gerald flushed. "That's just it, Ann. My family have always been a crazy wild lot and won't stay put. Can't anchor anywhere. Always popping off into the blue to search for something new. I couldn't ask any woman to share that sort of life, could I?"

"You might," said Ann. "Depends on the woman. I like a bit of change myself at times, and I've never seen the East. I suppose that's where you're heading for."

"Before," nodded Gerald, "we chuck it away for ever. Do you really think, Ann . . . ?"

Ann, as women do, changed the subject.

"I've only got one worry and that's my mother. The old dear does need someone to look after her, and she has lived with nice things about her all her life. She'd pass out if she knew the jobs I've done in the kennels and with the Land Army in the last five years. I can see my old father revolving in his grave at this moment, poor darling!"

"Well," said Gerald, "I've just been making a sort of arrangement about your mother. If it comes off, she won't lack companionship or comforts. . . ."

"You *have* been busy, haven't you?" said Ann.

"If," went on Gerald, "the arrangements I've made are O.K. . . ." he hesitated and his wind-bitten cheeks went redder still, "what about it, Ann, my dear?"

"I do wish," smiled Ann, "you cavalry-soldiers weren't so dumb. A girl does like to be proposed to properly, now and again."

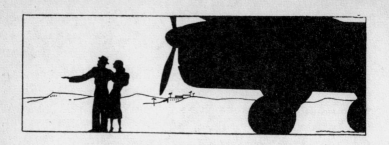

XXXIII. ENVOI

I will remember my old strength and all my forest-affairs.
    —*Toomai of the Elephants* by RUDYARD KIPLING

The ageless course of things begins again.—J. H. HALLARD

It was a mild evening in early May. Mr. Mannering sat at his littered desk, deep in thought.

He really must do something about the syndicate. Just when he thought he had got quite a nice little lot together, with the right proportion of dud shots and decent fellows, something always happened. This one had disintegrated quicker than most. He wondered idly which of His Majesty's "clubs for impoverished sportsmen" Sir William was now gracing and how he was getting on. Most likely just preparing to press his trousers under his palliasse. And not one novel seemed to have emerged from Mr. Lorrimer's dictaphone, ever since that unfortunate appearance of his as the *pièce de résistance* in Furzechester police-station. But he would come again! He was like some of those two-thousand-gallon Red Polls his neighbour kept. You couldn't really dry them off at all. And how he would flail the police in his next book when it *did* appear! And there was that nice young chap, Warde, who was beginning to pull down driven birds very neatly, wanting to be off to the back of beyond and to spend his honeymoon "travelling fairly light" on the edges of Tibet!

Anyhow, that meant he was three guns short of his quota for next September and it would never do to let anyone think his syndicate didn't "fill" for any reason. An advertisement now would mean time to vet applicants really thoroughly, and before the breeding-season could turn out disastrously. Probably be impossible to get beaters this year in any number at the rate they were demobilizing units all around. And farm-wages up too! If only they would de-control the price of game, he could make do on the old terms, but perhaps he had better make it a hundred guineas this year. He wished he could tell the partridges it was all over for five months.

Thoughtfully he took a clean piece of notepaper and wrote on it in capital letters:

"GUN WANTED
TO COMPLETE SYNDICATE SEASON 46–47. . . ."

Major Ogle was turning out the drawer of his gun-cupboard and mentally composing the first sentences of an article he intended for *Dog and Gun*. Hang it, if Lorrimer could make all that out of writing, there must be something in it for veterans with experience like his own. The words took shape: "At this time of the year, the thoughts of shooting-men naturally begin to turn from the lessons of the past season, towards the season which will be upon them in just over three months' time. Cartridges need seeing to, guns should be expertly overhauled, and an application of saddle-soap or neats-foot oil to the cartridge-bag will ensure . . ." Meantime he must put out the old dog's blanket in the sun tomorrow. It was getting quite noticeable.

Far away on Castel Benito aerodrome (perhaps we had better not enquire how he got there), Gerald Warde stretched his legs and sniffed thankfully a south wind blowing off the sand. "There, Ann, my darling," he said, "get a proper lung-full of that! There's some lovely desert only about a hundred miles in from here, and considering where it is, it's very little-known.

We'll have a peep at that and then wangle our way on eastwards somehow. You wait till you see the Taròn or the Chi-
mili. We haven't started yet! Happy?"

Ann Warde smiled. When happy, she was a young person of
few words.

On Colonel Bunbury's hearthrug old Daniel's muffled cooing, which took the place with him of snores, gradually ceased.
Then he twitched and quivered and little short strangled yelps
of ecstasy came from his aged jaws. After ten seasons he was, at
long last, just running into his hare, an absolute whopper of a
hare, too, after a stupendous chase, and was about to slay her in
fair fight. Very far away, across the sweep of the darkening
stubble, he could hear his Master's shouts of remonstrance
change suddenly into thunders of applause.

THE END